Warwickshire County Council

This item is to be returned or renewed before the latest date above. It may be borrowed for a further period if not in demand. **To renew your books:**

- **Phone the 24/7 Renewal Line 01926 499273 or**
- **Visit www.warwickshire.gov.uk/libraries**

Discover • Imagine• Learn • *with libraries*

Warwickshire County Council

ALSO BY MATT DUNN

A CHRISTMAS DAY AT THE OFFICE

MATT DUNN

LAKE UNION

PUBLISHING

Text copyright © 2016 Matt Dunn
All rights reserved.

Published by Lake Union Publishing, Seattle

www.apub.com

Amazon, the Amazon logo, and Lake Union Publishing are trademarks of Amazon.com, Inc., or its affiliates.

ISBN-13: 9781503938274
ISBN-10: 1503938271

Cover design by Lisa Horton

Printed in the United States of America

To Kai and Chiara: keep laughing . . .

1.

Sophie Jones took a deep breath. 'Well, it all started . . . Hold on a sec . . .' She checked the date – 14 December – on a discarded copy of today's *Metro* newspaper on the floor by her feet, wedging her mobile between her shoulder and her ear while she counted out the months on her fingers. 'Ten months ago. To the day, in fact. I fancied Nathan Field. He's the technical support manager at Seek Software – that's the company I work for – so I'd fixed things so Nathan and I would be alone together that evening. And I fancied my chances – as well as him, ha ha! I mean, it *was* Valentine's Day. And love was definitely in the air: Calum Irwin – he works in sales – hooked up with Mia-Rose from reception, and even my boss, Julie Marshall – and she can be a bit of a cold fish, let me tell you – got it on with Mark Webster. Oh, he's *everyone's* boss at Seek. *An-y-*way . . .' Sophie drew out the first syllable for effect. 'Suffice it to say, things didn't quite go according to plan, and Nathan and I – well, he ended up going out with someone else, but I – thanks to this amazing lingerie that I just happened to find that day in Selfridges – managed to bag myself a *doctor*, Vinay, and we went out for about six months, but then one day I asked him if I was ever going to meet the in-laws, and he told me . . .' Sophie took a few shallow breaths, fanning her face with her free hand to stop the tears she could feel welling up. 'Well, he said that I couldn't because of *his* in-laws – prospective ones, at least, given the dentist from Bolton his parents apparently had lined up for him to marry – a small fact he'd been keeping from me. And since then, well, I've been meeting these guys on Tinder, but maybe I shouldn't have put that I like *Mad Men* on my profile, because even though I meant the TV programme, they're all . . .' She put one finger to her temple and rotated it quickly while making a 'crazy' face. 'And even if they're not, they're generally only after one thing, and they don't only want to do it with one girl, so even though I've been thinking everything's been going fine, and I get my hopes up – and yes, I *know* I shouldn't – they always end up giving me the old "I never said we were exclusive" line . . .' Sophie stepped back quickly to avoid a spray of puddled rainwater caused by a passing bus, and nearly trod on the homeless man propped up against the wall behind her, leering at her while chugging down his 'breakfast' can of Special Brew. 'So yes, to answer your question, I *have* been hurt recently. Several times. And none of them have been my fault.'

'I meant in an *accident*,' said the woman on the other end of the phone, after a pause that lasted so long Sophie had begun to suspect she'd hung up. 'Not *emotionally*.'

'Oh. Sorry,' said Sophie. She felt a little guilty, unburdening herself like that to a complete stranger, but then again, the woman had phoned her out of the blue, and actually, it had been good to talk to someone about it. 'So there's no chance of any compensation, I suppose?' she asked half-heartedly, but the woman had gone.

She put her phone away, then hurried into Harrow-on-the-Hill tube station, brushing past the sparsely decorated (and even more sparsely needled) artificial Christmas tree hauled out every year by the owner of the key-cutting-and-shoe-repair shop (a combination of trades that always mystified her: did people sometimes snap a heel off while their key jammed in their front door lock, or perhaps they scuffed a toe when kicking the door in?), and that looked almost as miserable as Sophie felt. She'd been determined that this year – for the first time in three years – she wasn't going to be single over the holidays, but with less than two weeks to go, it was looking like all she'd be waking up with on Christmas morning was a hangover.

She tapped her way through the barriers with the new 'contactless' card that had arrived in the post the previous morning (it had been the only card she'd received so far this Christmas), and almost laughed at the irony. 'Contactless' just about summed up her life at the moment. She'd only signed up to Tinder in desperation (and after the best part of a bottle and a half of Pinot Grigio, which she'd downed when drowning her sorrows one lonely night after Vinay had made his announcement), but after close to fifteen dates (and countless more 'chats' that had her Googling some of the offers she'd received, staring open-mouthed at the definitions, then blocking the men just as quickly), she'd only come to one conclusion: that all of the good men on Tinder had already been 'swiped'.

Making her way along the platform, Sophie swapped the overnight bag containing the poshest, demurest dress she owned (though to offset its frumpiness, she'd paired it with the sluttiest of her shoes she could still dance in) to her other shoulder. Tonight was her office Christmas party – though not just *her* office's, she reminded herself. Seek had just been bought by (though the official line was 'merged with') another, much bigger, American-owned organisation, iFeel, with offices in oh-so-posh Fitzroy Square. And while that meant an extra ten minutes on her daily commute, and she'd miss working in Soho, any part of London was a bonus as far as the Eastbourne girl in her was concerned.

Manoeuvring herself towards the spot where the train's doors would open when it arrived (and Sophie was both chuffed and depressed by the fact she knew exactly where that was), she pulled her phone back out and swiped quickly through this morning's rogue's gallery of new faces on Tinder, then checked the personally addressed invitational email she (and everyone else at Seek) had received from Tony A. Wood, iFeel's (and Seek's new) owner. 'Happy Christmas!' read the header, closely followed by: 'I hope everyone in the Seek family can join me—' (although attendance was compulsory, so Mark Webster had informed them all at last week's emergency staff meeting, when the merger had been officially announced) '—this Friday, December 14, at a specially selected mystery London venue, for an evening of champagne, canapés and capers . . .'

Sophie speed-read the rest, relieved that there'd be 'external catering', which probably meant the 'capers' the invitation referred to were some sort of entertainment and not those strange little green things that looked like tiny olives and tasted like off ones, then sighed to herself. While she'd normally be grateful for any chance to let her hair down (especially when someone else was picking up the bill), partying was the last thing she felt like at the moment.

Still, she supposed she ought to be grateful. Whatever the circumstances were, at least the prospect of a party at a 'mystery London venue' was better than the usual Seek affair, forcing down crappy pub food before playing drunken games of pass-the-balloon (the first year, it hadn't even been a balloon, but some other latex inflatable thing that had caused Mary from accounts to run screaming from the room when she'd realised what it was) in some mouldy upstairs room in a nondescript pub near Oxford Street, especially with free champagne, perhaps even a DJ, and external catering (Sophie had never had external catering, unless you counted her daily trip to fetch a sandwich from the Pret A Manger across the street from the office).

But while there were bound to be men there, if iFeel was anything like Seek, all the eligible ones were probably already taken, and those who weren't . . . Well, experience told Sophie they weren't for a reason. And like she'd explained to the woman who'd cold-called her a few minutes ago, everyone at Seek was loved-up: Nathan – who she'd had a crush on since she joined three years ago – had taken a shine (if you excused the not-quite pun) to some Polish girl who worked in a café round the corner from the office. Her boss, Julie, was so obviously still shagging Mark Webster, a fact reinforced by how hard they were trying (and how badly they were managing) to keep it a secret. Even Calum, overweight, under-confident, and ginger-haired, was still getting his end away with Mia-Rose, the curvy, outgoing Afro-Caribbean girl on reception (though not actually *on* reception, Sophie hoped, given the odd hour she occasionally spent manning the desk when Mia was out at lunch). Everyone except *her*, that was.

Her tube arrived, and as it slowed to a stop, Sophie examined her reflection in the carriage window. She wasn't bad-looking, she'd been told, with the kind of figure that got her a lot of attention (especially from the guys working on the building site round the corner from the office), and the regular spinning classes she'd been attending for the last six months had given her what the gay American instructor at her gym had grabbed in both hands and described as 'thighs of steel'. It was just a shame that Vinay (or 'Vinnie', as she'd taken to calling him in a *sarf-London* accent whenever she'd wanted to annoy him, which had been more and more towards the end of their relationship) hadn't thought thighs of steel were a good basis for kicking his *other* girlfriend into touch. Which was ironic, if you thought about it.

The doors opened, and Sophie allowed the wave of commuters to carry her on board, then she elbowed herself towards a pole, trying to force herself into a party mood. Maybe she'd just get drunk tonight, throw both caution to the wind and herself at Nathan, or anyone decent-looking from iFeel. Although that wouldn't be the best first impression to make, she was almost past caring; Sophie had always wanted to meet 'the one' rather than the one-night stand, but the way things were going, almost *any* one would do. Besides, she was beginning to doubt 'the one' actually existed. For her, at least.

The carriage was crowded, so she clutched the bag containing her party gear tightly to her chest (the heels of her stilettos sticking painfully into her left breast) and told herself to cheer up. Perhaps there *would* be someone there this evening who'd take her away from all of this – though Sophie doubted it. 'This', she suspected, surveying her fellow passengers, miserably wedged into this airless cylinder hurtling towards the centre of London, was what she had to look forward to for the next twenty or thirty years, assuming this merger didn't mean she was going to lose her job. Now *there* was a jolly thought.

She glanced at the email one last time, almost laughing at the 'Happy Christmas!' part, then slipped her phone miserably back into her coat pocket. With her career up in the air and her love life dashed to the ground, 'happy' was the last thing her Christmas was shaping up to be.

∽

South of the river, Calum Irwin leaned heavily against the sink in the bathroom of the tiny Balham ex-council flat he shared with his mother as he tried to stop his heart from pounding. Tonight, after exactly ten months of dating (which was approximately nine months and two weeks longer than his next-longest relationship, a fact he felt simultaneously pretty good *and* more than a little worried about), he was going to tell Mia-Rose he didn't want her to be his girlfriend any more.

He stared at his reflection in the mirror, wondering (for what seemed like the hundredth time) how he was going to phrase it, when a loud knock on the door made him jump.

'Calum?'

His mother sounded anxious, and Calum groaned to himself. Oh, for the luxury of a second bathroom. Or even his own flat . . .

'Who else could it possibly be in here?'

'Are you going to be long?'

'No, Mum, I'm nearly done.'

'Is it safe? Or should I give it five minutes?'

'*Shaving!*' He splashed some aftershave into his palms, gingerly patted his freshly razored cheeks, then gritted his teeth as he waited for the stinging to subside.

'Right. Because I need the loo . . .'

'Okay, okay.'

'Soon.'

'Just give me a minute!'

'Honestly, you spend more time in there than I do nowadays!' His mother laughed from the other side of the bathroom door. 'It doesn't seem that long ago you used to burst into tears whenever it was bath day.'

'*Mum . . .*'

'That Mia's a good influence on you. You should think about making an honest woman of her. Before someone else comes along and snatches her away from under your nose.'

'*Mum!*' he repeated, his face turning the same deep shade of red as his hair. That was exactly what he was thinking about. And, if he was honest, exactly why he was thinking about it.

As Calum opened the door and glared good-naturedly at her, his mother laughed again.

'I'm just saying. After all, you're not getting any younger. None of us are. And I'd like to be around to at least see one of my grand-kids. God willing . . .'

'I think we can safely say that God's got your back, Mum.'

'It's not my back I'm worried about!'

7

She clutched her chest theatrically, and Calum rolled his eyes. His mother had been convinced she was dying (and trying to convince anyone who'd listen of the fact) for pretty much as long as he could remember, though recently he'd begun to suspect her continual references to her various aches and pains were more of a ruse to keep him here to look after her than any real health issues.

As he squeezed past her in the tiny corridor, a move that – given her impressive bosom, and the fact that he was hardly svelte himself – required some skilful manoeuvring, his mother narrowed her eyes. 'You're looking a bit pale, love. Are you feeling okay?'

'I'm always pale, Mum. On account of being Irish and—'

She ruffled his hair affectionately. 'Strawberry blonde?'

'Exactly. And I'm fine,' he added, although his stomach was still doing somersaults. 'Honest.'

His mother placed a hand on either side of his face and squeezed his cheeks, almost as if his head was a spot she was trying to pop. Then – with an expression that suggested her need for the toilet was suddenly urgent – she hurried into the bathroom, slamming the door shut behind her, so he headed into the kitchen and wondered whether he should have some breakfast, though he quickly decided against it. The way he was feeling, it might not stay down.

Calum didn't know what he was more nervous about: asking Mia-Rose to marry him, or telling his mum when – sorry, *if* – Mia-Rose said 'yes', then having to deal with the inevitable 'So you'll be moving out?' discussion. He hadn't dared say anything beforehand, partly because he wasn't sure he'd have the nerve to go through with proposing as it was, but mainly in case Mia-Rose gave the opposite answer. He didn't want the look on his mum's face to haunt him for the rest of his life – *or* for her to march into the office and let Mia-Rose have it with both barrels in front of everyone for turning down a proposal from her little (though he was anything but) boy.

Not that his mum and Mia-Rose didn't get on. Mia was a big, cheerful, Christian girl from North London (well, from Jamaica, technically), and his mum was a larger-than-life Catholic girl (her word, not his) from Northern Ireland, but despite their differences (or perhaps because of them) they always seemed to find something to talk about. In fact, there were times that Calum had just sat there and let the two of them get on with it (once, he'd even pretended he was nipping to the toilet, though he'd actually nipped out for a pint in the pub just down the road, only to come back an hour or so later and find them in the same position), such was their fondness for what his mum referred to as 'a good old chinwag'. Though strictly speaking, 'double-chinwag' would have been more appropriate.

It wasn't all one-way traffic either. He liked Mia-Rose's mum: a tiny, kindly West Indian lady who'd welcomed him with open arms that first nervous day he'd been introduced to – or rather, paraded in front of – Mia's rather large family. And while he'd have liked to have asked her dad for permission to wed his daughter, her dad wasn't around – and hadn't been for a good few years, apparently. So that was at least one hurdle he didn't have to haul his somewhat unfit body over.

Nor was worrying whether Mia-Rose would like the ring he'd bought – not an *actual* ring, but (the last remaining) one from a packet of Haribo jelly sweets he'd bought the previous weekend when – and Calum hadn't known what had come over him; perhaps he'd simply been panicking about what to get her for Christmas – he'd decided that proposing was on the cards. But this red-and-white sugary thing would do; it was symbolic, after all. And besides, given the relatively short time they'd been dating, plus Mia's somewhat 'eclectic' taste in jewellery, he didn't feel confident that he'd be able to buy one that she liked without her. He'd let her choose. Assuming she chose *him*, of course.

He'd planned the evening's events with military precision. A quick bite after work in the restaurant where they'd first got together (where he'd pop the question), then back to the office in time to catch the coach that had been laid on to take them to tonight's office Christmas party, where they'd pop the champagne, bask in everyone's congratulations, and – seeing as their new owner was picking up the tab – Calum wouldn't have to pay for the equivalent of his bodyweight in bubbly he'd be drinking. Which (given his bodyweight) would be a *lot*.

He'd even practised getting down on one knee – he had it down to an art form by now – and while getting up again was a bit trickier, Calum assumed he'd be holding Mia's hand at that point, and could therefore hoist himself up that way. And although he wasn't sure *which* knee it was traditional to get down on (and he'd practised both, just in case), tonight it would have to be his right: his left one was still a bit sore from his foolish attempt to play in the office Christmas five-a-side football tournament the previous week, when attempting to cover a Ronaldo-like sidestep from Nathan Field had sent him howling in anguish to the ground. Calum could only hope Mia-Rose's answer later today wouldn't produce the same result.

With a final check in his bag for the packet of Haribo (and its oh-so-important contents), he marched back down the hallway and knocked softly on the bathroom door.

'I'm off, Mum.'

'Right, son. Have a nice day. See you later.'

'Actually, you won't. Or rather, don't wait up. Tonight's the office Christmas party, so . . .'

She cracked the bathroom door open and squinted at him through the gap. 'Okay. Well don't forget, now . . .'

'Forget what?'

His mum mimed holding a phone to her ear. 'To give your best girl a ring later?'

Though if she wondered why Calum broke into a huge grin, she didn't say.

⁋

Across in Bermondsey, Mark Webster was standing in the front room of his flat, stifling a yawn as he counted down the minutes before he could leave for work. He'd been woken up at 5 a.m. by what had sounded like a full SWAT-team assault on his front door, but it had turned out to be the (extremely drunk) woman from the flat above, having accidentally got out of the lift one floor early, then (mistakenly and loudly) wondering why her key wouldn't work in 'her' front door.

Though he supposed he shouldn't be surprised he hadn't been able to get back to sleep, given that today might just be the biggest day of his professional life – assuming what he expected to happen happened. And it generally did – workwise, at least. Mark didn't really 'do' surprises, especially where his career was concerned. And although he'd never worked for a company that had been taken over by a software mogul before, he'd done his homework: iFeel didn't have anyone as senior as him, or as qualified as him (or as gagging for a promotion as Mark was, probably) here in the UK, so Tony A. Wood would surely have no option but to ask him to head up the new London office.

He hoped.

Not that he and Tony had ever had a conversation about it. Or exchanged emails on the subject. Or ever met. All Mark knew was that the billionaire was flying in specially for tonight's Christmas party, and that – according to the brief message Tony's PA had sent him – Mark should expect some one-on-one face time.

He'd done his homework, of course. Checked out the financials. Made sure there wasn't a question he wouldn't be able to answer, if the 'great man', as Tony A. Wood liked to describe himself on the TED talks Mark had watched on YouTube, decided to grill him. But then again, Tony didn't 'do' formal job interviews, apparently. Liked to trust his gut. And given the fact that he was worth just over a billion dollars (one-point-two-six billion, to be precise – Mark had looked it up), his gut must be pretty impressive.

And if he didn't get the job? He hadn't wanted to consider that possibility, but at least Julie Marshall would be there to offer him some comfort. Mark was in love with Julie, and this time, it was *proper* love, not the unrequited stuff that everyone said was the worst kind; given the couple of months he'd been infatuated with her before they'd finally gotten together, he could vouch for that. No, he was in love with someone who *loved him back*.

Or so he hoped. Julie hadn't quite used the three little words yet, and to be honest, he'd been too worried about scaring her away to say 'I love you' himself. This was uncharted territory for him: he'd never dated a divorcee before – or at least, someone going through a divorce – and he was doubly nervous for that very reason. Besides, she'd been in love with someone else enough to agree to marry him, presumably they'd told each other 'I love you' at some point, and then— Well, it had gone horribly wrong. If you followed that to its logical conclusion – and as an accountant by trade, Mark was all about logical conclusions – Julie was bound to be at least a bit suspicious of anything *he* told her, not to mention wary of declaring her love for him, especially after less than ten months of officially 'going out'. No, the way he saw it, she still had something – or rather, *someone* – she needed to get out of the way first. Then, and only then, would she – *they* – be free.

To her credit, when it came to her marriage, Julie had been prepared to just walk away, and it had taken Mark several weeks – and a couple of quite serious arguments – to convince her not to. But there was a lot of money tied up in the house she'd bought with

Philip, her ex-husband, and Mark knew she'd thank him once the divorce – and the proceeds from the sale of the property – came through. If, indeed, he and Julie were still speaking.

And though he'd wanted to shout about their relationship from the rooftops, Mark had agreed they'd keep a low profile in the meantime; after all, from what she'd said about her soon-to-be-ex, if he could use something like Mark against her in the divorce, he certainly would. So she'd rented a tiny bedsit in Elephant & Castle, just close enough to where he lived that they could share the commute, just far enough away that they'd end up spending a good proportion of their nights together rather than one of them walk the twenty minutes home alone in the dark (or rather, Mark walk *her* home, then surreptitiously flag down a cab to take him safely back through the 'mean' streets of Borough). Though he'd been careful to give Julie her space too; Mark knew he couldn't expect her to leave one relationship and rush headlong straight into another, even though he'd been desperate for her to do precisely that.

But once the divorce came through . . . Mark almost rubbed his hands together in glee. They'd be able to 'out' themselves at work. Spend some proper, quality time with each other without worrying who might see them. Go on holiday together without anyone from Human Resources raising their eyebrows at the fact that his and Julie's leave requests overlapped. And, thought Mark, have a good time, with no pressure, no third person in their relationship (as Philip had been for much of the past ten months). It would be great. Just the two of them. Unlike this evening . . .

He double-checked the contents of his suit carrier, well aware of the minefield that tonight's Christmas party might be. With the whole of the UK iFeel team there (not to mention Tony A. Wood), Mark knew he had to be on his best behaviour. And while that meant limiting his drinking, no dancing and *absolutely no repeat* of last year's erotically charged 'pass the balloon' game with Julie, it was only one night. He and Julie would have plenty of others. And with their first Christmas looming . . . Well, he still had no idea what to get her, hadn't even discussed what they'd be doing (or where they'd be doing it), but as long as they spent it together – perhaps in front of a roaring log fire somewhere (or even huddled by the dodgy storage heater in Julie's flat that Mark was convinced was a fire risk, so might well give them the licking flames he'd been hoping for anyway) – he'd be happy.

He pulled his phone out of his pocket, checked the time, then fired off a WhatsApp that simply said *Leaving now*, waiting until the two ticks turning blue confirmed she'd read it. Mark knew better than to expect a response, and certainly not some innuendo-charged emoticon. Julie just wasn't like that: not into small talk, or anything 'lovey-dovey' (her words). But that suited him (almost) just fine. He'd never been the most demonstrative or impulsive of people either – another reason the two of them were perfect for each other.

With a smile, he collected his briefcase, slung his suit carrier over his shoulder, and – triple-locking his front door behind him, then triple-checking it, as always – set off for the station.

∽

A mile or so down the road, Julie Marshall considered replying to Mark Webster's WhatsApp with *We need to talk*, then quickly decided against it, and instead, turned her attention back to the gadget in her other hand.

She double-checked the instruction leaflet, then frowned at the tiny grey screen, wondering whether she was reading it right, before finally concluding that, however you looked at it (and Julie had looked at it from a number of different angles), given how the device could only display either 'pregnant' or 'not pregnant', it was difficult to make a mistake. For good measure, she tapped the side of the tester smartly with her fingernail, just in case some blockage or fault in the wiring had prevented the word 'not' from showing, then with a sigh, dropped the small plastic device into the bin alongside the other two she'd used earlier. *This* was an interesting development – and not one that Julie was really sure she knew how to feel about. She and Mark Webster had only been a couple for little more than nine months, and now – and she almost laughed at the coincidence – in a little less than nine months' time, they might be *parents*. As to whether they'd be a family . . . Well, Julie wasn't quite sure about that either.

Nor was she sure as to how it had actually happened. No – strike that – she knew *how* it had happened, but as to why, or even when? She was on the pill, and Mark – well, Mark was a belt-and-braces kind of guy, and the chances of both of their precautions failing, unless he was producing the Michael Phelps of the sperm world . . .

Julie smiled grimly. Mark was the least sporty guy she knew. She'd run rings round him at the previous week's office Christmas five-a-side tournament, and Nathan Field at work had teased him that he was even developing a bit of a 'dad-bod' (something Julie had laughed about at the time, though she wasn't finding it at all funny right now). No, she doubted her 'Phelps' theory held any water. In which case, the blame must lie with her. Which meant it was her responsibility to deal with it.

She didn't know how Mark felt about having kids. She wasn't sure how *she* felt about having kids, to be honest, just assuming it was something she'd think about when the time was right. Trouble was, she'd always been too focused on ensuring her career went in the right direction, and then her marriage had begun to go in the wrong direction, so the time had *never* been right. As to whether she even *liked* kids . . .? Certainly, she and Mark preferred to steer well clear of cafés like Giraffe on the South Bank whenever they went out for a weekend brunch, but trying to linger over an Eggs Benedict and the Sunday papers while hordes of screaming toddlers ran riot around your table was surely nobody's idea of a relaxing morning. Though it was different when they were your own, everyone always said. Through gritted teeth, in Julie's experience.

She puffed air out of her cheeks, then stepped into the hallway to collect the official-looking letter that had just thudded onto her doormat, and as she slit the envelope open and speed-read its contents, her mood changed abruptly. *This* was what she'd wanted for Christmas: something worth waiting nine months for – her *divorce*. And while she'd been initially shocked when the solicitor she'd been referred to had asked her in their initial meeting if she 'fancied a quickie', by the looks of the letter, he'd been as good as his word. Philip, her husband, was now her ex-husband. History. Or at least, no longer a part of *her* story.

Excitedly, she retrieved her phone and began calling Mark's number, then stopped mid-dial. This kind of news was best passed on in person, and besides, in the light of this morning's other revelation, she might need to use it later in a good news/bad news kind of way. Though that was assuming Mark thought a baby *was* bad news.

She finished packing the holdall containing her party dress and a pair of shoes so uncomfortable that dancing was going to be interesting – just walking in heels that high was tricky enough – and placed it by the door. Tonight's office Christmas party was hardly the best place to celebrate news of your new-found freedom *or* of your impending parenthood, and while Julie would have preferred not to have gone, she understood from Mark that attendance was compulsory. Besides, it was kind of their anniversary; last year's event was when they'd first noticed a certain frisson between the two of them. And the first time they'd kissed, in the shared taxi Mark had insisted drop her off before him, even though he lived in the completely opposite end of London to where she had back then.

Julie blushed at the memory. She'd been married then. Still living with her husband (although in separate rooms) until Mark's admission of his feelings for her a few weeks later had moved her enough to move out, so she'd rented this tiny studio flat in Elephant & Castle, just down the road from where Mark lived in Bermondsey. And even though she'd moved here to be near him, the two of them had decided to keep their distance at work – at least until the divorce had come through. It had seemed easier that way. But not necessary any more, Julie realised, slipping the letter from her solicitor into her bag.

She headed out of her flat, rode the lift down to the ground floor, and made her way into the street, fastening her coat tightly against the cold December morning. Was it her imagination, or was the button over her stomach straining a little? She paused in front of the Wetherspoon's pub on the corner, and turned sideways on, examining her profile in the reflection in the window. No 'baby bump' – at least, not that she could see – and Mark hadn't said anything either, though he was too much of a gentleman to ever suggest she looked fat. Which meant she'd probably be able to avoid any awkward questions.

And if that was the case, then maybe for now, not telling him she was pregnant might be best. For one thing, she might not be pregnant; how reliable could a small plastic throwaway stick (or even, three of them) be? And even if she was, she might lose the baby, or choose not to keep it – being a mum certainly wasn't something that sat anywhere near the top of her list of ambitions (and yes, she had one, written out in a file marked 'Personal' on her laptop at the office).

Almost immediately the decision to keep this from Mark didn't sit particularly well with her. While Julie had always been a subscriber to the 'what they don't know won't hurt them' school of thought, that she hadn't told him she'd been married when they'd first got together *had* hurt him, and she was determined never to hurt him again. Besides, there was so much else going on, what with the merger and the corresponding office move, not to mention meeting their new owner this evening.

She reminded herself that – just like her divorce – this merger was a Good Thing. An opportunity, not a problem. The chance of a promotion, to advance her career, grow her department (at least to one that had more than herself and Sophie Jones in it), work with a bigger budget . . . This other business? It would all sort itself out over the next few weeks, Julie was sure, one way or another. Until she'd had it confirmed – professionally – she'd just put it to the back of her mind, and do her best to focus on today's positives.

And not today's positive results.

෧෨

Meanwhile, up in Bayswater, Nathan Field fastened the topmost of the two buttons on his single-breasted dinner jacket, then ran through his head-to-toe checklist, making sure he wasn't missing anything. Nathan loved dressing up – though not in a kinky way; he'd tried that with a girlfriend once when she'd suggested wearing a schoolgirl's uniform might spice up their sex life, and while he'd initially been enthusiastic, it had turned out that she'd expected *him* to don the short, pleated skirt and knee-high socks, and put his hair into pigtails: a sight that he'd been unable to unsee since then, no matter how hard he tried. But give him any excuse to wear a proper, smart suit, and he'd be lint-rolling his lapels quicker than you could say 'Ermenegildo Zegna'.

The box set of *Mad Men* Sophie Jones from the office had loaned him to watch the previous weekend had reminded him how stylish, how *cool* the office environment could be when people put in a little sartorial effort, though standards had certainly slipped since the 1950s; recently it seemed people had come to regard every day as if it were dress-down Friday. And although wearing suits to work wasn't really appropriate given that he worked in IT (the software industry tended to employ people who, while they might be coding geniuses, sometimes struggled to tie their own shoelaces, let alone produce the perfect Windsor knot), occasions like tonight's black-tie Christmas party were the ideal chance for Nathan to indulge himself.

He owned three suits: all Hugo Boss (they fitted his tall, broad-shouldered frame the best), each one hanging in its appropriate dust cover in his wardrobe, and bought (in the sales – Nathan may have been Seek's technical support manager, but he didn't earn *that* much) to cater for all occasions. The grey suit worked for interviews (not that he'd been to one of those for a while, though given Seek's recent merger with iFeel, he'd wondered whether he might be need-ing it imminently), weddings and the odd night out somewhere posh that didn't require a tie, like one of the number of rooftop or riverside bars that seemed to have sprung up around London lately, where the view took your breath away as much as the price of the cocktails did. The black one – well, he'd bought that so he'd have something stylish to wear to any funerals he went to, though fortunately so far it'd only been taken off its hanger the once, for a *Reservoir Dogs*-themed fancy-dress party he'd been to the previous year. The midnight-blue silk-trimmed dinner suit he was dressed in now was the one he wore the least, perhaps twice a year, at occa-sions like tonight's party, for example, and the odd posh dress-up do he occasionally got invited to at some pretentious friend's house. Though since Ellie had left him, he hadn't been to any of those. The pretentious ones had all sided with her. Which was something Nathan hadn't minded at all.

He carefully removed a stray hair from the lapel, then lint-rollered the rest of the outfit just in case. Attention to detail was important to Nathan. Working in technical support, you had to keep your eye on the little things – after all, any program or app was simply a series of smaller instructions or details designed to work together to perform an overall function; get just one of them wrong, and it wouldn't work – and Nathan saw dressing in a similar light. So for tonight, his shoes had to be black, and patent leather, the shine matched by the satin tape that ran up the side of his trousers. A black belt, too, with a silver buckle, which mirrored the vintage black-strap-with-silver-dial Jaeger-LeCoultre dress watch he'd inherited from his granddad, and which he only wore on special occasions like this. Then a simple, plain-collared cufflink-cuffed white shirt (from M&S, rather than any expensive designer make – credit where credit was due when the High Street got it right) instead of the fancy wing-collar type you'd see on the likes of Eton schoolboys, with a black bow tie – and not a clip-on one either. Nathan had learned how to tie his from a short instructional video on YouTube. It had been quite easy, really (after the fourth or fifth attempt) – just like tying a shoelace, but round your neck. And while this last item perhaps didn't look all that different from the ready-tied ones that most of the other men there would surely be wearing, there *was* a difference. As there would be later, when it was untied, and hanging oh-so-casually (with one end an inch or so lower than the other – Nathan had practised that look too) round his open-shirted neck.

With a final check in the full-length mirror in his hallway, he removed the outfit and slotted it carefully into his suit carrier, then dressed himself in his everyday casual jeans-and-denim-shirt workwear. Perhaps things would be different when they moved offices, but Nathan doubted it: iFeel was famous in the industry for having one of those workplaces that were more like student houses, with table-tennis tables, free vending machines, vintage arcade games and even hammocks for those 'contemplative moments' (or naps) the staff were apparently encouraged to take. He'd read about them in one of his style magazines – *GQ* or *Esquire*, he couldn't remember which – and had laughed at the photographs. Then a week later, he'd learned they were buying Seek, and he'd laughed even harder.

He jabbed a couple of buttons on his phone to summon an Uber, then slipped on his leather jacket, double-wrapped his scarf round his neck, slung the suit carrier over his shoulder, and headed outside, pausing to pass a handful of change to the homeless guy shivering on the bench outside his flat. As the man mumbled his thanks, a loud tutting made Nathan turn round.

'You shouldn't give them money, you know.'

'What?'

'The homeless.' The woman was about sixty, wearing a voluminous black puffer jacket with the hood up that made her look like an evil version of the Michelin man, and walking a tiny Chihuahua in matching attire.

'Why not?' said Nathan, frowning at her. Something about the way she'd almost spat out the words 'the homeless' told him all he needed to know about her privileged, sniffy attitude.

'Because they'll only spend it on alcohol.'

'Who am I to judge?' Nathan shrugged. 'That's exactly what I was planning to do with it.'

As the woman harrumphed off along the pavement, he shook his head. This was the downside to living next to Notting Hill: too many people who lived there thought life should be like a Richard Curtis film. Experience – or rather, *Ellie* – had taught Nathan the opposite was probably true.

He nodded goodbye to the homeless guy, then made his way across the street to where he'd parked his Vespa. While he'd normally ride the bike into work, given the amount he'd almost certainly be drinking this evening, he probably wouldn't be in any state to ride home – assuming he could even remember where he lived.

Besides, he didn't know where tonight's event was: transport had apparently been laid on to take them all from the office to the 'mystery London venue'. And though the word 'mystery' made him a little uneasy – Nathan always liked to know where he was going – the black-tie request meant that, for the first time in a long time, he was looking forward to it. Seek's office Christmas party usually only had the one dress requirement: an uncomfortable party hat, its thin elastic cord digging painfully into the underside of your chin, that someone (usually Mary from accounts) had thought it would be a 'great laugh' for you all to wear, while someone (again, usually Mary from accounts) tried to organise everyone into teams for the kind of party games you had to be either five years old or extremely drunk (though to be fair, by then most people usually were) to play. But this year, with iFeel's owner, the 'self-made billionaire Texan' (according to his LinkedIn profile) Tony A. Wood in attendance, it was likely to be a somewhat more refined occasion. Or at least, Nathan thought, checking his phone to see his Uber was a minute away, that was how it would start.

In any case, it would be a good chance to check out the competition. iFeel was . . . Well, even someone with Nathan's technical background didn't quite understand exactly what it was the company did: something to do with artificial intelligence, from what he could work out. They'd bought Seek because . . . Well, again, Nathan wasn't too sure why. Complementary technology, apparently, given the unique algorithms Seek's search engine used. But complementary or not, mergers usually meant job losses, and Nathan knew his opposite number in iFeel might be more senior than he was. So tonight was going to be an interesting evening from that point of view alone.

Brushing the light dusting of overnight snow from his bike's seat, he turned the key in the ignition and briefly fired up the engine, then smiled to himself. His scooter never let him down, and that was something he couldn't say about his past two girlfriends. First Ellie had dumped him – on Valentine's Day, *and* while he'd been in the middle of proposing – then Kasia . . . Well, he couldn't really blame her, he knew. She'd always said she was going to go back to her family in Poland once she'd finished studying, and to her credit, she had asked him if he wanted to come with her. But even Kasia being as hot as she was couldn't compensate for moving to a place where the summers weren't even as warm as this particular December London day, so, sadly, they'd parted. Just two short weeks ago.

Not that Nathan was feeling too upset about it. He'd always had a slight suspicion he and Kasia were what Sophie (or rather, one of the glossy magazines he often caught her reading in the kitchen – and sometimes even at her desk, if her boss, Julie Marshall, was out at a meeting) would describe as a 'sorbet' relationship: something to cleanse his palate of the (bad) taste Ellie dumping him had left. And it seemed to have done the trick; he hardly thought of Ellie at all nowadays. Well, no more than once or twice a day, at least.

A chill wind was blowing – Nathan hoped it wasn't an omen – so he gratefully climbed into the Prius that had silently glided to a halt in front of him (his Ubers so frequently seemed to be the Toyota hybrid that Nathan had once automatically climbed into one and told the driver where to go, only to be told the same – albeit somewhat *less* politely – by the angry occupant of the front seat in what had turned out to be a private car) and directed the driver down Queensway. The shop windows were full of decorations, their windows frosted with artificial snow; a large, brightly lit tree twinkled outside Whiteleys, and Nathan stared wide-eyed like a child as he passed them. Nathan loved Christmas; it just seemed to lift everyone's mood, even the normally surly black-cab drivers, many of whom worked these pre-Christmas days dressed in full Santa outfits, a sight that never failed to make him smile, especially when one of them was giving him the finger as he whizzed past them on his Vespa. And while the prospect of spending Christmas Day back home with his mum and dad (for the third year running!) wasn't the most exciting event on his horizon, Nathan didn't mind. Christmas was all about family, after all. And seeing as Ellie had turned down his offer to start a family of their own all those years ago, and he wasn't with Kasia any more . . . Well, his mum and dad were the only ones he had.

Except for his Seek family, of course (as Tony A. Wood had described them in his American way). Nathan loved where he worked, got on extremely well with the people he worked with – in particular Mark Webster and Calum Irwin; even he and Sophie (once she'd managed to get past the crush she'd admitted she had on him) were good friends now. As to whether he'd still be working with them after this merger with iFeel had gone through . . . Nathan knew he'd just have to wait and see.

Still, even if they did all end up going their separate ways, nothing would happen until the New Year. Getting sacked was like getting dumped: no one ever did it to anyone just before Christmas – that would just be too cruel. In any case, billionaire or not, surely their new owner wouldn't be wasting his money wining and dining a bunch of employees he was about to let go?

But whatever happened, Nathan knew he'd get through it. After all, he'd survived Ellie's dramatic dumping (just), and next to that, anything else life threw at him would be a walk in the park. Control was the secret; by not letting himself get close to anyone since then, he'd avoided being hurt again. By taking a firm grip of his career, he'd ensured he was where he wanted to be. If his job was safe, he'd decide if he wanted to stay at iFeel after the merger, although if they didn't want him, he'd choose where to go from the hundreds of jobs available online on the likes of *Indeed* and *Monster* – it was as simple as that. Besides, you shouldn't think of change as either good or bad, just inevitable; a wise man had told him that. Or it could have been Don Draper on *Mad Men*. Which, in Nathan's book, was the same thing.

No, he decided, as the cheerful driver let him out on the corner of Wardour Street (and thanks to his app, Nathan didn't have to worry about the uncertainty of how much to tip him), things were definitely changing. Even though it might be the end of Seek, or at least his time there, Nathan knew endings often had a funny knack of turning into beginnings.

Though you couldn't ever really know of what.

2.

Julie Marshall glanced up from her usual, speedy, head-down march along the pavement and caught sight of Mark Webster waiting for her by the entrance to Elephant & Castle tube station. Mark was never late; it was one of the things she most liked about him. It was just a shame that *she* was, which was why she'd bought those pregnancy tests from Boots on the way home the previous evening, though right now, she was wishing she hadn't. She fought her way through the crowds of early-morning commuters to where he was standing, stood up on tiptoe to kiss him briefly on the lips, then smiled as Mark's eyes flicked left and right.

'What's funny?'

She took him by the arm, then had to let him go as they swiped their way through the barriers. 'You always look like you're checking for paparazzi.'

'Well, you know. Until D-Day . . .'

Julie opened her mouth to tell him D-Day was in fact today, then remembered she actually had two pieces of news. And jammed into a crowded lift down to the Bakerloo Line was the last place she wanted to impart either of them.

'Sleep well?'

Mark shrugged as he followed her through the lift doors. 'Not great. Bed's too big without you, and all that. You should have stayed over. You should *always* stay over.'

'Mark . . .' Julie sighed. He'd been hinting they move in together for a while now, and Julie was beginning to run out of excuses. Not that she didn't want to be with him, but Mark lived in a one-bedroom flat. And after this morning's revelation, they might be needing two. 'I'm sorry. I just felt a little tired last night, and—'

'Are you feeling okay now?'

Mark's expression was suddenly all concern, and Julie realised with a start that this was one of the reasons she loved him. She made a mental note to tell him – one day – and gave his hand a squeeze.

'Fine.'

'Pleased to hear it.' He shifted his suit carrier to the opposite shoulder, and nodded down at the bag she was holding. 'Want me to take that for you?'

'Only if you give me yours to carry.'

'Point taken. Got your glad rags for tonight?'

Julie smiled again. Every now and again, Mark repeated a phrase he'd learned from Nathan, and it never sat well with his slightly clipped accent.

'Ye-es.'

He stepped a little closer to avoid the closing lift doors, careful to leave a polite distance between them. While she knew he couldn't wait for everyone at work to know about them, whenever they were together in public, Mark always acted as if there was a 'No Petting' sign on the wall, like they used to have in swimming pools.

'Should be a good bash,' he said, as they began their descent.

'Maybe.'

'Well, aren't you dripping with enthusiasm? A black-tie event, somewhere posh, with champagne, and me on your arm . . . Well, not actually on your arm, of course, but watching you from the other side of the room.'

'That sounds a bit creepy.'

'You know what I mean. Though I don't see why we can't have at least *one* dance . . .'

'Mark, we've talked about this. The last thing I want is for people in the office to be gossiping.'

'That's all some of them do all day anyway.'

'It just . . .' Julie exhaled loudly. 'No, you're right. I'm sorry. And I am . . . Well, to say I was "looking forward" to this evening would be overstating it a bit. I'd prefer it to be just you and me.'

'I would too. But at least Nathan will be there. And Sophie.'

'I know, but . . . I guess I'm just not the biggest fan of socialising with the people I work with. I see them every day, after all.'

'I'll try not to take that personally.'

'Not *you*. Nathan's fun. And so is Sophie. When she isn't having another personal crisis. But that lot from the main office—'

'Well, you're management. You don't have to speak to them. Besides, it's only once a year. If you don't count Nathan's *anti-Valentine's* bash.'

'I know, I know.' The lift doors opened, so they followed the crowd along the corridor and shuffled onto the already-packed platform. 'Though we could just . . . not go.'

'You did get the email? I think the head of marketing and UK country manager both not showing up might not be the best idea.'

'I suppose not.'

'Not to mention the rumour *that* would start.'

'Okay, okay.'

'Besides, Tony A. Wood's going to make an appearance. He's got some big announcement to make, apparently. And then he wants to talk to me privately about something, too.'

'Any ideas what?'

'Nope.' The train was approaching, so Julie allowed Mark to steer her back behind the yellow line on the edge of the platform. He always did things like this, including insisting on walking on the 'traffic' side of the pavement, and though Julie knew she should feel flattered, occasionally she had to fight the impulse to push him into the road. 'Well, it's about the merger, obviously, but I don't know any more than that. And you know how I hate surprises.'

Julie swallowed hard, and hoped he wouldn't feel the same about the one *she* had for him. 'It might just be about headcount. Redundancies.'

'I doubt they'd announce *that* at the Christmas party.' He stood back to give an old lady some space, then glared at the hoodie-wearing teenager who sidestepped into the gap. 'It's probably just about the new company name.'

'They're going to change it?'

Mark nodded. 'Change ours, at least. iFeel felt their branding was more important. And I can't see them compromising.'

'They can't combine the two?'

'To what? "iFeel-Seek"?'

Julie laughed, then suddenly realised sick – or at least, morning sickness – was the one thing she hadn't felt. Maybe the test *had* been a false alarm. She clutched her bag anxiously to her stomach, glad Mark was focusing more on the arriving tube than her expression.

'Anyway,' continued Mark, as they squeezed their way onto the train, 'how about we just stay as long as is polite? Say hello to whoever we have to say hello to. Hear whatever this big news is, drink some of Tony A. Wood's champagne, and then—' He ducked to avoid being decapitated by the closing doors. '—back home for our own private party. No, hang on. That sounded a little creepy too . . .'

As he tried to stop himself from blushing, Julie forced a smile, grateful that the noise of the tube was making conversation impossible, although now was hardly the time to tell him her big news.

No, she'd definitely tell him about the divorce *and* the baby tonight, once whatever this big announcement was had been made. That way, they'd have all the facts. Could make some decisions. And would be able to get on with their lives.

One way or another.

❦

Calum Irwin shivered as he half-walked, half-jogged down Wardour Street, regretting the fact that his best suit – chosen specially for this evening's *two* events – wasn't his warmest. Spotting Nathan climbing out of a Prius on the other side of the street, he gave him a cheery wave, then waited for him to cross the road.

'Mister Irwin!'

'Mister Field.' Calum tipped an imaginary hat, then fell into step alongside him. He liked Nathan immensely. It was hard not to – not only was he an all-round decent bloke, he also fixed Calum's computer whenever it went on the blink. Which was a lot more than it probably should have, Calum knew.

'All set for this evening?'

'I guess so,' said Calum, assuming Nathan was referring to the Christmas party. He hadn't told anyone at work his plans where Mia-Rose was concerned. 'Any idea what's happening?' he asked, as Nathan stopped at a cashpoint and fed his card into the slot.

'We get dressed up, jump on a bus to some posh venue, drink some billionaire's bubbly while he tells us how great we are, that together we're stronger, that this is more than just a marriage of convenience . . . What's the matter?'

'Sorry.' Calum hoped his friend wouldn't notice he was blushing. He'd already decided to ask Nathan to be his best man if – sorry, *when* – Mia-Rose said yes. He averted his eyes as Nathan punched in his PIN, then stamped his feet to get warm. 'Just got, you know . . .' His voice tailed off. He'd been about to say 'cold feet', and he didn't want to jinx himself for later. Still, at least he could use the temperature as an excuse for why his hands seemed to be shaking.

'Big change, though?' Calum said. 'New owner, new offices . . .'

'We'll see. In my experience, different job, same bollocks.' Nathan grinned as he stuffed a bundle of notes from the machine into his pocket. 'Still, you'll be alright. Top salesman and all that.'

'Only salesman.'

'Still means you're the best.'

Calum reddened again, but it was true. Since he and Mia-Rose had been going out, he'd been doing better at his job. Beating, not just meeting, his targets. More confident. And in sales, confidence was what mattered.

They hurried round the corner into Bateman Street, Calum anxious to get to the office and out of the cold, pausing only for Nathan to point out where someone had removed the 'e' from Bateman in his best *Christian Bale* voice.

'How about yourself?'

'Dunno.' Nathan pulled his key card from his pocket and swiped the door open. 'Still haven't met my opposite number. Probably some A.I. geek who never sees the light of day.'

'What makes you think they're from Newcastle?'

Nathan stared at him for a moment, then he laughed. 'No, "A.I.", not "wey-aye". "Artificial Intelligence".' Nathan glanced up at Mary and Carol, two of Seek's back-office team, who were comparing hideous Christmas jumpers by the top of the stairs. 'Which some of this lot could do with a bit of, I can tell you.' He rolled his eyes, then flashed a smile towards reception. 'Morning, Mia.'

'Morning, chaps.' Mia-Rose beamed up at them from where she was Sellotaping tinsel around the edges of the reception desk. 'How are my two favourite men in the world?'

Calum blushed again, and tried to bat down the spike of jealousy he felt whenever Mia so much as spoke to another man. As receptionist for the company, this of course happened a lot, plus Nathan . . . Well, everyone fancied Nathan – which meant Mia probably did too. Calum had shyly admitted his insecurities once. *But it's you I go home with*, Mia had said. And the smile hadn't left his face for the rest of the day.

As he glanced around to check no one was watching, then gave Mia the briefest of kisses on the cheek, Nathan mimed sticking his fingers down his throat.

'Get a room, you two.'

Mia-Rose glared affectionately back at him. 'Meeting Room two's available?'

'Please. I sometimes eat my lunch at that table.' Nathan made a face, then headed for the stairs. 'Right, off for another exciting day of telling people to turn it off and on again. Adios, amigos!'

'Adios,' said Calum, wondering why it didn't quite sound as cool when *he* said it.

He watched as Nathan launched himself onto the banister and slid acrobatically down towards the technical support room in the basement, then he leaned against the reception desk as casually as he could.

'Speaking of eating . . .' He took a deep breath, then hesitated. The reception phone was ringing, and Mia-Rose raised both eyebrows, but Calum suspected if he waited until she'd dealt with the call, he might lose his nerve. 'Did you fancy grabbing a quick bite later? Before the party?'

Mia-Rose nodded enthusiastically as she picked the receiver up. 'Love to,' she said, pressing the 'answer' button, followed by, 'Seek Software, good morning.'

And as she smiled at him, mouthing *Love you* before returning to the call, Calum virtually skipped up the stairs and into his office.

∽

Nathan Field leapt off the bottom of the banister, landing perfectly on both feet – something he imagined he'd probably get points awarded for once they'd moved into iFeel's building – and bounded into his office, switching his laptop on and slotting his phone into its charging dock in the same, practised movement. A quick scan of his emails revealed nothing urgent (except for one from Mary in accounts complaining she'd been hacked, though when Nathan read further, this was because her password box apparently showed a series of asterisks, and Mary was sure that wasn't the password she'd typed in).

However, as he scrolled further down through his inbox, he froze. There, sitting right in between a message from his mother entitled 'Christmas' (which Nathan decided he'd save for later) and another from someone called Saskia69 inviting him to see her 'sexy fakebook pix' (which he hesitated over before consigning it to 'spam') was one – no subject, but with an ominous paperclip-shaped icon signifying an attachment – from Ellie.

Nathan narrowed his eyes as he peered at the screen, then hovered his mouse over her name, checking it had really come from her address, and that Ellie's email hadn't been spoofed. The last thing he wanted was for the message to give his system a virus. It had taken him long enough to get over her in real life. He still wasn't convinced he had. Which was why any attachment from her, given his previous attachment *to* her, set alarm bells ringing.

He had three options, he knew: delete the message and nip any chance of a problem – technical, *or* emotional – in the bud; open it and hope either that it *was* actually from her, or if not, that his antivirus software was up to the job (and if it wasn't, then neither, surely, was he); or mail her separately to check whether she'd sent him something – but that could be opening a can of worms he'd thought he'd sealed well shut.

He sat back heavily in his chair. This was a woman he'd gone out with for nearly three years, lived with, even wanted to marry, but when he'd asked her, nearly four years ago, on Valentine's Day, she'd turned him down, then turned his life upside down by admitting she'd been seeing someone else. Nathan still didn't know how he'd gotten it so wrong. And even though he'd thought he could finally move on, the way he was feeling at seeing her email was telling him something different.

Though maybe he was just feeling sorry for himself. Perhaps Kasia leaving had left a void that was easier to fill with something familiar, rather than go through this whole cycle of getting-to-know-someone-new-then-waiting-until-it-eventually-went-wrong. Ellie had hinted – no, *suggested* (unless he'd imagined it) – they go for dinner when he'd seen her last, and that had been on Valentine's Day. And while he'd turned her down, maybe this was her way of testing the water again. Putting the feelers out. Seeing whether he was . . . What? Single? Interested? Or maybe just as lonely as she was? It was Christmas, after all. And no one wanted to be alone at Christmas.

He puffed air out of his cheeks, then – before he could change his mind – hit 'compose', and typed her name into the address box, wincing when autocomplete brought her address front and centre after just the first two letters, worried that would always be the case for him too. 'Did you email me? Worried it's a virus,' was all he wrote, then he quickly hit 'send'.

Then spent the next few hours wishing he hadn't.

❧

Julie Marshall strode up the stairs at Oxford Circus and made her way along Oxford Street, resisting the temptation to turn round and wave exaggeratedly at Mark Webster, wondering if she did so, whether he might suddenly leap into a doorway, or pretend to be fascinated by something in a shop window, like people did when they were tailing someone in the movies. Not that it was her he was trying not to be seen by. This was silly, she knew, that the two of them had to pretend they hadn't travelled into work together. What was she expecting – that Philip would be badgering the rest of Seek's employees, trying to find out whether they knew anything, or even worse, had spent the last nine months camped out in Top Shop's doorway with a camera, trying to secure photographic evidence that she was cheating on him?

Though that didn't matter any more, she reminded herself cheerfully. As of this morning, she was finally free of him. Divorced. Free to see whoever she wanted (though of course, it was only Mark she wanted). Free to concentrate on her career with Seek, or iFeel, whatever name the new organisation was going to have. And once she'd changed *her* name, the 'Marshall' period of her life would be nothing but a distant memory.

She frowned to herself as she walked briskly along the pavement. How did it work, this changing-your-name-back lark? When you got married, you just filled in a form, but as to the other way round . . . Would it happen automatically? Did she have to do the whole 'deed poll' thing, or could she just go back to being plain old Julie Pooley as soon as she wanted?

She turned into Bateman Street, sidestepping the three workmen it seemed to require for the ten-second job of replacing the missing 'e' on the street sign, though she doubted changing her name back would be *that* easy. Not that she'd ever particularly liked her maiden name, and besides, what had her parents been thinking? Giving your child a Christian name that rhymed with their surname . . . Well, it was akin to child abuse in her book. When – no, *if* – she had this baby, she'd make sure—

Julie stopped abruptly in front of the office. What would the child be called? Would it be a Pooley, or (if she didn't get a move on) even a Marshall? There was always Webster, of course – at least nothing rhymed with that – but it would be strange to have a baby that didn't have the same surname as she did.

Then again, if she had to go to the trouble of officially changing her name, maybe this was an opportunity to get something she liked, like Julie . . . She frowned again, unable to come up with something on the spot, though knowing this would be her last chance. She certainly wouldn't be getting married again; the years she'd spent with Philip had kind of taken the fun out of that particular institution for her. And while she hadn't told Mark this was how she felt, she actually hadn't told him how she felt about a lot of things. Including him, come to think of it.

She glanced back along the street to where Mark was waiting impatiently on the corner, no doubt wondering why she'd stopped outside the office, then quickly swiped herself into the building, mouthed *Morning* to an on-the-phone Mia-Rose, and took the stairs two at a time up to her office. Running the London Marathon earlier in the year had gotten her into pretty impressive shape, and while she never intended to attempt another one even if her life depended on it, she still ran every other day. She'd even convinced Mark to come with her once. Although given the quivering wreck he'd become after just one lap of the park, it had been just the once.

She marched in through the door, smiled at the unmistakeable sight of Sophie Jones glued to her computer – though as per usual, it didn't seem to be work-related – and cleared her throat.

'Morning!'

'Oh!' Sophie snapped her laptop shut. 'Sorry. You made me jump. Morning, boss.'

'What are you up to? Not looking at Monster, I hope?'

'Match dot-com,' said Sophie. 'Though "monster" would be a better name for it, given some of the profile pics that came up on my search.'

'Ah.' Julie had long ago stopped asking Sophie about her love life. Especially if they had some actual work to do that day. Besides, it would have taken a software package with data-mining capabilities even more sophisticated than Seek's to keep track of what was going on. 'Well, as long as you weren't looking for a new job.'

'Why? What have you heard? Are we all getting fired? Or is it just me?'

Sophie had turned pale, and Julie felt a stab of guilt. 'I didn't mean it like that. I'm sure you'll be fine.'

'How sure? Unless you're the one who's going? Because they'd have to keep me then, wouldn't they? I mean, I'm the only one who knows—'

'Relax, Sophie. I'm not going anywhere. And I'm pretty confident you aren't either. Just remember, you're my right-hand woman.'

'Which would be fine, if you were left-handed.'

Julie laughed, despite herself. She'd never met a more glass-half-empty person than Sophie. And while she was hardly the most glass-half-full person herself, meeting Mark had taught her that glasses were, in fact, refillable.

'But we're marketing,' continued Sophie. 'We're always the first people to be let go.'

'Only during a downsizing. This is a merger, remember? iFeel are buying us lock, stock . . .' Julie patted her arm reassuringly, 'and barrel.'

'So now I'm one of the barrels?'

'That's not what I meant. You've been here how long now?'

'Nearly four years.'

'Well, in that case, even if you do get fired, you should qualify for a decent redundancy package. Besides, being let go's not so . . .' Julie paused, mid-sentence, as Sophie had suddenly burst into tears. 'Don't worry! I'm sure they'll keep you on.' She marched around the desk and gave her a brief hug. 'And even if they don't, I'll give you a glowing reference.'

'Thanks a *lot*!'

'Why are you so upset?'

'Because I *have* been let go.'

'*What?*'

Sophie opened her laptop, tabbed through from Match.com, then rotated the screen to show Julie she'd been in the middle of changing her Facebook status from 'in a relationship'. 'I looked at the drop-down menu, but 'is giving up on Tinder' doesn't seem to be an option.'

'What happened to Doctor, um . . . ?'

'Doctor who?'

Julie made a face, unsure whether Sophie was making a joke. 'I don't . . . ?'

'What *always* happens. I think things are going great, and then, all of a sudden it turns out he has to marry some third cousin from India – well, Bolton – he's never met before.'

'That's what always happens to you, is it?'

'Not *exactly* that, no. It's what happened with him, and since then . . . I'm always the one who always gets dumped, and I can never see it coming.'

'Well, maybe you're picking the—'

'—wrong type of men? Tell me about it.'

Julie hoped that wasn't an instruction. She'd obviously picked wrong where Philip had been concerned. Though so far, Mark looked like being a much better bet. 'It's a difficult thing to get right, Sophie, believe me. But maybe, instead of dwelling on them, if you tried to *learn* from your mistakes—'

'If I learned from my mistakes, I'd be the Einstein of the dating world by now.' Sophie dabbed at her eyes with a tissue from the box Julie made her keep in her top drawer for whenever this kind of occasion arose. A box that was getting rather depleted, she couldn't help but notice. 'And besides, there aren't that many men left for me to make a mistake with!'

'I'm sure there are . . . No, wait, I didn't mean it like that.' Julie perched on the edge of Sophie's desk. 'Remember, it's the Christmas party tonight.'

'So?'

Julie wondered whether she should let on that Nathan was single again, but Mark had told her in confidence about him and Kasia splitting up, and she'd always prided herself that she was good at keeping secrets. Which was just as well, given this morning's developments.

'"Black tie". And at a "mystery London location". It sounds like fun.'

'Fun?' Sophie rolled her eyes sarcastically. 'Mark Webster said attendance was compulsory, which means they're going to be making some announcements, and probably about which of us are going to get fired. What kind of "fun" is that?'

'There'll be men there.'

'Julie, they're an artificial intelligence company. That means they're probably all techie geeks who make Stephen Hawking look like Keanu Reeves.'

'Nathan's a techie geek.'

At the mention of his name, Sophie perked up slightly. 'Yes, well, he's the exception that . . .' She frowned. 'Well, that either proves the rule, or disproves it. I never know which way that saying goes. But chances are—'

'—that there might at least be a few decent single men there.'

Sophie let out a short laugh. 'If men are decent, they're not single. And if they are single nowadays, then they're probably on Tinder, and all the men I've met on there are indecent.'

'Well, maybe you need to set your sights a little higher.'

'That's easy for you to say.'

'Come on, Sophie. Look at this office. What's the male/female ratio, do you think?'

Sophie shrugged. 'I dunno. About seventy-thirty, I guess.'

'And we're merging with a company, which, unless Tony A. Wood shares a hiring policy with Hugh Hefner, has . . .' Julie reached over and typed a couple of words into the Seek 'search' box on Sophie's laptop, then hit 'return'. 'Around a hundred UK employees. Which means, if they're anything like Seek, around—'

'Seventy men,' said Sophie glumly. 'I already did the maths.'

'Or "math", as our transatlantic colleagues, might say.' Julie smiled, then she put on her best American accent. 'And just wait till they get a load of you.'

'I'm not sure . . .' said Sophie, blowing her nose loudly into the tissue.

'I am. You turn up dressed to kill and you'll be fighting them off.'

'I've *been* fighting them off. And not in a good way.' Sophie looked up at her, and Julie was pleased to see a trace of a smile. 'Plus the only thing the dress I was planning to wear is likely to kill is passion.'

Julie thought for a moment, then she reached over and gave Sophie's shoulder the briefest of squeezes. 'Well, let's take a stroll along Oxford Street at lunchtime and see if we can't do something about that.'

Mark Webster swiped himself into the building, still picturing the pleasurable sight of Julie Marshall's rear view as he'd followed her – a respectable distance between them – down Wardour Street. He'd be glad when this little charade they'd been playing out every weekday since they'd got together last Valentine's Day would be over.

Not that he was desperate to walk into work holding hands or anything like that. Simply being able to walk side by side along the pavement, or go for lunch together, or even smile knowingly at each other whenever they happened to meet in the kitchen (which Mark did his best to make happen as often as possible) without setting tongues wagging was all he wanted. And once her divorce came through, well, surely all of those things would all be okay – assuming his new employers allowed it? He didn't know yet whether iFeel had any kind of policy about employees 'seeing' each other. He was pretty sure those kind of restrictions were illegal anyway. And besides, how could a company that apparently made business decisions based on the result of a game of table tennis possibly set rules about something like that?

He marched in through reception and nodded a curt hello to Mia-Rose, wondering what the best way to announce their relationship might be. Obviously an office-wide email would do the trick, but Mark was too private a person to do anything like that (plus Julie would probably kill him). Of course, he could 'accidentally' let it slip to someone like Mary in accounts – telling her anything was a sure-fire way to ensure everyone in the company would find out by the end of the day. But the problem with that was Mary was sure to embellish it a little, or get something wrong, and the control freak in Mark didn't want any of that going on. Besides, it wasn't as though they were announcing they were getting married, or anything. Mark smiled to himself. When Julie's divorce did finally happen, the coast was clear for that sort of thing, but one step at a time.

Though given that they hadn't even discussed what they were doing for Christmas yet – Mark assumed they'd be spending it together, though he knew better than to assume anything where Julie was concerned – and she'd changed the subject whenever he'd suggested she spend more than the night at his, those steps were seeming like rather big ones.

In any case, he had too much to think about at the moment, he knew, striding through the open-plan part of the office, trying not to notice how many people slammed their laptops shut or quickly 'minimised' whatever it was they had on screen as he passed. Not that he thought they were looking at anything untoward – except for possibly 'Eggs' Benedict from legal. Nathan had showed Mark his browsing history a few months ago, and it had made for a very interesting (not to mention embarrassing) conversation, followed by a very carefully worded written warning. It was more that everyone seemed to be updating CVs, or tweaking their LinkedIn profiles, or posting their details on job sites, rather than getting on with any work. Still, Mark didn't mind. It was to be expected; mergers made people jumpy, and it was only natural that they should be worried about the future. And besides, until tonight, when Tony A. Wood was going to hopefully reveal their new direction, no one was sure what work they should actually be getting on with.

He walked up to Julie's office, pausing in the doorway in readiness for their usual first-thing charade. 'Morning, Julie,' he said, perhaps a little loudly, making a sympathetic face when Julie looked up from where she appeared to be consoling a red-eyed Sophie Jones.

'Morning, Mark,' she replied, formally, and – job done/bluff continued – Mark headed on to his office.

He hung his suit carrier carefully on the back of his door, sat down at his desk, and switched his laptop on, watching it boot up with the same eager sense of anticipation he did every working day.

He had spreadsheets to pore over, org charts to memorise, removals companies to co-ordinate, and leases to cancel – so much, in fact, that it should be making his head spin. But in truth, Mark loved a project. Give him a problem, throw an issue his way, and he liked nothing more than to find a solution. It was why he was running the London office, after all.

No, Mark was confident that very little in life stumped him. So the fact that, right now, he was completely clueless about his and Julie's future, was something he tried not to read too much into.

3.

'Knock, knock.'

Nathan Field poked his head through Mark Webster's open doorway, then without waiting for a reply, marched inside.

'Was I supposed to say "Who's there?"' said Mark, glancing up from where he'd been peering intently at his laptop screen, and Nathan grinned.

'Java installation,' he announced, back-heeling the door shut behind him, before setting the two mugs of coffee that were just becoming too uncomfortably hot to hold in one hand down on Mark's desk.

'Great. Thanks.'

'Along with a rather large tin of Roses chocolates, courtesy of our printer supplier, that I thought I'd rescue from the kitchen before that lot out there got their hands on them, and all we were left with were the toffees.'

'The toffees are my favourite.'

'They would be.'

As Nathan gave him a pitiful look, Mark sat back in his chair. 'What's news?'

Nathan shrugged. 'Not much. Especially without Kasia.'

'You missing her?'

'A little.' In truth, he'd missed Kasia more than he'd thought he would. Though not enough to book a last-minute easyJet flight to Krakow.

'No one else on the horizon? Or even closer to home?'

'Nope. All quiet on the West End front.'

'Saving yourself for tonight's party?'

Nathan leaned heavily against the filing cabinet. 'Something like that.' He picked up his mug, blew across the top and took a sip. 'Where, of course, we'll be meeting our new lord and master. Any idea what he's like?'

Mark shook his head. 'Couldn't tell you.'

'Because you've been told not to?'

'No, because I've never met him. Or even spoken to him. This merger came a bit out of the blue, to be honest. And I don't know how much Tony A. Wood was involved in the negotiations.'

'You're Seek's UK country manager and you've *never even spoken to* the person who's bought us?'

'Er, no,' said Mark, awkwardly. He reached for his laptop and double-clicked on an email. 'All I got was this.'

As a video file began playing, which showed Tony A. Wood announcing how happy he was having bought Seek, Nathan gestured towards the screen with his mug.

'He talks like Forrest Gump.'

'Don't let that fool you. Reputation for being quite cut-throat, doesn't go in for popularity contests, and currently the hundred-and-seventh-richest man in America, apparently. Self-made too.'

Nathan made sure he looked suitably impressed. 'Any idea what he's going to do with us?'

'Not yet.' Mark reached over and paused the video. 'They've said there aren't going to be any redundancies, but . . .' He made a *we're all doomed* face, and Nathan laughed.

'They bought us, though? So if anyone's going, it's likely to be from our lot?'

'We'll see,' said Mark. 'Everything's a little hush-hush until tonight, to be honest.'

'Speaking of hush-hush, any news on' – Nathan leaned in – 'J-U-L-I-E?'

'Keep your voice down!'

'That *was* down.' Nathan gave him a pitying look. If there was a worse-kept secret in the office than Mark and Julie's relationship, he couldn't think what it might be. 'And don't worry. Like when you say W-A-L-K to stop a dog getting excited, I spelled it out, so none of them out there would work out what we're talking about. Clever, eh?'

'Oh yes. You're a genius. Not,' said Mark, dryly. 'And no change. Still waiting for the *you-know-what*—'

'D-I-V-O-R-C-E?' sang Nathan, in his best Dolly Parton accent, and Mark glared at him.

'Uh-huh. Should be any day now, though.'

Nathan widened his eyes. 'Excellent! So does that mean . . . ?'

'What?'

'You and her?'

Mark helped himself to a sweet from the tin. 'What about me and her?'

'Are you going to, you know . . . ?' Nathan swallowed hard. One of the legacies of being dumped mid-proposal, he knew, was that even thinking about the act of someone else getting down on one knee was tough to deal with. 'Do the decent thing?'

'As opposed to the *in*decent things we've been doing?' Mark leaned back and linked his fingers behind his head. 'I'd like to. One day. But not when the ink's hardly dry on her divorce papers. Not that it's even wet yet.'

'Don't want her to think things are moving too fast, eh?' Nathan unwrapped a caramel cup, popped it into his mouth, balled the wrapper up and lobbed it expertly into Mark's mug.

Mark ignored Nathan's whispered 'Get in!', fished the wrapper out and dropped it into the bin. 'Chance would be a fine thing. She won't even move in with me.'

'You've asked her?'

'I've mentioned it in passing once or twice, and she's pretty much blanked me. But it's probably for the best. Too much to sort out here, what with the office move and all that. This takeover—'

'Merger.'

'Merger, sorry, is actually quite a big deal. '

'That's what you should make it with Julie.'

'What?'

'A big deal.' Nathan looked up from where he was rifling through the sweet tin. 'Women don't want to be asked to move in "in passing". They want these things to be grand gestures. When I asked Ellie—'

'To move in? As opposed to the other thing? Because we all know how *that* worked out.'

Nathan glared at him. 'My point still stands,' he said. 'You've got a nice flat, so it's unlikely that's the sticking point – though admittedly, it could do with a bit of a woman's touch.' He slipped a handful of sweets into his pocket. 'As could I, come to think of it . . .'

'She might not want it to be a big deal.'

'Bet she does. Specially since she's pretty much ignored it when you've made it a small one. Once this D-I-V—'

'Okay, okay!'

'No, that's not how you spell it.'

'*Nathan . . .*'

'All I'm saying is, once this *you-know-what* of hers comes through, she might be feeling a bit low. Wanting some positive indication from you. A suggestion of commitment. Longevity. And remember, her recent memories of being shacked up with someone aren't the happiest ones. What have you said so far?'

'Well, just that there's no point her shelling out every month to rent some overpriced shoebox down the road when we're spending most of our time together at my place anyway.'

Nathan rolled his eyes. Hearing stuff like this made him feel grateful he was currently spared all this relationship anguish. 'That's the most romantic thing I've ever heard. I can't believe it didn't work.'

'I just don't want to make a fool of myself.'

'Like I did? Trouble is, sometimes women *want* us to make fools of ourselves. You just need to make sure whatever you do, however you do it, you come up smelling of . . .' Nathan drummed his fingers on the sweet tin, then showed it to Mark, as if presenting a game show prize.

'Roses. I see. Very good.'

Nathan grinned. 'At the very least, you need to sell her the idea.'

'Ah.'

'Ah what?'

'I don't know the first thing about sales.'

'Well, why not get some tips from a man who does?'

'Ask Calum?'

'Exactly. Oh, and if you want my advice, ease into it.'

Mark frowned, then he widened his eyes. 'Oh, you mean with Julie. Not Calum.'

'Right. Why not start by getting her to spend Christmas with you? Maybe at your folks' gaff. She can see what happy families are like, and then . . .' Nathan mimed shooting a basketball, then followed it with a celebratory fist-pump. 'What do you think?'

Mark stared at him for a moment. 'What do I think?' He put his coffee down, stood up, and clapped Nathan on the shoulder. 'I take back what I said earlier. You *are* a genius.'

∾

'Busy?'

Calum Irwin hadn't noticed Mark Webster standing in his office doorway, and his boss's curt enquiry had made him leap up from his chair in shock. 'No. I mean, yes! Well, not really, but . . .' Calum tried his best not to look guilty, but it was an unfair question for first thing in the morning. No one was ever busy as soon as they got into the office, were they? You needed to start gradually. Stick your phone on charge, delete your spam emails, grab a cup of coffee, discuss last night's *Game of Thrones* with someone. You couldn't just come straight in and *work*. You needed a warm-up.

'Relax.' Mark smiled. 'I've just got a quick sales-related question for you.'

'Fire away. I mean, sure.' Calum began to panic. Telling your boss to 'fire away' when redundancies were in the air possibly wasn't the best choice of terminology.

Mark peered back out into the corridor, then pushed the door to. 'Say you're trying to sell someone something . . .'

'You're trying to sell someone something.' Calum had done what he'd been told, then he realised Mark might have been talking hypothetically.

'That's right. And they're a bit . . . reluctant. To buy.'

'Reluctant?'

'Right. What's the best technique to make them less . . . ?'

'Reluctant?'

'Exactly.'

Calum mulled the question over for a moment or two. Not because he didn't immediately know the answer, but because he wasn't sure whether Mark was asking him genuinely, or testing him as part of something to do with the merger, and he wanted to make sure he responded appropriately. Then he realised that the answer would be the same in either case, and he felt bad about the delay. 'Well, normally, I'd suggest a demo.'

'A demo?'

'As in "demonstration". By which I don't mean walking up and down outside their offices with a placard saying "Please buy our software".' Calum grinned at his joke, but Mark only gave him the briefest of smiles in acknowledgement. 'I mean we offer them a trial. Give them a chance to use the software for a few days. So they can see how they get on with it. Whether it, you know, meets their needs.'

'I see.' Mark folded his arms. 'It gives them a chance to realise that it's better than where they're living – I mean, what they're living with – currently.'

Calum nodded. 'Exactly. It's known as the puppy effect. Lend someone a cute puppy, and after a few days they won't want to give it back.'

'And it works, does it?'

He nodded again. 'Assuming it doesn't, you know, do its business on their rug, metaphorically speaking. And, of course, that they like your particular . . .'

'Puppy?' Mark narrowed his eyes. 'Interesting,' he said. 'Thanks Calum.'

As he turned and left, Calum sat back down, a little puzzled at what had just happened. Selling was his department, so why on earth would Mark Webster be quizzing him about sales techniques? Either this *was* to do with upcoming redundancies, or there was something else going on that he didn't know about. Whichever, Calum suspected it might be time to up his game.

He double-checked his door was shut, then rifled through the suspension files in his desk drawer, trying to find the documentation from the refresher sales training he'd attended a month or so ago. The course – a half-day affair at some nondescript hotel in Canary Wharf, run by a husband-and-wife team who'd had a habit of finishing each other's sentences (something Calum had found sweet until he'd noticed the barely concealed look of anger on the wife's face whenever the husband had done it) – had been notable mainly because the all-you-can-eat buffet lunch (with a seemingly unlimited supply of Calum's favourite: chicken nuggets) had stretched even Calum's considerable appetite. But now, as he reviewed his notes, he could see there had been some useful nuggets of information too. Information that might help him keep his job. And could even come in extremely handy where his plans for tonight were concerned. After all, what was a marriage proposal but a sales pitch?

He skimmed through the pages in his notebook, mentally ticking the key points off as he did so. *Make sure you're speaking to the decision maker.* Well, Mia was the one who'd say yes or no, so he was pretty sure he'd got that right.

Make sure what you're selling meets a need in the person you're pitching to. Mia had said she wanted to get married. Didn't all women? And proposing to her was the most obvious way to satisfy that particular requirement.

Don't talk too much. Calum thought for a moment. 'Will you marry me?' was only four words, and even if he added 'Mia' to the front of that sentence (or 'Mia-Rose'), it was only five (or six). And that could hardly be regarded as 'talking too much'.

Oh, and *Know when to not talk at all.* Calum had always felt this was the hardest part of any sales pitch. Once you'd said your bit, the trick was then to keep shtum, even though the ensuing silence might grow uncomfortable, so the 'prospect' would feel a need to fill the gap by saying something. And while he knew that waiting for Mia's response to his 'Will you marry me?' (or 'Mia, will you marry me?' Or 'Mia-Rose, will you marry me?' – he hadn't decided yet) would be the hardest (and probably longest) period of silence he'd ever have to endure, he was determined not to break it. Until she broke into a grin. Or broke his heart.

Don't badmouth your competitors. Calum batted that one down straight away. As far as he knew, he didn't *have* any competitors. He hoped.

Has your prospect been qualified? Well, Mia was over the legal age to get married, and he assumed she could, in that she wasn't married to someone else, or going through a divorce, or anything that rendered her ineligible. She came from a religious family, and believed in God, which surely meant that marriage rather than 'living in sin' was on her agenda.

Sell the sizzle, not the steak. Calum smiled to himself. He knew not to take this one literally, even though he was carrying quite a lot of steak, but to sell the *benefits* of what he was offering, not just, well, him. And while what he was offering *was* just him, there were benefits too: a ring, for one thing. Two, in fact (and Mia loved jewellery). A new surname, if she wanted it (though Mia-Rose Irwin meant she'd have the initials 'MRI', which was a bit too medical-sounding for his liking). A wedding (and most women wanted one of those, didn't they?) and everything that went with that, including (he swallowed hard) kids. And he knew Mia wanted kids – she'd often stop and remark about some cute child they'd seen when they were out and about. And while Calum sometimes woke up in a cold sweat wondering what a child of theirs might look like given her Afro-Caribbean heritage and his pale, red-haired Irishness (and Google Images had done nothing to alleviate his fears), a baby was a baby. And the sooner they got married, the sooner she – *they* – could start a family . . .

At the thought he might be a dad soon, Calum felt his palms start to sweat, and he wiped them anxiously on his trouser legs. Suddenly, tonight was taking on a whole new level of seriousness. He'd thought of it simply as proposing, but in reality, it was much more than that. They'd have to set a date for the wedding, then actually *get* married, and then what? Would Mia move in with him and his mother in Balham, in their flat with paper-thin walls? Would he move in with Mia's family in North London, where there was hardly enough room for Mia and her three sisters as it was? Or, would he abandon his mum, and he and Mia buy a flat somewhere they could both afford (which, given the current state of the London property market, might not actually *be* in London)? Either way, it surely wouldn't be long before they heard the patter of tiny feet (or the thump of large ones, given that he and Mia were unlikely to produce small offspring).

He was sweating all over now, so he got up from his desk, walked over to the window, and cracked it open. When you thought about it, proposing actually went against all the fundamentals of sales training, which could essentially be boiled down to one thing: *ABC*. Not that it meant it was as easy or simple as that: ABC stood for *Always Be Closing*, whereas as far as he could tell, proposing this evening was more *Close Once, Calum, Keep Shtum*, which didn't make quite as good-sounding an acronym. But he had to remember it above all the others. Go straight for the commitment. No preamble, no setting out your stall, just straight in there with the world's most binary question.

They were only four words (or five, or six – depending on whether hyphenated words counted as two), and yet to Calum they seemed like the hardest words in the universe to say. But he and Mia had already said 'I love you' to each other: that had been easy. All he had to do was come out with a sentence thirty-three per cent longer (or sixty-six per cent, or more. Calum decided to forget about the maths).

He'd tried it out loud a couple of times, placing the emphasis on different words, even recording it on his phone so he could hear how it sounded, but each time, the gravitas seemed to be lacking – it was as if he was asking Mia if she wanted a cup of tea or to go for a walk, not spend the rest of her life with him. No, he could see why people spelled it out in big letters on the sand, or hired airplanes to write it out in the sky. Though given *where* he was planning to ask her, writing it with ketchup on Mia's plate while she was in the toilets seemed his only option this evening.

Maybe it was easier when you were actually down on one knee, though, like when you did a parachute jump – shouting 'One thousand, two thousand, three thousand!' face down on the floor of an aircraft hangar felt ridiculous, but once you'd actually jumped out of the plane it was a lot more appropriate. Not that Calum had ever done a parachute jump; his vertigo put paid to that idea, and while he'd gone through the training on a corporate team-building event a few years ago, the relief he'd felt when the jump had been cancelled due to bad weather had been immeasurable. Though right now, jumping out of a plane seemed a piece of cake compared to what he was planning to do later.

He pushed his chair back to make some room, then knelt down to see how it sounded in situ, but just as his mouth was forming the shape for the 'w' of 'will' (he still hadn't decided between 'Mia' and 'Mia-Rose'), his door flew open. By the look of the Ugg boots he could see from his under-desk vantage point, it was Mia, and Calum froze. He could hide, he knew, though just as he decided that was the best plan, Mia's 'What are you doing down there?' put paid to that strategy.

'I, um . . .' Though he was down on one knee, Calum knew he had to think on his feet, and all of a sudden, he had a brainwave. He double-checked he wasn't actually wearing his glasses, then hauled himself to his feet. 'Dropped a contact lens.'

'Want me to get down there with you and help you look?'

Calum blinked furiously for effect, then dabbed at his eye. 'Don't worry. Found it,' he said, before realising Mia's 'Shame' meant she'd been flirting with him. *This* was why he needed her to say 'yes' later. He just wasn't good at this stuff. But women were complicated. Especially to someone who often found himself struggling to push open doors with *PULL* written on them.

He looked up to find Mia smiling broadly at him. 'Post,' she said, depositing a couple of envelopes on his desk.

'Great. Thanks,' he said, brushing the dust from his knee. 'So I'll see you later? For dinner?'

'You already asked me that. Don't worry. I'm a dead cert.'

Calum hoped so. 'Five-thirty? I'll meet you at the restaurant, if that's okay?'

'Sure,' said Mia. 'Where did you have in mind?'

'I thought we could grab a quick bite at Old Amsterdam,' he said, as nonchalantly as possible, and Mia-Rose widened her eyes.

'You old romantic. It's not our anniversary, is it?'

'No. Nothing like that. Unless you count ten months and a day something worth celebrating?'

Mia-Rose leaned across his desk and kissed him quickly on the forehead. 'Every day with you is worth celebrating, Calum,' she said, and Calum found himself hoping that this one particularly would be.

As Mia headed back to reception, he checked his notes again. There was only one more entry: *Don't take 'no' for an answer* – and Calum stared at it.

That was the one he was the most worried about.

༄

Sophie Jones was scrolling through iFeel's website, and getting more than a little excited, though not at the various photos of iFeel's (predominantly male, predominantly unattractive) staff playing ping-pong or table football in the office. Nor was she especially attracted to any one of the half-a-dozen or so executive profiles of the UK management team; as she'd suspected, none of them were particularly good-looking either. But Tony A. Wood (always with the 'A', she noted, though so far she'd been unable to find out what it stood for) was a different matter, not in the least because iFeel's founder and majority shareholder was a *billionaire*. ('On paper', at least, whatever *that* meant – surely all money except for loose change was made of paper?) And while, from what she could make out from the photos that showed him standing on the deck of (what was no doubt) his yacht that graced his profile page, he was perhaps a little older than she'd ideally have liked, Tony A. Wood would be at the party this evening.

She'd never been on a yacht before. Even the rowing boats you could rent by the hour on the Serpentine in Hyde Park made her feel a little queasy, although she supposed that might have been from the bottle of prosecco she'd drunk during lunch before she and her last Tinder date had hired one (Sophie was ashamed she couldn't remember his name, but he'd probably been trying to forget hers on purpose, seeing as she'd thrown up on him the moment they'd got back to dry land). But by the looks of it, Tony A. Wood's yacht was so big she didn't think the largest of waves would trouble it much, and even if they did, if your favourite film was *Titanic* (as Sophie's was) then drowning at sea wasn't such a bad way to go.

As she gazed out of the window, Sophie allowed herself a little daydream: A billionaire as a boyfriend, just like in those *Fifty Shades* books she'd seen everyone reading on the tube a while back! And even if *Fifty Shades* was true (not that Sophie had read it, apart for the odd snippet over peoples' shoulders that had made her blush), and all billionaires were perverts, if all she had to do was put up with a bit of kinky sex every now and then, perhaps wearing a blindfold (and let's face it, with some of the guys she'd met on Tinder, wearing a blindfold would have been the only way she'd ever have got through the experience), it seemed a small price to pay.

She glanced across to check that Julie Marshall was still safely ensconced at her desk, typed 'Fifty' and 'Shades' into Seek's search engine, and quickly scanned through the results. While she certainly didn't have time to read all three of the books before this evening, she could download the film to watch later, perhaps from one of those dodgy streaming sites she'd badgered Nathan to find for her (though she'd have to hope he didn't find her browsing history afterwards), just in case there were any areas she needed to – if you excused the phrase – *bone up on.*

Excitedly, she located it within a couple of clicks. Judging by the movie poster, the actor playing Christian Grey was young, hot, and fit, which Sophie guessed probably made some of his 'demands' easier to agree to. According to the 'yacht' photo, Tony A. Wood was probably at least twice his age. Which made him twice *her* age.

Sophie pursed her lips as she stared at her laptop. She'd never been into older men. Though it occurred to her that perhaps that was where she'd been going wrong: she and her childhood sweetheart Darren had been the same age, and that hadn't worked out. The doctor she'd just split up with had been a couple of years younger than she was, and truth be told she'd found him a little childish. The guys she'd met through Tinder . . . Sophie pulled her phone out and skimmed through their profiles (the ones she hadn't deleted, or blocked, at least, which admittedly didn't leave that big a sample), but not one of them was more than a year or two older than she was. Whereas Tony A. Wood . . . She quickly found his Wikipedia profile. Born in 1960, which made him . . . Well, that was a few years after Sophie's dad, so at least no one could say he was old enough to be her father.

She scrolled down the page to the 'personal life' section. Born in Texas, currently living in San Francisco, seven (*seven!*) children, three divorces – possibly because he'd been too busy building up his first internet company before 'selling it to Apple for two hundred million dollars just before the market crashed in 2001', then, through a series of acquisitions and disposals, turning that into one-point-two-six billion dollars at the last count . . . Sophie's hands trembled on her keyboard. *One-point-two-six billion dollars!* That bought you a lot of . . . well, anything you wanted, really. And while his record in the 'disposals' area – both in terms of companies *and* wives – worried her a little, the thought of all the acquisitions *she* could make while going out with a billionaire more than made up for that.

She ran a quick image search on the Seek engine, and found photos of Tony with his various wives, or with different women, out at various events: fundraisers, emerging from a limo with Brad Pitt at the Oscars (a sight which made Sophie's heart beat even faster), and even on a yacht (the same yacht, which meant it must be *his* yacht!) at the Cannes Film Festival. *This* was the kind of life she wanted. Not having to get up at six o'clock on a cold December morning, make her way along freezing streets to Harrow-on-the-Hill tube station, and then endure the same, dull journey clanking along the Metropolitan Line into work every day, jostling for position (and with no hope of a seat) on an overcrowded tube. Surely after four years of that she was due a life of chauffeur-driven cars, helicopters, private jets and yachts at Cannes with her very own Steve Jobs, rather than the no-jobs wasters who had been contacting her recently.

Strike that, thought Sophie. This was the life she *deserved*. Forget work; she could happily spend her days shopping or lunching or (if she had to) running some sort of philanthropic foundation like she'd read in *HELLO!* that that Microsoft bloke's wife seemed to do, hosting charity gala dinners in the evenings, on first-name terms with rock stars and celebrities and actors and footballers . . .

As much as she liked Harrow, she'd always wanted to live some-where exotic, and as far as she was concerned, you couldn't get more exotic than San Francisco. The Golden Gate Bridge. Antique trams running up and down breathtakingly steep streets. Alcatraz. The Forty-Niners . . . Okay, Sophie had never been to San Francisco, and didn't know who Alcatraz was (some famous gangster, she'd guess) or what 'Niners' were (all forty of them), but she wanted to. And how better to get to know a city than to tour it from above in someone's private helicopter, or sail around it on the deck of a luxury yacht?

She peered closely at the photos of Tony with his various wives and exes, trying to work out whether he had a 'type', though as far as she could see, his only type was 'female', 'younger than him', and 'blessed in the chest department' – which, Sophie knew (particu-larly with reference to the latter, as some of her kinder respondees on Tinder had pointed out in their initial approaches to her), actu-ally summed her up quite well. Plus, from what she could tell, those women all had fake boobs. Hers were real. Which had to count for something.

With less than two weeks to go until Christmas, Sophie knew she didn't have a lot of time if she wanted to be whisked off to, say, Aspen, or the Maldives, which was probably where someone like Tony A. Wood spent the holidays. And while she worried a little that, in *Fifty Shades* terms, being 'whisked off' was possibly some perverse sexual practice with a kitchen implement, she'd try any-thing once. And who knew? She might even grow to like it.

With a smile, Sophie clicked confidently back through the vari-ous photos. Tonight was going to be her night – well, hers and Tony A. Wood's; she'd make sure of it. So what if he was a little older than her? That might just be a good thing. And while the only fifty shades she might experience would be of red if her plan didn't come off, what was the worst that could happen? Apart from being found out, she realised, when Julie's voice from behind her made her jump.

'Who's *that*?'

Embarrassed, Sophie hit 'close' as quickly as she could, only to reveal the other web page she'd been looking at: a *Daily Mail* article titled 'The Men To Avoid on Tinder', which Sophie could have almost written herself, or at least summed up in three words: all of them.

'Our new boss, apparently.' Sophie angled the laptop round so Julie could get a better look, then typed Tony's name into the paper's 'search' box. 'I was just doing a bit of research.'

'Research?'

'Apparently, he's single,' she said, skimming through a recent feature showing the 'billionaire playboy' 'cavorting' on his 'floating gin palace' with a 'bevy' of supermodels who, according to the paper, were 'showcasing their curves' (which seemed to be *Daily Mail*-speak for 'wearing bikinis'). 'Or rather, "currently single". Just divorced, apparently.'

'Sophie, you're not thinking of . . .?'

'You're the one who told me I should set my sights higher.'

'Yes, but . . . not *that* high!'

'What's wrong with dating the boss?'

'Well, nothing,' spluttered Julie, and Sophie grinned. Julie knew she knew Julie and Mark were seeing each other. And while they never talked about it, Sophie was aware it gave her a bit of leeway.

'So?'

'It's just . . . well, men like that . . .' Julie thought for a moment, then threw her hands up dramatically. 'Who am I kidding? I don't know what men like that are like. Mainly because I don't know any men like that. All I'm saying is: be careful.'

'Of what?'

'Well, for one thing, getting a reputation.'

'For what?'

'Sleeping your way to the top.'

'It's hardly sleeping your way to the top if you *start* at the top, is it?' said Sophie, indignantly, and Julie laughed.

'I suppose not.'

'Do you think I'm his type?'

Julie leant over and scanned through the *Daily Mail* story. 'Well, you may not be a supermodel, but you've got curves that make this lot look like they need a good meal or two,' she said, tapping the screen. 'And if we can find you the right dress this lunchtime, there's no reason you can't "showcase" the hell out of them.' She checked her watch, then made for the door. 'Though if I were you, I'd be more worried as to whether he's *your* type.'

As Julie shut the door behind her, no doubt on her way to the kitchen to make her usual mid-morning tea, Sophie stared at the article again and quickly came to a decision. When it came to Tony A. Wood, she *definitely* would.

∽

Mark Webster waited till he heard the unmistakable sound of Julie Marshall's office door closing, then he checked his watch – ten o'clock precisely – and smiled. Julie liked her routines – it was one of the (many) things he liked about her – and ten o'clock every morning was tea time. He waited a couple of minutes, then picked up the tin of Roses Nathan had left on his desk, strolled as nonchalantly past the kitchen as he could, and – pretending he'd only just noticed her once he'd passed – sidled in to join her.

'Hello.'

'Hello, Mark.' Julie held up the 'Marketeers Do It on a Budget' mug he'd given her (the one he'd hunted far and wide for, and that no one except Julie seemed to find funny – though he had his

61

doubts that she was being genuine), and waggled the herbal teabag it held by its little tag. 'Want one?'

Mark did his best not to grimace. Herbal tea was one of those things he knew adults were supposed to like, but immersing a bag of strange-smelling leaves in a cup of boiling water then having to wait at least half an hour until it was cool enough to drink always seemed a bit strange to him. The whole point of (proper) tea and coffee was the instant hit – plus the whole biscuit-dunking thing just didn't work with this herbal stuff. Mark had tried it once, dipping a custard cream into one of Julie's strawberry-flavoured brews, thinking he might end up with something that wouldn't be out of place during Wimbledon fortnight, but the soggy mess he'd ended up having to fish out of the bottom of his mug hadn't looked in the least bit appetising. Besides, he was more of a coffee man, and the real stuff, too, properly brewed, or at least from the Bodum press he and Nathan did their best to hide from the office's instant-coffee crowd.

'Same question to you,' he said, depositing the tin of chocolates on the counter.

'You brought me Roses? How sweet. And why not?' She peered into the tin and removed a coconut cream. 'It is Christmas, after all.'

'It is.' Mark poked his head back out through the doorway to check they weren't being watched, but the office was half empty, and those people who were at their desks seemed to have their headphones in, probably engrossed in 'amusing' videos of cats, or catching up on last night's TV. 'And speaking of Christmas, I was wondering . . .' He took a step closer and lowered his voice. ' . . . what your thoughts were. You know. *About* Christmas.'

Julie chewed her chocolate as she considered the question. 'Well, it's a Christian festival where people commemorate the alleged birth in the poorest of circumstances of someone called

Jesus by indulging in an orgy of consumer spending and food and alcohol consumption. Always struck me as a little strange, really. Like Easter. Celebrating the same guy being crucified by eating fruity buns with little pastry reminders of that horrible event baked onto the top. And I don't want to think about what the chocolate eggs are supposed to represent.'

'No, I meant—' Mark caught sight of Julie's expression, and realised she was teasing him. 'Yes, very good. I mean *our* Christmas. Whether you'd had any thoughts about what we were going to do. And . . .' he coughed nervously, 'where we were going to do it.'

Julie waited for the kettle to click off. 'Well, um . . .' She poured water into her mug, cursing under her breath as the teabag's tag followed it in, as if it and the bag had signed a suicide pact. 'That's a good question. I mean, no. I hadn't. Not especially.'

'Oh. Well, what would you normally do?'

'Sit and watch Philip get steaming drunk. Though I'm spared that particular ordeal this year, thank goodness,' she added, fishing the tag out with a teaspoon. 'There's always my mum and dad in Birmingham, though it's a long drive for an even longer day, and my sister usually draws the short straw where that particular family chore is concerned. How about you?'

Mark frowned, though mainly because this was the first time he'd heard about a sister. 'Well, I'd normally go and have lunch with my parents.'

'Ri-ight.'

'Which, um, you know you'd be more than welcome to do.'

'With you, right?'

Mark shrugged. 'Or on your own. Whatever you'd prefer. I'm sure they wouldn't mind.'

'Where do they live?'

'Pickering.'

'In Yorkshire?'

'You know it?' said Mark, a little surprised. When he'd told a previous girlfriend he'd like to take her to Pickering one weekend, she'd mistakenly assumed he was about to propose, which had made for a *very* uncomfortable road trip.

'That's an even longer way to go for lunch.'

'It's not so bad. Of course, we'd stay over. I mean, like you say, it's a long way, and no one wants to drive back home on Christmas night. And it'd be a great chance for you to meet them. And them to meet you. Obviously.'

'Ah.'

'"Ah?"'

Julie blew across the top of her tea, then took a cautious sip. 'Do we have to? It's just . . . Can't we do something on our own? The two of us? It might be the last chance we get to do that, and—' She corrected herself quickly. 'I mean, how often do you get a chance to avoid all this family rubbish?'

'I quite like this "family rubbish",' said Mark, quietly. 'And besides, they've said they'd love to spend Christmas with you. I think my mother's out buying you a present even as we speak.'

'You've already told them I'm coming?'

Mark felt the colour start to rise in his cheeks. 'Well, no. Not definitely. But I phoned them this morning, and happened to mention we didn't have any plans, and they invited you – well, *us* – and I didn't exactly say we wouldn't . . .' He grinned sheepishly. 'After all, Christmas is a time for family, and all that.'

'They're not *my* family,' snapped Julie.

'No,' said Mark, trying desperately to stop himself from adding 'not yet'. 'But they're mine. And seeing as I obviously don't exist as far as yours are concerned – and in fact, I've only just found out you've got a sister – they're the only family I've got. So I thought it might be nice—'

'Nice for *who*?' Julie angrily put her mug down on the kitchen surface. 'Why would you possibly think I'd like that? Christ, Mark. I've only recently managed to extricate myself from my home situation, and all of a sudden you want me to give up my new-found freedom. Well, I'm sorry, but excuse me for wanting a bit of breathing space before I go rushing headlong into playing happy families all over again.'

'I don't understand. Earlier, when I suggested you might want to spend a little bit more time at my place, you hardly reacted in the most enthusiastic of ways, and now—'

'Mark, I just . . . Moving . . .'

Julie stopped talking abruptly. Mary from accounts – Hairy Mary, as she was known around the office (due to the beginnings of a beard any prepubescent hipster would be proud of) – had just walked into the kitchen. As she set the mug emblazoned with 'Mary' she'd brought in with her down onto the work surface (having learned the hard way not to leave it in the kitchen when someone had changed the 'Mary' to 'Hairy' with just a couple of pen strokes – quite ingeniously, Mark had thought, when she'd stormed into his office and tearfully shoved it under his nose), Mark cleared his throat.

'Don't mind me!' she said, eyeing them both suspiciously.

'Sorry, Mary. Julie and I were just discussing, well—'

'Moving,' said Mary. 'I heard you.'

'That's right,' said Julie, quickly. 'The office move. Mark was thinking we ought to try and be in before Christmas, but I was saying it was better to wait until after Christmas. That trying to do it before Christmas was too soon. Too much . . . pressure.'

'Right,' said Mark. 'Whereas I thought . . . Well, you already know what I thought. What do *you* think?'

Mary raised both eyebrows, as if genuinely chuffed to have been asked. 'Well . . .' She briefly tapped the side of the kettle to check if it was hot, picked it up to estimate whether there was enough water for another boil, then placed it carefully back on its base and clicked it on; Mark guessed it was probably the most work she'd do all day. 'I'd get Christmas out of the way first. Wouldn't you? After all, no one wants to move before Christmas, do they?'

Mark mumbled his thanks, then headed glumly out of the kitchen. By the way Julie seemed to be doing her best to study something apparently floating in her mug, he feared she might not be too keen on moving *after* Christmas either.

❦

Julie Marshall knew she should chase after Mark Webster and apologise, though what she wasn't sure about was why she'd flown off the handle so quickly. Normally, time of the month would have been a good excuse, but she hadn't had one of those for a while now. She also knew that Mark was just trying to do something nice. He didn't have it in him to be duplicitous, or to scheme, or have any kind of ulterior motive – the opposite of Philip, in every way – and after what she'd been through, that was important. More importantly, she was sure he'd never cheat on her – Julie had never even seen him so much as glance at another woman – and she owed it to him to at least say she'd think about Christmas. Although the sound of Mark's 'always open' office door loudly slamming shut made her suspect that now might not be the best time, and besides, Mary's rather large bulk was preventing her from getting out of the kitchen.

'Want one?' she said, trying to lure her to one side by sliding the tin of Roses along the counter – a tactic she'd seen someone in *Jurassic Park* use successfully on a T-rex, although with a flare and not a tin of chocolates – but instead, Mary just peered at the tin, inhaled, then shook her head.

'Can't,' she said. 'Five two.'

Julie looked at her watch. 'What does the time have to do with it?'

'Not five to,' said Mary, walking over to the fridge and removing a bag of sliced lemons with 'Mary' written on the label in indelible marker. 'Five *two*. I'm on the diet. And today's a fast day.'

Julie tried to hide a smile. Mary was as wide as she was tall, and constantly dieting, hence the hot water and lemon she always drank at the office. Plus, the concept of Mary doing anything 'fast' was one that was a million miles away from her nature.

'Right. And, um . . . Is it working?'

Mary looked a bit offended. 'Can't you tell?'

'Well . . .'

'Although Mister Whiskers doesn't seem to enjoy it that much.'

'He's . . . your cat, right?' said Julie, tentatively. Given Mary's facial sproutings, she'd made the mistake of assuming that was a pet name for Mary's husband the first time she'd heard it, rather than Mary's pet's name (though in her defence, while Mary didn't *have* a husband, you could be fooled into thinking the cat *was*, given how she referred to it).

'That's right.'

'He prefers you, ahem, *larger*, does he?'

Mary scowled at her. 'No. He's doing the diet too. It's good to have someone to share these things with. Keeps us both motivated.'

Julie stared at her. If this was her future – living on her own, just a mangy old cat for company, then perhaps this baby was a blessing in disguise.

'Although it beats the cabbage soup diet we were on last month,' continued Mary. 'Forget fast days, that made every day a *fart* day, I can tell you.' She grinned at her own joke, then gave Julie's slim figure the once-over, though Julie couldn't stop herself from covering her stomach with her free hand. 'You're lucky. You never seem to put on weight. Me, I've got an underactive thyroid—'

Or overactive jaws, thought Julie.

'—which is why I have to constantly try these different diets. Mix it up a bit.'

'Sure.' Julie made what she hoped was a sympathetic face, though she wondered whether the chunks of chocolate she'd seen Mary 'mix up' into her Special K the other morning counted. 'So how does it, I mean, what do you—?'

Mary waited until the kettle clicked itself off, filled her mug up with hot water, then leaned heavily against the kitchen counter, as if the effort had been a little too much. 'It's easy. You fast for two days a week, then you can eat what you like for the other five.'

Julie peered at her, wondering whether she should suggest Mary tried it the other way round. 'And is that . . . difficult? The fasting?'

'Not really. You're allowed five hundred calories. And you know you can eat normally the next day, so it's not really a problem.' She leaned across to Julie and nudged her. 'Though it's ironic. They're called "fast days", but they really drag.'

'Bit unfortunate you're fasting today, though. What with the office party?'

'Why?'

'Champagne?'

Mary shook her head. 'If you think about it, champagne's mostly bubbles, isn't it? And bubbles are made up of air . . .'

'Well, strictly speaking, I think they're carbon dioxide.'

'Either way, there's no calories in them. So if I don't eat anything all day, I'm allowed . . .' She pulled a small, well-thumbed book out of her pocket. 'Well, a glass of wine is about ninety calories. And if champagne is half bubbles, then that makes it around forty-five a glass. So I can have . . .' Mary frowned as she tried to do the maths in her head.

'Eleven glasses?' suggested Julie, and Mary smiled.

'Excellent!'

'And is that wise, on an empty stomach?'

'What do you mean?'

'You don't want to get drunk and make a scene in front of your new colleagues, surely?'

'Oh, it won't matter, even if I do.'

'Why ever not?'

'It's Christmas,' she said, carefully removing a slice of lemon from the bag. 'A time for forgiving.'

'For *giving*,' said Julie.

'That's what I said,' said Mary, dunking the lemon briefly into her mug, before drying it off on a piece of paper towel and replacing it in her plastic bag.

And as Julie helped herself to another chocolate, and steeled herself to go and apologise to Mark, she could only hope Mary was right.

4.

Nathan Field shook his head slowly. Mike from pre-sales was on the phone from his home office with more printer problems (last week, his new wireless printer had failed even to switch on, though after Nathan had investigated further, it had turned out to be because Mike had thought it didn't require *any* wires. Including the one that plugged into the mains).

'Have you tried turning it off and on again?'

'I knew you were going to say that.'

Well, if that was the case, then maybe you could have tried that before you called me and wasted my time, thought Nathan.

As he wondered whether he could set that piece of advice as a recorded message that would play automatically whenever people dialled his number, there was the sound of grunting, then a switch being pressed – twice – and then: 'It seems to be working now.'

'You're welcome,' said Nathan, ending the call before Mike could ask him anything else. Some days he despaired about his job. A deep understanding of database technology, the ability to take apart and put back together any PC almost in his sleep, and still it was mostly about the press (or two presses) of a button.

He leaned back in his chair, wondering whether it was too soon for another coffee, then jerked back upright as an alert popped up on his laptop. While there'd been no response yet from Ellie, the email that *had* just appeared in his inbox was giving him cause for concern. And while normally he'd consign any message entitled 'you and me' straight to 'spam', this one was from a 'Stacey Garrity', with an iFeel address that made him think it might be genuine.

Her email signature said 'Technical Director' – Nathan was only 'Technical Support Manager', which immediately made him a little wary as he scanned through the message. Despite the difference in titles, Stacey was introducing herself as his 'opposite number' at iFeel. Apparently she'd 'heard a lot about him' (though Nathan couldn't think who from) and was 'looking forward to comparing notes' this evening.

Nathan peered suspiciously at his laptop. He had no idea whether his job was safe post-merger, and perhaps there might be room for the two of them, but if not, whether he could work under a woman . . . Worried, he punched Stacey's name into Seek's search engine and found her LinkedIn page, disguising his IP address so she wouldn't know it was him viewing her profile, though as soon as he caught sight of her photo, Nathan decided that working under this woman might not be such a bad thing. Stacey was a looker – a rarity in the IT industry, in his experience – and though what he was doing was perhaps a little unprofessional of him, he suddenly found himself looking forward to tonight's party even more.

His interest piqued, he hurriedly did some background searching, even locating an old Friends Reunited entry, then found her profile page on Facebook. There was no mention of her being 'in a relationship', and no sign of a boyfriend in the several hundred photos he hurriedly scrolled through on her Instagram, though he was double-checking the ones of her on a beach in her bikini just in case when a voice from his doorway made him jump.

'Working hard, I see?'

As Mark walked into his office, Nathan slammed his laptop shut abruptly. 'Sorry. Just . . .' He stopped talking, unable to think of an answer that'd explain what he'd been up to.

'Who was *that*?'

Nathan waited until his heart stopped hammering, then he opened his laptop again. 'My opposite number at iFeel, apparently. She just emailed.'

'And sent you that photo?'

'No, I was, um, doing a background check.'

Mark made the 'yeah, right' face, then angled the laptop towards him to get a better view of the screen. 'It looks more like you were doing a foreground check to me. So what have you learned? Apart from the fact that she's attractive.'

'Who's attractive?'

Julie Marshall was standing in the doorway, and Nathan smirked as Mark leapt back from the screen as if it had suddenly delivered him an electric shock.

'Just Nathan's new—'

'Boss,' said Nathan, hurriedly, as Julie walked across and peered at Stacey's photo.

'They have an interesting office dress policy.'

Mark grinned. 'I assume Tony A. Wood hired her for her brains?'

'That's a rather sexist thing to say.' Julie narrowed her eyes at him, and Mark looked like he'd just been caught looking at something dodgy on the Internet. Which, Nathan thought, was a pretty good description of what had just happened.

'No, I don't mean . . .' Mark sighed. 'It's just that it's rather well reported that our new owner values, shall we say, aesthetics *and* intelligence.'

Julie made a face, then jabbed a thumb back out into the central office, where the majority of the Seek workforce were lolling around at their desks. 'Well, that's half of this lot out on their ears, then.'

Mark let out a short laugh. 'Now *that's* sexist.'

'Only if I was talking about looks . . .' She nodded back at Nathan's laptop, 'like you two obviously were.'

'Not at all,' spluttered Mark. 'I was, I mean, we were . . .' He held his hands up resignedly. 'Were you looking for me for something?'

Julie's eyes flicked back to the laptop screen. 'Not any more, no,' she said, turning on her heel and striding out of the office.

Nathan watched her go, then he nudged his friend. 'You're in trouble later.'

'I'm in trouble *now*.'

'The "Christmas" discussion went well, then?'

'What do *you* think?'

'That we're both in trouble.'

Mark pointed at Nathan's laptop. 'You're not worried, are you?'

Nathan scrolled down through Stacey's details on LinkedIn. A good degree, from a good university, plus an MSc in programming, whereas most of Nathan's skills had been acquired on the job. 'A little. I mean, if you were taking over a whole load of staff you didn't know, and you already had loads you did, *and* who looked like that, who would *you* keep on?'

'That's assuming they're any good at their jobs.'

'Well, Stacey Garrity's obviously good at *everything*, judging by the number of people who've "endorsed" her.'

'Are you being rude?'

'On *LinkedIn*, Mark.'

'So you're just taking a professional interest?'

Nathan hurriedly closed the browser window. 'I'm just checking out the competition.'

'And is there any? Competition?'

Nathan knew exactly what Mark was asking, and he held both hands up in a 'guilty as charged' way. 'Okay. Not as far as I can tell. According to Facebook she doesn't have a boyfriend. And she's still got the same surname as when she was at school, so I'm guessing she's never been married—'

'I don't even want to know how you found *that* out.'

'Mark, in case you'd forgotten, Seek's a search engine company. And a good one, which is probably why iFeel have just bought us. There's very little I can't find out, if I put my mind – and our technology – to it.'

'So, what's your plan?'

'Plan?'

Mark tapped the screen. 'For whatshername.'

'I don't *have* a plan.'

'Well, maybe you should come up with one. Christmas is coming, you know? And unless you want to spend it sitting alone at home—'

'Slitting my wrists in front of the inevitable repeat of the *Morecambe and Wise Christmas Special*, you mean?'

'What's wrong with Morecambe and Wise at Christmas?'

'I think I'm beginning to understand why Julie doesn't want to spend it with you.'

Mark shot him a look. 'All I'm saying is, you and Kasia split up, what, four weeks ago? And it's been nearly four years since Ellie . . .'

'Dumped me mid-proposal? I was there, remember? I don't need to be reminded.'

'And if it were me – Well, obviously not *actually* me, but if it was a case of an empty Christmas stocking hanging by the fireplace, or *her* and, you know . . .' He lowered his voice. 'Stockings . . .'

'Mark, *please*. She might be my new boss.'

'So? There's nothing wrong with . . .' Mark coughed awkwardly. '. . . internal relations. If you know what I mean?'

'Yeah, you would say that, wouldn't you?'

'And *she* emailed *you*.' He smiled. 'What's she been saying?'

'Be my guest.'

Mark sat down in Nathan's chair, and scanned silently through the message.

'Well?'

'Well, bear in mind that I'm no expert . . .'

'That's true.'

'But even to my untrained eye, she is totally flirting with you. It's the email equivalent of a booty call. Or as you lot in technical support might call it, a re-booty call.'

'That was quite funny. For you.'

Mark ignored Nathan's sarcasm. 'And tonight, you'll be meeting her. At a posh venue, where everyone's up for a good time. And quite possibly drunk. And there'll be music . . .'

'So?'

'And dancing. *Slow* dancing.'

Nathan sighed. Mark was right, of course. The prospect of spending Christmas alone wasn't a particularly appealing one, and he didn't really want to make the long trip home to watch his mother and father insisting he have the turkey breast. Nathan had always been a leg man. Which, given some of Stacey's short-short-wearing gym selfies on Instagram, meant she was right up his street.

'Come on.' Mark looked up expectantly at him. 'What have you got to lose?'

'My job, for one thing.'

'Well, like you said, that could happen anyway.' Mark hauled himself out of Nathan's chair, and offered him his seat back. 'Either way, you might get an attractive payoff.'

Nathan hesitated for a moment, then sat back down in front of his laptop and hit 'reply'. Mark was right. With no Ellie, no Kasia, and his job future probably already decided, what *did* he have to lose?

A strange, animalistic wailing noise coming from the main office made Julie Marshall realise with a start that she'd been staring out of the window since coming back from catching Mark doing she-didn't-know-what, and she shuddered involuntarily. Last month's 'bring your pet to work' day was still notorious for Doug (Mike in legal's pug) chasing Mary's cat round the office and (unbeknownst to Julie) Mister Whiskers taking refuge on her office chair, and the sound she could hear at the moment was identical to the one Mister Whiskers had made when Julie had accidentally sat on him. While she must have missed the email (and was surprised Mary had brought the traumatised feline back into the office so soon), a repeat of the incident was something she was keen to avoid.

As she quickly got up from her desk and pushed the door to, Sophie frowned at her, then got up and cracked the door back open.

'Sophie, do you mind? I don't want that . . . thing in here.'

'That "thing"?' Sophie looked surprised at Julie's terminology. 'Aren't you going to come and see it?'

'Why on earth would I want to do that? To apologise?'

'Apologise for what?'

'Exactly. In fact, that stupid dog is the one who should be apologising.'

'Aisleen from HR?' Sophie looked confused. 'I know she can be a bit of a slapper, but "dog" is a bit harsh.'

'What?'

'Aisleen.'

'What about her?'

'She's here.'

'I thought she was on maternity leave . . .'

'She is. But,' Sophie nodded through the open doorway, 'she's here.'

Julie decided she wasn't getting any sense from Sophie, so she got up and checked for herself. Sure enough, Aisleen was standing in the middle of the office, surrounded by clucking and cooing women, which meant that unholy wailing wasn't coming from some animal, but from . . . a baby.

A few broody men had joined the group, though Julie suspected they could simply be there to get a better look at Aisleen's nursing-enhanced chest, especially given the low-cut top she was wearing, Julie imagined, for easy access at feeding time, and she glanced down at her own cleavage. When she'd started her marathon training last year, her breasts were the one place on her body she hadn't lost weight, a fact she'd regretted from about mile twelve onwards (and thanks to a rather severe bout of 'jogger's nipple', for a good few days afterwards), so the prospect of them getting even bigger . . .

She paled at the thought, then followed Sophie dutifully into the main office area, where Aisleen's baby (and Julie couldn't remember its name, or even if it was a boy or a girl) was being handed around, like in some weird music-free game of pass the parcel. As she peered at the child from a safe distance, still none the wiser as to what sex it was, and hoping the non-music wouldn't 'stop' and make it her turn, Aisleen turned to face her.

'Would you like a cuddle?'

'Of the baby?'

'I wasn't suggesting from *me*.'

Julie went white. 'No. Thank you. I—'

'I will.' Sophie took the child, who stared wide-eyed at her chest like a student at an all-you-can-eat buffet.

'So, is it . . . ? I mean, does it . . .' Julie hesitated. Baby small-talk was so far off her radar she didn't have a clue what to ask, though the child was dressed primarily in blue, so she took a chance. 'Sorry, I mean, does *he* . . . ?' She took a deep breath, then out of nowhere, managed to come up with a question. 'How's, you know, motherhood?'

Aisleen made a face. 'Knackering, to be honest, what with the 3 a.m. feeds, and the constant being sick—'

'I thought that happened when you were pregnant?'

'Him, I meant, not me. Though the toilet issues—'

'All those dirty nappies?'

'No, that one's me. I'm a bit leaky, to be honest. Still, it was that, or being cut open, which is no fun, I imagine. Besides, I wanted to have a natural birth.' She smiled. 'But as tough as it can be, you just have to look at him to realise it's all worth it.'

'Ri-ight,' said Julie, as convincingly as she could manage, although when she played it back in her head, it didn't sound that convincing at all.

'Here.' With a mischievous grin, Sophie passed her the baby, and Julie held the child at arms' length, not knowing exactly what to do with it, though handing it on to someone else as quickly as possible seemed as good an option as any.

'See?' Aisleen was beaming at her, and Julie did her best to make approving noises, though give Doug the pug a quick shave and wrap him in a blanket, and he and Aisleen's baby could be twins.

' . . . plus I just love that incredible newborn smell. Don't you?'

Julie tentatively brought the baby towards her nose and inhaled deeply, then tried not to gag. 'I think he might need his nappy changed . . .'

'Oops!' Aisleen giggled. 'Who's a dirty boy?'

As a few of her male colleagues exchanged guilty looks, and Benedict slunk away – perhaps to delete his browser history – Julie grimaced good-naturedly. She handed the baby back, just in time to see Mark emerge from his office, work out what all the fuss was about, then beat a hasty retreat, so she did the same, heading back to the safety of her office and shutting the door firmly behind her. She'd always suspected she wasn't the motherly type, but she'd thought that when – sorry, *if* – she ever became pregnant, some sort of switch would flick inside her and she'd suddenly develop her maternal instinct (or at least not detest babies quite as much as she seemed to). Now that she *was* pregnant, she'd hoped perhaps seeing a baby, holding one, might feel a little more natural. But that quite plainly hadn't been the case.

People always said it was different if it was your own, but Julie doubted it. She was one of these cooks who loved it when other people made dinner for her, but if she had to spend a few hours in the kitchen slaving away over a hot stove, she kind of lost her appetite – and that was when she'd had something in the oven for a couple of hours, tops, not nine months!

Mark's reaction had spoken volumes to her. And it would be alright for him; he'd get to escape to the office every day, while Julie was stuck at home with just this crying, pooing, peeing, vomiting, screaming-to-be-fed *thing* for company . . . She almost laughed at the irony. Here she was, finally free from Philip, and soon she was going to be beholden to something even worse. Plus, she'd be feeling constantly knackered, with sore nipples, a sore back, depressed about the baby weight she'd gained, Mark not wanting to touch her – not that she'd let him, ever again, after this . . .

The more she thought about it, the less she could see an upside. She wasn't like Sophie, desperate to get married, all clucky whenever she saw a baby. The only thing Julie wanted to nurture was her career, and if that was selfish, well, that was just the way it was. The world already had too many babies, as far as she was concerned, so in actual fact, she'd be doing a public service by not having this one. As for Mark . . . He didn't know anything yet, and that was the way it should probably stay. After all, if she did decide to get rid of it, well, it was *her* body. Her decision. There was no sense saddling him with the guilt.

She did a quick search on Seek's engine, and soon found the information she needed. Nine weeks, she had, if she just wanted to take a few tablets. There was even a place just north of Oxford Street – she could go one day in her lunch hour, get it over and done with in the time it took to grab a sandwich from the Pret across the street. And if she took the medicinal option, there was no need for Mark to find out – she'd just say she was feeling a bit poorly, go and do the deed, then go home, and see him the next day. He'd be none the wiser. No harm done.

Apart from to the baby, of course.

Julie pursed her lips grimly. It wasn't a baby yet, she reminded herself, as she made a note to delete her own search history (and wondered whether deleting her pregnancy would be just as easy). Just a mistake that somehow she and Mark had made.

And as Aisleen's baby emitted another blood-curdling scream that penetrated even the closed office door, Julie promised herself that it was one mistake she wouldn't let affect her.

৩৶

Mark Webster ducked back into his office, hoping no one had seen him blank Aisleen and her baby – though fortunately, they'd all seemed too distracted by the godawful noise it had been making – and sat back down at his desk. He didn't have time for babies today; in any case, they were usually sick on him, or cried as soon as he picked them up, and the last thing he wanted was for Julie Marshall to see how bad he was with them. Especially when he was so desperate to get (back) in her good books.

He'd still heard nothing from Tony A. Wood, though he was trying to see that as a good thing. After all, it gave him some time to think about his other big problem. As far as he could see, there were two possible reasons why Julie wouldn't move in with him: either because she didn't like his flat, or because she didn't like him. And while he was too scared to ask her directly about the latter, raising the idea of him moving (in a no-pressure 'come and look at a few places with me' kind of way) would surely provide him with an answer to the former.

He did a quick check on Seek's share price. When the takeover had been announced, it had shot through the roof, meaning Mark was, although by no means rich, certainly comfortably off. Comfortable enough to buy a bigger place, at least. And while he loved where he lived (though he'd hardly describe himself as either 'hip' or 'trendy', Bermondsey certainly was), he only had a one-bedroom flat, and Julie – though she was only renting a studio now – had come from a house, which was why he'd spent the last hour idly browsing through larger properties online.

Besides, he needed to at least be sure them living together was a viable option. Because women had *stuff*, didn't they? Clothes, and shoes, and make-up, and jewellery, boxes of trinkets, and photographs, and keepsakes, and smelly candles, and handbags, and more shoes, and bowls of those little decorative things that he'd once assumed were snacks but had turned out to be potpourri (either that, or the weirdest-tasting, softest vegetable crisps he'd ever eaten).

And there was no way his minimalistic flat could cope with soft furnishings. He'd seen it happen before. The one time he'd lived with a girlfriend, his smart, uncluttered bachelor pad had been transformed into something resembling a child's soft-play area, with so many throw cushions (whatever they were for – though Mark had eventually found that throwing them *out* was extremely satisfying) it had been impossible to sit anywhere comfortably unless you'd piled them up into a little defensive fort in the space next to you. Eventually, he'd come to dread weekend couple-trips to the shops, knowing that they'd invariably end in the attempted purchase of some other pointlessly decorative *thing* from Habitat, or Heal's, or any of the stores' home furnishings departments. Which meant they'd often also end in an argument.

But that had been a long time ago. And with a girl who he'd only asked to move in because he'd feared she was going to dump him (though, ironically, he'd ended up dumping *her*, then taking several trips to the dump to get rid of all the stuff she'd accumulated). Whereas Julie? He'd live in a tent if it meant being with her.

He still didn't quite know the 'grand gesture', to use Nathan's term, that he was going to use in order to convince her, or even when he was going to ask her. To be honest, he wasn't entirely sure *if* he was going to ask her, seeing as she'd just rebuffed his plans for them to spend Christmas together. And maybe now was the wrong time; after all, there was a lot going on, what with her divorce coming through any day now, and the Christmas party, and all this stuff with the takeover. He'd been assured that this wouldn't mean redundancies, but they *always* said that, and while he was pretty sure his position was safe, Julie was head of marketing, and marketing was always where they made the first cuts. And while he knew he couldn't show any favouritism, he'd do his best to keep her on – after all, if nobody knew about him and Julie, then no one could accuse him of that. He hoped.

He minimised Rightmove on his laptop, and considered getting on with some work, but then realised that until Tony A. Wood had actually clarified exactly what was happening, he couldn't actually make many decisions. The last couple of weeks since the takeover announcement had been strange; no one had known what they were supposed to be doing. Whenever he'd walked past more than one workstation in the past few days and seen people (understandably) hurriedly rewriting their CVs, he'd done his best to reassure them, though he'd felt bad doing it. iFeel were buying Seek because of their technology, not because of their people, and he had to be concerned about that. What was the old joke – mergers and acquisitions were more like murders and executions? And as UK MD, Mark knew he might be the one wielding the knife.

He dreaded the prospect of having to get rid of anyone. It had taken him a guilt-racked year to fire his cleaner, a woman he never saw (although given the less-than-pristine state of his carpets, he'd suspected his Hoover didn't spend that much time with her either), so to have to get rid of these people, some of whom were his friends, one of whom was his *girl*friend . . . He suppressed a shudder. That was a bridge too far, and one he didn't want to cross if he came to it, if you excused the mixed metaphors.

Perhaps he should start compiling a list. This could be a good chance to get rid of some of the dead wood around the office – that Benedict in legal, for example, and maybe even Mary (though Mark knew firing her because she'd taken Julie's side earlier wasn't the most honourable of actions). Even so, the more he could legitimately get rid of, the safer Julie was bound to be. Though of course if Julie *was* let go, then maybe she couldn't afford to rent her apartment, and moving in with him would make more sense . . .

His stomach rumbled, and he checked his watch, surprised to see it was nearly lunchtime, and he realised the morning had passed in a blur. All would become clearer after tonight, he hoped. Tony A. Wood would be making his big announcement, Mark would have some one-on-one time with the man himself, and after that . . . Well, maybe *he'd* be the one looking for another job.

He swallowed hard, did his best to put Seek's predicament out of his mind, and went back to his property search on Rightmove. Though given how Julie had reacted when he'd asked her about Christmas, he still wasn't convinced asking her to come and live with him *was* the right move.

∾

Calum Irwin's desk phone was ringing, so he swallowed the last mouthful of the 'Fitness' cereal bar he'd been eating (given that it was his third of the day, he reckoned he could safely skip the gym at lunchtime) and picked up the handset.

'Calum Irwin.'

'It's Mia.'

Calum's heart began to beat a little faster – though whether that was just at the sound of her voice, or the fact that he was scared Mia was going to dump him every time she called, he wasn't sure.

'Hello you-a,' he said, instantly cringing at his bad joke, though when Mia let out a little giggle, he relaxed a bit.

'Call for you. A Linda Smith.'

'Ah. Right,' he said, though he didn't know a Linda Smith. She certainly wasn't one of his sales prospects, or an existing client. And the fact that she hadn't given a company name was setting alarm bells ringing. 'Do you know who she's calling from?'

'She says it's a *personal* call.'

Calum could almost hear Mia-Rose's eyebrow arching, and for a moment, he wondered whether it was one of the women he'd met on the dating site he'd tried earlier in the year. The one he'd 'met' Mia on, funnily enough, even though she'd only worked on the floor below him, and he saw her every day. But it would be strange for any of them to be calling now (unless they'd finally worked their way through all the other men on the site) and besides, he'd been careful not to put his work details on his profile – a profile that he'd deleted virtually the moment he'd got home from his first date with Mia.

'Hold on,' he said, wheeling his chair over to his office door, kicking it shut, then wheeling himself back to his desk. 'Okay. Put her through.'

There was the sound of a click, then: 'Calum Irwin?' he said, tentatively.

'No, it's Linda Smith.'

'*I'm* Calum Irwin.'

'And I'm Linda Smith. Well, not really.'

'Huh?'

'No. Don't want to be recognised, you see?'

Calum frowned at the handset. He didn't see. Like sending a Valentine's card without putting your name on it, what was the point of calling someone if you didn't want them to know who you were?

'Not really, no.'

'I'm a *headhunter*. Well, "recruitment consultant", to give my job its official title.'

'Oh. *Oh*.' Calum found himself sitting up straighter in his chair.

'So I can't use my real name. Otherwise I'd never get through.'

'Right,' said Calum, not sure she was getting through at the moment.

'And I'm calling because I was wondering whether you were perhaps looking for pastures new?'

'"Pastures new"?'

'That's right. What with everything going on.'

'What do you mean, "with everything going on"?' said Calum, suspiciously.

'Hello? The iFeel business?'

Calum stiffened in his seat, not sure whether the merger was common industry knowledge, and not wanting to give it away if it wasn't. 'How did you know about that?' he said, then kicked himself. If she was fishing, then he'd pretty much just confirmed her suspicions. 'I mean, what iFeel business?'

Linda – or whatever her name was – laughed down the phone. 'It's a small industry, Calum. And I wouldn't be very good at my job if I didn't keep my ear to the ground. Have my finger on the pulse. Couldn't work out which way the wind was blowing. Know what I mean?'

Calum still wasn't sure he did. 'So what's any of this got to do with me?'

'Well, they say it's a merger, don't they? Except it's actually more of a takeover. Which means there are going to be casualties, Calum. Lots of them. Bodies piled up by the side of the road. HRmageddon!' She paused for Calum to laugh at her joke, though all there was to hear was the sound of him gulping loudly. 'And at times like these, it's generally better to jump before you're pushed, and all that.'

'What makes you think any of us are going to be pushed?'

'It's what always happens.'

'Well, what makes you think *I'm* going to be pushed?'

'You might not,' said Linda, though in what sounded to Calum like a less-than-reassuring tone. 'But just in case . . .'

'I'm Seek's top salesman.' Calum tried to say it as confidently as possible. Though he was actually Seek's only salesman. Which should surely count in his favour?

'But Seek are a database company, aren't they?'

'Well, strictly speaking, we're a search engine. Like Google, but—'

Linda laughed. 'Calum, if Seek were like Google, you and I wouldn't be having this conversation. But think about it. You sell databases. And someone's just gone and bought you. Which means . . .'

Linda stopped talking, and Calum wondered whether he was supposed to complete the sentence. Though 'That . . . ?' was the best he could come up with.

'Well, who knows?'

'I thought you said *you* did?'

'All I'm saying is, it doesn't hurt to have alternatives. That way, when – sorry, *if* – security suddenly turns up at your desk, makes you pack all your stuff into a cardboard box, and escorts you smartly off the premises, you don't have to worry.'

Calum gripped the receiver even more tightly. He hadn't *been* worried, but Linda's phone call was having exactly that effect on him. And more alarmingly, call him old-fashioned, but he could hardly ask Mia-Rose to marry him if he was unemployed.

'How do I know you're for real?'

'What do you mean?'

'You read these stories about women who hire other women to try and seduce their husbands to test how faithful they are. You could be working for iFeel, and doing the same thing. To test whether I want to stay or not.'

Linda laughed. 'Hardly, Calum. But hey, even if you do get given your marching orders, I'm sure you've got nothing to worry about. People like you are in demand.'

'People like me? Or actually me?'

Linda laughed again. 'Actually you, Calum. So if you wanted to meet up, have a chat about your options . . .'

Calum hauled himself out of his chair and strode towards the window. Perhaps it wouldn't do any harm. 'When?' he said, peering out at a busy Bateman Street. 'And where?'

'How about right now? I've set up camp in the Pret A Manger across the street.'

Calum ducked down as if he'd been shot, nearly dropping the phone in the process. Linda was *here*. And probably working her way through Seek's internal phone directory.

'Is that wise? In full view of everyone?'

He could almost hear Linda shrug. And he was sure he could probably have *seen* her shrug, if he hadn't been ducking down beneath the window like someone trying to avoid sniper fire.

'Why not? It doesn't hurt for them to see you're in demand.'

Calum didn't like to think who 'them' was. *And* that they might be watching him.

'Fifteen minutes. That's all I need,' she continued. 'Come on, Calum. What's the worst that could happen?'

'I could lose my job.'

'That might happen anyway. At least this way, you might have another one to go to.'

'I can't. Not right now, at least.'

'This afternoon, then?'

Calum thought for a moment. He'd never been headhunted before – he'd never been made redundant either – but as his mind whirled, he realised that while this was one more thing to worry about on a day when he already had too many concerns, maybe this could work in his favour. After all, if he *was* going to get sacked then there might well be a juicy redundancy package coming his way. And that, combined with the raise that any move to a new company might bring . . . Well, there was the deposit on a flat for him and Mia.

'Okay.'

'Great. Four p.m.?'

'Fine. How will I recognise you?'

'Oh, don't worry,' said Linda. 'I'm sure I'll see you coming.'

Though as Calum put the phone down, he was worried she already had.

ভৎ

'I knew it!' Sophie Jones angrily deposited the cup of coffee and chocolate muffin she'd bought her boss on Julie's desk. 'I *am* being let go.'

'What?'

'You're firing me!'

'What are you talking about, Sophie?'

'"How to go about a termination". It says it right there on your computer.' She jabbed a finger at the screen accusingly. 'And to think I just bought you a coffee—'

'Sophie, relax,' said Julie, though her expression suggested she wasn't feeling particularly relaxed herself. 'It's not you. It's me.'

'That's the oldest line in the book.' Sophie walked miserably back to her desk, and slumped down into her chair. 'And it *is* me. It's *always* me.'

'Not this time.'

'Yeah, right!'

'It's me,' said Julie, quietly.

'What?'

'I'm looking up "terminations" for me.'

'You're firing *yourself*?' Sophie looked puzzled. 'What for?'

Julie sighed. 'Sophie, no one's getting fired. I'm, well . . . It's not that kind of termination.'

Sophie stared at her for a moment or two, then her jaw dropped open, and before she could stop herself, she'd jumped up from her desk, run over to the door, and slammed it shut.

'You're *pregnant*?'

Julie sat back in her chair, then she nodded, and Sophie didn't know what to say. From what she knew of Julie, getting pregnant certainly wasn't on her agenda, and as for her getting pregnant accidentally? Julie didn't do 'accidentally'. Besides, Julie didn't 'do' babies either, or at least, as had been quite obvious earlier, she didn't do other people's.

'I'd say "congratulations", if you weren't looking at what you were looking at.'

'Thanks,' said Julie, flatly. 'Though I'm just doing a bit of checking, really. Just in case.'

'Oh. Right. Of course. And are you sure . . . ? I mean, is it . . . ?'
She stopped talking. Neither of those two questions would be particularly helpful, under the circumstances.

'Of course it's Mark's!' Julie snapped. 'What do you take me for?'

'That wasn't what I meant,' said Sophie, though of course, it had been. 'And how does he feel about it?' *A little more excited than you*, Sophie hoped.

'I don't know. Mainly because *he* doesn't know.'

'You haven't told him?'

When Julie didn't respond, Sophie stared at her in disbelief. 'Why not?'

'I've only just found out. This morning.'

'You've been to the doctor's?'

Julie shook her head. 'Not yet. But several pregnancy testing kits can't be wrong.'

'Oh *no*,' said Sophie. 'I mean; I don't mean "oh no" that you're pregnant. I mean "oh no" that you've got to tell him. Not that I think he won't be happy . . . And what a bummer! Not being pregnant, obviously, but finding out today. The morning of the Christmas party. 'Cause you can't drink if you're pregnant. I can't think of anything worse! Not being able to have alcohol, I mean – not "being pregnant". Though of course I'm glad I'm not. Pregnant. *Or* not allowed alcohol. Ha ha! Particularly because I don't have a boyfriend. And that's a time when you really need, you know . . . Alcohol.' She stopped talking again, mainly because Julie's face appeared to have glazed over. 'Don't you think you ought to? Tell him, I mean?'

'Of *course* I do.' Julie slid the muffin across the desk towards Sophie as if it was poisonous. 'It's just . . . I only found out this morning, like I said, and Mark's had so much on his plate, what with the merger, and everything.'

Sophie stared at the muffin, weighing up whether eating it would affect how she looked in the knockout dress she was planning to buy for this evening, then decided it looked so delicious it was worth the risk. 'Do the two of you want kids?' she asked, through a mouthful. 'Because I do. I've always wanted them.'

'You can have this one if you like,' Julie patted her stomach, then forced a smile. 'To be honest, we're still working out whether we want each other. This is . . .' She puffed air out of her cheeks. 'It's just come at the wrong time.'

'Out of interest, when would the right time have been?'

'I don't know. Just . . . Not now.'

'So you *do* want kids?'

Julie shrugged. 'I suppose I'd just kind of put it out of my head when I was married because I didn't want to start a family with Philip. But Mark's . . .'

Sophie swallowed a particularly chocolatey lump, and wondered whether she could steal a mouthful of Julie's latte to wash it down with. 'I think he'd make a great dad. Don't you?'

'I don't know. I mean, he's a great . . .' She shifted awkwardly in her chair, as if uncomfortable with the word. 'Boyfriend, but . . . These things go in order, don't they? Meet someone, go out for a while, get to know each other, then maybe move in together, get married, *then* start a family. We've only been dating for nine months.'

'That's ironic!'

'Not funny, Sophie.'

'Sorry.'

'It's just . . .' Julie took a sip of her coffee. 'Something like this? It could mess everything up. Because they can, can't they, children? And just when . . .'

'Just when what?'

She lowered her voice. 'My divorce finally came through this morning.'

Sophie did a little clap. 'Yay?' she suggested, tentatively.

'Yes, yay.'

'At least Mark must have been pleased about . . . Sorry.'

Julie finished glaring at her. 'And then, like some sick joke, the same day I find out about that, this happens.'

'Well, technically, this didn't actually happen today. I mean, I'm not a doctor – not even going out with a doctor any more – but I'm pretty sure you'd have had to have done it a good few weeks ago to get the results now—'

'*Sophie.*'

'Anyway, it's not a sick joke. Quite the opposite, if you ask me.'

When Julie *didn't* ask her, Sophie soldiered on. 'Because actually, I think – well, believe – that in life, everything happens – when it happens – for a reason. My dumping. Tonight's party. Tony A. Wood flying in specially . . .'

'Yes, Sophie, it does. And the reason this happened was one of Mark's sperm defying the odds, medical science, and the best the London Rubber Company had to offer for a cosy tête-à-tête with an egg halfway up one of my fallopian tubes.'

Sophie made a face that was part 'eew', part 'too much information'. 'No, that's *how* it happened. Not *why* it happened.'

'So "why" did it happen, then?'

Sophie folded her arms. 'I don't know. Maybe because it's helping you make a decision you wouldn't normally have made. Maybe because it's stopping you from doing something else that would be a wrong move. Maybe because it's making you think seriously about your relationship with Mark. Maybe it's so you can go on maternity leave and I can steal your job.' She grinned. 'All I'm saying is, you might not know why it's happened yet. All you can be sure of is that it's happened for a reason, and while that reason may not be clear right now, it will be in the fullness of time. You may not believe this, Julie, but we're not all in complete control of our destinies, no matter how hard we try to be. Otherwise things like this wouldn't happen.' She paused for breath. 'Listen, all I'm saying is, this pregnancy, coming at the same time as your divorce . . . Well, I don't think it's a coincidence.'

'You don't?'

'No. It's a sign. And as for Mark . . . Well, he'll probably be delighted when you tell him.'

'You think so?'

Sophie frowned. 'I mean, that depends on whether he wants kids, like you said. And whether now's the right time to have them. Although there's still another nine months to go before you actually have them. It. Though it could be "them". Do twins run in your family? Or Mark's?'

'Sophie!'

'Sorry. Again.' Sophie giggled sheepishly, then lowered her voice, even though the door was shut. 'In any case, whatever Mark thinks, I think it's wonderful news.'

'Oh yes,' said Julie, sarcastically. 'It's a real Christmas miracle.'

And though Julie didn't seem to share her enthusiasm, Sophie smiled to herself. After all, if Christmas miracles did happen, and especially to people like Julie who didn't need them, then there was no earthly (or heavenly) reason why one couldn't happen to *her* later.

5.

Nathan Field was bounding up the stairs, wrestling with the tricky dilemma of which of Soho's many and varied eateries was going to supply him with some lunch, when his phone rang, and while he didn't recognise the number, for a moment, to his surprise, he found himself hoping it might be Stacey.

'Hello?'

'It's a Christmas card!'

'What?' Ellie's voice, still unmistakeable, had brought him to an abrupt halt, and though he'd heard her clearly, his 'what?' was just to buy him a bit of recovery time.

'My email. It's a Christmas card,' said Ellie. 'You know, one of those animated e-cards? I was going to email you back and tell you, but then I thought you might worry my email back to you was dodgy, so you wouldn't open it, and then you'd send me another mail, and that could go on and on . . .' She giggled down the phone. 'So anyway, I thought it was easier to call.'

'Hold on.' Nathan headed back to his office, shut the door behind him, and sat down at his desk. 'Why did you send me an e-card?'

'Well, I normally send everyone *actual* cards – charity cards – but I always worry when I buy them that not a lot of the purchase price goes to the actual charity because of the manufacturing cost of the card, and then there's all that money you waste on stamps when you post the things that could go to some starving child in Africa instead.' She giggled again, which Nathan thought was a bit inappropriate given the subject matter. 'So anyway, this year I thought I'd send e-cards instead, and just make a donation to charity directly . . .'

'I meant, why did you send *me* an e-card?'

'Because it's Christmas?'

Nathan wasn't sure, but he thought he heard a question mark at the end of that sentence. 'Ellie, I . . .' He stopped mid-sentence. Why had he been so stupid? Ellie hadn't sent him a physical card because that was a very binary thing, something he could rip up and throw in the bin so easily, whereas an email invited a response. It was just too easy to click 'reply'. As Nathan had virtually done. 'I was worried it was a virus.'

'From me?' She huffed indignantly, then went quiet. They both knew that, when she'd been sleeping with someone else behind his back, that that had been one of the things he'd been worried about.

'So,' she said, after an uncomfortable silence that Nathan hadn't the first idea how to fill. 'How have you been?'

'What? Me? Fine.' He hesitated, and then, against his better judgement, said: 'You?'

'I'm good. Thanks for asking.'

'Good.'

There was a longer pause this time, then Ellie said: 'Aren't you going to watch it?'

'Watch what?'

'Your *card*, silly!'

'I'm not at my desk,' lied Nathan.

'No?'

'No, I'm . . .' Nathan hesitated again. He wasn't proud of the fact that he was still suspicious of Ellie, nearly four years after she'd cheated on him, but some things took a bit of time to get over. If, indeed, you ever did. 'Wait a sec,' he said, then he stood up and – holding his phone out to ensure Ellie could hear – stomped loudly on the spot as if he was walking somewhere, opened and shut his door, stomped 'back' to his desk, and sat down again. Feeling a little ridiculous after his little pantomime, he found her email, clicked on the attachment, then sat back from the screen with a start. Ellie – at least, Ellie's face, superimposed on a dancing body in a reindeer costume complete with antlers – had appeared in front of him, and – once he'd cranked up the volume – appeared to be dancing to the Macarena.

Fascinated, he watched, knowing it wasn't her body (it might even have been a man's, Nathan was ashamed to realise), but there was still something sexy about seeing her moving on the screen in front of him. Nathan had always enjoyed watching her dance, and even this was stirring feelings he thought he'd buried.

The music finished, Ellie/the reindeer adopted an arms-folded 'gangsta' pose, and after a close-up of her face – antlers decorated with tinsel – had wished him a happy Christmas, he sat there in a stunned silence.

'What did you think?'

'What?' Nathan had forgotten she was on the other end of the phone, and he almost fell off his chair. 'Oh, um, nice outfit.'

'Thanks.'

'And those dancing lessons have paid off.'

'Ha ha.'

'Though I think you might have forgotten to shave your legs.'

'It was that or a singing elf.'

'Right.' Nathan glanced at his watch. 'Well . . .'

'Don't feel you have to send me one back.'

'I'm not sure I'd do the costume justice.'

'Thanks. I think. And I don't know about that.'

'I do.'

'So . . .'

'So?'

'Christmas, eh?'

'Christmas B,' replied Nathan, automatically. It had been their standard response, and he almost kicked himself at how easily he'd fallen back into it.

Ellie laughed. 'I'd forgotten about that.'

'Me too.' Nathan glanced at his watch, wondering how soon was polite to end the call. This conversation was . . . while not unpleasant, exactly, certainly a little uncomfortable. And while they'd parted on okay terms when he'd bumped into her earlier in the year, he'd kind of been resigned to the fact that he wouldn't be hearing from her again. Perhaps ever. 'So . . . How's work?'

'Really good. Great, in fact.' Work was always great with Ellie. Though maybe if you worked in PR like she did, you ended up PR-ing yourself. 'You?'

'Same. Though we've been bought. iFeel.'

'What?'

'iFeel.'

'What do you feel, Nathan?'

'No, that's the name of the company who's bought us.'

Ellie laughed again. 'I know. I'm teasing you. I read about it. You're so easy to get.'

'Maybe,' Nathan conceded.

A ping from his laptop made him look up: another email from Stacey Garrity, and Nathan immediately felt as if he was doing something untoward. 'Listen,' he said, batting down the feelings of guilt. 'I've got to go. Something urgent has just come in.'

'Okay. Well . . .' Nathan heard Ellie take a deep breath. 'Listen, silly idea, probably, and possibly completely inappropriate, but did you want to meet for a quick Christmas drink after work?'

'What for?' He'd said this too quickly, and he could hear the hurt in Ellie's reply.

'For old time's sake?'

'When?'

'Tonight? There's something I'd like to . . . No, that I *need* to talk to you about.'

Nathan shook his head. Was this what it was all about? The card out of the blue, then the call – Ellie was feeling lonely. And who did she think she could turn to? Good old reliable Nathan.

He sighed, leant back in his chair, and stared up at his office ceiling. This was the last thing he needed. So why he found himself saying 'sure' was beyond him.

ლ

Sophie Jones stepped out of the office, and stopped dead in her tracks. A large, white feather was fluttering down to the pavement in front of her, and as she bent down to pick it up, a closely following Julie Marshall almost sent her flying.

'Sophie! What are you doing?'

'Sorry. It's . . . this.' Sophie showed her the feather reverentially. 'It just landed at my feet.'

'Yuck!' Julie wrinkled her nose as she glanced upwards, then she grabbed Sophie's arm and frogmarched her smartly along the pavement.

'What's the hurry?'

'Sophie, I don't know about you, but the last thing I want to happen is for the rest of that dead seagull to fall down and hit me on the—'

'It's not from a seagull.'

'Well, unless there's such a thing as an albino pigeon . . . No, hang on. That would be a dove, wouldn't it?'

'No, it's . . .' Sophie felt herself start to colour. 'Do you believe in guardian angels?'

Julie started to laugh, then she saw Sophie was serious. 'Um, no, not really. Sorry.'

'So you don't sometimes feel there's someone watching over you?'

Julie glared at a couple of leering workmen as they walked past the building site on the opposite side of the street. 'Not in the way you mean, I imagine.'

'It's just . . . in my life, whenever anything bad has happened, I always find a feather.'

'From your guardian angel?'

'Well, yes.'

'It must be getting a bit bare by now.'

'Don't be like that. And I don't mean it's an *actual* angel's feather. It's more of a sign.'

'A sign?'

'That things are about to get better.'

'Come on, Sophie. You'll be telling me you believe in, I don't know, *homeopathy* next.'

Sophie blushed again. 'You can't tell me there isn't something in that?'

'I can, actually. Because there isn't anything in it. At all.'

Sophie rolled her eyes as they turned into Wardour Street. 'You're always so practical. So matter-of-fact. But that's because everything's always worked out for you.'

'Hello?' Julie mimed knocking on Sophie's forehead. 'Divorced and pregnant?'

'Which are both positive things, if you think about it.'

As Julie frowned at her, Sophie soldiered on. 'Anyway, my point is that some of us – *most* of us – we're not like that. We need to believe that life isn't this . . . shitty. That someone's looking out for us. That there's some magic for us just around the corner, and someone's there to give us a nudge in the right direction. And this,' Sophie waved the feather as if it were a mini Union Jack flag and the Queen had just driven past, 'is a sign that there is.'

Julie was shaking her head. 'I'm sorry, Sophie, but the way I see it, life is all action/reaction. You study hard, you get a good degree. You work hard, you get a promotion. Your relationship isn't working out – you change it. You're in control. Not some . . .' she looked up to the sky, where a plane was flying across the gap in between the buildings, 'mystical force from up there.'

'But don't you see? This feather might be telling me that Tony A. Wood could be on that exact plane right now, that he may even be the key to my life going forward, and to me getting what I've always wanted. Tell me it's a coincidence how every woman wants to meet a rich man, and one of the richest in the *entire world* is coming to my office Christmas party this evening, *and* he's just got divorced right when I've been dumped—'

'Again.'

Sophie glared at Julie, then she realised she was probably referring to Tony A. Wood's recent (third) divorce, and not her recent (she'd lost count) dumping.

'And besides,' Julie added. 'There's someone else who's just got divorced, *and* will be at the Christmas party tonight as well.'

'Who?' said Sophie, excitedly.

'Me.'

'That's not the same thing!'

Julie smiled sympathetically. 'Okay. So what is your guardian angel telling you right now?'

Sophie thought for a moment. 'Well, we're on our way to get a dress for me to wear at the party, where Tony A. Wood's going to be. So it's just his way of—'

'It's a 'he'?'

'All angels are,' said Sophie.

'Charlie's aren't. And nor are Victoria's Secret's, now I think about it.'

'Anyway,' continued Sophie, ignoring her. 'It's *his* way of telling me I'm doing the right thing. And that I'm going to find the right dress. Either that, or . . .'

'Or?'

Sophie narrowed her eyes at Julie, and held the feather up again. 'Maybe this actually came from *your* guardian angel.'

'Well, if that's true, then he's got a sick sense of humour.'

'I'm serious! Your little speech just now about being in control? Well, given recent developments, I'd say that, actually, you're not as in control as you think you are, and so maybe this is his way of telling you that finding out you're pregnant on the day your divorce comes through means you're supposed to have this baby. And with Mark.'

Julie gave her a look. 'I'm sorry, Sophie; I know you believe in this kind of thing, but I just don't, especially when there's no supporting evidence. All that feather means is that somewhere up there some poor seagull is going to spend the rest of the day feeling a little bit chillier.'

'But—'

'So I'm afraid we'll just have to agree to disagree on this one.' She glanced impatiently at her watch in the same 'discussion over' way she often did when Sophie was going on a bit in meetings, then tapped the dial. 'Now, come on. Let's go and find you that dress. With or without help from above.'

Sophie grinned sheepishly, then tucked the feather into her handbag and followed Julie obediently along the pavement. She knew there was no science behind something like homeopathy, no proof that there were such things as guardian angels. To tell the truth, that didn't matter. What mattered was whether you *believed* in them or not. And right now, Sophie believed with all her heart.

∽

Mark Webster was sitting in his office, fastidiously picking the avocado out of the chicken and avocado sandwich from the Pret A Manger across the street that Julie had popped in and handed him as a 'peace offering' before telling him they'd 'talk about Christmas' later. Though when he'd suggested that 'later' could perhaps be now, she'd informed him she had something to do this lunchtime – and her lowered-voiced 'Sophie' in response to his raised eyebrows hadn't encouraged him to ask any more.

He hated avocado. It was the devil's vegetable, or fruit (or whatever classification it belonged to), as far as he was concerned, even the tiniest fragment of nastily textured Incredible-Hulk-coloured stuff giving whatever it was in a disgusting sliminess. Pound for pound it seemed to cost more than gold, plus the actual buying process involved picking up and squeezing every single of the reptilian-skinned things in the section in order to try and determine which one had reached optimum ripeness (which seemed to be during some micro-sized window of opportunity between rock-hardness and the thing almost exploding mushily in your grip). Even then, there was no guarantee that you wouldn't get home, slice them open, do that complicated thing with a spoon to get the flesh (and the word gave Mark the shivers) out of the skin, only to find out that at least one of them had turned brown, and yet despite this, Julie *loved* the stuff, adding it to sandwiches and salads at every opportunity.

Still, he knew he couldn't expect the two of them to be compatible on every level, and it was his own fault she'd brought him this – out of all the other delicious sandwich-filling combinations he'd have preferred – from Pret. He'd never quite gotten around to telling her how he felt (and there was a lesson there, Mark suspected)

– mainly because the first time she'd cooked him dinner she'd made guacamole as a starter, and Mark hadn't wanted to hurt her feelings (or appear awkward) so he'd forced a half-a-dozen or so tortilla chips-worth down. Now he worried if he ever let on, she was bound to ask him why he hadn't said anything back then, and to admit that part of the reason was he'd been scared she'd read something into it just seemed too, well, silly.

Although given their argument, it was nice that she'd bought him a sandwich to say 'sorry', which led him to assume that she knew she was in the wrong, and therefore that she'd come round eventually. Though even if she didn't, and if they did have to spend this first Christmas apart for whatever reason, Mark had decided not to let it worry him. Once they were living together, he'd have all the time with her he wanted. And then some, he realised, with a smile.

He reached into his briefcase and removed the jewellery box he'd popped out and bought from the H Samuel shop on Oxford Street a few minutes earlier, checking that the key he'd had cut beforehand was still firmly lodged in the foam slit where a ring would normally sit. And while he was a bit miffed that the woman in the shop had charged him four ninety-nine for what was essentially an empty plastic box – getting the key cut had only cost him a fiver – he supposed that (just) less than ten pounds wasn't too much to pay for what would surely qualify as the 'grand gesture' Nathan had been talking about earlier.

He knew Julie was a modern, independent woman. She'd probably want to insist on paying something towards her board and lodging, so he'd tried to work out what would be reasonable. Her flat in Elephant & Castle cost a little over fourteen hundred pounds a month, and when you factored in her bills, plus council tax . . . Well, Mark had drawn up a spreadsheet, mainly so he could show it to her (he'd even considered putting it in the box alongside the key) to prove that, emotions aside, them living together made financial sense too. And a saving of what effectively added up to just short of seventeen hundred pounds a month . . . Well, they could do all sorts of things with the extra money, like . . . In actual fact, Mark hadn't dared to think that far ahead. But a holiday was certainly on the cards. Skiing, maybe. Or somewhere where there'd be sun.

He stared out of the window at the grey December sky and allowed himself a little daydream about sitting round a pool some-place warm, Julie in her bikini, him perhaps sipping one of those cocktails from a hollowed-out coconut while trying not to poke his eye out on the little decorative umbrella . . . Oh yes, Mark decided. It would be good to get away, once all this merger stuff was done and dusted.

But first things first. He'd find an appropriate moment (i.e. this evening, and once she was drunk enough), present Julie with the key, and then – as his dad always used to say about his mum's brother Robert – Bob's your uncle. Then the only other sticking point would be Philip, who was proving a little harder to get rid of than the avocado had been.

He wrapped the offending pieces of green nastiness in a balled-up serviette, reconstructed the sandwich, took a tentative bite, then threw the rest of the sandwich into his waste bin. This was the problem, Mark realised, and not just with unwanted sandwich fillings: though you did your best to remove every last trace of something, the memory that it was once there could still leave a bad taste in your mouth.

❧

Calum Irwin was sitting at his desk, alternately poring over the document on his laptop screen and checking that Mark Webster hadn't suddenly reappeared at his door. He didn't want to be caught updating his CV, but Linda – or whatever her real name was – would be needing a copy, and although he was feeling guilty for attending to this rather than doing any actual work, from what he'd seen when he'd walked through the main office floor earlier, he wasn't the only one.

In truth, he didn't have that much work to do, given the company's current up-in-the-air status, and the combination of that and tonight's Christmas party meant today felt a bit like being at school on the last day of term, when everyone was allowed to bring games in. Besides, what was the point of getting on with your job when you might not have that job tomorrow? Mark Webster might have reassured everyone there were no planned redundancies in the rather curt email he'd circulated when the merger had been announced, but Calum had been on the receiving end of too many out-of-the-blue dumpings to take that particular promise with any more than a pinch of salt.

He took a deep breath, even more resolved to go through with it this evening, and especially if he was going to get fired soon. After all, Mia might not want to marry someone who was unemployed. No, Calum decided; he'd propose, she'd say yes, and they'd get married as soon as possible. He might lose his job, but there was no way he was going to lose Mia.

He'd be sad to leave, though. He'd joined as a telesales person, then quickly worked his way up to sales manager (though all that meant was he'd sometimes go out to meet prospects, rather than simply call them on the phone), and sales manager (though he didn't actually 'manage' anyone except for himself) had been where (or rather, what) he'd remained. Ever since. For eight years. Not because that had been his top level, but because there hadn't been anywhere else to go, and the UK office hadn't needed any more salespeople than him. Or at least that was how Calum had justified it. And while he'd always been proud of that fact, thought that it showed loyalty, he was also worried it showed a lack of ambition, or rather, worried that was how any prospective employer might see it. 'If you're not moving forwards, you're actually moving back-wards' was what the motivational speaker at the last team-building event he'd been on had been preaching. But how could you move forwards if there wasn't anywhere to go? And besides, Calum really liked where he was.

He lined up an Excel spreadsheet by the side of his CV, and tabbed through the columns, updating the figures for the last few quarters. He'd always at least made his target, or beaten it, so he had nothing to worry about on that front. As for the 'Achievements' sec-tion below . . . Well, in actual fact, he saw his biggest achievement as maintaining his relationship with Mia-Rose since Valentine's Day, although he could hardly put that . . . Or could he? Quickly, he added 'Relationship Management' to the list. It was a Thing, after all.

With a final check for spelling errors, he re-read his CV, then sat back in his chair, feeling pretty satisfied with his efforts. If he did lose his job, well, he was sure there'd be others. He only wished this was how he felt about Mia-Rose. Life without her . . . Well, he couldn't even contemplate having to re-enter *that* particular market.

Not for the first time, he began to doubt the wisdom of what he was doing. After all, they were getting on just fine right now. Things were going well. Why rock the boat? But Calum knew the answer to that. The longer they dated, the more he was sure she would get bored of him and leave. But this way? With a ring on her finger, they'd be engaged. Then married. Moving in together. Then perhaps even starting a family. These were all steps forward. Progress. *And if you're not moving forwards* . . . he thought again, as he printed his CV off and slipped it into his jacket pocket.

With a start, Calum suddenly realised the second thoughts he was having weren't about proposing – every time he thought about

Mia-Rose, or she put a call through to him, or he walked past her on reception, he was surer she was the girl for him – but about what he was going to propose *with*. He'd felt his sugar levels drop a bit mid-morning, so he'd eaten the Haribo jelly ring, and on his way to buy another packet, he'd walked past a jeweller's on Oxford Street and caught sight of the array of shiny, diamond-topped engagement rings in the window.

At the time, he'd dismissed them, reminding himself that he and Mia could choose one together once he'd done the deed. But Mia was a traditional girl. From what she described as a 'God-fearing' family – though the couple of times he'd met Mia's sisters, a pair of huge Afro-Caribbean girls as loud as the multicoloured headscarves they always wore, he was sure if they and God were ever in the same room, it'd be Him who'd be quaking in his boots. Would she really want to be proposed to with a sugar-coated sweet?

Suspecting he already knew the answer to that, Calum leapt up from his desk, grabbed his coat, and hurried back to the jeweller's, hanging around in front of the window for a few minutes as he drummed up the courage to go inside. With a final check that no one from the office was watching, he pushed the heavy glass door open and slipped inside. As he made his way nervously toward the counter, the shop assistant looked up from where she'd been polishing one of the glass cabinets.

'Are you here to rob the place?'

'What? No! Of course not. Whatever makes you think that?'

'I saw you through the window. You looked like you were casing the joint. Plus you're sweating like it's the middle of summer . . .' She leant in close and lowered her voice. 'Though between you and me, the really valuable stuff's in the safe out the back . . .'

'Honestly, I'm not, I—' The woman was probably as old as his mum, and Calum felt like he was being scolded. He glanced up at the CCTV camera pointing down at him, and suddenly felt doubly guilty. 'I'm a customer. Not a, you know, *robber*.'

'Well, that's a relief.' The woman beamed at him. 'In that case, can I help you?'

'Um, yes.'

'With?'

'Oh. Yes. Telling you would help, wouldn't it?' He did his best to crack a smile. 'Sorry. I'm just a bit nervous.'

'Whatever for?'

'Because I'm after . . . I mean, I need . . .' Calum swallowed hard. 'I'm planning to propose. Tonight. So . . . engagement rings.'

'Rings, plural?' The woman laughed. 'How many girls are you planning to propose to?'

'No, I meant . . .' He smiled politely back. She was obviously trying to lighten the situation, but so far, Calum wasn't finding much of today funny.

'I know what you meant. Did you have a budget in mind?'

Calum shrugged. The packet of Haribo had cost a pound, but he suspected he might have to spend a little more than that. 'What's . . . usual?'

'Well, it depends how much you love her. It is a *her*, isn't it?'

'Of course! Well, not "of course", obviously. I mean, there's nothing wrong with, you know—'

'Only we have to ask, nowadays.' The woman smiled. 'And I was joking about the "how much you love her" part. Traditionally, it's one month's salary. Two, if you're feeling generous.'

'I don't know how much she earns.'

'*Your* salary.'

'Oh. Right.' Calum thought for a moment. As a salesman at Seek, he got paid a base salary with a quarterly bonus, but did she mean base, as in the two months he didn't get a bonus, or one base plus one bonus, or should he average it out over twelve months? 'Um . . .'

As the woman watched him patiently, he did a quick calculation in his head. He'd been having a good year, so if he included his bonus . . . But that was an awful lot of money for what was just a piece of jewellery. And besides, if they were going to get married, well, weddings were expensive, and she didn't have a father, and her mum didn't work, so they could hardly be expected to do the traditional bride's-family-footing-the-bill thing. Plus, he'd need all the money he could lay his hands on if he was going to be moving house. Especially if he was going to lose his job. 'Maybe . . .' Calum swallowed hard. 'A couple of thousand.'

'A couple?'

'Three, tops.'

'And do you know the kind of thing you're looking for?'

'Um, no. Not really,' said Calum. He wasn't even sure he knew what an engagement ring looked like – was it the one with the stone, or the plain band thing?

'Well, what kind of thing does she like?'

Calum considered the question carefully. Mia-Rose was quite . . . flamboyant. She wore a *lot* of jewellery – not over the top in an A-Team Mr T kind of way, but she was always finding things at the various London street markets she'd drag him round most weekends. Generally, the stones were large (and often plastic – though he was sure that wouldn't cut it this time).

'You mean what kind of jewellery, right?'

'Right,' said the woman. 'We already know she likes you, obviously. Or at least, let's hope she does. Anyway, I'm sure you'll find that out when you ask her to marry you later.'

'She quite likes, well . . .' Calum knew the description he was about to give applied to him as well, and he hoped the woman wouldn't make a joke. He'd always been sensitive about his weight, and even though Mia was a similar size, it still made him uneasy to think about it, as if he was sure she'd run off with someone slimmer given half the chance. 'Big stuff.'

'Oh dear,' said the woman, though her expression suggested the opposite. 'Well, how about one of these?'

She reached down under the glass counter and retrieved a tray full of the shiniest, most expensive-looking rings that Calum had ever seen, each one he looked at seemingly sporting a diamond larger than the previous shockingly large one. Mia-Rose had always told him that size wasn't important, and while he'd always assumed she was referring to his weight (at least, that's what he told himself), he had a sneaking suspicion that when it came to diamond rings, that particular phrase wasn't true.

'Right. Well, um, how about . . .' He clutched the edge of the counter for support, then gestured vaguely towards the middle of the tray, hoping the rings there might strike the right kind of balance, careful not to actually touch one, worried that if he did, like when looking at donuts in Greggs, he'd be legally bound to buy it. 'That silver one,' he said, before realising they were *all* silver.

'This one?'

The woman was indicating one with a diamond that seemed just about right – not too big that he'd be losing any deposit he had for a flat, not too small that Mia might turn her nose up at it, so he nodded. 'Yup.'

'An excellent choice. Though technically, it's white gold.'

'Right.' Calum peered at the ring. It was neither white, nor gold, though he knew he'd just have to take the woman's word for it. 'And how—'

'Many carats? Hold on . . .' The woman extracted the ring from the tray, and Calum stared at it. He'd heard something about carrots helping you see in the dark, but he suspected the same might be true about *carats*, given how amazingly it was catching the light.

And while he'd actually wanted to ask how *much* it was, suddenly that didn't seem so important.

'Two,' said the woman.

'And, um, how much . . . ?' He'd managed to get the word out this time, and he waited, nervously as the woman fiddled for the tiny label attached to the underside of the ring.

'Two thousand—'

'Oh. Right,' he said, pleasantly surprised.

'—nine hundred and ninety-nine pounds.'

'Ah.' Calum caught his breath. It was more than he'd wanted to spend. But how could Mia – how could *anyone* – refuse when presented with something as beautiful as this? 'I mean, er, great.'

'Lovely. Do you know what size she is?'

'A sixteen,' said Calum, quickly, pleased with himself that he knew the answer to that one. 'Though I don't see what that has to do with—'

'Her ring finger,' said the woman, flatly. Then, when she saw his blank expression, she made what almost looked like a rude gesture. 'Which is this one.'

'Oh. Um . . .' Calum frowned. He'd held her hand often enough, but he didn't have a clue. 'Is it important you know now?'

'Well, we can adjust it to within a size or so, but if she's planning to put it on after she's said yes, and most women do – put it on, I mean, not say yes . . .' The woman let out a short, high-pitched laugh, but Calum didn't feel like joining in. 'It's better if it fits.'

He frowned again. To get the wrong size could well spoil the moment. Buy one too small, make her struggle to squeeze it onto her finger, and Mia-Rose might be embarrassed about her weight, or might even say no just because she didn't think she could put it on in the first place – and that wouldn't be fair. But to buy one that was too big, and run the risk that she might think he thought she was larger than she actually was . . .

'I'd better go and find out, in that case. What time do you close this aftern—'

'Calum!'

At the sound of the loud Caribbean twang from behind him, Calum froze. Why did Mia always catch him when he was doing something like this? And what could he say – that he was in here buying her Christmas present? Maybe something for his mother. That would have to do. Although the tray of engagement rings in front of him might make that sound a little creepy. He made a face at the woman behind the counter, willing her to understand that he needed a cover story, then nervously turned round to find Nathan grinning at him from just inside the door.

'Hello, sweetheart,' Nathan said, in a more-than-passable impression of Mia-Rose's voice.

'You . . . bastard!' Calum leant against the counter and waited for the hammering in his chest to subside, then glared at Nathan as he strolled jauntily over.

'Whatcha doing?'

'Me?' Calum felt himself start to colour. Not only was he embarrassed about what he was up to, he also knew Nathan didn't really go for any of this 'marriage bollocks', as he'd heard him call it once or twice. Though, Calum supposed, when you were told mid-proposal by your girlfriend that she was seeing someone else, he could understand why. 'Getting, um, *something* for Mia.'

'Oh, right.' Nathan glanced down at the tray of rings, then his eyes widened. 'Oh, *right!*'

'It's not what you think,' said Calum, hurriedly. 'Okay, it might be what you think. But—'

'Relax.' Nathan grinned at him, and as the shop assistant slipped the tray away and moved away to serve someone else, he lowered his voice. 'I've got a spare one of those, if you want. I mean, it's used. And doesn't exactly have the best track record.'

'Thanks, Nathan, but—'

'I'm kidding! I'm happy for you, mate. Really I am, you sly old dog! When are you planning to do the deed?'

'Tonight.' Calum made a 'terrified' face, though he didn't have to do much acting. 'Just before the party. Over dinner. In Old Amsterdam.'

'Good on you!'

'Yeah. I'm hoping she'll say, you know . . .'

'Yes?'

'Yes.'

'How could she possibly say no? And you'll be dressed the part, so that should count in your favour.'

'What do you mean?'

'Hello?' Nathan rapped him lightly on the forehead with his knuckles. 'The Christmas party?'

'Oh. Right,' said Calum, sheepishly. He hadn't paid too much attention to the invitation. His mind had been on other things. 'Where is it again?'

'Dunno,' said Nathan. 'There's a coach coming to pick us up at six thirty, apparently. But it's going to be somewhere posh.'

'What makes you say that?'

Nathan made the 'duh' face. 'Well, perhaps the fact that there's a coach coming to pick us up? Or maybe because our new owner's a billionaire? In any case, it's bound to be somewhere nicer than upstairs at the Frog and Ferret like last year.'

'Right. And, sorry, but rewind a few moments, what does how I'm dressed have to do with it?'

'You did notice that it said "black tie" on the invitation?'

'I'm not completely stupid, you know?' Calum wiggled the knot on the black necktie he'd put on that morning. The one he'd bought from M&S especially for this evening. The one, when he'd showed it to his mum, she'd asked if he was buying things to wear at her funeral already. 'Ta-da!'

Nathan widened his eyes. 'Calum, "black tie" doesn't mean you just wear a black tie. It means you wear a black *bow* tie.'

'What?'

'And a DJ? And by "DJ" I mean the full penguin suit.'

'Sure,' said Calum, though he was anything but. Was Nathan implying it was animal fancy dress?

'Do you *own* a dinner suit?'

'A dinner suit?' As the penny finally dropped, Calum shook his head. He didn't own that many suits full stop.

'Well, you need to get one. There's nothing worse than standing out like a sore thumb because you don't look like everyone else.'

Calum began to panic. That was how he'd felt all his life. 'Oh. Right. Of course.' He looked anxiously at his watch. 'And I can get one from—?'

Nathan smiled. 'Relax. You could rent one, but to be honest, they're available everywhere on the high street nowadays, and not much more expensive. And who knows when you might need one again?'

'Well . . .' Calum knew exactly when he might need one again – assuming Mia-Rose said 'yes' this evening.

'Tell you what,' continued Nathan. 'I'll come with you now, if you like. Help you pick one out.'

Calum thought for a moment. Nathan was a snappy dresser: He'd make sure he got a decent dinner suit, then if he wore it to Old Amsterdam, and proposed to Mia-Rose in it – well, like Nathan said, that'd be even more of a reason for her to accept.

'That'd be great,' he said.

Julie Marshall stifled a yawn, and checked her phone for messages for what seemed like the fiftieth time. She'd been waiting outside the changing room for so long, she'd begun to suspect there was a back entrance she didn't know about and that Sophie had made a run for it. With a last look at her watch, she hauled herself up from the seat she'd commandeered in the shoe section, pushed her way through the impatient queue that had formed by the entrance to the cubicles, and cleared her throat.

'Everything okay in there?'

'Just a sec,' said Sophie.

After more than a sec – possibly even sixty of them – Julie stuck her head through the curtains. Sophie was staring at her reflection in the changing room mirror, the expression on her face suggesting she was beginning to regret coming to Zara. Which – if Julie were being honest – made two of them.

'Do you need a hand?'

Sophie sighed loudly, then pointed at the selection of outfits hanging on the hooks next to her, frowning at their unseasonably plunging necklines and bottom-skimming hemlines. 'All these dresses seem to be more appropriate for a summer's evening.'

'Well, that's because shops generally stock a season or two ahead.'

'Don't they know that people generally come clothes shopping because they need something *now*, rather than something that they might want to wear in six months? I *never* know what I'm going to need that far ahead. And certainly don't know what size I'll be.'

Julie nodded. Even she had several outfits hanging in her wardrobe that would need several weeks of dieting (and some she'd need to binge-eat for them to fit) before she could even contemplate trying to get into them. Still, maybe that was one upside to the pregnancy. At least they'd fit her again. If only briefly.

'Although maybe the lack of *coverage* makes them perfect for seducing a billionaire husband-to-be. Especially on a cold winter's evening, where everyone else will be wrapped up.'

'You'd think so,' said Sophie miserably. 'Though so far, nothing's giving me the look I'm after.' She spun round to show off the one she'd just squeezed herself into. 'They either thrust my boobs so far forward that walking downstairs will be dangerous – especially in the killer heels I'm planning to wear – or make me worried that every time I so much as shrug my shoulders, the bottom's going to ride up and expose, well, *mine*.'

'And the problem with that is?' asked Julie, gathering up the pile of dresses Sophie had discarded on the bench. 'What sort of look *are* you after?'

Sophie examined her reflection again. 'A little bit sexy without being tarty. Approachable, but not easy. Something that shows off my curves, but doesn't make me look fat. And in a colour that doesn't make me look washed out.'

'Hmm.' Julie thought for a moment. 'Size?'

'Ten,' said Sophie, quickly. 'Though actually, I might need to breathe, rather than let *them* breathe,' she said, nodding down at her rather exposed chest. 'So you'd better make that twelve.'

'Okay. Back in a mo.'

Julie reversed out of the changing room, and – ignoring the angry looks from the even longer queue – dumped her armful of dresses on the table in front of the bored-looking assistant, then – after an accidental excursion into the 'baby clothes' section sent her quickly scurrying back to the main part – hurried round the shop floor. She hadn't been clothes shopping for what seemed like years, apart from to buy the new work outfits she'd needed after her marathon training had seen her drop a couple of dress sizes. And while Zara might be a bit, well, *young* for her, surely there was plenty here that would be just right for Sophie?

She headed over to a rack of dresses in the corner, picked up a slash of bright-red material and examined it, then hastily put it back, not sure which way round it went. The dress might have been okay on her, but on someone with Sophie's 'assets' (as the *Daily Mail* would describe them), it was asking for trouble.

Then again, wasn't that what Sophie was after? Not trouble, exactly, but attention. She needed to turn up tonight wearing something memorable. And this particular dress – or rather, Sophie in it – would certainly be that.

She quickly found a size twelve, and carried it back to the changing rooms, rapping her knuckles on the curtain with a loud 'Knock-knock', followed by a 'Ta-da!'

'Um . . .'

As Sophie regarded the dress with suspicion, Julie held it up against her. 'What's wrong with it?'

'It's a bit . . . There's not a lot of material.'

'I thought that was the point?' Julie smiled patiently. 'Don't you want to try it on?'

'The dress? Or with Tony A. Wood?'

'I think the former might well lead to the latter.'

As Sophie pulled the curtains shut, Julie prepared herself for another long wait, but she was just reaching for her phone again when Sophie appeared in front of her.

'What do you think?'

'I . . . It's . . . Wow! I mean . . .'

'Too much?' Sophie did a quick twirl. 'And by that, I mean "too little"?'

'No, I think . . .' Julie pointed to Sophie's chest. 'Perhaps it shows a little too much of your bra.'

'Oh. Right. Hang on . . .' Sophie reached behind her, undid the clasp one-handedly, and quickly shrugged it off. 'How's that?'

'It's . . .' Julie's jaw dropped in admiration. 'Well, as the saying goes, you look like a million dollars. If that doesn't get his attention . . . And impressive trick, by the way!'

Sophie turned and paraded up and down in front of the full-length mirror. 'He won't think it's cheap? I mean, he's a billionaire, and this . . .' She checked the price tag. 'Is twenty-nine ninety-nine. It's hardly the designer stuff I'm sure he's used to.'

'Trust me, Sophie. In my experience, men only notice how little a woman is wearing, not how little it costs. And if that's true where Tony's concerned, then he's *really* going to notice this. Just remember me when you're rich and famous. Or even just rich.' She smiled. 'So – do we have a winner?'

Sophie took one more look at herself in the mirror, and beamed at her reflection. 'We do!'

'Great!' said Julie, pleased with herself. The dress was a knock-out, and she was sure Sophie would be too. If this didn't do the trick? Well, she might as well give up.

She hesitated for a moment, then leaned in and gave Sophie a hug, though mainly because she was grateful that the shopping ordeal was over. Perhaps this was what it was like to have a grown-up daughter? If only you could fast-forward to this point.

She reached up to help with the flimsy straps that just about kept the top half of the outfit in place, then stood back as Sophie fumbled for the zip.

'It's a lot harder to take off than my bra was,' laughed Sophie, and Julie let out a short laugh.

'Sophie, if everything goes to plan later, taking it off isn't going to be *your* problem.'

6.

Calum Irwin and Nathan Field were striding along Oxford Street
– or rather, Nathan was striding along Oxford Street, while
Calum was somewhere between a walk and a run as he did his
best to keep up with his long-legged friend. In truth, he was relieved
to be out of the jeweller's, though he knew it was only a temporary
respite. He had a plan to find out Mia's ring size later – a plan that
involved Sophie Jones – so he'd head back to the shop after that
particular mission had been accomplished.

'What's your budget?' Nathan asked, during a welcome respite
from their (at least, so it seemed to Calum) headlong charge, while
they waited to cross the road. 'For the suit, I mean. Not the . . .' He
tapped the middle of his ring finger, as if he couldn't bring himself
to say the word.

Calum stepped back as a bicycle rickshaw mounted the pavement at breakneck speed in front of him, a couple of elderly, scared-
looking tourists clinging to each other for dear life in the back, and
considered his answer. He might need the majority of his money to
spend on the ring, he realised. 'Budget?'

'Yes, budget. How much do you—?'

'That's what I mean. Something towards the, you know, *budget*
end. I mean, I'm not going to be wearing it that often, am I?' Twice,

he thought. Or rather, hoped. 'So should we perhaps look in here?' he said, leading Nathan into the doorway of TK Maxx.

Nathan looked up at the sign above the shop door, then shook his head. 'Next,' he said, decisively.

'I don't have any other suggestions. And sometimes TK Maxx have bargains that—'

'No, I meant Next. The shop. You want good, cheap suits on the high street, that's the place to go.'

'Next. Right.'

They made their way a block further down to the Oxford Street branch, where Calum stopped in front of the window to catch his breath.

'Are you . . . sure?' he asked, staring at the athletically shaped, impeccably suited mannequins in the window.

'What's wrong?'

'The dummies.' Calum pointed at the nearest one, worried Nathan might think the term might include him after his 'black tie' faux pas. 'They're all a bit . . . *thinner* than me.'

'Calum, they're not modelled on real people,' said Nathan, leading him inside. 'And besides, they pin the jackets at the back so they look this fitted. Trust me, the actual clothes are a lot more . . . forgiving.'

'Phew.'

Calum followed him upstairs to the men's section, where Nathan swiftly located the dinner-suit rack. 'Right. What size are you?'

'Thirty-eight.'

'And the trousers?'

Calum could feel his face burning. 'I *meant* the trousers. Jacket forty-two.'

'Oh-kay . . .' Nathan flicked through the rack. 'Here you go,' he said, handing Calum a suit in the appropriate sizes.

They strolled towards the changing room, where a pretty, stick-thin girl was disinterestedly slotting clothes back onto their hangers.

'How many?' she said, smiling shyly at Nathan, and Calum gritted his teeth. Women always acted like this around him, and Calum always tried not to feel too jealous. And always failed.

'Two,' said Nathan. 'Well, technically, it's one, seeing as it's a suit.'

The girl burst out laughing, a little overenthusiastically, Calum thought. Nathan's observation hadn't been *that* funny. 'Straight through,' she said, indicating the curtained booths behind her.

As Calum stared at Nathan, he winked. 'As appealing as the thought of watching you get undressed might be, I think I'll wait here,' he said.

Aware he was probably in double figures already for the day, Calum blushed again, then carried the suit into the changing room, removed his own grey work two-piece, and hurriedly pulled on the trousers. Relieved they fitted him without too much of a constriction, he took off his tie, slipped on the jacket, then nervously regarded himself in the mirror like a plastic-surgery patient seeing himself without the bandages for the first time. He'd never worn a dinner suit before, and the effect was . . . well, if not quite James Bond, certainly closer to 007 than his usual zero.

As he peered at himself from all angles, liking what he saw, a voice from outside the cubicle interrupted his reverie.

'How are you getting on?'

'Good,' said Calum. 'I think. I mean, it fits and everything.'

'What's "everything"?'

'I can still breathe with the trousers done up. And I can fasten the front of the jacket,' said Calum, though he'd have settled for either of those things.

'Cool!' Nathan laughed, then he stuck his head through the curtain and wolf-whistled. 'Oh, and one more thing.'

'What?' said Calum, still admiring his reflection.

'The "black tie" part.' Nathan handed him a bow tie. 'You'll need this.'

'But I don't know how to tie one.'

'It's easy,' said Nathan. 'Particularly when it comes pre-tied, like this one.'

Calum slotted the tie underneath his collar, fastened the Velcro, levelled the bow, and turned back to the mirror. *Oh yes*, he thought. This was definitely worth the money. Mia was going to be a push-over. Or at least, he might get her just enough off-balance to say 'yes'.

He did a couple of spy-like 'action' poses in front of the mirror using the jacket's hanger as a gun, then blushed a third time when he realised the cubicle's curtain was still open, and the girl was peering at him strangely from the entrance.

'Right. Your belt's the right colour, as are your shoes,' said Nathan, looking him up and down, 'so I'd say we're pretty much done here.'

'Do I need one of those Cumberbatch things?'

'Huh?'

'You know. Around my waist. Assuming they make them that bi—'

'You mean "cummerbund". And no. It's formal dress, not fancy dress. Though a fancy dress is what Mia will be shopping for soon.' He raised both eyebrows in quick succession, like a ventriloquist's dummy. 'Does she have any idea?'

Calum shook his head. 'Nope. At least, I don't think so. I mean, we've talked a bit about the future. She's told me she wants to get married.'

'Well, there you go then.'

'Although she didn't actually say to *me*.'

'Ah.' Nathan grinned, then clapped him on the shoulder. 'I'm sure it'll be fine. Have you thought how you're going to do it?'

'What do you mean?'

'You know: drop the ring in her glass of champagne, or hide it in her dessert, or get a specially trained dove to fly in with the ring in its beak and drop it onto the table in front of her?' He narrowed his eyes. 'Actually, I'm not sure you can do that.'

Calum paled. Aside from getting down on one knee and saying 'Will you marry me?' he hadn't thought he might need some sort of gimmick. 'Do you think I need to? Do something memorable, I mean?'

Nathan shrugged. 'I didn't. I just asked Ellie outright. And she said "no". Although that was possibly something to do with the guy she'd been planning to leave me for who she'd been seeing for weeks. But . . .' Nathan stopped talking, perhaps because he'd seen the look of panic on Calum's face. 'All I'm saying is, she might want it to be memorable. Imagine she's chatting with her friends, and she tells them you've asked her to marry you, and – once they've stopped jumping around and screaming at the tops of their voices – they ask her how you did it, and Mia says, "Well, he just asked me". And then she sees their faces fall ever so imperceptibly, and she feels miserable, and she forever remembers her proposal as something . . .'

'Disappointing,' said Calum, dejectedly.

'Hey.' Nathan held both hands up, as if Calum were pointing a gun at him. 'Like I said, I'm the last person to give advice where proposing is concerned. But I've never been able to stop wondering whether if I'd done it a little more differently, made it a bit more special, more—'

'Memorable.'

'*Memorable*, then maybe the outcome might have been different.' He shrugged again, in a *what-can-you-do?* kind of way. 'Still, it's not me we're talking about here.' Nathan punched him affectionately on the arm. 'You look great, mate. Even if you *do* simply go for the traditional get-down-on-one-knee thing, Mia's going to be speechless.'

Calum forced a smile as he unfastened the bow tie from around his neck. 'Not completely, I hope,' he said.

⌒

Julie Marshall had left a beaming Sophie Jones at the till in Zara, but now, staring perplexedly at the festively decorated information board in John Lewis, she wasn't feeling at all like smiling herself. She didn't have a clue what to buy Mark for Christmas, and despite a couple of circuits of the store, Julie still found herself none the wiser.

What hadn't helped was that the shop was full of bratty, mid-tantrum scarlet-faced toddlers, most of them screaming their heads off from strollers (a name Julie always found ironic, since they encouraged exactly the opposite) not much smaller than a Smart car, and accompanied by stressed-out mothers who looked like they wanted to be anywhere but here. And while Julie had tried to be sympathetic as they'd alternately bashed into her ankles or attempted to spray the contents of their drinks bottles, fruit pouches, or even their stomachs over her shoes, she was rapidly running out of patience. If she'd wanted to be subjected to constant high-pitched whining and childish unreasonableness, she might as well have stayed with her ex-husband.

She'd always loathed Christmas shopping. Back when she'd been married, Philip had pretty much gone out and gotten himself whatever he'd wanted (including a shag from a woman he'd met at some literary festival, which was the reason they'd got divorced in the first place), so present-buying had always been a bit of a moot point between them. Mark seemed to be pretty much the same (apart

from the 'shag' part) – at least, as far as she could see, he didn't seem
to want for much. He dressed pretty well (though perhaps a little
older than Julie might have liked, if she was honest), didn't wear
jewellery, seemed happy with the old Seiko watch he always wore,
and though he was into gadgets (she still couldn't work his hi-fi –
the remote control looked like something you could fly the space
shuttle with – or his flat's central heating system, and his kitchen
contained the widest and most sophisticated range of coffee-making
apparatus she'd ever seen), the last thing Julie wanted was to get him
something that would no doubt become obsolete by the New Year,
or that didn't top the 'best of' lists she'd often see him poring over
in the tech magazines he subscribed to. He'd even recently stopped
wearing a tie (though he'd been one of the last people in the office
to do so – something that had gained him much ribbing from the
likes of Nathan Field), which had cut off that particular avenue of
gift-giving, so apart from socks – and Julie couldn't believe she was
even considering *that* – she was plain out of ideas.

As she frowned at the board, wondering which of the floors
might provide her with a solution, a kindly faced middle-aged lady
in a John Lewis uniform approached her.

'Are you looking for something?'

'Inspiration.' Julie sighed. 'I need a Christmas present.'

'For . . . ?'

'My . . .' Julie hesitated. She still didn't quite know how to
refer to Mark. 'Boyfriend' sounded a little childish, 'other half' a
bit pathetic (and don't get her started on 'better' half), while 'part-
ner' always seemed a bit impersonal – not to mention ambiguous
– to her. 'He and I . . . Well, we've only been together for about
nine months. So it's our first Christmas together. Assuming we are
together. I mean, we probably will be. Spending it with each other,
that is. Though we've just had a bit of an argument about that . . .'

Julie stopped talking, as the woman was looking a little uncomfortable. 'Sorry. Too much information.'

'And what does he like?'

'Chicken and avocado sandwiches, hopefully,' Julie grinned guiltily. 'I'm sorry. I'm not normally like this. It's just been a bit of a funny day so far, that's all.'

The woman smiled. 'Don't worry. Were you thinking of something for him to wear? Or is he sporty, at all?'

'I wish,' said Julie. 'I mean, not really, no. And no. He's got his own taste in clothes. And it's a bit early on for me to try and impose mine on him.'

'What about something from our male grooming range?'

Julie made a face. 'I'm sorry, that always sounds a bit pervy to me. "Grooming"; isn't that what paedophiles do over the Internet?'

'I meant some aftershave,' said the woman, dryly. 'Or moisturiser. Men are into that kind of thing nowadays.'

'You're telling me,' said Julie. 'His bathroom cabinet's got more products in it than mine does, and don't get me started on the amount of time he spends in there every morning . . .' She clapped a hand over her mouth. 'I'm sorry. I don't know why I'm oversharing today.'

'That's okay,' said the woman. 'Trust me, I've had people tell me a lot worse. So . . .' She thought for a moment. 'Does he like surprises?'

Julie let out a short laugh. 'Oh, don't you worry. I've already got him one of those. And it's a corker!'

'Oh. Because I was going to suggest that you could get him one of our "Experience" packages. We've got a range to suit all kinds of people. Driving a Ferrari, learning how to mix cocktails . . . Does that sound like the kind of thing he might like?'

'As long as they're not at the same time.' Julie looked at the woman, and then, despite her best efforts not to, found herself bursting into tears. 'I'm sorry,' she sobbed. 'I don't know what's come over me. It's just— I know we haven't been together for that long, but I'm really worried by the fact that I don't have a clue what to get him. And that might sound silly, but he's been living on his own for such a long time before he met me, and he's kind of got everything sorted. The way he likes it. Without a ripple. And I'm about to come and jump in with both feet, and make the biggest of splashes . . .' She took the tissue the woman was handing her, and dabbed at her eyes. 'I'm sorry. Your badge says "ask me anything", not "tell me everything".'

She stepped back to let another harassed mother pushing a stroller past, wincing at the look of quiet desperation on her face, and the assistant smiled again.

'When's it due?'

'What?'

'You're pregnant, yes?'

'How can you—?'

'Well, let's see. Maybe from the fact that your emotions are quite obviously all over the place, plus the way you're looking at every baby and toddler in here with an expression of absolute terror on your face.'

'I've only just found out.' Julie blew her nose loudly. 'This morning.'

'I don't need to ask if it's your first.'

'It will be, if I decide to have it.' Julie felt awful the moment the words had left her lips. 'I'm sorry. That sounded terrible, didn't it?'

The woman shook her head. 'It's your right. Your choice. And don't let anyone tell you otherwise. Even that husband of yours.'

'He's not my husband. That's part of the problem.'

'Is he someone else's?'

'No!'

'Well, what are you worried about, then? Or should I say, *who* are you worried about?'

'I'm worried . . .' Julie blew her nose loudly, then balled up the tissue, '. . .about *me*. That I can't do this. And even if I could, that *he* doesn't like me enough to want to have a baby with me.'

'You don't even know what he wants for Christmas. So how can you possibly know *that* about him?'

'But don't you see? That's exactly my problem.'

'Or your solution. Because you know what they say about children.'

Julie thought for a moment. In her experience, her friends said a lot of things about children, and they weren't usually complimentary. 'Um, that they're better seen and not heard?'

'No.' The woman smiled patiently. 'That they're the greatest gift of all.'

Julie made a face. Even if that was true, she had a feeling she should keep the receipt.

༄

Mark Webster's ears were burning, though he knew it was his own fault for sitting so close to the patio heater outside Bar Italia. But all the inside tables had been taken, and desperate to get out of a depressingly empty office (and desperate to get rid of the taste of avocado), a cup of the best coffee in central London had seemed like a good idea.

He edged his chair forward an inch or two, careful not to get too close to a man his age vaping away like a steam train at the table next to him, and sipped his cappuccino. He'd never seen the point of e-cigarettes. Or e-books, for that matter. Perhaps not the healthiest attitude for someone who worked for a company at 'the cutting edge of technology' (according to the brochures that came from Julie's department), but sometimes, new things appeared because they could, not because they should. And when it came to making a change, Mark generally needed a better reason than that.

His phone rang – Nathan had set Sir Mix-A-Lot's 'Baby Got Back' as his ringtone when he'd accidentally left it on his desk the other day, and Mark hadn't got around to changing it back yet – a fact he was always reminded of whenever a call informed everyone in the vicinity that Mark 'liked big butts', and as the man with the e-cigarette smirked at him through a cloud of vapour, he scrambled for it in his pocket. The number said 'withheld', so he hit the answer key and barked a suspicious 'Yes?'

'Webster?'

'This is Mark Webster.'

'Tony A. Wood here.'

At the sound of the drawling American tones, Mark jerked himself bolt upright, nearly losing his grip on his phone, spilling his cappuccino all over the table in the process. 'Oh hell! Oh. I mean, "Hello?"'

'Have ah caught you at a bad time?'

'Not at all,' Mark lied. He grabbed a serviette from the dispenser and dabbed frantically at the pool of coffee on the table, trying to prevent it from running off the edge and dripping onto his trousers. 'It's a pleasure to finally—'

'Ah'm just callin' to check everything's okay for tonight?'

'Yes, er, *sir*. We're all looking forward—'

'And you're goin' to be there, Webster?'

'Of course, sir.'

'Less of the "sir" business, Webster. It's "Tony". Ah run an informal ship.'

'Oh. Right, um, Tony. Well in that case, please call me "Mark".'

'Sure thing, Webster. So, remember, there's transport coming at 6.30 p.m. In the meantime, there's somethin' we need to talk about, so listen caref—.'

The call faded out for a moment, and Mark frowned. 'I'm having difficulty hearing you. Where are you?'

'On mah plane.'

'On a plane?'

'*Mah* plane. Hold on, Webster, ah'll tell the pilot to fly a bit lower.'

There was the sound of a muffled conversation, and Mark did a double take. Could you phone from a plane? And what was with all this 'Webster' business? The exaggerated American drawl was like something out of the movies, and cogs started to turn in Mark's head. This was typical of one of Nathan Field's wind-ups. And though he'd told Nathan many times that he didn't find them funny, Nathan would always remind him that he wasn't the one who was supposed to.

'Is that better?'

'Much better. But tell me something, Tony. How did you get this number?'

'Ah bought the company, remember? Which includes all the people. And their company phones.'

'Ah. Yes. Of course.'

'Which effectively means that ah own you.'

'Oh. I thought it was actually more of a merger, so—'

'What are you suggestin'?'

'Well, nothing. I—'

'Relax, Webster. Ah'm yankin' your chain. Sheesh. Ah thought you Brits were supposed to have a good sense of humour. What's that?'

'I didn't say anything.'

'Not you, Webster. Apparently we're about to land, so we'll have to wind this up, but one question first. Are you happy here?'

'How do you mean?'

'Here. Are you happy? Ah can't make it any clearer.'

Mark thought for a moment. Was this a leading question? Then again, most questions were leading ones, if you thought about it. 'I am, yes.'

'Not thinkin' about movin'.'

'I wasn't—'

'Because ah'd like you to.'

'Think about it? Or actually, you know, move.'

'Both.'

'I'm confused. Are you *firing me*?'

'The opposite. Ah wanna make you a VP.'

'*Vice-president*?'

'That's right.'

'Of iFeel?'

'No, of the United States of America. *Of course* of ahFeel.' Tony let out a short laugh. 'You'd be mah right-hand man. Runnin' EMEA.'

'But I already run them here.'

'*EMEA*,' Tony laughed. 'Europe, Middle East and Africa.'

'Wow. That's— That *is* a promotion. I— I don't know what to say.'

'Say yes.'

'Um . . . Yes!'

'And you're okay with movin'?'

Mark nodded, then felt a bit stupid. Unless Tony A. Wood had told the pilot to fly *really* low, there was no chance of him seeing. 'Fitzroy Square's nice. And it's only a couple more stops on the tube than Soho is now, so—'

'To San Francisco.'

Mark nearly dropped his phone again. 'What?'

'You'd need to move to San Francisco.'

'I'm sorry?'

'What is it with you Brits and your constant need to apologise?'

'Sorry.' Mark had to stop himself from slapping his palm to his forehead. 'It's just . . . Wow. That's a big decision.'

'Take some time to think about it.'

'Thanks.'

'Let me know this evenin' at the party.'

'That's not exactly a *lot* of time.'

'Well, that's what you've got. You snooze, you lose, Webster!'

Mark pulled his phone away from his ear and regarded it suspiciously. The bad accent, the 'tell the pilot to fly a bit lower', the clichés, the constant calling him 'Webster' . . . 'This is Nathan, isn't it?'

'What was that?'

'Well, not funny, Mister Field, not funny at all.'

'Mister Field? Who's—?'

'I'm sorry. I'm having difficulty hearing you. You must be flying so low that you've flown up your own backside!'

Happy to have caught Nathan out, Mark ended the call with a flourish, slipped his phone smugly into his pocket, and downed what was left of his coffee, just in time to see Nathan Field walking along the opposite pavement, happily working his way through a sandwich. And to Mark's horror, Nathan's phone was nowhere to be seen.

~

Nathan Field spotted a somewhat flustered-looking Mark Webster waving at him from the other side of the road. He waited for a hipster-type on a jet-black-with-white-rim-tyres-fixed-wheel bike to whizz past, then he hurried across to the other pavement.

'Wotcha!'

'You didn't just call me, did you?'

'Nope.' Nathan dropped his sandwich wrapper in a nearby bin. 'Been out helping Calum not embarrass himself.'

'Ah. And, er, quick technical question: can you call someone from a plane?'

'Course you can.' Nathan stifled a burp with his napkin. 'As long as your phone's in "aeroplane" mode.'

'Even I know that's not what it's for! Serious question.'

'I think so, nowadays. Why?'

'In that case, I've just done what you helped Calum not to do. And with our new owner.'

'How so?'

'Never mind.' Mark shook his head as the two of them began the short walk back to the office. 'And how was Calum going to embarrass himself?'

'By taking the party invitation a little too literally. Oh, and keep this hush-hush, but he's planning to propose to Mia-Rose tonight.'

'When tonight?'

'Before the party.'

'Is that wise?'

'Proposing? Or doing it before the party?'

'Take your pick.' Mark smiled humourlessly. 'So, do you have time for a quick drink before the bus leaves?'

'I do.' Nathan lobbed his balled-up napkin into a nearby waste bin, and missed. 'But not with you,' he said, retrieving it from the pavement.

Mark widened his eyes. 'You old dog. You're not meeting that iFeel girl—?'

Nathan took another shot, succeeding on the second attempt. 'Not exactly.'

'You're not exactly meeting her? Or . . . ?'

'I'm meeting Ellie.'

'Ellie?' Mark stopped walking abruptly. 'Your Ellie?'

'Well, technically, she's not *my* Ellie any more.'

'The Ellie who dumped you, mid-proposal?'

'That's the one.'

'The one who suddenly announced she'd been two-timing you with someone else?'

'Yup.'

'The one who broke your heart, and stopped you dating anyone else for the best part of three years? The one whose office you used to regularly ride past on your Vespa in the hope that you'd "accidentally" bump into her? Or run her over. I was never sure which one it was, exactly.'

'Um, yeah.'

'Well, excuse me if I'm asking the blindingly obvious question, but why?'

'Because it's Christmas?'

'So? It was Christmas this time last year too. And the year before that. And I don't remember you having a drink with her either of *those* times.'

'Yeah, well, this is different.'

'How so?'

When Nathan didn't answer, Mark gave him a pitiful look. 'And how did this come about?'

'She sent me a Christmas card.'

'Ah. *That* explains it.'

As Nathan glowered at him, Mark sighed. 'You're not going to do anything stupid, are you?'

'Such as?'

'Get back with her.'

Nathan made a face. 'I haven't really thought about it,' he said, though in truth, that was exactly what he'd been thinking about. In between sending flirtatious emails to Stacey, of course.

'Well, that's probably what she wants.'

'I doubt it.'

'Why else would she send you a Christmas card out of the blue?'

'At the risk of repeating myself, because it's Christmas?' suggested Nathan, though tentatively this time.

'And at the risk of repeating *myself*, it was Christmas this time last year too. And the year before that. And I don't remember you getting a card from her either of *those* times.'

'Yeah, but . . .' Nathan threw his hands up in the air. 'She might just want to be my friend.'

'That's what Facebook's for, isn't it?'

'And so what if she wants to get back together? It doesn't mean I do. And even if I did. And she does. And we do . . .' Nathan was confusing himself, so he decided to change tack. 'The reason she didn't accept my proposal all those years ago was because she didn't want to get married to me *then*. Not that she didn't want to get married to *me*. And now . . . Well, it's not "then" any more, is it?'

'Yes, but you're not you either, are you? In that you've moved on, remember?'

'Maybe.'

'So, you'd take her back, would you?'

'I don't know.'

'A woman who cheated on you.'

'She had her reasons.'

'You're defending her now?'

'No, I'm just . . . There are two sides to every story, aren't there?' Nathan began walking briskly again. 'Besides, people change.'

'No they don't.'

'Yes they do. Otherwise Julie would still be happily married to Philip, wouldn't she?'

As Mark gave him a look, Nathan grinned triumphantly. 'Don't worry. I'm just going to have a quick Christmas drink with her. A catch-up. Check she's okay. Nothing's going to happen. Especially not in an hour.'

'Just be wary.'

'"Wary" is my middle name.'

'So that's what the "w" stands for. I'd always thought it was something else.'

'You're a funny guy. Did you know that?' said Nathan, as they rounded the corner into Bateman Street.

'Funny ha-ha?' said Mark, 'or funny strange?'

Nathan grinned. 'The two don't have to be exclusive,' he said.

'A bit like Ellie thought you and she weren't?' suggested Mark, and Nathan had to bite off his reply.

∞

Sophie Jones, her headphones pushed into her ears, was sitting at a corner table in a Costa Coffee several blocks north of Oxford Street, sipping a latte and munching on a piece of millionaire's shortbread (she'd thought it might help her get in character) while she speed-watched the rest of *Fifty Shades* on her laptop. While she'd normally have just gone to the Pret on the corner of Bateman Street, she'd needed a bit of privacy given the subject matter, and besides, for some reason, all day there had been a steady stream of her colleagues disappearing into Pret (then emerging fifteen minutes later, not even clutching a coffee).

And although watching the film in fast-forwarded bursts in a coffee shop – ensuring the screen was angled away from prying eyes, given the risqué scenes that she certainly didn't want to be caught watching in public – perhaps wasn't the best way to perform detailed research, one thing was becoming clear: she didn't have any experience with S&M (though Sophie had nearly had sex once in the changing rooms in M&S, she was pretty sure that wasn't the same). If *this* was the kind of thing that, as a billionaire, Tony A. Wood was into, then she'd better make sure she knew what she was doing.

The café was busy, so Sophie hunkered down over her screen and turned the volume up to full, cursing the poor quality of the headphones she'd grabbed from her desk drawer – or maybe it was the bad sound on the dodgy download – trying to ignore the raised eyebrows and shocked glances she seemed to be getting from the people at the nearby tables. It was almost as if they knew what she was watching – though she couldn't see how. She wasn't wearing glasses, so no one could see her screen reflected in those, and there wasn't a mirror on the wall behind her – although maybe her shock at what she was seeing was showing in her face. But so what? She'd seen loads of people reading the book blatantly on the tube, and that hadn't caused anything like the reaction she seemed to be provoking, and besides, surely what Sophie was doing was the equivalent of reading the eBook version, in that no one could see the cover?

Undeterred, she watched on, fast-forwarding from sex scene to sex scene, studying them closely, sometimes replaying them, occasionally making notes on her phone. From what she could tell, the world of S&M had its own language (and Sophie blushed when she remembered when someone on Tinder with the username 'Dom69' had asked her whether she was a 'sub' girl, she'd assumed they meant her sandwich preference), so she made a note of all the relevant terms, just in case they – along with anything *else* – came up later.

Still, from what she could see, the girl in the film seemed to be enjoying herself, and Sophie told herself to be more open-minded. She wasn't in Eastbourne any more; this was *London*. People were more adventurous here. And who knew how adventurous they were in California? Besides, the 'rope' stuff was something she could do – if you excused the phrase – with her hands tied behind her back. Growing up in a seaside town, she'd been in the Sea Cadets – it was a good place to meet boys, she'd been (mis)led to believe – and Sophie was pretty sure her knot-tying skills hadn't deserted her.

As for the other stuff, well, maybe that was something that was an acquired taste, like Brussels sprouts, or real ale, or that posh tea that tasted like bonfires smelled (though she still couldn't stomach any of those, despite her best efforts). In any case, whatever she thought of the various practices, she enjoyed the scenes of helicopter flying, and gliding, and the chauffeur-driven cars, and the jewellery, and the various other pursuits and trappings of the super-rich that Sophie was sure she'd soon be experiencing. And if the odd smack on her backside was the price she had to pay, then so be it.

She was watching the first 'whipping' scene one more time – just to be prepared – when she became aware of someone standing over her, so she hit 'pause' and looked up. The man was good-looking, and while Sophie might normally have flirted with him, she had a richer target in her sights.

'Can I help you?' The man winced, and Sophie realised she'd shouted the question, so she pulled her headphones out of her ears. 'Sorry.'

'Um. We've had a few complaints.'

'Complaints?'

The man, Sophie noticed, was wearing a 'Costa' uniform, and he cleared his throat awkwardly and nodded down at the table. 'That's right.'

'I'm not surprised,' said Sophie. 'Your barista tried to draw a heart in the foam on the top of my latte, but then he gave it to me upside down, and it looked like someone's naked bottom—'

'Not about *us*,' said the man, whose name tag read 'Baz' – though Sophie assumed it might just be a new trendy abbreviation of 'barista'. 'About you.'

'*Me?*'

'More specifically, what you're watching.'

'What I'm . . .' Sophie frowned. 'Why is it anyone's business what I'm watching?'

'Well, for one thing, there are kids in here.'

Sophie looked around angrily. Sure, there were a couple of mothers with infants glaring at her from the other side of the café, but no one who could possibly see her screen. 'They're babies. Even if they could see what I was watching, they'd probably just think it was some weird episode of *Peppa Pig*.'

'Maybe. But the noises—'

'What noises? I'm not making any noises.' Sophie began to feel a little awkward. 'Am I?'

'Not you.' The man – Baz – tapped the top of Sophie's laptop. 'They're coming – and I mean that literally – from here.'

'How can they possibly—?'

'Your headphones.'

'What about them?'

'They're not plugged in properly.'

Sophie's eyes traced the headphone's wire down to her laptop, until she noticed the slightly protruding bronze-coloured prong. With a growing sense of dread, she jabbed the 'play' button again, and as Dakota Johnson's ecstatic screams filled the otherwise-quiet coffee shop, Sophie turned redder than she thought possible.

'Yes, well, they shouldn't be listening,' she announced, as she fumbled for the 'stop' key.

'It, um, was hard not to. So, if you don't mind—?'

'Sure. Sorry. I'll just, you know, push it in deeper. If you excuse the—'

'—leaving.'

'What?'

'Like I said. People have complained.'

Sophie shook her head, her mouth agape. She couldn't believe she was being thrown out of Costa Coffee. Still, she reminded herself, when she was Mrs Tony A. Wood, she wouldn't need to come into places like this any more. She'd probably be able to afford one of those Nespresso machines. *And* the capsules.

'It was for research,' she insisted. 'For *work*.'

Baz looked at her disbelievingly. 'What kind of work do you do, exactly?'

'I'm in *marketing*,' said Sophie, as if that would clear everything up. Then she slammed her laptop shut, stuck it under her arm, picked up her Zara bag, and hurried for the door as quickly as her legs would carry her.

7.

Calum Irwin was walking back along Oxford Street, hurriedly finishing off the turkey and stuffing sandwich he'd bought himself for lunch. Okay, so he had the suit, and soon he'd have the ring, but Nathan had got him panicking, and now he was sure that unless he did something special as far as proposing to Mia-Rose was concerned, she was never going to accept his hand in marriage (or any other body part, for that matter). But what? He'd already booked the table at Old Amsterdam, and even if they had time to go somewhere further afield before the coach left, it was probably too late to find another, posher venue.

Maybe he'd just have to resort to hiding the ring in her glass of champagne like Nathan had suggested, though surely ordering champagne would give the game away (and he wasn't sure Old Amsterdam served champagne anyway)? Besides, what if Mia ordered Coke? Calum could hardly hide the ring in that: the dark-brown colour of the liquid might mean she'd miss (or swallow!) it. Or, knowing his luck, it might dissolve before she could fish it out; Calum had seen a video on YouTube recently where someone had left a molar in a glass of the stuff, and the speed at which it had been eaten away (combined with his terror of going to the dentist) meant he hadn't touched it since then.

He supposed he could ask the chef to hide it in her pancake, but that was hardly the most romantic thing to do (plus she might eat it accidentally, or break a tooth on the diamond, or the waitress might give it to someone else by mistake). Alternatively, he could place it decoratively on top of the chocolate fudge cake they always shared for dessert whenever they ate there, but he knew if he waited until dessert to propose, his nerves would be so bad for the whole of the meal that Mia was bound to know something was up.

He tried to reassure himself as he walked. Old Amsterdam meant as much to them as anywhere in London, because it was where they'd first revealed their feelings for each other, back on Valentine's Day. And while he could perhaps have found a more impressive venue nearby – on the London Eye, for example, or up on the observation deck of The Shard, Calum knew his fear of heights would put paid to either of those. They were both *properly* high, and he'd be feeling sick enough without vertigo giving his stomach an extra jolt, not to mention the fact that Mia's potentially glass-shattering scream of surprise wasn't the best thing if you were on the seventy-second floor of a building made primarily out of the stuff.

And while it perhaps wasn't the most romantic setting in which to propose, Old Amsterdam served the best pancakes in London, and he'd long ago learned that the way to his fiancée's heart was through her stomach. Besides, those other clichéd proposal venues – up the Eiffel Tower, or in front of Niagara Falls . . . He'd probably have had to share them with loads of other people doing the same thing, with less nervousness, plus they'd all probably be good-looking, and trendily dressed, and so smooth at their proposals that Mia-Rose was bound to look at them, then at Calum, and wonder what she was doing with him.

He reached the office, and peered in through the door. Mia-Rose was on reception, and Calum couldn't face any 'where have you been?' questions, plus he didn't want her to see the dinner suit he'd bought, so he fished his phone out of his pocket and surreptitiously called the switchboard number as a diversion. As Mia picked the phone up, he darted in past her and up the stairs to his office, nearly knocking Sophie Jones over in the process.

'Someone's in a hurry?'

'Sorry, Sophie.' Calum smiled apologetically. 'Just trying to avoid Mia.'

'You two fallen out again?'

Calum made a face at Sophie's 'again' reference. He and Mia were known as the office lovebirds. Even Benedict from legal would pretend to stick his fingers down his throat whenever he'd see the two of them holding hands outside of work, though Calum told himself that he was just jealous. Or bulimic.

'Just trying to hide this from her.' Calum steered Sophie into his office, and showed her the contents of his Next suit bag. 'Thought I'd do the big reveal later.'

Sophie widened her eyes. 'Mia's a lucky girl.'

'Thanks.' Calum did his best not to turn his usual shade of red, and for once, succeeded. 'Listen . . .' He beckoned Sophie into his office, and pulled the door shut behind them. 'Remember that favour I did for you on Valentine's Day?'

'Yup.'

'Well, now *I* need a hand with something.'

'Name it.'

'I need you to find out Mia's ring size for me.'

'Sure. Are you getting her one for Christmas?'

'Actually, for life. Hopefully.'

Sophie stared at him as the penny dropped, then she placed a hand over her mouth and mimed a scream. 'Calum, that's—' She did the 'scream' mime again for effect. 'When are you planning to ask her?'

'Tonight.'

'At the party? I knew there was going to be some big announcement, but I assumed that was about the company merger. Not yours and Mia-Rose's.'

'Ha ha. No, beforehand. Over dinner.'

'Well, good luck!'

Calum's face fell. 'Do you think I'll need it?'

'Not at all.' Sophie nudged him. 'Mia's crazy about you. I'm sure she'll say "yes".'

'I wish I was.'

'You'll be fine.' She rubbed his arm encouragingly. 'What do you want me to do?'

'Well, you know how Mia wears a lot of jewellery? I thought you could perhaps go up to her, pretend to admire one of her rings. And by "one of her rings", I mean—'

'The one she wears on her ring finger? I'm way ahead of you.'

'Then if you could perhaps ask if you could try it on. See which of your fingers it fits. That way—'

'Got it!'

'Then we just need to measure *your* finger. You know, to see what size—'

'Calum, I get it. Just leave it to me.'

'Thanks.'

Sophie did another silent scream, though by now, Calum was feeling like letting out a real one. 'How exciting! Our first office wedding.'

'Sophie, please don't say anything to anyone. *Especially* to Mia.'

'Don't want to spoil the surprise, eh?'

Calum nodded. Though more than that, he didn't want anyone knowing in case Mia said 'no'.

Sophie winked conspiratorially. 'Don't worry,' she said, as she headed back out of his office. 'My lips are sealed.'

∾

Sophie Jones walked back along the corridor, not knowing whether to feel happy or sad. Calum was getting married. *Calum*! And Mark and Julie were having a baby, and . . . Well, she wasn't sure what Nathan was up to, but even so, why was *she* the only one who hadn't been able to move forward with her (love) life?

She felt terribly guilty for feeling so jealous, but she couldn't help herself. Just a few short weeks ago she'd been out shopping with Vinay, and they'd walked past a jeweller's, and . . . Well, Sophie had seen him glance slyly through the window, and at the time, she'd assumed it was because that'd be where her Christmas present was coming from. What she hadn't suspected was that the ring he'd been staring at was for someone else, and the only thing she'd be getting from him would be the brush-off.

Suspecting she wasn't quite in the right frame of mind to go and compare jewellery with Mia-Rose, she popped into the toilets, checked her make-up, then headed miserably back to her office. When she walked in through the door, Julie looked up from her laptop.

'What's the matter?'

Sophie slumped disconsolately down into her chair and burst into tears. 'Calum and Mia-Rose are getting married.'

'Oh. That's . . .' Julie's face went through a complicated series of expressions. 'Wonderful?'

'Isn't it?' sobbed Sophie.

'Then, um, why are you crying? If it was Nathan, I could perhaps understand you being upset, but *Calum*? Unless these are tears of happiness?'

'I'm not crying because Calum's getting married.' For the second time that day, Sophie helped herself to a tissue from the box in her desk drawer. 'I'm crying because *Calum's* getting married.'

'Oh. Right.' Julie smiled sympathetically, then she frowned. 'I'm not sure I understand.'

'It should be *me*.'

'I didn't think you thought of Calum in that way.'

'Not marrying Calum. Marrying *anyone*.' Sophie blew her nose loudly, then balled up the tissue and threw it expertly into the waste bin on the other side of the office – a shot she'd become unfortunately well-practised at. 'I work for a search-engine company, and I can't even find a boyfriend, let alone a husband, so how on earth I'm going to convince a billionaire to even give me so much as a second glance this evening . . .'

Julie regarded her for a moment, then reached into her in-tray, removed an envelope, and Frisbee'd it onto her desk. 'This is for you.'

Sophie stared suspiciously at the envelope, convinced it was her P45. She wouldn't be surprised; she'd been sure that her day couldn't get any worse, but at every stage, it seemingly had.

'What is it?'

'Call it an early Christmas present.'

'Oh.'

'Aren't you going to open it?'

'Um . . .' said Sophie, scared to pick it up despite her boss's reassurance, and Julie let out a long-suffering sigh.

'It's a *voucher*. For one of those beauty salons in Soho. I was going to wait and give it to you nearer Christmas, but needs must, and all that . . .'

'Thanks very much!'

'I meant that in a "you shall go to the ball" kind of way.'

'Julie, I know you're trying to be my Fairy Godmother, but—'

'Less of the "mother" references, please.' Julie shuddered, then she smiled. 'You can pop down after work today. Get your nails, or your eyebrows, or . . .' Her eyes flicked downwards. 'Anything – or anywhere – you like done. For this evening. Might as well give it your best shot, if you're going to convince him to get down on one knee in front of you. Though by the looks of him, you might have to help him back up again.'

Sophie laughed, despite herself, then she picked the envelope up and removed the voucher. 'Thanks, Julie,' she said, scanning through the information on the front. 'That's really kind.'

'Don't mention it. Oh, and Sophie?'

'Uh-huh?'

'It's not all about marriage, you know.'

'Yes, it is! At least, it is for me. I want all that stuff. The happy-ever-after. The love of your life. That special someone who'll mess up my lipstick, not my mascara . . .'

'Sophie . . .' Julie thought for a moment, then she got up, walked across the office, and perched on the edge of Sophie's desk. 'It's lovely that you think like that. That you're such a romantic. Really it is. But life . . . It's just not like that. Philip and I . . . Marriage can make you . . . Well, sometimes you kind of think you should stay together because you're married, not because you want to, but because you don't want to get divorced, and add to the statistics. If you ask me – and I'm conscious you're *not* asking me, but even so – sometimes, being not married is better. Takes more commitment. You haven't got society, or a piece of paper, or a promise in front of a god you don't necessarily believe in, keeping you together. It's the quality of your relationship, the love you feel for each other that does. And that's much more important than the fact that you've stood up in a draughty old church in front of several dozen distant relations who you'll never see again until the next family funeral and said "I do".'

'So, what would you do if Mark proposed?'

Julie made a 'mock horror' face. 'He's not planning to, is he?'

'He might tonight. After you've told him about . . .' her eyes flicked towards Julie's stomach 'a certain someone else.'

Julie's jaw dropped open, as if she certainly hadn't anticipated that kind of response.

'Anyway,' continued Sophie, 'you're getting divorced, so you're bound to be cynical. But I still believe in finding the one.'

'Even though you haven't yet?'

'Precisely. He's so hard to find because there *is* only one,' she said, looking at Julie as if she was stupid. 'And even if I don't ever find him, I still just want to be *asked*. Just the once. By someone who means it.'

Julie leaned over and patted the back of Sophie's hand. 'And you will. I'm sure of it. Maybe even tonight, if you play your cards right in that dress. But . . . just don't think being proposed to is the ultimate goal, or that marriage is this amazing, wonderful thing, because statistically, most of the time, it isn't.'

'So you wouldn't get married again? Even if Mark asked you?'

'I doubt it, no.'

'Been there, seen that, got the T-shirt?'

'Which I'm going to set light to, then dance in the ashes.'

Sophie reached into her desk drawer for another tissue, but all she found was an empty box. 'I just don't want to be left on the shelf.'

'Trust me, Sophie, there isn't a shelf big enough to hold you— No, hang on, that didn't come out quite right. My point is— Actually, I'm not quite sure what my point is. All I know is, if you want something to happen, then if you give yourself the best possible chance, well, it might just.'

'Do you really think so?' sniffed Sophie.

'Why not?' Julie rubbed her stomach. 'If there's one thing I've learned, it's that you never know what might be just around the corner.'

And standing in the corridor outside of their office, *literally* just around the corner, Mark Webster couldn't believe what he was hearing.

⁓

Mark Webster made his way back along the corridor, feeling a little dazed. Nathan was in the kitchen, sniffing the milk carton suspiciously, so he went in and closed the door behind them.

'Do you want one of these?' Nathan nodded at the latte he was making, having evidently decided the milk was fit for purpose.

'What? Oh, no thanks. Though something stronger might be appropriate.'

'An espresso?' Nathan grinned. 'Everything okay? You look like you've just had some bad news.'

'Julie doesn't want to get married.'

'Well, *that* escalated quickly.'

'Pardon?'

'I thought you were only going to ask her to spend Christmas with you?'

'Huh?'

'And maybe walking into her office straight after lunch and proposing wasn't exactly the most romantic way of asking her. What did you say? "Here's your expenses form back, and by the way, will you marry me?"'

'What? Oh no, I didn't propose.'

'Oh. Right.' Nathan pressed the plunger on his coffee maker, careful not to exert too much pressure and squirt coffee everywhere, then filled his mug up. 'So how do you know?'

Mark lowered his voice. 'I overheard her just now. Talking to Sophie. And there was something about . . .' he swallowed hard, 'someone else.'

'*Someone else?*'

'That's what Sophie said: "A certain someone else." Which would explain a lot, now I come to think of it.'

'Such as?'

'Recently. She's been acting a bit funny.'

'Funny?'

'Moody. Argumentative. Like I can't do anything right.'

Nathan let out a short laugh. 'Mark, she's a woman. That's how they act all the time.'

'No, I mean . . . It's as if she's wrapped in cotton wool. I feel like I have to tiptoe around her all the time. And then this morning, I ask her about us spending Christmas together, suggest her maybe meeting my parents, and she flies off the handle. It's almost as if the closer this divorce of hers gets, the more she seems a little . . . miserable. As if she's disappointed it hasn't worked out with her ex or something.'

Nathan sipped his coffee, grimaced, then splashed a little more milk in. 'She probably is.'

'Thanks very much!'

'No, I mean, in the same way as if a marketing campaign hadn't worked out the way she'd wanted it to, or if she hadn't managed to finish the marathon. You know what Julie's like: very . . . driven. Doesn't want to fail at anything. Admit any kind of weakness. So this divorce is bound to make her a bit wistful.'

'Maybe.' Mark said, though he didn't feel all that convinced. 'There was just something else. Something I couldn't quite put my finger on.'

Nathan opened his mouth as if to mention something, then frowned. 'I've got nothing apart from my earlier "she's a woman" observation,' he said. 'But why the rush to get married? I thought the plan was simply to get her to move in with you?'

'There's no rush, exactly. Although there's something else I haven't told you.'

'Which is?'

'I had a phone call from Tony A. Wood earlier.'

'I take it there's more?' said Nathan, when Mark didn't continue.

'He offered me a new job. It's a promotion. Quite a big one, as a matter of fact.'

'Wow – congratulations!' Nathan held his mug up in a 'cheers' kind of way. 'I'm guessing there's a "but" coming?'

'It's in the US. At head office.'

'*California?*'

Mark nodded.

'You lucky—'

'But there's a problem.'

'Which is?'

'Julie?'

'Ah.' Nathan put his mug down and folded his arms. 'Have you told her yet?'

Mark glared at him.

'Can she come with you?'

'Oh yes,' Mark said. 'If we're *married.*'

'Ah. *Ah.*'

'Exactly. Good old US Immigration. It's fine for me, given that the company will be sponsoring me.'

'As in a pound a mile, that kind of thing?'

As Mark gave him a look, Nathan smiled at his own joke. 'Not a fan of long-distance relationships, then?'

'It's hard enough with her twenty minutes down the road.' He sighed. 'Besides, I just . . . I guess I'm just quite traditional.'

'No kidding?'

Mark ignored him. 'And marriage? It's something I always thought I'd do.'

Nathan smirked. 'It's normally girls who have this idea of the big wedding from back when they were little. Not us men.'

'It's not like that,' said Mark, awkwardly. 'There are just some things I always assumed I'd get to experience. University. Qualifying as an accountant. Falling in love. Running a company. Getting married. If this merger works out for me, then I'm nearly there on those first four. And I can't see why Julie wouldn't want to do number five.'

Nathan thought for a moment. 'Remember that time we went out for that company dinner last summer, and I had the mussels, and they made me so sick I was projectile vomiting in the toilets for the rest of the evening?'

'What's that got to do with any of this?'

'I haven't been able to eat shellfish since then.'

'This is hardly the same thing.'

'It might be to her. She had a terrible time in that marriage. So you can understand her being a bit . . . reticent.'

'Yes, but . . .' Mark threw his hands up in the air. 'That's hardly a good reflection on me, is it? I mean, the reason her marriage to Philip was so awful' – he lowered his voice to a whisper – 'is because she married a selfish shit. Not—'

'Shit shellfish?'

'Very funny. No, I meant it was his fault, and not because marriage *per se* is so, you know . . .'

'Shit?'

'Exactly.'

Nathan took another mouthful of coffee, then spat it back into the mug and poured the rest of it down the sink. 'Is it such a deal-breaker for you?'

Mark perched on the edge of the kitchen table. 'I think so, yes.'

'Isn't just being with her enough?'

'No.'

'Shouldn't it be?'

'I'm sorry, Nathan, but marriage means something to me. And if the person I'm with doesn't want to get married . . . Well, that means something too.'

'Shouldn't you be telling her that?'

Mark hesitated as Benedict opened the door, saw the two of them, then beat a hasty retreat. 'I guess. But all this kind of puts the brakes on my "asking her to move in" plan.'

'Maybe. Or maybe not. Nothing like a bit of pressure on a relationship to get everyone to reveal their true colours. And I wouldn't worry too much about that marriage thing.' Nathan stifled a burp. 'I mean, when's the best time for us to sell someone a new software license?'

'Just when their old one is about to finish.'

'You *have* been speaking to Calum.'

'This is hardly the same thing.'

'Isn't it? You just wait till that divorce of hers finally comes through.' Nathan stifled another burp, rubbed his stomach, then headed anxiously for the door. 'See if she feels the same way about marriage then.'

'Maybe,' said Mark, as he watched Nathan leave. Although his problem, he realised, was that he didn't know how Julie felt about *anything*.

He walked back to his office, pleased her office door was closed as he passed. This marriage issue was a biggie – particularly in the light of his lunchtime telephone call – and as for the 'someone else' . . . Mark certainly didn't know what to make of that. But like every problem he encountered, all he had to do was tackle these things one at a time. There were bound to be minor bumps in the road, and after the offer Tony A. Wood had made him, Mark was heading along his career path in a 4x4.

First of all, he needed to find out exactly what was going on with Julie, and the party this evening would be the perfect time. She relaxed after a drink or two – he sometimes suspected if she hadn't had those half-a-dozen cosmopolitans at last year's Christmas party, the two of them would never have gotten together. So he'd wait until they were half-a-bottle of champagne in, ask her what was going on, then casually mention that he was up for promotion – not that he'd already been offered it, and float the idea of moving past her. Julie hated the London winters; where better than the balmy climate of San Francisco to tempt her away? Then maybe he could present marriage as a logical step so they could go there together, rather than the poisoned chalice she seemed to regard it as. And whatever way he got it – though he wouldn't be particularly proud of himself – they'd be married.

And wasn't that the important thing?

❦

Nathan Field had felt better. Why hadn't he gone with his normal choice of lunch from Pret, instead of something he hadn't tried before? There was a lesson there, he was sure, if only he wasn't too ill to think about what it might be.

But Calum's mission had taken up most of his lunchtime, and meeting Ellie later had meant he wouldn't have time to grab a bite after work, so he'd needed something to line his stomach. And while the pulled-pork mac-and-cheese toasted sandwich had seemed a good idea when he was standing in the queue, had smelt great when he'd ordered it, had even tasted fantastic as he'd polished it off on the way back to the office, the moment he'd washed it down with the first mouthful of his usual post-lunch coffee, he'd suspected there was something a little dodgy about it.

He loved pulled pork, but now he was feeling like he'd pulled a stomach muscle, and while the explosion of street food was something Nathan had been welcoming since the first food trucks had appeared, right now he feared there was another sort of explosion coming.

He'd known he didn't have much time to lose, so he'd left Mark Webster in the kitchen, taken the stairs two at a time, and now he was running headlong into the toilets, dreading a repeat of last year's shellfish-related session. Fortunately, the cubicles were unoccupied, and with a sigh of relief he shut himself into the nearest one and dropped to his knees in front of the bowl.

Nathan hated being sick. Like most other aspects of his life, his drinking was something he was careful to control, so he avoided hangovers (and the associated loss of his breakfast) as a rule, but now he felt like he was in danger of projectile vomiting on the kind of scale you'd see in *The Exorcist*. He almost expected his head to start spinning – physically, as opposed to the way the room had begun to. Knowing there was nothing for it – he had to get the sandwich out, and fast – Nathan decided that sticking his fingers down his throat was the easiest way. Or not – as it turned out: as he rolled up his sleeve and braced himself to do the deed, a patter of feet and the slamming of the cubicle door next to him was swiftly followed by the sound of someone else throwing up. And that was all the incentive Nathan needed.

For the next two minutes, it was as if they were egging each other on. Nathan would throw up, followed noisily by whoever was in the cubicle next door, which in turn made him throw up again, and vice-versa, until he was sure his stomach couldn't get any emptier. Finally, thankfully, there was the sound of a toilet being flushed, followed by a groan, and then: 'Are you taking the piss?' said Julie Marshall, from the adjacent cubicle.

'Julie?'

'Who's that?'

'It's me. Nathan.'

'Are you ill?'

'No – just getting some practice in for tomorrow morning.' Nathan flushed his toilet, then wiped his mouth with a handful of toilet paper. 'Food-poisoning. What's your excuse?'

'Oh, er, same thing.'

'Don't tell me *you* had a pulled-pork mac-and-cheese toasted sandwich as well—?' But Nathan didn't get any further, as his description of his lunch had set Julie off again.

'Thanks a lot!' she said, eventually, and Nathan grinned, though he still felt more than a little queasy.

'Don't mention it.'

'I wish you hadn't.'

'Can I get you anything?'

There was a pause, and then: 'Toilet paper. I seem to have run out.'

Nathan grabbed a handful of tissues from the dispenser on the wall, and carefully passed them under the dividing wall. He wondered if iFeel's offices had separate toilets for men and women, though he doubted it. Given what he'd read about them, they probably didn't even have separate cubicles. Or doors.

'What did you say you had?' asked Julie, weakly.

'Pardon?'

'To eat?'

'Toasted mac-and-cheese . . .' Nathan stopped talking. The thought of the sandwich was making his stomach flip again. Though not as much as Julie's, given the new retching sounds coming from next door. He passed her another handful of paper under the dividing wall, and – using the cistern for leverage – hauled himself gingerly to his feet.

'Thanks,' said Julie. 'Are you going to be okay? For this evening, I mean?'

'I think so. Mainly because I don't have anything left to sick up.'

'Thanks for the imagery.'

'Sorry.'

'Still, better out than in, I suppose.'

'Right.'

'So . . .'

'So?'

'Did you want to leave first?'

'Sure.'

'I think I'll just wait here for a minute. Just in case.'

'Okay. On second thoughts, me too.'

'Fine. Oh, and Nathan?'

'Uh-huh?'

'Can we perhaps not talk?'

'Sure.' Nathan closed the toilet lid and sat there for a minute or two, then he flushed his toilet again, opened the cubicle door, and made his unsteady way to the sink. 'Have you got your phone with you?' he asked, splashing water on his face.

'My *phone*?'

'In case you need anything. And you can't move.'

'No, I'll be—' There was the sound of retching again, though Nathan was pleased to note his stomach didn't respond in kind.

'Shall I fetch Mark?'

'No!' said Julie, quickly. 'I mean, no thank you. No sense worrying him. It's just a bit of . . .'

'Food poisoning. You said.'

Nathan half-smiled at his reflection, conscious he was supposed to be meeting Ellie in a couple of hours. He looked a little pale, he thought, and red-eyed; this had been a common look for him in the months after Ellie had dumped him, and he was shocked to be reminded of how bad it felt. Hopefully she wouldn't make him feel the same way when they met later for a drink, though he doubted it. His failsafe trick for realising what it was that had made him sick was to think through everything he'd eaten that day, and when he'd get to the offending item, his stomach would confirm it – just like it did earlier when he'd mentioned his sandwich. But thinking of Ellie . . . The old feelings of hurt, of *despair*, didn't seem to be there any more. Though he'd find out for sure later.

In the meantime, he knew he ought to try and eat something else – the last thing Nathan wanted was a drink on an empty stomach going straight to his head, and him doing something he'd regret later. He already had so many regrets when it came to Ellie, and he certainly didn't want to add to that list.

Though whether he meant with Ellie, or with Stacey, Nathan couldn't quite decide.

∽

Julie Marshall walked gingerly back to her office, disgusted with herself. She'd told Sophie she didn't believe in signs, yet the fact that she was throwing up in the afternoon and therefore couldn't even get morning sickness right was the surest indicator she wasn't cut out for this motherhood lark.

At least, she assumed it was morning sickness. Nathan had said he'd been suffering from food poisoning, so maybe the milk in the kitchen had been off (and it wouldn't be the first time; Julie had lost count of the number of times she'd opened the fridge to find the question 'One lump or two?' could apply to the contents of the carton). Then again, she hadn't had milk in her herbal tea, she realised dejectedly, and she'd skipped lunch due to her shopping trip(s), which meant there was probably only one cause of her being ill.

Still, at least she was feeling better now – physically, at least. The trip to John Lewis had done nothing to reassure her about other things. If anything, it'd had the opposite effect. Which wasn't something Julie wanted to think about.

It didn't help that she was bored. 'Only boring people get bored' was her motto, and yet, she had *absolutely nothing to do*. Normally at this time of year, Julie would be busying herself (and Sophie) organising Seek's attendance at the upcoming spring trade show, re-writing their publicity fliers, updating case studies, or even creating a series of New Year banner ads to use on their website, but given the company's up-in-the-air status, all of that seemed a waste of time.

And while she could have at least had a coffee with Sophie, Sophie was . . . Well, Julie didn't know where Sophie was – again. Chatting to Calum, perhaps, or more likely, off doing some last minute research about Tony A. Wood, or making eyes at Nathan . . . Sophie's life seemed to be dominated by her hunt for a man, though she never seemed to have much luck – something Julie always found ironic, given how much practice she put in.

A distant memory fired in her brain, so she flicked quickly through the 'motivational' calendar on her desk she'd got (from Nathan) in last year's office (not-so) Secret Santa, and found the quote from a certain golfer who'd been accused of making a 'lucky' shot, and who'd replied with 'The more I practice, the luckier I get'. Julie smiled to herself, though the following month's Einstein quote about insanity being doing the same thing over and over again and expecting different results was perhaps more appropriate where Sophie was concerned. Still, maybe that would all change this evening, when Tony A. Wood caught sight of her.

She got up and peered out of the window to see if there were any pigs flying by (or angels flying past), then briefly considered popping down to see if Mark was free for a chat, but quickly decided against it. Nathan might have mentioned that he'd seen – well, *heard* – her throwing up, and the last thing she wanted was to accidentally blurt something out about being pregnant, especially with today being so important for him – and with her hormones sending her emotions all over the place. No, she'd stick to Plan A and wait until this evening – when he'd got all the important stuff out of the way (and, more importantly, had a couple of drinks inside him) – before she dropped this particular bombshell on him.

Probably.

She walked over to Sophie's desk and fired up her calendar, wondering whether she was perhaps in a meeting – but then again, what would she be in a meeting about? And besides, any meetings Sophie had usually involved her. No, Julie concluded, Sophie had to be skiving.

Maybe things would be different when they moved; iFeel's offices were in Fitzrovia (Mark and she, a respectable distance between them on the pavement *just in case*, had taken a walk there one evening), which was a bit more sedate. Refined, even, with less going on, which was good for work, she supposed. Fewer distractions. Not quite as close to the shops of Oxford Street, where Sophie seemed to spend a good deal of her time. And her salary. And where she possibly was now. Unless, of course, she'd headed off to the beauty salon already . . .

Julie pulled open Sophie's top drawer in search of the voucher she'd given her, spotted a pile of magazines – *Cosmopolitan*, *Glamour*, and something called *Take a Break* – and smiled. Sophie could often be found in the kitchen, coffee going cold beside her, engrossed in one of these. The various articles – usually about getting a man, keeping a man, making a man happy, and tricks you could use to make your man keep *you* happy – seemed to be the same, month in, month out, and Julie couldn't understand the fascination.

Faced with nothing else to occupy her, she helped herself to *Take a Break*, and sat back down at her desk. This was *Britain's biggest-selling women's magazine*, the strapline told her, though as she stared at the cover, she had to wonder why. It was nothing like the other two – no glossy model or airbrushed celebrity boasting about their perfect lives on the cover – in fact, it was quite the opposite. Normal people determined to (over) share just how *im*perfect their lives were – from their husbands running away with their sisters, to (and Julie had to re-read the title a number of times to make sure she'd got it right) someone whose new boyfriend turned out to be her ex-husband's ex-girlfriend.

Intrigued, she leaned back in her chair, put her feet up on her desk, turned to the first page of a piece entitled 'My Lover Turned Out to Be My Brother', and started reading. If anything was going to make her feel better, this was.

8.

Calum Irwin was sitting in his office, kitted out in his outfit for this evening, admiring the selfie he'd just taken. He'd thought it best to have a dress rehearsal outside of the cramped confines of the shop's changing room, and he was pleased with the results; walking out of Next ninety-seven pounds lighter had put a definite spring in his step. For the first time, he could see how the phrase 'Clothes maketh the man' was true (even if, like the originator of the saying, you had a lisp). He felt confident, assertive, slimmer, better looking, more powerful, even, and that he didn't owe anyone anything (apart from Nathan, and big time, for saving him from being the odd one out and embarrassing himself this evening). Assuming he didn't embarrass himself beforehand with Mia-Rose.

But how could he, dressed like this? She'd turn up to Old Amsterdam to find him sitting there looking like 007, which couldn't do him any harm. Maybe he'd even order himself a vodka Martini, shaken not stirred – though given how badly his hands would probably be shaking, if they gave him a glass with the vodka and Martini in it, he could do the shaking part all by himself.

He deleted the photo, killed his camera app, then noticed the time, and leapt to his feet – he was late for his meeting with Linda, and didn't have time to change back out of his dinner suit. But how to get past Mia-Rose on reception without spoiling the surprise?

Grabbing his coat, he slipped it on, turned up the collar, buttoned it up fully, then bounded down the stairs two at a time, waving quickly in response to Mia's inquiring expression as he passed the reception desk and barrelled out through the front door. Calum had never met a headhunter before, and he tried to put the image of an Amazonian tribeswoman out of his mind as he crossed Bateman Street and made for the Pret on the corner. Which was just as well, given the middle-aged, dumpy woman sitting behind a laptop at a table in the corner and watching the door expectantly. He assumed it must be her.

When she smiled at him – a rare event from a woman in public, in Calum's experience – he was sure it was, so he fixed a friendly grin on his face, stood up straight, and walked on over.

'Linda Smith?'

'No,' said the woman, and Calum hesitated. She'd said she wasn't using her real name earlier, so maybe it *was* her, and of course she wasn't going to admit to being someone she wasn't. Or *was* she? As he considered the possibilities, she winked conspiratorially. Or she could have been flirting with him. Or just have something in her eye – Calum wasn't sure. This was why he needed to get Mia to say 'yes' later, he knew. He was just so bad at reading women.

'It's Linda Jones, actually.'

'Ah. Okay,' said Calum, none the wiser. 'You are the headhunter, though?'

'I am,' she said, winking again.

As he shrugged his coat off, she widened her eyes. 'Either you're Calum Irwin and Seek does dress-up Fridays, or someone's sent me a strippergram.'

Calum tried to stop himself from blushing, but as ever, failed miserably. 'It's our office Christmas party this evening.'

'Ah.' The woman – Linda (Calum was fairly sure of *this*, at least) – indicated the seat opposite. 'Please, sit. Coffee?'

Calum glanced down at his crisp white shirt as he lowered himself into the chair. 'Actually, I'm fine, thanks.'

'If you were fine, Calum, we wouldn't be having this conversation.' Linda winked at him again, something Calum was beginning to find a little disconcerting, then let out a short laugh that sounded like an opera singer going through a scale. 'So, sorry about the cloak-and-dagger approach, but you know how it is?'

Calum nodded. 'Sure,' he said, even though he didn't.

'Great. Well, why don't we start with you telling me a little about yourself?'

Calum frowned. 'You headhunted me, remember? I thought you had a job you wanted to tell me about . . .'

'I do, I do. Lots of them, in fact. I'm simply trying to get a picture of you first so I can make sure I don't waste your time talking to you about unsuitable opportunities. My job, Calum, is like that child's game where you have to fit the right-shaped peg in the appropriate hole. At the moment, everything I know about you has come from your LinkedIn profile. And without knowing what shape your peg is—' She laughed again as she picked up the huge, half-full mug of cappuccino sitting next to her laptop; given how animated she was, Calum suspected it wasn't her first of the day. '—I won't know which hole you're right for.'

Calum smiled politely. He'd filled in that profile a while ago, after he'd read some article about LinkedIn being good for networking, though it had actually seemed to be more like a Facebook for people with jobs (and who wanted to brag about how good they were at them, rather than post photos of their cats). Ever since, he'd struggled to free himself from the site's endless update emails telling him to congratulate people he hardly knew on their 'work anniversary' (as if that was a Thing), or asking him to endorse so-and-so for being good at this and that when he hardly knew what *his* skills were, let alone someone he had only the most tenuous connection to.

'Well, there's not that more to tell, really.'

Linda paused, her coffee halfway to her mouth. 'There must be.'

'Er . . . Why?'

'Well, do you at least have an up-to-date CV?'

'I do.'

'And can I see it?' said Linda, after a pause.

'Oh, of course.' Calum reached into his jacket pocket, just as he remembered his CV was in his *other* jacket pocket. 'I'll, um, have to email it to you.'

'Fine.' Linda was sounding a little exasperated. 'Well, perhaps you could run me through your career history?'

'Sure.' Calum's mouth was feeling dry, and he found himself wishing he'd taken up Linda's offer of a drink. The way things were going, that might be the only thing he'd be getting out of this meeting. 'It's just Seek, really.'

'Just Seek.'

'That's right.'

Linda drained the rest of her coffee – no mean feat given the size of the mug and therefore the amount of liquid left – slid it out of the way, and glanced down at her laptop. 'So you went to Seek immediately after you left university?'

'Yup.'

'Where you studied . . . ?'

'That's right.' He stared at her, waiting for her next question, before twigging that he hadn't actually answered her previous one. 'Business. Well, business studies, to give it its full title. Though I don't suppose it's strictly true to say I studied business studies. That would be studying the studies, and not—'

'And you've been doing the same job since then?'

'Well, not exactly.'

'Oh. Right.' Linda had perked up suddenly, though Calum realised it could simply have been the effect of chugging down half a gallon of coffee.

'I started as telesales, then got promoted. To, you know, sales. So technically I've had two jobs.'

'Both in sales.'

'That's right.'

'At Seek.'

'Yup. I'm their only salesman.'

'So, you *have* pretty much done the same job for eight years?'

'Um . . . Well, that would be one way of looking at it.'

Linda sighed. That was obviously *her* way of looking at it. 'And is it all new business? Or mostly account management?'

'A mix, really.'

'How much of a mix?' Linda asked, when Calum didn't elaborate.

'About eighty-twenty.'

She widened her eyes. 'Eighty per cent new business?'

'No.' Calum tried to ignore the sinking feeling in his stomach. 'The other way round.'

'That's doesn't exactly make for the most impressive of CVs, does it?'

'Why not? It shows loyalty. Commitment. Staying power.'

Linda sat back in her chair. '*Ambition*, Calum. Where's that?' She shut her laptop firmly. 'In my experience, no one's going to take a chance on someone who doesn't have at least a bit of variety in their career. If I were being critical, your career history sounds like someone who's taken the first job he could get, and just done enough to not get sacked.'

'Sacked? Why would they sack me? I'm Seek's top salesman.'

'Seek's *only* salesman.'

'That's not my fault.'

Linda reached over and patted his arm. 'All I'm saying is, why would a prospective employer employ someone who only had experience selling the same product to the same people year after year? People want variety. Breadth. They'd be worried that you only know the one way of doing things. The Seek way. And that by now, it'd be too ingrained in the way you work to change it.'

'But . . . I can learn new things.'

'That's easy for you to *say*, isn't it? Where's the *proof*?'

As Calum stared miserably at the table, Linda stood up and slipped her laptop into her handbag. 'Fact of the matter is, it's a competitive world. People are changing their jobs as often as they're upgrading their phones. And when there are lots of candidates out there, all after the same thing, most of them a lot hungrier than you.'

'I *am* hungry. I'm always hungry . . .' Calum's voice trailed off. He suspected Linda might not mean that in the sense he did.

'Don't worry,' she said, squeezing him comfortingly on the shoulder. 'I'm sure you'll be fine.'

But as Calum turned and watched her leave, he wasn't sure at all.

❧

Nathan Field, sipping gingerly from his (second) can of Red Bull, smiled as another email from Stacey Garrity appeared in his inbox. He was quite enjoying this email flirting that seemed to be going on between the two of them, though he warned himself not to get too carried away. She may only be doing this to gather evidence to get him sacked on some trumped-up sexual harassment charge, which – seeing as the two of them were possibly competing for the same position – wasn't actually a bad strategy. But surely that wasn't the case, he thought, zooming in on the picture he'd cut-and-pasted from her LinkedIn profile (just to familiarise himself with so he'd recognise her later, he'd told himself). She didn't look the type.

It could simply be that she was bored too, of course. Nathan knew better than to take anything for granted, and admittedly, he was a little out of practice where this 'flirting' lark was concerned. Ellie had pretty much ruined it for him for the three years after she dumped him, and Kasia . . . Well, flirting was a two-way thing, wasn't it, like being in love? You couldn't just flirt with someone if they weren't doing it back. That would be pervy. Or stalking.

He quickly fired off a response to her 'Hasta luego' (having first of all doubled-checked with Google Translate that the Spanish phrase meant what he suspected it did), typing (then deleting) 'alligator' from his own 'See *you* later', then shut down his laptop. If any important emails came in . . . Well, Nathan hadn't had anything as important as the ones from Stacey all day. Not including Ellie's, of course – though he didn't yet know how important that might turn out to be.

While he'd started to feel hungry again (usually a sign that the nausea had passed), he didn't want to risk eating anything and maybe make a mess of his expensive suit. And though going for a Christmas drink with Ellie on an empty stomach might not be the best of ideas, he could always stick to water. Even though the thought of being around her was already making him desperate for something stronger.

His hands shook as he buttoned up his shirt, though he told himself that was just the caffeine from the Red Bull kicking in. Sure, he was nervous about seeing her again, but the one-hour time slot he had before the bus left would be just the thing to stop him doing – or saying – anything stupid (he hoped). And while turning up in full evening dress was perhaps a little over the top, Nathan didn't have much choice; he'd be nervous enough sitting there without worrying he had to get back to the office and get changed in time for the bus. Plus, there was a part of him that wanted to turn up dressed up to the nines, looking sharp, just to show Ellie that he was doing okay/what she'd been missing. It was childish, he knew, but he couldn't help himself.

Her choice of venue – the Long Bar at the Sanderson Hotel – was an interesting one. It was where they'd had their first date, and Nathan suspected she'd chosen it on purpose – and not just because it was halfway between their respective offices. He hadn't been back there since; bad memories were easier to forget if you didn't give yourself reminders. Still, it might be good for him to revisit their old haunts. Go over some old times (the good ones, at least). Therapeutic, perhaps. He'd see.

He tied his bow tie, using the selfie camera on his iPhone to check he'd fastened it correctly. Nathan hated selfies – Ellie used to want to take them (of the two of them) all the time – but with no mirror in his office, he could see they sometimes had their uses. Although she'd go a step further and print them out, then distribute them around their flat on those little blocks with a bit of wire sticking out and a crocodile clip on the end, so wherever Nathan went, there'd be photos of the two of them waving in his face. He'd complained once, but Ellie had refused to get rid of them. 'We're such a good-looking couple,' she'd said. Then she'd left him the following week.

With a final check he had everything, Nathan downed the last of his Red Bull, made his way shakily up the stairs, then strode out through reception, where Mia-Rose and Sophie were comparing jewellery over the front desk. As he did his best to sneak past them, Mia let out an ear-shattering wolf whistle.

'Looking good, Nathan!'

He waved at her as he headed out. If only that was all there was to it.

෧

Calum Irwin was back at his desk, wondering whether his day could get any worse, when a breathless Sophie Jones came bounding in through his office door.

'Mission accomplished!'

'What?'

'Mia. She's a ring-size twelve.'

'You're sure?'

'Yup. Same as me.'

'You know your ring size?'

Sophie shrugged. 'Be prepared, and all that.'

'Right. Well, thanks for doing that.'

'No worries. Are you going to get the ring now?'

'I suppose so.'

'You don't sound too excited.'

Calum sighed. 'Sorry, Sophie. I'm grateful, really I am, but the more I think about it, the more proposing seems like a terrible idea.'

'What?' Sophie sat herself down in the chair on the opposite side of his desk. 'Why?'

'I'm wondering if it's the right thing to do.'

'What do you mean?'

'Well . . .' Calum thought for a moment. 'You know how they say that you shouldn't buy the first house you see?'

'You should if it's the right house.'

'Maybe, but . . . Say the opposite is true.'

'The opposite?'

'Yes. In that you'd be wary of selling your house to a person who hasn't, you know,' Calum coughed awkwardly, 'viewed any other houses.'

'Pardon?'

'I mean, I've viewed *lots* of houses, obviously. Just, you know, from the street. I've not actually . . .' Calum pulled nervously on his ear as he tried to come up with the right phrase, 'been through the front door.'

Sophie shook her head. 'I'm sorry, Calum. I didn't have any lunch, so my brain's probably not functioning at a hundred per cent, but are you saying Mia's your first-ever girlfriend?'

Calum fought to stop the colour rising in his cheeks. And failed. 'Not first ever, no.'

'First *proper* girlfriend, then?'

'Yes.'

'Oh. Right.' Sophie stared at him for a moment. 'And I'm guessing that by "proper"' – she made the 'speech marks' sign with her fingers – 'you mean . . .'

'Yup.'

'That Mia's . . .'

'Uh-huh.'

'The first girl you've ever . . .' Sophie cleared her throat awkwardly, 'slept with.'

Calum didn't think it was possible for his cheeks to turn any redder, but given how much they were currently burning, he suspected they were now the right colour to stop traffic. 'Keep your voice down!'

'I'll take that as a "yes", shall I?' Sophie grinned. 'And *that's* what you're worried about?'

'Kind of.'

'That you haven't been out and sowed your wild oats?'

'Well, yes. But not for *that* reason.'

Sophie folded her arms. 'I'm sorry, Calum. You'll have to enlighten me again.'

Calum sighed again. 'It's just – I'm not worried I haven't, you know, what you said, enough for *my* benefit, but for *Mia's*. Supposing I'm no good? I mean, sex is a bit like flying, isn't it?'

'Not in my experience, unfortunately!' Sophie laughed. 'Unless you mean there's not enough leg room, and you end up paying big time for any excess baggage,'

'No, I mean like when you're *learning* to fly. You've got to get a certain number of hours before you can fly solo.'

'Isn't it the other way round?'

'No, hang on, that's not what I mean. Before you're *qualified*.'

'So you're worried you haven't put enough hours in? Or is it that you don't have sufficient experience in . . .' Sophie thought for a moment. 'Enough other aircraft?'

'Something like that.' Calum couldn't meet her eyes. 'I mean, if you were about to go on a long-haul flight, would you want to go with a pilot who hadn't done that much flying? Or someone with more time in the, you know . . . ?'

'Cockpit?' Sophie sniggered childishly. 'So you're worried that Mia might not want to marry you because you haven't had sex with anyone else so you're not good enough in bed with *her*?'

'Tell the whole office, why don't you?'

Sophie regarded him across the desk. 'Calum, you and Mia have actually *had* sex, haven't you?'

Calum nodded.

'More than once?'

He nodded again.

'And at her, you know . . . ?'

'House?'

'Instigation.'

Calum began to fidget in his chair, then he nodded a third time, and Sophie smiled.

'Well, the sheer fact that she's let you sleep with her more than once – *and* that she's kicked off the proceedings on occasion – would indicate that you're at least okay at it.' She lowered her voice. 'I take it she seems to be enjoying herself?'

Calum mumbled his assent, though mainly because all the nodding was making his neck ache. 'Assuming she's not pretending to,' he said. He'd sat through the 'faked orgasm in the diner' scene in *When Harry Met Sally* too many times with Mia for his liking. And once, even more embarrassingly, with his mother. 'Because you do, don't you? Sometimes? To spare our feelings?'

Sophie sat back in her chair. 'Calum, trust me: if she'd been having to fake it all this time, you'd know, mainly because the two of you wouldn't be together any more. And if she initiates things . . . Well, that probably means you're pressing all the right buttons, *and* in the right order. So I'd say you've got nothing to worry about.'

'Do you think so?'

'I *know* so.'

Calum forced a smile. 'Thanks, Sophie.'

'Don't mention it.'

'Same to you,' said Calum. And he really hoped she wouldn't.

ꙮ

Sophie Jones hurried back along the corridor, worried she'd been gone a little too long, and that Julie Marshall might tear her off a strip, but as she walked back into her office, she couldn't believe what she was seeing. Slumped at her desk, Julie was bawling her eyes out.

She stared at her for a moment, then kicked the door shut, deposited the diversionary-tactic cup of coffee and remainder of the tin of Roses chocolates she'd rescued from the kitchen on her desk, grabbed a packet of Kleenex from her coat pocket, and rushed across to where she was sitting.

'What's wrong?'

Julie took the tissue Sophie was offering her, and blew her nose loudly. '*Irgel durdel curgalla*,' she said – or at least, that was what it sounded like to Sophie, insofar as she could make anything out between Julie's loud sobs.

'Is it Mark? Is something up with you and him? Did you tell him about the baby? Doesn't he want it? Or does he want it, but you don't? Because that would be worse, wouldn't it?'

Julie shot her a glance, then shook her head violently as she tried to regain her composure. 'No,' she sniffed. 'Nothing like that.'

'Don't you feel well?'

'I'm fine,' insisted Julie, though Sophie thought she was doing a very good impression of someone who was the opposite.

'You're quite obviously not.' Sophie hesitated – she and Julie had never been particularly touchy-feely, and Julie certainly wasn't a girl's girl – then she lightly rested an arm round her boss's shoulder. 'Do you want to talk about it?'

Julie looked up at her for a moment, then she burst into tears again. 'It's just . . .' she said, eventually. 'He's run off. With her *mother*.'

'Who has? Mark? When? And whose mother?' Sophie folded her arms. 'It just goes to show you can never tell about some people—'

'Not *Mark*,' said Julie, in between chest-heaves.

'Then who?'

'*Him!*' Julie jabbed a finger at the magazine open on her desk, or more specifically at a photo of a couple on their wedding day that the magazine's art department had artfully 'ripped' down the middle.

Sophie peered at the magazine. 'Is this my *Take a Break*?' she said, picking it up and scanning quickly through the piece.

'It was in your drawer. I hope you don't mind, but . . . It's just so *sad*.'

'What is?'

'Everything! Here.' Julie snatched the magazine back, and leafed a few pages forwards. 'This poor woman bought a pot-bellied pig off eBay, but . . . It turned out to be a normal pig, and it was eating them out of house and home. And they lived in a flat, and couldn't . . . Well, they had to sell it to the local farmer. And he . . . he . . .' She dissolved into tears again, before wailing what Sophie could just about make out as 'sausages'.

Sophie gave her a squeeze. 'But that's what happens to *all* pigs.'

'Not if they've been *pets*. And this . . .' Julie flicked on a few pages. 'She met the brother she never knew she had for the first time when she was thirty-one.'

'Well, that's a good thing, surely?'

'On a *dating site*. And only realised after they'd . . . Well, you can guess . . .'

Sophie started to giggle, and Julie glared at her.

'It's. Not. Funny!'

'It is. A bit.' Sophie forced the smile from her face, which took a fair amount of effort. 'But why is it making you so upset?'

'Because . . .' Julie blew her nose loudly. 'Because it's Christmas.'

'And a pig is for life, eh? And not just . . .' Sophie started to laugh again, then she fetched Julie's coffee and the chocolates and put them down in front of her. 'Here. These should make you feel better.'

'Thanks.'

As Julie took a sip of coffee, unwrapped a chocolate, then grabbed at her stomach, Sophie peered at her. 'Are you sure you're okay?'

'Yes, I'm . . .' She waved a hand frantically in front of her nose. 'It's . . . The chocolate smell. I think I just need a . . . To go to the . . .'

Just in time, Sophie grabbed the open tin, passed it to Julie, then held her hair back as she threw up into it.

'Thanks,' said Julie, eventually, her voice muffled by the tin. 'Must just have been something I ate.'

'What do you think it might have been?'

Julie thought for a moment. 'I'm not sure. I haven't eaten that much, to be honest, apart from a few chocolates. Not that we'll be having any more of those.'

She fumbled for the lid, grimacing as she fastened it back onto the tin, then placed it carefully in the bin underneath her desk, and Sophie frowned. Given Julie's emotional response to *Take a Break*, and now this . . .

'Well, at least we've got the answer to the question as to whether you're pregnant.'

'It's certainly looking that way,' said Julie, wiping her mouth with a tissue. 'I just . . .' She slid the magazine across the desk, then exhaled loudly. 'My hormones are all over the place. And I just don't know what to do.'

'About the baby?'

'About *anything*.'

'Which is precisely why you shouldn't be making any decisions right now. These things need a cool head. And . . .'

'And?'

'Mark has the coolest head in the office.'

Julie narrowed her eyes across the desk at her. 'You're saying I should go and tell him?'

'Right.'

'Now?'

'Yes. Right now. Though I'd get ready for tonight first, if I were you. Just in case the conversation takes a little longer than planned.'

Julie stared at her for a moment. 'You're right,' she said. 'Thanks. In the meantime, haven't you got somewhere you need to be?'

Sophie looked at her watch, then got up and grabbed her coat and bag from the rack in the corner. Unlike Mark Webster, she didn't need to be told.

◯◯

Mark Webster was pacing around his office, wondering whether there was a right way up for his Velcro-fastening bow tie, when a knock on the door made him jump. As Julie Marshall stuck her head round the door, Mark felt himself begin to panic. Even though he still hadn't decided whether to present her with it this evening, the ring box containing his front-door key was sitting on the middle of his desk. Before she could see, he hurried across and hastily slipped it into his jacket pocket.

'You scrub up well!'

'Thanks.' He looked her up and down, admiring the way the black cocktail dress Julie was wearing fitted in all the right places, then he smiled.

'What's funny?'

'I was just thinking, when they say a dress fits "in all the right places". What would be one of the wrong places for it to fit?'

Julie smiled at him. 'You take things very literally, you know?' She walked over and removed a speck of dust from his collar. 'Nervous about tonight?'

'Not really,' said Mark, though he was feeling the exact opposite. He'd already fluffed his first 'meeting' with Tony A. Wood thanks to what he thought was Nathan's prank call (though he'd decided to withhold that particular snippet from Julie), and still

177

hadn't decided what to do about Tony's offer (assuming it still stood after his faux pas on the phone). If it did, he had the all-important conversation about it with Julie to come, and thinking about it, that was the thing he was most nervous about. 'Well, yes. A bit.'

'Remember, it's also the Christmas party. So try to have a good time too.'

'Like last year?' Julie had coloured quickly, and Mark felt a little guilty. 'I didn't mean . . . At least there won't be a round of "pass the balloon" this year.'

'Shame,' said Julie. 'So, do we know any more about it?'

Mark shrugged. 'Coach is leaving at 6.30 p.m. It's black tie. That's all I know.'

'No clues as to this mysterious announcement?'

'No. Nothing.'

'It's probably just him bragging about how much money he's worth now.'

'I'm sure he's not that bad.'

'No?' Julie had hitched her dress up a little in order to perch on the edge of his desk, giving Mark a provocative glimpse of thigh, and he had to fight the temptation to lock his office door and ask her if she fancied a quick 'meeting'. 'Most billionaires either make their money by inheriting it, or shafting other people to get it. From what I can work out, Tony A. Wood didn't inherit anything. Which means he's done an awful lot of—'

'Shafting?' Mark grinned, then his smile faded rapidly. 'Well, as long as he doesn't shaft anyone tonight.'

'That's not what Sophie's hoping.'

'Pardon?'

'Nothing.'

'Listen, Julie . . .'

'Listen, Mark . . .'

They'd spoken simultaneously, and Mark let out an embarrassed laugh. 'Sorry. You first.'

'No, you.'

'Okay. Here goes.' Mark cleared his throat. 'Well, I just wanted to say . . . You and me . . . This "Christmas" thing—'

'Mark, before you—'

'No, please, let me finish. I don't want to put you under any pressure, or anything, so I just wanted to say, I'm fine with things the way they are.'

'The way they are?'

'Just you and me. Like this. If it never changes . . . I'd still be happy. Even if we have to live . . .' He swallowed hard. 'Apart. Anyway, I just wanted you to know that . . .' Mark stopped talking. Julie looked like she was welling up. 'What's the matter?'

'Nothing.'

'You're sure?'

'Yes!' she snapped, and he wondered if he'd overstepped the mark again. This was the trouble with women. Offer them something you thought they might like, and you got your head bitten off. Take it back a bit later, and you got the same reaction. iFeel's financials had been easier to understand, and that had been a hundred-page document full of some of the worst management-speak imaginable. He shook his head imperceptibly, then worried Julie would round on him for that.

'Right. Whatever you say. And speaking of which . . . ?'

'What?'

'You were going to say something. Just now?'

'Oh.' Julie hopped off the end of the desk. 'Don't worry. It can wait.'

Julie looked at him for a moment, and from her expression, Mark wondered whether it couldn't, but she simply gave him a brief smile.

'Fair enough. So, see you at six-thirty?'

Julie saluted him smartly. 'Yes, *sir*.'

Mark forced himself to smile back at her. The way things were going, those might as well be the exact words he was going to say to Tony.

❧

Julie Marshall hurried back along the corridor, determined to reach the safety of her office and shut the door behind her before she burst into tears. Hormones aside, she couldn't work out why she felt so bad – Mark had effectively given her a 'Get Out of Jail Free' card. So why had it felt like the opposite?

Of course there was a part of her that wanted this baby – though not enough to have it on her own. And here was Mark, the one person in the world she'd thought she could rely on, dismissing their relationship as something, well, *casual*. And if that *was* the case, well, maybe it was best that she did get rid of it.

The single mothers she knew were single in all senses of the word – apparently, a baby wasn't the kind of accessory most men looked for in a woman – and Julie couldn't contemplate being on her own for ever (or at least, for the next however-many-it-took-before-the-child-left-home years – which, the way the economy was going, might be more than she could contemplate). She liked being in a couple – or at least, liked being with Mark. A lot more than she'd liked being with Philip, even before their marriage had gone south. But if he wasn't committed to her, to their relationship . . . Well, what was the point?

Julie almost laughed. The scene at the end of *Four Weddings and a Funeral* where Hugh Grant asked Andie MacDowell if she could possibly consider being 'not married' to him had always made a lot of sense to her, but now, when Mark had said pretty much the same thing, she'd found herself feeling disappointed.

But this was her problem, she realised. Waiting for other people to make decisions, rather than taking the initiative yourself, meant you didn't always get the result you wanted. She should have told him about the baby earlier, presented him with all the facts as soon as she'd known them, and then they could have come to a sensible conclusion, rather than her waiting for him to say what he probably thought she wanted him to say, based on the idiotic way she'd been presenting herself since her emotions had locked the sensible side of her brain in a darkened room and thrown away the key. Well, not any more.

There had been a feature on Beyoncé in Sophie's magazine (though there seemed to be a feature on Beyoncé in every magazine), and Julie had always loved that Destiny's Child song about independent women, partly because that was how she saw herself. A child wasn't necessarily in *her* destiny – it was her body, and while she might not have had any control over what had gone into it, she was in charge of what would come out of it. She'd read enough 'parental nightmare' horror stories in *Take a Break* – and in only the one issue. Given her lack of empathy with children, if she *did* have this one, she was sure she had a real risk of appearing in the magazine herself.

She got up from her desk and walked across to the window, taking in the sights in the street below. Coffee-carrying workers were hurrying to their offices; a couple of the girls from Spank-o-rama, the hostess bar round the corner from the office, were huddled in a doorway, chain-smoking while the builders renovating the office block opposite ogled them. A workman wearing camouflage trousers and a high-visibility jacket, as if he couldn't decide whether he wanted to be seen or not, was tinkering with a streetlight; next to him, a homeless man chatted animatedly with a cycle courier. As a shouting match broke out between two motorists vying for a parking space, Julie sighed. London was fun, vibrant, exciting, and work . . . Well, apart from today, it was the same. She wasn't prepared to give this all up for a life of play-groups, or posting pictures of poo on Facebook; there was only one kind of run she wanted to do, and it didn't have the word 'school' in front of it. Before she could change her mind, she gathered up her things, hurried downstairs, and headed for the address she'd looked up earlier.

She made her way towards Oxford Street, passing a group of carollers dressed in Dickensian outfits in the centre of Soho Square. As she walked by, a woman at the front of the group rattled a charity box at her, so Julie fumbled in her purse for a few coins.

'*Christmas is coming, the geese are getting fat,*' they sang, and Julie quickened her pace. If she didn't take action right away, that was exactly what was going to happen to her.

༄

Sophie Jones hurried along Dean Street, Julie's voucher safely stowed in her Zara bag. With an hour and a half to go before the coach left, she surely had enough time to go for her makeover, get changed, and get back in time for the bus. But what to have made over?

She found the salon, and stared at the brightly lit sign above the window. Okay, so Get Nailed perhaps wasn't the most enticing-sounding place, but it was short and to the point, and as someone who worked in marketing, Sophie appreciated that.

As she scanned through the list of treatments on the board out-side, a black girl with the longest, pinkest nails Sophie had ever seen came walking gingerly out through the door. Sophie stood to one side, and the girl nodded her thanks, then she gave a friendly grimace.

'Hollywood,' she said, in response to Sophie's enquiring look.

'That's a coincidence,' said Sophie, brightly. 'I'm hoping to move to San Francisco.'

The girl smiled. 'That's nice for you,' she said, as she held the door open.

Sophie walked inside, and made her way to the reception desk, where a heavily made-up woman was sitting, flicking through a copy of *Heat* magazine.

'Can I help you?' she said, in response to Sophie's throat-clearing.

'What can I get done in an hour?'

The woman reluctantly pushed the magazine to one side, then slid a price list across the desk. 'Well, pretty much anything you want. Nails, eyebrows, Botox . . . And we're having a waxing special today.'

Sophie peered at the price list, and tapped the treatment at the top. 'Hence the Closing Down Sale?'

'Oh, sorry. That's the men's list.'

'Men come in for waxing?'

'They do. And that top one's very popular.'

'And, er, what exactly is the Closing Down Sale?'

The woman grinned. 'Everything must go! Otherwise known as the Back, Sack, and Crack. But that sounds a little coarse, so . . .' The woman flipped the leaflet over, then waited as Sophie read through the various women's options. 'Anything take your fancy?' she said, eventually.

'Well, um, Brazilian I know, obviously,' said Sophie. 'Though why it's called a Brazilian is always a mystery to me. I mean, from what I remember from my school geography lessons, most of Brazil is covered by rainforest. And not, you know, deforested . . .' She let out a nervous laugh. 'Sorry. So, um, these others . . .'

'Which others?'

Sophie pointed at the first item on the list. 'The "English Country Garden"?'

'Just a little tidy up. Kind of a short back and sides. But . . .' The woman pointed a finger downwards. 'Down there.'

'The "Love Heart"?'

'More appropriate for Valentine's Day.'

'The "Cocktail Glass"?'

'Shaped like a cocktail glass.' The woman hadn't added 'obviously', but Sophie heard the implication.

'The "Desert Island"?'

'Just a small bit left. For those afraid of going completely bare.'

'And, um, the "Hollywood"?'

'That would be completely bare.'

'Ah. Right,' she said, suddenly twigging what the girl she'd met on the way in had been on about. 'And, um, men like that, do they?'

The woman nodded. 'Some do. So . . . ?'

Sophie was beginning to feel nervous. 'What's the most popular treatment?'

'Well, that depends. What does your boyfriend like?'

Sophie opened her mouth to say that she didn't have a boyfriend, then she shut it again. *Think positive*, she reminded herself. 'Tonight's our first date.'

The woman widened her eyes. 'Well, in that case, he's probably going to expect you to be waxed, plucked, plumped, and primped to within an inch of your life.'

'Right. Well, I've got this' – Sophie pulled the voucher from her bag, and slapped it down on the desk – 'and an hour and a half. So what can I have done?'

The woman gave Sophie a quick once-over, picked up a calculator, and tapped the keys. 'The lot!'

Sophie frowned at her. 'Is there time?'

The woman jabbed a thumb towards a back room, where half-a-dozen bored-looking women in white uniforms were sitting around, sipping coffees and reading magazines. 'It'd be a challenge, but why not?'

Sophie thought for a moment. She only had one shot, she knew, and this was it, especially given the fact that she may never meet Tony A. Wood – or *any* billionaire – again. And particularly if the redundancies she suspected would happen in the New Year happened.

'Then the lot's what I'll have,' she said.

9.

Calum Irwin was sitting in Old Amsterdam, sipping his beer nervously as he waited for Mia-Rose to arrive. He didn't know where the phrase 'Dutch courage' came from, but in this Netherlands-themed restaurant, where the waitresses all wore clogs and tulips adorned every table, his glass of Heineken might be as good a place as any to find some.

He'd reassured himself that, given their history here, this was *where* to ask her to marry him, and thanks to some last-minute rehearsals, he finally knew *how* to ask her (a simple 'Will you marry me?' – Calum had decided the fewer words the better). But now he was actually sitting in the restaurant, the one thing he hadn't quite decided on – *when* to ask her – was troubling him.

Before they'd eaten seemed just wrong, as if it was something he wanted to get out of the way so they could have dinner, and while that was true (and while he *was* hungry), he didn't want Mia to think of it like that at all. Waiting until the end of the meal meant he'd have to pretend nothing was up for the whole time, and Mia was sure to see through that. That only left doing it between courses, which, knowing his luck, was sure to mean the waitress would come over and interrupt him just when he was in full flow. And he was nervous enough without having to look over his shoulder the whole time.

Maybe *while* they were eating was best. Halfway through their mains, maybe. The casualness might look cool, the surprise could have the desired effect. He'd make sure she didn't have her mouth full, then pretend to drop his napkin on the floor, kneel down to pick it up, surreptitiously remove the ring from his jacket pocket and . . . Bingo. In theory, at least.

He glanced round at the Edam-cheese-shaped clock on the far wall, then double-checked the time on his watch. Mia was late, but then again, she *was* getting ready for a party, and even in Calum's limited experience, the serious primping this involved usually took a considerable amount of time. Not that it annoyed him. He loved the fact that even after ten months of dating, Mia still made an effort. Still wanted to dress up, even when they were just going somewhere casual, like the cinema, where they'd be spending most of the evening in the dark. Still took the time to put make-up on, even when she was just popping to the corner shop . . . No, actually, Calum could do without that last one.

He wondered if she'd still be the same when they were married – *when they were married*. His heart started racing at the thought. In an hour or so, if he played his cards right, he'd be walking into the office Christmas party with his *fiancée* on his arm. And people would know, too, without him having to tell them – maybe from the huge grin he'd probably have to have surgically removed from his face, but definitely from the glinting of the diamond on Mia-Rose's finger. He'd even tried the ring on himself to see how it looked – though on his little finger, where it had gotten stuck, necessitating an embarrassing walk through the office to the toilets with his hand in his pocket to hide it from prying eyes, then an anxious five minutes and most of the contents of the soap dispenser until he'd managed to get it off again.

The one person he *would* have to tell was his mother (who'd probably *actually* have that heart attack she'd been threatening for the past twenty or so years). Then all they'd have to do was let Mia's mother and sisters know (though he might just leave that particular trial to Mia herself), and then they could start making plans – for the wedding, for their *future* . . . Oh yes, Calum thought, forget what that stupid headhunter had said earlier; tonight was going to be the beginning of a new, better stage of his life. The life he'd always dreamed about. *Married* life. This was shaping up to be the best Christmas ever.

He stood up and brushed the front of his suit down, and a couple of other diners whispered to each other and pointed in his direction, but Calum didn't mind. So what if he was a little over-dressed for a place like this? Who cared if an elderly couple had thought he was the head waiter earlier and asked him for a menu as he'd been making his way back from the toilets? It was no big deal that someone else had looked at him as he'd been waiting outside, and wondered out loud why Old Amsterdam had started employing a bouncer. The only thing that mattered was what Mia thought. And he'd find out soon enough.

The ring box made a rather embarrassing bulge in his trousers, so he moved it into the inside pocket in his jacket, then glanced round at the door, just in time to see Mia pushing it open. She looked beautiful, in a dress Calum had helped her choose in Top Shop the previous Sunday, and his heart leapt again. This was it. Now or never. The most important evening, or rather, *meal* of his life.

With a last, nervous adjustment of his bow tie, he drained the rest of his beer, checked the ring box was still in the pocket he'd only just put it in, fixed a smile on his face, and waved her over to his table.

∽

Julie Marshall double-checked the address on her phone, worried the modern, glass-fronted building was too much like an office, the huge windows at odds with the private, personal nature of what went on inside. It all seemed a bit too businesslike, too clinical, but then again, Julie supposed, it *was* a clinic. What she was going to speak to them about was simply a medical procedure, just like the same kinds of procedures she imagined Sophie was going through at the moment – and besides, there was no mistaking the sign above the entrance. She looked up and down the street, took a deep breath, then strode purposefully through the door, and made her way to the reception desk.

'Can I help you?'

The woman behind the counter had done a double take at what she was wearing, so Julie shrugged apologetically. 'Christmas party.'

'Coming or going?'

'Going. And I'm also "going" to have a baby. Or, you know, not. Which is why I'm here.'

'Do you have an appointment?'

'Er, no. Sorry. Do I need one?'

'Well, normally, yes. But we're never that busy before Christmas. After is a different matter.'

'Like pets' homes, I'll bet. "A dog is for life" and all that . . .' The receptionist's smile had wavered a little, and Julie wanted to slap herself on the forehead. 'Not that this is the same as an unwanted . . . I'm sorry. I didn't mean it like that. I've . . . I'm having a funny day, is all.'

'Don't worry. Let me just take some details.' The woman tapped a few keys on the laptop in front of her. 'Name?'

'I haven't decided yet. And I suppose that depends if it's a boy or a—'

'Not of the *baby*.'

'Ah. Well, actually, same answer. The first part, at least.'

The woman frowned up at her. 'You don't have to worry. This is completely confidential.'

'No, it's not anything like *that*. I've just got divorced. This morning. So I don't know whether I should be giving you my married name, or—'

'Either is fine.'

'It's Julie. Pooley.' Julie shuddered. She hadn't said her maiden name out loud for so long she'd forgotten how ridiculous it sounded. 'That's p-double-o . . .' Julie laughed. 'Which, again, is what I'm trying to avoid.'

The receptionist gave her a look. 'Thank you,' she said, flatly, typing her name into the computer. 'Date of birth?'

'Well, I'm hoping there won't be one . . .' Julie let out an embarrassed snort. 'Sorry. Again. You meant mine, didn't you?' She *actually* slapped herself on the forehead this time. 'I'm sorry. I thought "baby brain" only happened after you'd had it, but mine seems to have come on prematurely.'

The woman smiled patiently, then passed Julie a clipboard and a pen. 'Just take a seat, and fill this in for me. Someone will be with you shortly.'

Julie bit her tongue. That was exactly what she was trying to prevent.

∽

Sophie Jones was sitting in the beautician's chair, about to have her first-ever Botox session, and – given the collection of what looked like the kind of torture implements that you'd see on an episode of *Game of Thrones* on the table next to her – wondering what on earth she was letting herself in for.

'Trust me,' the therapist rested a comforting hand on her shoulder, as if sensing her nervousness. 'You won't look back.'

'Or sad, or happy, or frightened . . . ?'

'It's not that bad.' She leant in to study Sophie's face. 'Tell me: have you been frowning a lot recently?'

'Why do you ask?' said Sophie, defensively.

'No reason. It's just—'

'I look old, don't I?'

'No. In any case, wrinkles aren't always a sign of ageing. Technically, they're just creases that've been worn into the skin after you've made the same expression several thousand times. Now, if you could frown for me . . .'

Sophie did as she was told.

'As I thought.' The woman smiled encouragingly. 'Don't worry. We can do something about that.'

'You can't do something about the *reason* I've been frowning, by any chance?'

'Man trouble?' The woman laughed. 'Well, I could, but that'd take a bigger syringe.'

At the word 'syringe', Sophie eyed the needle nervously. 'So, tell me how this works again?'

The woman smiled again. Or, at least, her mouth did, and Sophie hoped that was because she'd had the treatment too, and not just that she was trying to falsely reassure her. 'There's nothing to worry about. Botox might be a toxin, but—'

'A *toxin*? As in "toxic"? Like in the Britney Spears song?'

'Just like that,' said the woman, patiently. 'But like I said, even though it is toxic in huge doses, the doses you'll be getting are tiny.'

'Doses. As in the plural?'

'That's right.'

'And is it . . . natural?'

'Oh yes. In actual fact, it's made from the *Clostridium botulinum* bacteria.'

Sophie grimaced. If that was meant to reassure her, it wasn't working. 'Like in botulism? Food poisoning?'

'Not exactly.'

'But similar?'

'Ish,' said the woman. 'But like I said, the amounts we use are extremely small, so there's an incredibly tiny chance they'll spread throughout the body.'

'How tiny?'

'Incredibly.'

'How incredibly?'

'Very. As in really, really small.'

'Right.' Sophie swallowed hard, trying to forget the 'My Botox Nightmare' story she'd read recently in *Cosmo*. 'Great. And does it, you know . . . ?'

'Hurt?' The woman rested a hand on Sophie's arm. 'Have you been for a waxing yet?'

'Not yet, why?'

'Well, it's not as uncomfortable as that.'

'So it *does* hurt?'

'A tiny bit.'

'How tiny?'

'There'll be a few little pricks.'

Sophie almost laughed. That pretty much summed up her recent encounters on Tinder.

'So,' continued the woman, holding the syringe out of Sophie's line of sight. 'I'm just going to inject a tiny bit into the muscles underneath your wrinkles, and what that'll do is' – Sophie gripped the arm of the chair tightly as the needle went in for the first time – 'block the nerve impulse from reaching that particular area. So when you try to frown, you won't be able to. Which means the skin gets a chance to relax' – Sophie wished *she* could, as the woman jabbed the needle in again – 'so it won't wrinkle. And the less it wrinkles, the more the existing lines disappear. Like magic.' The woman dabbed a piece of cotton wool against Sophie's forehead (and Sophie tried to ignore the fact that it came away bloody), and stood back to admire her handiwork. 'Although of course, it's not magic. It's poison. But you get what I mean.'

The needle went in for a third time, then a fourth, then Sophie decided to stop counting. Her eyes were watering, and she considered telling the woman to stop, but annoyingly she'd only done the one side of her forehead, and the last thing Sophie wanted was to spend the next three months looking as if she didn't believe anything anyone said to her.

She told herself to just breathe deeply, that it'd all be over in a minute, though it didn't seem fair. Watching *Fifty Shades* had made her think that she might have to experience a little pain *during* sex, where at least she was getting some pleasure to offset it, not *before* she'd even met her billionaire. Still, if this was what it took for a life of yachts and shopping, then so be it.

'All done,' said the woman, after what had felt like an eternity to Sophie but in reality had probably been little more than five minutes.

'Really?'

'Really.'

Excitedly, Sophie took the mirror the therapist was handing her, and examined her reflection. Apart from a few tiny spots where the needle had gone in, she couldn't see anything.

'Don't worry,' said the woman, as if reading her mind. 'They'll disappear in an hour or so.'

'And how long before it, you know, kicks in?'

The woman smiled. 'It's different for everyone. But you should feel your face begin to relax over the next few hours. So as the night gets older, you'll look younger!'

'Great!' Sophie put her face through all sorts of complicated expressions, relieved to find everything still worked, then rubbed her hands together. So far, this beauty voucher was the best present anyone had ever given her. 'Right,' she said, as she followed the woman back out into reception. 'What's next?'

❦

Calum Irwin licked the last piece of chocolate fudge sauce from his spoon, then glanced worriedly at the clock on the wall for what seemed like the hundredth time. Mia-Rose hadn't stopped talking since she'd sat down – it was as if she had her 'play' button stuck in the 'on' position – but if he didn't interrupt her and make his move soon, they'd be in danger of the coach that was taking them to the party leaving without them. And while he loved hearing Mia talk – her accent, her enthusiasm, her stories were things he could happily listen to for hours – right now he didn't *have* hours.

There was nothing for it, he decided, but to distract her. He surreptitiously felt for the ring in his pocket, ignoring the mild heart attack he had at not finding it before realising he'd reached into the *wrong* pocket, then, reassured by the comforting shape of the box in his fingers, he took a deep breath, stood up, and 'accidentally' dropped his napkin. But before he could do anything else, Mia's arm had shot out like a striking cobra, and she'd caught it.

'Whoops!' Mia handed the napkin back to him. 'Here.'

'Oh, er, thanks,' he said, though he didn't know what to do now, on his feet, but with no reason to kneel on the floor. Without a distraction, it seemed an awfully long way down, so instead he just stood there.

'You okay?'

'I, um . . . I thought I needed the toilet.'

'But you don't now?'

Calum shook his head. If he left the table to go to the gents, he suspected he might not have the nerve to come back, so even though (now he thought about it) he *did* need the toilet – in fact, he'd felt an anxious pressure in his bladder since he'd arrived at the restaurant, and the beer he'd gulped down earlier wasn't helping – he sat back down.

As Mia-Rose continued with her story – though Calum would have been hard-pressed to answer questions about it – he decided to have another try, so he animatedly shifted position in his chair and dropped the napkin again – careful this time that it fell out of Mia's reach. But just as he was taking the ring box from his pocket, a loud 'Let me get you a clean one' sounded in his ear. He looked up, just in time to see a smiling waitress handing him a replacement from the next-door table.

'No, that's okay. I—'

'It's no bother.'

'I don't want another one!' snapped Calum, picking the original angrily off the floor.

As the waitress gave him a funny look and stomped off, Mia-Rose frowned. 'Calum. There was no need to be rude. She was only trying to do her job.'

'Yes, well, she wouldn't have to, if you'd let me get a word in edgeways.' Almost immediately, Calum realised he'd made a mistake. 'I'm sorry, I didn't mean—'

'Are you saying I talk too much?'

'No, not at all. I . . .' Calum let his voice tail off. How could he extract himself from this one?

'No? "If you'd let me get a word in edgeways," you said. What did you mean by that, exactly?'

'Well, I—'

'What's so important that you need to say that you couldn't wait until I'd finished?'

'I just . . . It's . . . I wasn't sure you were ever *going* to finish. No – I didn't mean it like that . . .' Calum could feel the moment slipping away from him. '*When* you were going to finish. You just . . . I mean, I wanted to talk to you about something, and—'

'What?'

'I said I wanted to talk to you about—'

'And I said "what?" As in, what did you want to talk to me about?'

Mia had folded her arms now, and Calum worried he was in trouble. This certainly wasn't how he wanted to propose – in the midst of an argument. 'Well . . .' He wondered whether it was too late to drop his napkin on the floor again, but he suspected he already knew the answer to that. Instead, he slumped back on the banquette, and gazed hopelessly up at the ceiling. 'Never mind.'

Mia-Rose reached over and grabbed his hand. 'Sweetie, is everything okay?'

'Yes,' Calum lied. 'Why wouldn't it be?'

'You seem a little jumpy.'

'I'm sorry. It's just . . .'

'Is it the merger?'

He half-smiled. It wasn't the first time he'd been aware of the irony. 'Yeah.'

'You're not worried you'll be gotten rid of?'

Calum blanched. He hadn't thought of *that*. All along, he'd been expecting Mia-Rose to say yes. At the least, he'd been hoping she might say she'd think about it. But he hadn't considered what he'd do if she said 'no', or what it might mean for their relationship – after all, from what he knew about Nathan's failed proposal, Ellie had left him pretty much there and then. And besides, how did you move on from something like that: just go back to the way things were? He didn't know about Mia-Rose, but he was pretty sure *he* couldn't stay with someone he knew didn't want to marry him – and why would *she* stay with him if she didn't?

He sighed miserably. He'd been a fool, all this time thinking that the big proposal he had planned was going to be the start of a great new phase of their relationship. Because not once had he considered that it might actually be the end of it.

'Let's just not talk about it, shall we?' he said, then he carefully slipped the ring box back into his jacket pocket, and tapped his watch. 'Should we get the bill?'

Mia-Rose nodded. 'Don't want to miss the bus,' she said. Though Calum suspected he already had.

॰৹

Sophie Jones was lying on her back on a treatment bed, feeling like one of those cars moving along a production line while one person worked on the lights, another fitted the windows, and someone else attended to the doors. And while she hadn't got to the 'carpets' part yet, she was getting increasingly nervous, The only other time she'd tried waxing was when she'd bought one of those home depilatory kits; while she was preparing it she'd accidentally dropped one of the strips, and when she'd seen the damage it had done when she'd peeled it off the rug, she'd chickened out and thrown it in the bin.

But these people were professionals, she reminded herself. They knew what they were doing. And if they were half as good down there as they had been on the gleaming new nails and exquisitely shaped eyebrows she was now sporting, then Sophie knew she had nothing to worry about.

She hoped.

Her (latest) beautician came into the room, a small, wiry Chinese girl with forearms bigger than Sophie's thighs. 'What are you having?' she said, cracking her knuckles, then hoisting Sophie's gown up matter-of-factly.

Second thoughts, Sophie wanted to say, remembering the woman she'd met on her way in. 'Just a bit of a tidy up. Maybe that pint-glass thingy.'

'Cocktail glass,' said the woman, though her expression suggested she thought a pint glass might be more appropriate. 'Okay, please open your legs, then lie as still as possible.'

Sophie let out a snigger. She'd heard that line before. Or at least had acted it out once or twice. 'Aren't you even going to buy me a drink first?'

The beautician smiled politely, and Sophie supposed she'd probably heard them all before, though as she fussed around with some hot wax by the bed, Sophie wondered whether she should try and make polite conversation. But say what? Asking someone if they enjoyed their job when *this* was their job seemed a little, well, weird. In the end, 'I'm a bit nervous,' was what she settled for.

'You don't look nervous.'

'Well, at least the Botox is working!'

'Right.' The therapist placed something warm against the inside of Sophie's thighs. 'Take a deep breath, and try to relax . . .'

'That's easy for you to—AAARGH!'

'There,' said the woman. 'That wasn't so bad, was it?'

'*Not bad?*' panted Sophie. 'I can't believe *childbirth's* that bad.'

'The stinging will stop in a moment or two.'

'I hope so.'

Sophie, her eyes watering, reached for her knickers, but the therapist put a restraining hand on her arm. 'Where do you think you're going?'

'That was it, wasn't it?'

The woman shook her head. 'It was the cocktail glass we were going for. At the moment, it's more of a . . .' She regarded the area between Sophie's legs quizzically. 'Measuring jug. And we can't leave it like that.'

'How many more?' said Sophie, gripping the edge of the bed so hard she feared her new nails might pop right off.

The beautician took a step backwards and narrowed her eyes, as if measuring up a wall for wallpaper. 'Two should do it.'

'Two. Okay.' Sophie took a few shallow breaths, imagined herself on the deck of a yacht, gritted her teeth, and gripped the edge of the bed even harder.

∽

Nathan Field marched into the Long Bar at the Sanderson Hotel, feeling more than a little self-conscious in his dinner suit. Up until he'd walked into the lobby, he hadn't been sure he was going to come, then he'd spied Ellie waving at him from the far end of the bar, her hair shorter than it used to be, her chic, fitted business suit emphasising the Pilates-honed curves he was pleased to see she'd managed to maintain, and he'd felt a wave of nostalgia rush through him.

He gave himself a second for his eyes to adjust to the low light – Nathan always wondered why cocktail bars did this; given the price of the drinks, it wasn't as if they couldn't afford to pay their electricity bill, and tripping over someone's outstretched feet or handbag wouldn't be the best of entrances – and made his way towards where she was sitting.

'This place certainly lives up to its name,' he said, once he'd eventually arrived at her side.

'Try doing it in heels!' Ellie smiled at him, then jumped down off her stool, hesitating for a moment as if she didn't know whether a hug would be inappropriate, then she stood up on tiptoe, and kissed him quickly on the cheek. 'You didn't have to dress up for me.'

'I didn't,' said Nathan, then he felt guilty as Ellie's face twitched. 'Sorry. I didn't mean it like that. It's our Christmas party tonight. It's black tie. I'm going straight from here.'

Ellie looked him up and down, then reached out a hand to straighten his bow tie, and Nathan had to stop himself from flinching. 'Either way, nice suit.'

'This old thing?' Nathan grinned as he helped her back onto her stool, then he hauled himself up onto the one next to her. 'What are you drinking?' he said, waving the barman over.

'Are you trying to get me drunk? I haven't finished this one yet . . .'

'No, I meant what is it? It looks nice.'

'Old-fashioned.'

Nathan knew enough about cocktails to be sure she wasn't talking about him, and while the Old-fashioned was Don Draper's cocktail of choice, he didn't think his stomach was quite ready for whisky. 'I'll have an espresso Martini,' he told the barman.

Ellie raised one carefully manicured eyebrow. 'Sounds posh.'

'It's the perfect drink. Vodka to get you drunk, and coffee to sober you up at the same time.' He picked her glass up, took a sniff, and hastily put it back down, confident he'd made the right decision as his insides gave a slight lurch. 'I didn't know you were a Scotch girl?'

'I'm not. It's a work thing.'

'A *work* thing?' Ellie's job had always been beyond him. Then again, she'd never understood his. He'd always suspected that had been part of their problem.

'We're doing the PR for a whisky company, so I'm trying to develop a liking for it.'

'And have you?'

'Let's just say it's an acquired taste.' Ellie took a sip of her cocktail, and made a face.

'Which you look like you haven't acquired yet.'

'No.' She let out a short, tinkling laugh. 'So . . .'

'So?'

'It's nice to see you.'

Nathan looked at her. 'Uh-huh,' he settled for, non-committally, knowing he should be able to forgive her by now. Every time he read stories in the papers about prisoners from the Second World War who'd managed to forgive their captors, he'd felt a bit pathetic about his ongoing antipathy towards Ellie. And even though as he sat next to her, and a small part of him still wondered what his life would have been like if she had said 'yes' back then, he realised it was the same small part that might do the same upon hearing that some famous actress or supermodel he fancied had just got divorced, or found themselves suddenly single, and *they* met.

As he stared at the barman, enjoying the spectacle of the cocktail-making process (though perhaps you *should* expect a show at these prices) while simultaneously willing him to hurry up with his drink, Ellie laughed again.

'What's so funny?'

'We used to have so much to talk about. Now we're sitting here like we're on the world's most awkward first date.'

'This is where we had our first date. Did you know that?'

'I'd forgotten. The place has changed.'

'As have we.'

'Have we?'

The barman chose that moment to deliver Nathan's Martini, and he was grateful for the interruption. He picked his glass up, and chinked it against Ellie's.

'To . . . ?'

Don't say 'us', he thought. *Don't say 'us'*.

'Us?'

'To us.' He took a cautious sip from his glass, wary of the alcohol's effect on an empty stomach. Then, when there were no ill effects, Nathan gratefully swallowed a much larger one. 'So, your card was a . . . surprise.'

'A nice one, I hope?'

Nathan reached for a handful of the complimentary popcorn from the bowl the barman had just set down on the bar, hoping it would stay down after his rogue grilled cheese sandwich, and thought about her question as he chewed. In truth, it *was* nice to see her, he realised. Sitting here, in one of their old haunts . . . While perhaps he *could* forget what had happened, the jury was still out on whether he *should*.

'Yes,' he said, surprising himself with how genuine it sounded.

'Good. So, listen.' Ellie put her glass down, and shifted round on her stool to face him. 'There's a reason I asked you here today.'

Here it comes, thought Nathan, though whether Ellie meant 'here' as in their first date venue, or 'here' as in 'out for a drink', he still wasn't sure. Either way, he braced himself.

'You always said to me that when you met the right person, you just knew. And back when you and I . . . When you proposed, the only thing I knew was that I didn't want to get married. Not because it was you, but because of me. How I felt back then. And now . . .' She reached out and rested her hands on top of his. 'I do.'

Nathan didn't dare move. He'd always loved Ellie's hands, the feel of them in his. They – she – had been so tiny, it had made him feel protective. But now . . . It was all he could do not to pull away.

'Ellie, I'm . . . flattered, really I am,' he said, staring into his drink. 'But what we had . . . It was a long time ago. And relationships – they're not like computers. You can't just turn them off when they're not working, then turn them on again, and expect that to fix everything. People move on. They change. It's like operating systems.

They get regular updates, and things that used to be compatible, well, sometimes they don't work together any more . . .' He looked up to find Ellie was grinning at him. 'What?'

'Have you finished?'

'I think so. Why?'

'I'm not talking about me and you, dummy. I . . . I've met someone. And . . .' She wiggled the fingers on her left hand, and as the bright lights in the bar twinkled on the stone, Nathan saw the engagement ring.

Playing for time as much as anything else, he took her hand and pretended to study the ring. He could feel his heart pounding in his chest, but to his surprise, Nathan realised it was pounding with relief, like whenever he had a near-miss on his Vespa.

He took a couple of breaths to calm himself, then he let go of her hand, picked up his glass, and chinked it against hers. 'The diamond's not as big as the one I gave you.'

Ellie folded her arms, and regarded him mock-sternly. 'Nathan, you should know more than anyone that size isn't important.'

He looked up sharply, to see she was teasing him, and rolled his eyes. 'So, you're getting *married*?'

She nodded.

'But – in February – when I last saw you, you weren't even seeing—'

'I know!' Ellie made the 'aargh!' face. 'It's been a bit of a whirlwind, to be honest, but like I said – or rather, like *you* said – when you know, you know, and this time . . . I do.'

'Thanks very much!'

'Oh, Nathan.'

'I'm kidding.' He smiled at her, then took another mouthful of Martini. 'Well, congratulations!'

'Thank you.'

'So, what's he like?'

'Do you really want to know?'

Nathan began nodding, then quickly changed it to a head-shaking. 'Nope.'

'Because he's sitting over there, if you wanted to meet him . . .'

Nathan looked around with a start, nearly falling off his stool in the process, and Ellie burst out laughing. 'Got you again. You are *so* easy. Or not, now I come to think of it.'

'Ha ha.' Nathan set his cocktail down carefully, relieved he hadn't spilled any on his trousers. 'So you're happy?'

'I am.' She gave his hand a quick squeeze, and to his surprise this time, Nathan found himself not wanting to recoil. 'But I wanted to see you. To tell you in person. So you didn't find out from someone else. I owed you that much, at least.'

Nathan frowned. He and Ellie didn't move in the same circles any more, didn't even have any of the same friends (most of them had sided with him after what she'd done, and the ones who hadn't, Nathan had refused to have anything to do with), so how he'd actually have found out was beyond him. But it didn't seem like this was all a charade to hurt him one more time, or even see whether he'd make some huge declaration of eternal love, or even challenge Ellie's new fiancé to a duel. She had nothing to gain from that – not after all this time. And, of course, nor did he.

'Thanks.'

'So . . .' Ellie regarded him over the top of her glass. 'You're okay with this?'

'Yeah,' said Nathan, still stunned as to exactly how okay with it he was. 'Of course.'

'Great.' Ellie helped herself to a piece of popcorn. 'So, what about you?' she said, popping it into her mouth. 'Anyone on the horizon?'

Nathan thought for a moment, wondering whether he should tell her about Kasia, then he remembered the day's email exchanges with Stacey, and all of a sudden, he realised Ellie wasn't the only one who'd been caught up in a bit of a whirlwind. 'Maybe,' he said, checking his watch. 'Early days, but . . .'

'Good.' Ellie smiled. 'You deserve to be happy, Nathan.'

'Everyone does.'

'They do. Except for that Syrian dictator chap. And, you know, *paedophiles*.'

'Well . . .' Nathan removed his wallet, deposited three ten-pound notes on the bar to cover the bill, then drained the rest of his drink. 'And for no other reason that I've got a bus to catch, I have to go.'

'A *bus*?' Ellie looked horrified. 'What's happened to your Vespa?'

'In this?' He indicated his dinner suit with a sweep of his hands. 'Besides, I don't want to drink and ride.'

'But . . . public transport dressed like that?'

Nathan shook his head. 'They've laid one on specially for us this evening.'

'Classy. Where are you going?'

He grinned. 'I don't know,' he said. And for the first time in a while, the prospect didn't fill him with dread.

As he climbed down from his stool, Ellie looked at him fondly, and to his surprise, he found himself reciprocating. They hugged this time, then when Ellie let him go, she took his face in her hands and kissed him briefly on the lips.

'Bye, Nathan.'

'Bye.'

'And good luck.'

'With?'

Ellie shrugged. 'Everything. Oh, and . . .'

'And?'

'Merry Christmas!'

'Merry Christmas,' said Nathan, then he marched out of the bar, leaving Ellie, his resentment, and all those unhappy memories behind.

It was funny, he thought, how for all this time, Ellie not saying 'yes' to his proposal had stopped him from moving on. But now that she'd said 'yes' to someone else, he finally knew he could.

∽

An exasperated Mark Webster was standing with his arms folded, directing everyone onto the coach that had pulled up outside Seek's office. This 'mystery venue' lark was supposed to add a level of fun, but Mary from accounts had already complained to him that the vehicle didn't have a toilet, and the place might take ages to get to (which, even if it was just down the road, given the usual London pre-Christmas rush-hour traffic, might well be the case), and if that was true, given the amount of hot water and lemon she'd been drinking all day she might end up wetting herself, something Mark was filing under 'too much information'. Still, a simple 'Is it far?' to the driver had gotten a bored shake of the head in reply, so Mark reasoned it had to be somewhere in central London. He did his best to reassure her, then made a mental note to sit at the other end of the bus, just in case.

'Come on,' he said, like a schoolteacher, as everyone trooped onto the coach. 'The quicker you get on, the quicker we'll get there.'

'That's not strictly accurate, is it?' said Benedict.

'What?'

'Sooner. Not quicker.'

Mark glared at him. 'Eggs' Benedict would be out if he had his way, maybe even this evening, if Tony A. Wood got wind – if you excused the phrase – of his body-odour problem.

He shepherded the stragglers/smokers on board (Mia-Rose and a somewhat bewildered-looking Calum Irwin bringing up the rear), then he climbed on, and took the seat up front, as far away from Mary *and* Julie Marshall as was possible. As the bus made its way down Frith Street, Nathan Field stuck his head through the gap between the seats.

'Any idea where we're going?'

Mark peered out of the window as the bus turned right into Shaftesbury Avenue. 'Looks like West London,' he said, as they joined the queue of slow-moving traffic heading towards Piccadilly Circus.

'Well, that narrows it down a bit. And speaking of narrowing things down, dare I ask?'

'You first. How did it go with Ellie?'

Nathan pursed his lips thoughtfully. 'Pretty good, considering.'

'Considering?'

'She's getting married.'

'Nathan, I'm so sorry.'

'I'm not. That was why she wanted to meet me. To tell me.'

'To get your blessing?'

'Not exactly. I guess she just wanted to do right by me. Which was good of her. So now we can both move on.'

'She already had.' Mark gave him a long-suffering look. 'So that's it, then? The Ellie chapter of your life is closed?'

'Seems that way.'

'And you're okay with that?'

'Seems that way too.'

'Great.'

'Yup.' Nathan turned and stared out of the window as they carried on past The Ritz, raising a chorus of boos from the back of the coach when they didn't stop.

'Well, *that* narrows it down a bit.'

'I guess he's rich, but not Ritz rich,' said Nathan, and Mark laughed, then he glanced at Julie Marshall, who seemed to be glued to her phone, gesticulating animatedly with her free hand, and Nathan caught his eye.

'I haven't asked her yet, alright?'

Nathan sat back in his seat. 'Okay, okay.'

They rounded Hyde Park Corner in silence, then passed Harrods, Mark doing his best to ignore the cries of 'Are we nearly there yet?' from some of the younger staff members occupying the back seat. As they approached the Natural History Museum, Nathan stuck his head back through the gap. 'But you're going to, right?'

'*Nathan . . .*' But Mark couldn't say any more, as the coach suddenly came to a halt. Instead, he glanced across to the driver. 'Are we here?'

The driver nodded, then jabbed a thumb towards the main doors. 'Front entrance.'

'Right.' Mark stood up in the aisle. 'Okay everyone. Off we get.' He clapped his hands, then stood back as everyone ambled past. 'Chop chop.'

'I love it when you act all masterful,' Julie whispered as she filed past him, and Mark blushed.

With a final check the coach was empty, they followed the group towards the building, which was lit up imposingly against the night sky, and Nathan grabbed Mark's shoulder.

'Crikey!'

'I know!'

They filed nervously inside, dropped their coats off at the cloakroom, and walked into the main hall. Mark had been here before, several times, and grand architecture – not to mention the huge dinosaur skeleton standing proudly in the middle – always took his breath away. The iFeel crowd were already there, congregating by a pop-up bar at the far end of the room, and as the Seek staff formed a defensive circle next to what looked like a dance floor, he smiled.

'I hope that's not a metaphor,' he said.

'What?'

'The dinosaur. That's us, and . . . Well, I don't know what it means, really. Though that lot don't seem to care, especially now the drink's arrived.'

Like a swarm of locusts, the Seek staff had quickly stripped the circulating waiters of the drinks on their trays, and Mark thought about saying something, perhaps telling them to not get too drunk too quickly, but it *was* the Christmas party. And besides, why shouldn't they? Who knew what the New Year would bring?

'Look at them,' he said, pointing at the two groups of employees. 'It's like a group of lions and a group of wildebeest.'

Nathan helped himself to a couple of glasses of champagne from a passing waiter. 'Yeah, but which is which?' he said, handing one to Mark.

'We'll soon find out. But whatever happens, it's been nice working with you.'

'Yes,' said Nathan, chinking his glass against Mark's, before downing his drink in one. 'It has, hasn't it?'

❧

Sophie Jones couldn't feel her face. Normally, this was something she'd experience towards the end of a typical evening out (depending on how many cosmopolitans she'd consumed), but so far today, she hadn't had a thing to drink. Still, she reminded herself, as she changed out of her gown and into her party gear in the salon's toilets, she shouldn't be worried. It was just the Botox doing its thing, and every time she caught sight of her reflection, she was sure she looked a little younger.

She also looked a little younger *down there*, of course, although a lot younger than she'd wanted. Sophie had been squirming so much at the pain that the waxer had struggled to get the sides of her 'cocktail glass' straight, and subsequent attempts to even them out had been so sore that in the end, Sophie had told her to just take the lot off – something she hoped she wouldn't regret as soon as she'd left the salon, given the icy December wind that had been whistling up her skirt on the walk there.

Slipping her bra off, she stuffed it into her bag, pulled her new dress on (making sure everything went where it should for maximum effect), squeezed her feet into her party shoes, then re-applied her lipstick, happy with what she saw in the mirror. She'd been primped, plucked, painted, and pricked to perfection, and now, clad in Zara's finest, she was ready to face the world. Even if that was with a face that didn't quite work the way it used to.

She peered closely at her reflection and frowned, then she feigned surprise, then pouted, then smiled broadly, happy to see that nothing above her beautifully sculpted eyebrows wrinkled when she did so. And while the rest of her features didn't perhaps quite move as freely as they used to, Sophie decided she could live with that. It was certainly a lot better than the 'something-out-of-Madame-Tussauds' look she'd feared might be the end result.

Taking a step back from the mirror, she ran through her mental pre-night-out checklist. The shoes she was wearing, while they might be a little tricky to dance in later, made her legs look longer (and more importantly, slimmer) than normal. The dress – well, it just about covered what she needed it to, and 'showcased' (her new favourite word, thanks to the *Daily Mail*) everything else – which was kind of the point, if you thought about it. Her hair was pulled up in a simple topknot, elegant rather than sexy, though she knew letting it down and shaking it free like those models in those shampoo adverts who looked like they were having an orgasm every time they washed their hair did (and Sophie had practised that in front of the mirror a thousand times) would achieve the second of those two definitions. And what was more, her breasts would jiggle when she did that, because they were *real* – something Tony A. Wood was bound to appreciate.

And while she hoped that, for him to appreciate anything, she wouldn't have to be bound *to* anything like in some of the bondage scenes she'd seen in *Fifty Shades*, Sophie realised something: where she was concerned, and to paraphrase another film title, this was as good as it got. She *did* look like a million dollars. And maybe, just maybe, she'd soon look like a billion.

She performed a few last-minute pouts in front of the mirror, like an athlete warming up before an important game. This was how she had to treat this evening, she told herself. Like a game. And Sophie was tired of being on the losing team.

Her phone rang, and she fished it out of her bag to see Julie Marshall's name flashing insistently on the screen. With a grin, she hit 'answer'.

'Julie! I just want to thank you. This beauty voucher you gave me has been great. I really think Tony A. Wood's going to be putty in my—'

'Sophie, where on earth are you? We're all on the coach, and it's about to go.'

Sophie went pale, and she glanced at her watch. 'Fuck! Sorry. I mean . . .' She thought for a moment, but 'fuck' was pretty much the most appropriate response. 'I'm still at the salon.'

'Doing what?'

'Getting ready.'

'Hold on . . .' There was a muffled conversation, then: 'We have to leave.'

'I thought it was coming at six thirty?'

'*Leaving* at six thirty.'

'But it's only just six thirty *now*,' said Sophie, desperately.

'And your point is?'

'Leaving at six thirty doesn't actually mean *leaving* at six thirty, surely?' Sophie said, desperately, though she feared this was an argument she knew she wasn't going to win. 'Can't you ask the driver to hang on? *Please*.'

'I just did. He won't.'

'Hang on . . .' She hit the 'hands free' button on her phone, frantically gathered the rest of her belongings together, stuffed them in her bag, grabbed her shoes in her other hand, and pelted out of the salon past a bemused receptionist. 'I'm leaving right now. I'll be there in . . .' Sophie stopped talking. The unmistakeable sound of a coach revving and pulling out into traffic booming out from the speaker told her all she needed to know.

As she stared at her phone in disbelief, Julie came back on the line.

'Get yourself a cab. Now!'

'Where to?'

'I don't know yet.' There was another muffled conversation, then: 'Phone me back once you're in one.'

Sophie stared up and down the street, trying to ignore her growing sense of dread. It was Christmas party season, and cabs would be like gold dust. She thought about calling an Uber, but where would she say she was going? And besides, they'd probably all be booked up too. There were regular buses on Oxford Street, of course, but get the wrong one and she might end up on the other side of London. The tube would be quickest, but probably rammed, and she couldn't call Julie from there to find out where she was supposed to be going. And while there were dozens of bicycle rickshaws going up and down the street, their drivers all in fancy dress, one even dressed as Rudolph, complete with antlers and a very shiny red bicycle light for a nose, they all charged an absolute fortune. Sophie may have set her sights on a billionaire, but she wasn't confident enough to be spending any of that money yet.

She sprinted (as best she could, given her heels) onto Oxford Street, searching frantically for the nearest bus stop, but even if she knew which bus to take, given the volume of Christmas shopping traffic, they weren't going anywhere fast. Miserably, she pulled her phone back out of her back and dialled Julie's number.

'Are you in one?'

'There aren't any. Where are you?'

There was a pause, and then . . . 'The Ritz! No, hang on . . .' Julie sounded disappointed. 'I thought we were stopping, but it was just at the lights.'

'Keep talking!' Sophie jammed her phone between her ear and shoulder, crammed her shoes into her already overstuffed bag, and – at a loss for what else to do – began walking briskly west along the pavement.

'Are you on your way?'

'Sort of. Where are you now?'

'Hold on . . . We've just passed Green Park, now we're approaching Hyde Park Corner, and . . . Ooh, Harvey Nichols is looking really Christmassy . . . Sorry. Down Knightsbridge. Past the top of Sloane Street, so it looks like Chelsea's out. Definitely West London, though. Or west of London. I'll call you back.'

Sophie looked around miserably. The number ten bus would take her in that general direction, but would also take ages, and time wasn't something she had on her side. Besides, what if Tony A. Wood had hired some posh country-house hotel somewhere out along the M4? How on earth would she get *there*?

She slumped against the nearest lamp post, stared at her phone, and willed Julie to call, trying her best not to burst into tears. All of this – the research, the new dress, the injections, the *waxing* – if she couldn't get to the party, it would all be for nothing. And while she always used to look forward to Christmas . . . Well, right now, Sophie was beginning to think it was her least favourite holiday of all.

All of a sudden, she heard a bell ring, and she looked up to see a bicycle rickshaw – made up to look like a Harley-Davidson motor-bike – in front of her.

'Are you okay?'

The driver was about her age, nice-looking, and – and Sophie did a double take – sporting what appeared to be a pair of white angel's wings fixed to the back of his leather jacket.

'I'm fine,' she sniffed.

'Excuse me for saying this, but you don't look fine. I mean, you look really fine, if you know what I mean? But just not . . . fine.'

Sophie did her best to swallow her tears. 'I'm sorry. I just . . . I've missed the bus to my office Christmas party, and now I don't know where they're going, and if I don't get there in time . . . Well, let's just say I've spent the whole day – no, the whole of my *life* getting ready for tonight, and . . . Excuse me.' Her phone had started ringing again, so she broke off to answer it. 'Julie?'

'It's the Natural History Museum.'

'What is?'

'The party. It's at the Natural History Museum. Where the dinosaurs live. Well, not live, exactly. And Tony A. Wood will be giving his big speech in about fifteen minutes . . .'

'Natural History Museum. Fifteen minutes. Got it. Thanks, Julie.'

'Oh, and Sophie?'

'Yes?'

'Hurry up!'

Desperately, Sophie tapped 'Natural History Museum' into her Citymapper app, then sighed. Even if she could get a cab, she'd never make it in time. She looked around in desperation, and saw the bicycle rickshaw was still in front of her.

'Problem?'

'I have to get to the Natural History Museum, and in fifteen minutes, or *I'm* history. Or at least, any chance I have of future happiness is.' She stared at the gridlock on Oxford Street in front of her. 'And by the looks of it, it might take me that long just to *get* a cab, and even then . . .'

'I'll take you.'

Sophie grimaced. Her one experience of London rickshaws – a five-minute trip from the pub to the station so she could catch the last tube home – had ended up costing her so much money that a taxi all the way back to Harrow would have been cheaper. 'I'm sorry, I can't afford—'

'No charge.'

Sophie scowled at him suspiciously. In her experience, there was always a charge, but the man just spread his hands out, as if showing her he was unarmed.

'Seriously, it'd be my pleasure. I'm on my way home between shifts, and I live in Fulham. We can cut through the park. Miss all the traffic. And we might just make it.' He tapped the dial of his watch. 'If we leave right now.'

'Why are you doing this?'

The man shrugged, causing his wings to flap. 'It's a nice RAK.'

'Well, you shouldn't be looking,' said Sophie, pulling her coat tighter across her chest.

'No – R.A.K. It stands for Random Act of Kindness.' The man smiled. 'Just remember to pay it forward later.'

'It's probably not the smartest thing for me to just jump into some stranger's—'

'In that case . . .' The man held his hand out for Sophie to shake. 'My name's Richard, but everyone calls me—'

'Rick?' Sophie rolled her eyes. 'And you'll be telling me your surname's "Shaw" next.'

The man – Richard – stared at her for a moment, then he burst out laughing. 'Very good! No, my friends actually call me "Rich". And you are . . . ?'

'Sophie. Sophie Jones.'

'Well, it's nice to meet you, Sophie. And seeing as we're not strangers any more . . .'

'I'm not sure . . .'

'What have you got to lose?'

Sophie swallowed hard. 'Everything' was the first word that had sprung to mind.

'Besides,' he glanced up at the decorative lights spanning the road. 'It is Christmas, after all.'

'So?'

'So just think of it as my gift to you.' Richard nodded at the seat behind him. 'Come on. Get in.'

Sophie looked at her watch, looked again at the traffic, then quickly climbed into the back of the rickshaw. 'You're an angel,' she said, as he pedalled them out into the traffic.

'*Hell's* Angel, if you don't mind.'

Sophie smiled to herself as they sped along Oxford Street. From where she was sitting, 'Guardian' was probably more appropriate.

10.

Sophie Jones shouted a hurried 'Thank you!' over her shoulder as she leapt out of the rickshaw, then she sprinted in through the museum's main entrance, tore off her coat, then threw it and her bag towards the white-dinner-jacketed man standing by the cloakroom. Bursting in through the door, she slowed abruptly to a glide, then – as if she'd had the most relaxing journey here ever – made her way as elegantly as she could into the hall.

The party venue was impressive, she had to admit. She'd been here once before, when she was eleven, on a school trip from Eastbourne, though shamefully she hadn't been back; one of the reasons she'd moved to London was to take advantage of the galleries and museums, but it was the shops that had taken up more of her spare time. Tonight, however, the museum looked somewhat different to how her schoolgirl self remembered it: the great hall decked with Christmas decorations, multicoloured balloons tied in decorative bunches in the corners, a bar at one end, a dance floor (with a real-live DJ!) in the middle, and even what appeared at first glance to be a selection of fairground games at the other. And everyone looked so smart; the men all in black, the women clad in their finest (though their dresses typically utilised a *lot* more material than the one Sophie was sporting).

Pausing to grab a glass of champagne from a passing waiter, she quickly checked out the competition, glad she'd dressed to stand out – although it had meant she'd been a little chilly on her rickshaw ride, despite the blanket she'd been huddled under, and parts of her were standing out a little more than she'd have liked. Still, at least the stinging *down there* had subsided. Or perhaps been numbed by the cold.

She downed her champagne in an attempt to calm her nerves, helped herself to another, then scanned the room, trying to spot Tony A. Wood among the sea of faces. Sophie had memorised his features from his profile picture on iFeel (though given his bio, she suspected it had been taken a while ago) and although he wasn't the most attractive man she'd ever laid eyes on, she hoped it was a face she could grow to love. Though even if she couldn't, with the sun in her eyes as she reclined on the deck of his yacht, or rather, through the pair of diamond-encrusted Versace sunglasses he'd probably present her with as a welcome-aboard gift, she wouldn't be able to see it clearly anyway.

Assuming she ever saw him when they were married, that was. According to an article she'd read on *The New York Times* website, Tony was a well-known workaholic, which left him little time for anything (or anyone) outside of business, including his ex-wives and (current) children. Presumably he wouldn't want any more (children, not wives), but Sophie was okay with that. She knew you couldn't make an omelette without wasting a few eggs, or something like that, and the billionaire lifestyle would more than make up for her forgoing the 'miracle' of motherhood. And besides, she'd have seven ready-made stepchildren. Even though a couple of them were older than she was.

She moved through the room, smiling politely at the eyes that swivelled her way, feeling more than a little self-conscious in the dress Julie had helped her pick out – she'd wanted to be noticed by Tony, not by everyone – but so what? This was how winners behaved. They didn't care what other people thought. She'd just walk on through, her head held high, her chest thrust out, as if she owned the place. Which, in a few weeks, she quite possibly would.

It was warm in the great hall, and Sophie was beginning to sweat – surprising, she knew, given how she was wearing so little – so she downed her second glass of champagne in two gulps, hoping it'd cool her down, but instead, her head began to swim. Hurriedly, she looked around for somewhere to sit, but just as her legs began to give way, she felt a strong hand take her arm, and a deep American voice boomed into her ear.

'Are you okay, li'l lady?'

Sophie swivelled round, distraught that her first meeting with Tony A. Wood should be with her on the verge of collapsing, then she breathed a sigh of relief.

'Nathan!'

'You okay, Soph? You're looking a little . . .'

'I'm just a bit hot.'

'You're telling me,' he said, steering her over to a nearby bench. 'Nice dress!'

Sophie flushed even more as she lowered herself carefully onto the bench. She'd always fancied Nathan – who didn't? – and it had taken her a long time to feel okay about the fact that the feeling wasn't mutual. Still, at least he'd forgiven her for trying to trick him into going out with her on Valentine's Day. She hoped.

'Thanks.' Sophie fanned herself vigorously with her free hand, then stopped when she realised it made her chest jiggle, though Nathan – ever the gentleman – was pretending not to notice. 'Are you enjoying yourself?'

Nathan frowned for a moment. 'Oh, you mean the party?' He sat down next to her. 'It's okay, under the circumstances. Though I'd be surprised if our new owner would be spending this amount of money if he was planning on firing us all.'

'Let's hope so,' said Sophie. 'Have you seen him yet?'

Nathan shook his head. 'Nope. Rumour has it he always likes to make a big entrance. Maybe he'll come in riding the pet velociraptor he's cloned from some dinosaur DNA. Or more likely, he's probably waiting until everyone's here, and with a drink in their hand. Speaking of which, can I get you one?'

Sophie's head began to swim again, though that could have just been the effect of sitting so close to Nathan that their thighs were touching. 'Just some water, if they have it?'

Nathan hauled himself back to his feet, and patted her on the hand. 'Coming right up,' he said. 'And be careful.'

'What of?'

Nathan pointed to the space above her head, and Sophie looked upwards and almost jumped out of her skin, before realising she was sitting underneath the head of the large dinosaur skeleton that occupied the centre of the hall. If you believed *Jurassic Park* – and the first time Sophie had seen it, she'd mistakenly thought she was watching a documentary on National Geographic – dinosaurs once ruled the earth, and now they were on their way back, and she couldn't help wondering if Tony A. Wood had chosen this venue to make a point.

She surveyed the rest of the room. There must have been over a hundred people at the party, most of them stood around in small groups, chatting animatedly while knocking back glasses of champagne as if they were in some sort of competition. Tony A. Wood was nowhere to be seen, and Sophie was starting to worry he might not be turning up at all.

'Here.' Nathan was back already, and handing her a glass of iced water, which she gulped down quickly.

'Thanks. I needed that.'

Nathan took a sip of the champagne he'd fetched himself. 'And I need this.'

'How come?'

'See that girl over there?' He nodded towards the huddle of iFeel employees, where a tall, dark-haired girl in a tightly fitted red cocktail dress was chatting with a group of spellbound men, while occasionally throwing a quick glance in their direction.

'What about her?'

'Stacey Garrity. My opposite number—'

'Who *wants* your number.'

'Huh?'

'She's totally checking you out.'

'Only because she wants the tech-support job.'

'Zere can be only one,' said Sophie, in her best French accent, adding '*Highlander?*' when Nathan frowned.

'Nah, I think she's from London.'

'No, I meant . . .' Sophie sighed, and hoped Tony A. Wood would get her sense of humour better than Nathan apparently did. 'You should go and talk to her.'

'What about?'

'The weather?' She pressed her glass against her forehead, hoping to feel its coolness, although thanks to the Botox, she couldn't even feel *it*. 'Anything. Find out what she's like. The one thing working in marketing has taught me is that you've got to know your competition.'

'I'm not sure, I—'

Sophie stood up abruptly, grateful that her head didn't spin when she did so. After her Valentine's Day escapade, she owed it to Nathan to try and introduce him to someone, plus – and she felt a little guilty about this – she didn't want Nathan cramping her style if Tony A. Wood were to suddenly appear. 'Come on.'

'What? No—'

Grabbing three glasses of champagne from a passing waiter (and Sophie was amazed how they were passing so frequently, though she supposed if you were a billionaire this was to be expected; Tony A. Wood probably filled his swimming pool with the stuff), she handed two of them to Nathan, took him forcefully by the elbow, then dragged him across to where Stacey was standing.

'Hi,' said Sophie. 'I'm Sophie Jones. And this is . . .'

'Nathan Field, I'm guessing,' said Stacey, as the men she'd been chatting to melted away, as if in deference to Nathan's alpha-maleness. 'Stacey Garrity. Nice to meet you both.'

'Would you like a drink?' said Sophie, nudging Nathan, who seemed to be in a bit of a daze.

'Thank you.'

Nathan still hadn't moved, so Sophie took a glass from him and handed it over, then against her better judgement, she lifted her own, full glass to her lips, and downed it in one. 'Well, I seem to have finished mine,' she said, her voice made funny by the bubbles. 'I better go and get myself another.'

Ignoring Nathan's glare, she started to move away, and nearly tripped over the edge of the dance floor.

'Are you going to be okay?' said Nathan, and as a hush fell over the room, and all heads turned to look behind her – Sophie could only assume that finally, Tony A. Wood was making his entrance – she smiled.

'Oh yes,' she said confidently, quickly following it with 'Oh no!', realising to her horror that the man walking down the stairs at the far end of the great hall; the man waving presidentially as an entourage that Sophie guessed consisted of the iFeel board followed him a respectable few stairs behind; the man who'd just bought the company she worked for; the man who was to all intents and purposes her new boss; the man who she was intending to seduce this evening; the man in the *white dinner jacket* – was the man she'd thrown her coat at as she'd rushed in through the door.

❦

Mark Webster took a deep breath, then he nudged Julie Marshall. 'Here we go,' he said, as all eyes swivelled towards the staircase.

'Is that him?'

'Can't you tell?'

'He looks like a Bond villain.'

'We're about to find that out.'

A hush fell over the room as Tony A. Wood stopped on the bottom step, then – as if realising no one could see him – he walked back up a few stairs and clicked his fingers. Once a waiter had rushed forward and handed him a glass of champagne, he cleared his throat.

'Evenin', y'all.'

'Evening, Tony,' chorused the iFeel contingent, followed a few seconds later by some begrudging 'hellos' from the Seek team.

'Thank y'all for comin' to mah little soirée.'

'Like we had a choice,' whispered Sophie, who'd sidled up next to them.

'And welcome to the Natural History Museum. It's magnificent, isn't it? Remember, you can look, but don't touch. If you try, a team of security professionals will wrestle you to the ground.' He paused to let the ripple of polite laughter die down, then pointed to the various exits, where a number of uniformed guards were standing. 'Ah'm not kiddin'. Seriously, they will. Anyway, this is a venue ah chose because, well, tonight, *we're* makin' history. Of sorts.'

'Oh *please*,' said Sophie, rolling her eyes, and Mark flashed her a look.

'As you know,' continued Tony, 'ah've been through a few mergers in mah time . . .'

'Did he say "murders and executions"?'

' . . . but nothin' will give me more pleasure . . .'

'Want to bet?' said Sophie, a little too loudly, and Mark shushed her.

' . . . or has the potential to make me more money – than this one. Not that ah'm in it for the money.' He gave a theatrical wink, which, to Mark, just came across as creepy. 'But now, with ahFeel's predictive technology, coupled with Seek's search-engine capability, we've got a company that can compete with the best of them. And not just compete: win. In a few years, they'll be saying "Google who?" In fact, they'll have to use Seek to find out just who Google is. Sorry, *was*.'

There were a few cheers and whoops from the iFeel contingent – Americans, probably, thought Mark, though Sophie seemed to be jumping up and down and clapping *really* loudly, as if something about Tony's speech had struck her as pretty motivational. And while he wasn't sure she knew exactly what iFeel actually did (according to Julie, she'd only recently got a handle on what *Seek's* technology was, and that had taken her the best part of three years), he was pleased to see her enthusiastic response.

'But tonight ain't about talkin' business,' continued Tony. 'It's about havin' fun. Celebratin'. And so we're gonna get this party started the only way ah know how. With a drink!'

As if on cue, and Mark realised it probably was, a troop of waiting staff appeared from a side door, a bottle of Moët in each hand, and quickly moved around the room topping everyone's champagne up. Once everybody had a full glass, Tony A. Wood held his hand up, and the room went quiet.

'Y'all ready?'

'Ready,' came the chorus, slightly more enthusiastically from the Seek contingent now they had another drink, Mark noted cynically.

Tony A. Wood scanned the room (and for a moment, Mark thought he detected a slight smile when the billionaire looked in his direction, though when he noticed Sophie biting her bottom lip flirtatiously next to him, he realised he'd been mistaken). 'To us!' he said, raising his glass and 'cheers'-ing the room. 'Now, what are y'all waitin' for? Christmas?' He downed his champagne, threw the empty glass over his shoulder (where it was caught expertly by a member of his entourage), and clapped his hands together, signalling the DJ in the corner to start the music. 'Let's have a good time, people!'

Mark took a sip of champagne, then thought *what the hell*, and drained the rest of the glass. It was Christmas, he'd been offered a promotion, and the woman he loved was standing by his side. Who cared what the rest of the company – no the *world* – thought? Tonight, he and Julie would have a good time if it was the last thing they did.

Then he glanced down at Julie Marshall, who was staring glumly at her untouched drink, and he suddenly feared that it might be.

ᕣᕖ

'To us!'

Calum Irwin chinked his glass against Mia-Rose's, then he leaned across and kissed her shyly on the cheek.

'What was that for?'

'Do I need an excuse to kiss you?'

'Like I'm your sister, you do.' She grabbed Calum by the arm, and pulled him into an alcove on one side of the great hall. 'Come here.'

He held her tight as they kissed, using one of the exhibits as cover from the rest of the revellers, then she suddenly pulled away.

'What's the matter?'

'There's something hard in your pocket.'

Calum blushed. 'I'm *so* sorry . . .'

'No, in your *jacket* pocket.'

Calum paled. He'd transferred the ring to his jacket pocket for safety, but now he could see it was spoiling the line of his suit – not to mention digging into Mia-Rose's chest whenever he held her close. 'Oh, that's just . . .' He paused, mid-sentence, and wondered whether now was the time and the place, but standing behind some scary-looking dinosaur skeleton wasn't quite how he wanted to do this. Besides, the thing was looking like it might pounce (or collapse) on them at any moment, and he was nervous enough without the fear of being buried under a pile of old bones. 'My, um, keys. Sorry.'

'That's okay.' Mia kissed him again, then peered coyly up at the skeleton. 'Do you think he saw us?' She stared at Calum for a moment, then she nudged him. 'Geddit?' she said, collapsing in a fit of giggles.

'Yes, very good.'

'Try and at least pretend you found it funny!' Mia scolded him, then she peered at the neighbouring exhibit. 'Look at this weird tree! It's like it's made of stone.'

'It's petrified,' said Calum, realising that description also applied to him. 'So, are you enjoying yourself?' he asked, in an attempt to change the subject.

'Oh yes! It's a lovely party.' Mia nodded towards the centre of the hall, where a few brave individuals had ventured onto the dance floor. 'And look – there's dancing.'

As Mia-Rose began to move to the music, Calum felt a growing sense of dread. Like most men, he wasn't very good at dancing; why it wasn't taught to boys in school as an essential life skill alongside maths and English had always been beyond him. You had classes where they'd teach you useless things, like how to chase after and kick a ball (or puff around a field avoiding one, in Calum's case), but something so important to a spotty, unconfident kid (and even a slightly-less-spotty just-as-unconfident adult) was left to your own devices. Sure, you could try and practise in front of the TV at home (assuming your mum didn't laugh at you, or even worse, try to join in, as had happened to Calum on more than one occasion), but mastering anything more than the simple step-left-feet-together-step-right-feet-together while randomly waving your arms around (simultaneously trying not to poke anyone else in the eye) surely needed professional instruction? And lately, thanks to what seemed like the never-ending series of dancing programmes on TV, there seemed to be an expectation that *anyone* could dance, from eighty-year-old weathermen to portly actors to ex-rugby stars. But to dance well (and for Calum, dancing well meant dancing well enough so people didn't point and giggle) you had to have a sense of rhythm – and where he was concerned, matching the movements of his feet to the beat was, if you excused the pun, a step too far.

He'd tried going to a class once – Salsa Fit, it had been called, at the gym he'd joined when he was still single. Salsa dancing, so the instructor told him, could burn a thousand calories in an hour, and seeing as the only other time Calum had burned a thousand calories that quickly was when he'd forgotten about the meat-feast-stuffed-crust-with-extra-cheese pizza he'd left in the oven, it had seemed an ideal opportunity for him to slim down. But he'd kicked himself afterwards, having realised that an ability to salsa dance was a fundamental requirement for the class (and he'd kicked himself during the class a couple of times too, not to mention the woman in front of him), so he'd sneaked out through the fire doors after fifteen embarrassing minutes. And ever since then, the only salsa he'd ever been interested in came with a huge bowl of nachos.

What was worse was that Mia-Rose *loved* dancing. And despite her size, she was very good at it too: fluid, languid, and lots of other words that suggested sexy, slinky movements, which, of course, made Calum look (and feel) even worse whenever the two of them were dancing together. And though he loved to watch her, this was preferably from a comfortable chair with a pint of beer by his side, rather than from a foot or so away with (what he was sure were) all eyes on him. What he *didn't* love was the way other men – single men who could dance – would sidle their way up to her, jig a little alongside, and then attempt to 'cut in'. While Mia always politely ignored them, it never failed to make Calum jealous, and although he'd say he didn't mind – that she *should* dance with them (it wasn't fair to not let her have her fun) – it was no fun for him to watch.

Though the one thing he hated even more was, on the rare occasions he *did* get up to dance with Mia, how she'd take pity on him, and tone her moves down, or even – and he detested this the most – grab his hands and attempt to lead him through the basics, like you might a dressed-up toddler at a wedding.

Which – as he realised the price tag was still on his jacket, and right now, was hanging from his top buttonhole as if *he* was for sale for ninety-seven pounds – was exactly how he was feeling.

❦

'So . . .' Stacey Garrity's lingering once-over was making Nathan feel a little self-conscious. 'You're the famous Nathan Field?'

'"Famous"?'

'Oh yes. You have quite the reputation.'

'With who? And for what?'

Stacey smiled. 'With the girls at iFeel, since we began checking out you Seek lot.' She took a step back and looked him up and down again. 'You don't look like a techie.'

'Yes, well, it's dress-down Friday. Or, actually, dress-up Friday. And neither do you.'

She clinked her glass against his. 'I'll take that as a compliment.'

'Nor does he, come to think of it.' Nathan peered towards the staircase, where Tony A. Wood was basking in the applause. 'What's he like, our new lord and master?'

'Tony?' Stacey shrugged. 'What you see is what you get.'

'That's a good thing?'

'In some cases.' Stacey was eyeing him again, though this time, he wasn't finding the sensation unpleasant.

'Do you know him . . . ?' Nathan paused as he worked out how to phrase the question, ' . . . well?'

'What's that supposed to mean?'

'Just that . . . Well, you've been at iFeel for a while, haven't you? According to your LinkedIn profile. Not that I've been checking *you* out – I mean, checking up on you.'

Stacey frowned. 'Oh. Right. Sorry. No, he's a bit . . . eccentric. Comes out with some strange requests from time to time . . . And no, not in *that* way,' she added, in response to Nathan's raised eyebrow. 'His personality doesn't make him the most popular of people. But in general, he kind of leaves us to get on with it. Which is all you can ask for from a boss, right?'

'And what's he planning to do with us?'

'Is there an "us", Nathan?' Stacey said, quickly, which made Nathan blush, and she laughed. 'I'm just teasing you. Big data?'

Nathan did a double take. 'Not really,' he spluttered. 'I mean, I've been going out with someone for a while, but I'm not on Tinder, or anything like—'

'D-a-t-a!' Stacey laughed again. 'Thanks for the personal info, but I'm talking technology. Predictive analytics. With Seek's search capabilities, and our reasoning algorithms . . .' She shook her head briefly. 'It sounds like I'm trying to recruit you for some super-geek crime-fighting organisation. Anyway, Tony's got some vision for the future technological direction of the company that he decided it was easier to buy Seek for than to do all the work in-house, so here we are, merging!'

'And what happens once we've, you know, *merged*?'

Stacey took a sip of champagne. 'Well, you lot are moving over to our offices *en masse*, as you probably know, after Christmas. You're going to be taking over the whole of the ground floor. Though you're technical support. So you'll be coming upstairs. With me.'

Nathan bit off his reply. 'But nothing's been decided yet?'

'Decided?'

'As in who's getting the top job.'

'Tony's got the top job.' Stacey took another sip of champagne, and regarded him over the top of her glass. 'Everything else is up for grabs.'

'Really?' said Nathan, meeting her gaze. He knew he was a little rusty, but Stacey seemed to be flirting with him big time. And while he'd usually have preferred to be the one making the moves, he was surprised to realise that he liked it.

'Really,' said Stacey. 'He's keen to put everyone together and just see how they get on.'

'But he's American, right? So is he keen for us all to be, you know, touchy-feely?'

Stacey set her glass down on a nearby table, then motioned for Nathan to do the same. 'Ask me to dance, and maybe you'll find out.'

❧

Sophie Jones nipped to the toilet to check her makeup (and to make sure her dress hadn't sprung any leaks), then headed back into the great hall, hoping Tony A. Wood wouldn't hold the fact that she'd mistaken him for a cloakroom attendant against her. At least it would be a funny story to tell their grandchildren, she told herself. Or their children. He might not still be around by the time *they* reproduced.

She found a vantage point in front of the dinosaur skeleton and scanned the crowd. Tony A. Wood wasn't that easy to spot, despite his white jacket, mainly because (as she'd seen when he'd stepped off the staircase) he was a head shorter than most of the other people in the room. But Sophie wasn't worried about that. After all, everyone was the same height lying down.

She walked briskly round the perimeter, then cut back through the middle, eventually finding herself standing by what looked like one of those old fairground hook-a-duck games, which she guessed had been laid on as part of tonight's entertainment. As she watched a couple of extremely drunk girls fumbling with their fishing rods, then failing to get the hooks on the end of their lines anywhere near the small metal loops fixed to the backs of the bright yellow rubber ducks floating around in the blue plastic 'pond', an American voice behind her made her jump.

'Thinking 'bout tryin' your luck?'

'Nathan, you're not funny,' she said, wheeling around, though where Nathan's handsome face would normally be, there was only . . . space. She caught her breath, then lowered her gaze by a dozen or so inches.

'Why does everyone from your company keep callin' me "Nathan"?'

'Oh, I'm sorry, Mister, um . . .' Sophie didn't know how to abbreviate him. 'A. Wood?'

'Tony, please.' Tony A. Wood looked her up and down, his eyes lingering on her cleavage, though Sophie knew she shouldn't be offended; that had been her intention when she'd bought the dress.

'Tony. Sorry.'

Tony A. Wood took her hand, and kissed the back of it. Up close, he looked a little older, with a slightly artificial air about him, as if he'd had some 'work' done, but Sophie decided there was nothing wrong with that. After all, if – sorry, *when* – she had his money, she certainly wouldn't think twice about going under the knife to preserve her looks. Though she might give waxing a miss.

'And who maht you be?'

'I might be – well, I *am* – Sophie. Sophie Jones.'

'Is that hyphenated?'

'Is what hyphenated?'

'As in Sophie Sophie-Jones? Ah never quite get it with you Brits and your posh names.'

'Oh. Sorry. No. It's just the one "Sophie".'

Tony A. Wood clicked his fingers, and an aide materialised at his shoulder with two glasses of champagne. 'I hope that's not what they call you?' he said, passing her one.

'No, they call me Sophie. Sophie Jones.'

Tony A. Wood looked a little confused, and when Sophie played their conversation back in her head, she could see why. 'Please. Just call me Sophie.'

'Well, Sophie, d'you think you maht be able to land a li'l feller this evening?'

'I, um, well . . . Oh, you mean the *ducks*.'

'That's right.' He nodded at the game behind her, then picked up one of the rods and handed it to her. 'Here. See if you can't—' he licked his lips '—catch somethin'.'

Sophie smiled, and did as she was told. She'd always been good at fairground games; coming from Eastbourne, where things like this (until she'd been old enough to make her own) had been the only entertainment on the pier, she'd certainly had a lot of practice. Which meant that, even after three glasses of champagne, she was still able to hook a duck at the first attempt.

'What now?' she said, dangling it provocatively in front of Tony A. Wood's face.

232

'You look at its tush.'

'Its . . . what?'

'Tush. Butt.'

'But what?'

Tony A. Wood let out a short laugh. 'Two countries divided bah a common language, eh? Its tush. Ass. Or, as you Brits say, "bottom".'

'Oh. Right.' Nervously, Sophie unhooked the little plastic bird from the end of the line and turned it over. On its bottom, the word 'vodka' was written in black marker pen.

'What's this?'

Tony A. Wood smiled. 'It's a duck shoot.'

'With fishing rods?'

'I'll show you. Every time you hook a duck—' Tony took her by the arm and led her over to the adjoining bar. He handed the duck to the barman, who peered at the word on its bottom, filled a shot glass full of vodka, and set it down in front of her '—you get a shot.'

'What do I do with this?'

'Dahn in one.'

'I'm not sure. I—'

'Ah'm the boss, remember?'

Sophie obediently downed the glassful. She'd never been a vodka girl, and the liquid burned her throat, but she managed it without coughing – something Tony A. Wood seemed impressed by.

'Now it's your turn,' she said, handing him the fishing rod. 'Quid pro quo. Or should that be *dollar* pro quo?'

He frowned at her for a moment, and Sophie wondered whether she *was* the only person who got her jokes, but then he slapped his thigh. 'Ah get it! Dollar instead of "quid". What's your name again?'

'Sophie.'

'Sophie Jones. Ah remember.' Tony A. Wood turned his attention to the pond, and hooked a duck so quickly Sophie wanted to check the end of his fishing rod for magnets.

'You've done this before.'

'When you get to mah age, there's not much you haven't done before,' he said, with a wink, then he smiled, revealing a set of slightly too-perfect teeth. 'What does it say?'

Sophie unhooked the duck, and flipped it over. 'Tequila. Double,' she said to the barman, and Tony A. Wood narrowed his eyes at her in disbelief.

'Really?'

Sophie quickly dropped the duck back into the water. 'You'll just have to take my word for it,' she said, handing him the glass the barman had just given her.

The billionaire gave Sophie a look, then he chugged the contents, and slammed the glass back down onto the bar. 'Tell me, Sophie Jones. What exactly is it you do for me?'

Sophie took a deep breath, suspecting it was now or never (though she already knew that if he hadn't been a billionaire, 'never' would be the appropriate response). 'Whatever you tell me to,' she said.

Tony A. Wood placed one hand on the small of her back, and steered her onto the dance floor. 'In that case, you and ah are going to get on just fine,' he said.

❧

Julie Marshall was beginning to regret accepting Mark Webster's offer of a dance. It was warm in the great hall, and what with the lights, the music, the stress of having to tell Mark she was pregnant, *being* pregnant, and the people spinning around her on the dance floor, she felt in danger of passing out. The fact that she'd thrown up pretty much everything she'd eaten today wasn't helping, so unsteadily, she grabbed Mark's arm, led him back to their table, and slumped into the nearest chair.

'Are you okay?' Mark rolled up his shirtsleeves as he sat down next to her.

'Just a little . . .' Julie couldn't quite find the right word, though she suspected 'pregnant' wasn't it. 'It's hot in here. Let's go outside for a bit.'

Smiling at Mark's not-needing-to-be-asked-twice expression, she allowed herself to be helped up, then, as he collected a couple of glasses of champagne, she grabbed the jacket from back of his chair. They made their way through the doors at the front of the building and out into the cool night air, and as Julie slipped the jacket gratefully over her shoulders, he handed her a glass.

'Thanks.'

'How are you feeling?'

'I just needed some air.'

'Are you warm enough?'

The two of them had found a bench outside the main entrance, sheltered from the light dusting of snow that had fallen while they were inside, which made the Romanesque surroundings look frankly magical, though Mark was doing his best not to shiver in his shirtsleeves, and Julie felt a little guilty for pinching his jacket.

'Are *you*?'

'I'm fine,' he said, his teeth chattering.

'Let me know if you want your jacket back.'

'I will,' he said. 'Though we could share . . .' He slipped an arm round her waist, and rested his forehead against hers. 'Finally, it's just the two of us. And soon it really will be, once you've gotten rid of you-know-who.'

'Pardon?'

Mark grinned, then lowered his voice. 'Your d-i-v-o-r-c-e.'

'I'm not five years old, Mark. You don't have to spell things out for me.'

'Sorry.' He grinned again, then took her lightly by the hand. 'Listen, Julie, I don't want to rush things, but there's something I need to talk to you about. and I know it's only nine months . . .'

Julie shot him a look, then she realised he must be talking about their relationship.

' . . . but something's happened. Something big. And so I don't think you should move in with me in Bermondsey any more.'

Julie almost dropped her glass. Did he *know*? Or was he breaking up with her? Though surely not. Even so, Mark seemed uneasy, and as he took a large gulp of champagne, Julie had to stop herself from doing the same. She knew you weren't supposed to drink if you were pregnant, though how much you could drink – and how pregnant you had to be before it was dangerous – she wasn't so sure about, and of course, she'd 'been pregnant' for a while – and she'd had more than the odd drink, given the run-up to Christmas, so to suddenly stop now might be silly. Besides, it might kick off a conversation she wasn't quite ready to have.

As he nervously clinked his glass against hers, she took the tiniest of sips, and hoped he hadn't seen her spit it surreptitiously back into her glass.

'Not to your liking?'

'Sorry?'

'Can I get you something else? Or do you want to wait until that one's evaporated first?'

'I'm sorry, I . . .' Julie took a deep breath. Whatever big thing Mark needed to tell her, surely hers was bigger, and besides, it might affect what he wanted to say to her. Plus, she owed him full disclosure now, at least, if only to stop him saying something he might regret. 'There's something I need to talk to you about first.'

'What's the matter?'

'I'm pregnant.'

'*Pregnant?*'

'Keep your voice down!'

'I'm sorry.' Mark had stood up, and was pacing back and forth in front of the bench. 'It's just a bit of a shock.'

'For you and me both.'

'When did you find out?'

'This morning.'

'And, um, is it—'

'*Yours?* How can you ask me such a thing? Do you think I've been sleeping with—?'

'"Something you're pleased about", I was actually about to say.'

'Oh. Sorry.' Julie slumped forward and rested her head in her hands. 'I'm not sure, to be honest.'

'Ah.' Mark sat back down next to her. 'We've never talked about kids. Wanting them.'

'And do you?'

Mark shrugged. 'I've never really thought about it, to be honest. I kind of just assumed that if the woman I loved wanted them, then I'd be having them.'

'Well, think about it, will you?'

'Sorry, sorry. Yes.'

As he stared off into the distance, Julie let out a loud sigh. 'Not *right now.*'

'Sorry.'

'And stop saying sorry!'

'Sor . . . Yes, of course.' He leant back and gazed up at the night sky. 'Wow. A baby. How . . . ? Well, I don't mean "how", obviously. Any fool knows that. It was more of a "when". Though it came out as a "how". And now I'm babbling.'

'There's something else I haven't told you.'

Mark was staring at her now, but before she could tell him about the divorce, a loud 'Webster! There you are!' came echoing from behind them. Tony A. Wood had emerged from the building, and was striding towards them, the whiteness of his jacket (and his teeth) making him difficult to spot against the snowy backdrop.

'Oh. Yes. Mister . . . I mean, Tony.' Mark had jumped up from the bench again. 'Hello. Can I introduce you to Julie Marshall? She's Seek's . . .'

'Marketin' di-rector. Ah know. Ah've heard good things about you, Julie. And ah like your assistant. Very . . .' Tony paused, and Julie smiled.

'Yes, it's hard to think of a word that sums Sophie up, isn't it?' she said.

'So . . .' Tony put his arm around Mark's shoulders. 'Are you kids having a good time?'

'Yes,' said Mark. 'It's a fantastic party. Thanks so much for, you know, paying for it. And about earlier, on the phone. I'm sorry. I thought you were—'

'*Nathan Field.* Ah know. It seems to be a common misconception.' Tony waved him away. 'But you can stop the brown-nosin', Webster. We're here to have fun.'

'Yes, sir,' said Mark, though Julie wondered if it was ironic.

'We're having a lovely time,' she said. 'Thank you. It's a fantastic venue.'

Tony A. Wood looked round at the building, as if seeing it for the first time. 'Certainly cost me a bundle – not to mention the deposit in case y'all broke anythin'.' He jabbed a thumb back towards the museum's entrance. 'You won't believe what an old dinosaur is worth.'

About one point two six billion dollars? wondered Julie, then, to her horror, she realised she'd wondered it out aloud.

'That's funny.' Tony A. Wood narrowed his eyes. 'Though if it's such a great party, what are the two of you doin' out here?'

Mark flicked his eyes at her. 'We just came out for some air.'

Tony looked at the two of them suspiciously. 'Air. Right. Well, Julie, assumin' you're fine breathin' on your own, can ah just borrow Webster here for a moment? There's somethin' important we need tuh discuss.'

'Of course,' said Julie, shrugging off the jacket and handing it back to Mark, but he waved it away.

'I'll be right back,' he said, the expression on his face suggesting there was something *they* needed to discuss too.

⁊

From the table they'd been seated at, which seemed to consist of most of Seek's senior management team, Calum Irwin scanned the dance floor anxiously. He and Mia-Rose were the only ones yet to venture out there, where the Seek group had occupied a central position: Mary so drunk it was as if she was dancing to a different song to the one playing, Benedict . . . Well, people were leaving a respectable distance around him, and given how much he was sweating, you didn't have to be Sherlock Holmes to work out why. Nathan was with some gorgeous woman Calum didn't recognise, the two of them moving like they'd been rehearsing their routine for weeks. Sophie had briefly managed to get Tony A. Wood up there too, though their 'dancing' seemed to consist mainly of Tony trying to grab her, and Sophie expertly sashaying just out of his reach, before Tony had given up and left her to it. Even Mark Webster had been dancing with Julie Marshall earlier, though they'd been so formal with each other it almost looked like they were brother and sister, and they'd abandoned the floor after just a few minutes.

As one of his favourite tracks came on, he turned and gazed at Mia, nodding his head in time to the music, and – too late – realised he'd made a mistake.

'Come and dance with me?'

'Do I have to?'

Mia pretended to look hurt. 'I didn't realise it was such a chore.'

'That wasn't what I meant. It's just that dancing and me—'

'*Calum . . .*'

'Sorry.'

'Come on. It'll be *fun*,' she said, though Calum doubted it as – reluctantly – he allowed himself to be led (or rather, dragged) into the midst of the gyrating bodies.

As Nathan greeted him with raised eyebrows, he stood there hopelessly, then realised that just standing still would make him stand out even more, so he began his usual shuffle, hoping that with everyone this drunk and with the dance floor this crowded, no one would notice how bad he was. And then, the worst thing possible happened. *No, it couldn't be*, he thought, wishing he was back at the safety of his table. Because, to the strains of Snap!'s 'I've Got the Power', the group was forming a *circle*.

Calum knew what would happen next. Some brave (or drunk) person would leap (or stumble) into the middle, where they'd perform a bit of exaggerated dancing for a few moments before happily re-joining the perimeter, only for someone else to take – or be shoved into – their place. And inevitably, one of those 'someones' would eventually be him.

Sure enough, Benedict stepped his way into the centre, making what Calum understood were 'rave'-type moves with his arms (and causing those people nearest to him to wrinkle their noses), before sidling back to his original spot to a round of applause. Then Sophie . . . Well, he wasn't sure what her moves were called, but they involved a lot of upping and downing, and certainly had the attention of every man in the circle, maybe hoping that the flimsy straps on her dress might give way. Next came Mary, whose hands-on-the-ground backside-shaking moves that Mia had enthusiastically exclaimed 'Twerk it, girl!' at were followed by her storming off the dance floor in tears, protesting how she'd simply slipped and was actually trying to get back up. Even Nathan took his turn (having been reluctantly encouraged into the centre by the girl he'd been dancing with), stopping dead still for a few seconds before launching into what was probably an ironic (yet pretty smooth, Calum had to admit) *Saturday Night Fever* finger-pointing hip-shaking take-off.

He looked on in horror, knowing it would be his turn soon, but what to do? He could try and be funny like Nathan and run the risk of people thinking it was his normal dancing, or just *do* his normal dancing, and have people *think* he was trying to be funny. But be funny how? Apart from a Seventies disco parody like Nathan had already nailed, a bad moonwalk (i.e. Calum's best moonwalk), or pretending to be one of those white-faced mimes you saw in Covent Garden, what else could you do? His backside was certainly big enough to give twerking a go, but get that wrong, and he could be thrown out for indecency. Plus his trousers might split.

Maybe he should grab Mia, take her into the centre of the circle with him, and let her lead them. Perhaps they could even attempt some *Strictly*-type ballroom moves – all he'd need to do was let himself go loose in Mia's arms, and she'd do the work . . . It was that or suddenly feigning an injury.

Then, like a flash of the most brilliant lightning, it occurred to him: the centre of the circle would be the perfect place to propose. He'd drag Mia there, then, while she danced, and as all eyes were on her, he'd slowly sink to the floor in some kind of move – maybe The Twist, he hadn't decided yet, or maybe even without a twist, and more like just a kneel – surreptitiously slip the ring from his pocket, and do the deed.

The more he thought about it, the more he was convinced this was the perfect plan. So what if his plans for a romantic proposal had fallen by the wayside? That was hardly his fault. Old Amsterdam hadn't worked out, and the quiet corner of the museum they'd found themselves in earlier hadn't seemed quite romantic enough – he wanted her to remember the moment for his sincerity, not for the skeleton of the giant sloth they'd been standing next to (though Calum knew if he didn't get a move on, 'Giant Sloth' would describe him pretty well).

As he danced with Mia, enjoying the fact that the focus on the dancer in the circle meant he could just continue to rock from side to side while clapping half-heartedly without having to make any elaborate moves, it struck him that this was in fact a better way to propose than in front of some dusty old pile of bones, or a mouldy, stuffed, long-extinct specimen. Here, in the middle of the dance floor, to one of his favourite songs, and in front of everyone they knew, *he* had the power. Not Snap! And while he'd seen videos on YouTube of public proposals gone wrong, men who'd assumed the position in the middle of packed baseball stadiums or on the 'kiss cam' at ice hockey games, only to see their intended throw their hands over their mouths in shock, and then make for the exit as if pursued by a ravenous bear, surely Mia wouldn't do that to him. Not *here*.

He took a deep breath, trying to stop his heart from hammering – though that was as much from the exertion of dancing as his nervousness – and suddenly, a feeling of extreme emotion came over him. This was it! Something he wanted to ask only once. The biggest question he'd ever ask in his life. And the most important one too. To the most important person in his life.

The only problem, Calum realised, was that the ring was still in his jacket pocket, and he'd left his jacket on the back of his chair, and to go and get it . . . Well, Mia would wonder where he was going, or might follow him, and maybe they'd miss their 'turn' in the circle, plus he might lose his nerve and not come back. Besides, this way, it'd seem more spontaneous. In any case, he could present it to her later.

He rehearsed the question a final time in his head, slightly worried that the more he repeated it, the more it didn't make sense, a bit like when you repeated a word over and over and it lost all its meaning. But how could 'Will you marry me?' ever lose its meaning?

To his surprise, Calum felt himself getting a little teary. He'd never been a crier, but now he was worried he was about to break that habit, and as he fought to stop the lump in his throat from becoming full-on waterworks, Mia leaned across to speak into his ear.

'Are you okay?'

'More than okay,' he said, or rather squeaked, and Mia smiled.

'Me too,' she said, kissing him briefly, and Calum's heart almost burst.

'Mia,' he said. 'I have a question for you.'

'Okay. But are you sure?'

Calum nodded. He'd never been more sure of anything in his life. But then he noticed that Mia was looking at him strangely, so he took a step back. 'What?'

'Are you sure that you're okay?'

'Why?'

'Your eyes are watering.'

'Are they?' Calum blinked a few times. 'It must be my contact lenses playing up,' he said, trying to make light of it. He reached up to rub his eyes, surprised how wet his hands were when they came away, then told himself it was now or never. Though that wasn't strictly true, he knew. He'd propose a hundred times, if that was what it took for her to say yes.

With a final nervous glance around the dance floor, he pulled Mia into the middle of the whooping circle of Seek employees and dropped to his knee, then looked up at her. The tears were coming thick and fast now, but Calum didn't care. This way, she'd know exactly how strongly he felt about her. And (he hoped, sneakily), the sight of him crying might influence her decision a little more in his favour. He caught Nathan's eye just in time to see him make an 'oh my God' face, then opened his mouth and began to speak, but he hadn't got any further than the 'w' of 'will' when – to his horror – Mia knelt down in front of him.

'Have you dropped a contact lens again?'

'What?'

'A contact lens. Like earlier, in your office. Is that why your eyes are watering?'

'What, no, I . . . I wanted to ask . . .' Calum began to panic. With Mia down at his level, this was hardly the proposal he'd been planning. 'Will you . . . ?'

'Will I what?'

'Stand up for a second.'

'Hold on.' Mia-Rose hauled herself to her feet, though now she was towering right over him.

'And could you move back a bit?'

'Sure,' said Mia, then, to Calum's dismay, she began to clear people away from the area where they'd been dancing. 'Bit of space, please, people,' she said, loudly. 'Contact lens emergency.'

'No, I . . .' But before Calum could explain, someone had rushed over and had a word with the DJ, and then – to make matters worse – the lights went up and the music suddenly stopped.

As everyone stopped dancing, he began to feel ridiculous, as if he was in some weird reverse flash mob. Mia was still standing over him, so his window of opportunity was technically still open, but to propose *now* would surely lose its impact, especially since a number of people had dropped to their knees next to him to help him comb the floor.

Not knowing what else to do, he began peering around the floor himself, through the only thing he was trying to find was an excuse to get back up again – either that, or a switch he could flick that would erase the last two minutes. Then, suddenly, Nathan was squatting down next to him.

'Found it,' he announced loudly, with a wink in Calum's direction.

'What?' Calum, frowned, then as Nathan pretended to hand the imaginary lens to him, he twigged what was going on. 'Oh, er, thanks, Nathan,' he said, equally loudly.

'Don't mention it!' Nathan leapt back to his feet, then hauled Calum up by the arm. 'Nothing to see here,' he announced, then he waved at the DJ, and the music started up again. 'As you were.'

Calum made a play of re-inserting his lens, then he took one look at Mia, who'd begun dancing again, brushed the dirt off his knees, and moved over to join her.

Though as Lionel Richie launched into the opening bars of 'Easy,' Calum was starting to believe that this proposal business was anything but.

11.

'So, Mark.' Tony A. Wood had his arm around Mark Webster's shoulders as they walked, which Mark found more than a little awkward. For one thing, he had never been a particularly touchy-feely kind of guy – even he and Julie hardly ever walked like this – and for another, he was a good foot taller than Tony, and therefore was having to stoop quite considerably. 'It is Mark, ain't it?'

'It is,' said Mark, relieved they'd moved on from the 'Webster' phase of their relationship.

'Ah didn't interrupt anythin' back there, ah hope, between you and the li'l lady?'

Mark raised both eyebrows. If this was the 'no employee relations' thing, then quite frankly, he was prepared to tell Tony to get stuffed. Though perhaps not using those exact words.

'No,' he lied, just to be on the safe side. 'We were just . . . talking.'

'Talkin'. Oh-kay.' Tony A. Wood winked at him. 'So, have you thought about mah offer?'

'Well . . .' Mark's heart began to hammer. He'd done nothing but think about it (apart from when he was thinking about his dilemma with Julie). He'd even decided to accept it. Right up until Julie's bombshell five minutes ago.

'It'd be a significant raise, obviously.'

'Great.'

'And you'd get more options.'

Mark almost laughed. Given the conversation he'd just had with Julie, options were the one thing he didn't have. He shivered again – not surprisingly, he realised, given that it had started to snow again, and he was outside in his shirtsleeves.

'And ah'm sure ah don't need to tell you how much better the weather is in San Francisco than here in this godforsaken country,' continued Tony. 'So. Whaddaya say?'

'I . . .' Mark stared down at him, unable to believe what he was about to do. '. . . can't.'

Tony A. Wood removed his arm from Mark's shoulders. 'What?'

'I can't. Take the job. Move to America.'

'Wah not?'

'Because . . .' Mark took a deep breath, 'I'm having a baby.'

Tony A. Wood glanced down at his stomach.

'Well, not me personally.'

'So bring your wife with you.'

'She's not my wife. She's still married to someone else. Well, to all intents and purposes, she's his ex-wife—'

'Not one of mine, ah hope?'

'No! Of course not—'

'Well, what's the problem? Marry her, bring her.'

Mark looked at him. Tony was obviously someone used to getting his own way. Or not, given his three divorces. 'I'm not sure she'd want to.'

'Marry you? Or come to the US?'

'It's not as simple as that.' He glanced back over his shoulder, though he couldn't see Julie any more.

'Aha!'

'I'm sorry. What does "aha" mean?'

247

'It *is* her, ain't it? Julie Marshall.' Tony A. Wood folded his arms. 'This is your career we're talkin' about, Webster. Don't throw it all away over some woman.'

'She's not just "some woman". She's the woman I love. And she's having my – sorry, *our* – baby. So I'm sorry, but I can't just up and hotfoot it across the Atlantic at five minutes' notice.'

'Oh-kay.' Tony A. Wood sighed. 'What's it gonna take?'

'Pardon?'

He reached into his jacket pocket, removed an envelope, and handed it to Mark. 'This is your official offer. Ah generally like to do things on a handshake, but mah legal team has told me that ain't worth the paper it ain't written on, so . . .'

Mark stared at the envelope, then tore it open and extracted the piece of paper from inside.

'What do you think?'

'It's . . .' His knees went slightly weak as he saw the figure, '. . . very generous.'

'So say "yes".'

'I can't.'

'Playing hardball, eh? Okay. Another ten thousand dollars.'

'No.'

'Twenty.'

'It's not about the money.'

Tony A. Wood let out a short laugh. 'It's *always* about the money.'

'Not for me, it isn't.'

'She's just a woman, Webster. Take it from me, there'll be plenty more where she came from. Especially when you're rich—'

'You'll excuse me if I don't take relationship advice from a man with three ex-wives?'

Tony A. Wood shot him a warning glance. 'Don't make me angry, Webster. You wouldn't like me when ah'm angry.'

'Yes, well, from what I've heard, no one likes you anyway.'

As Tony A. Wood stared at him, Mark swallowed hard. He hadn't known what had come over him, but he feared he might have just quite possibly committed professional suicide, and with a baby on the way, that perhaps wasn't the most sensible of moves. Then, to his surprise, Tony A. Wood started laughing.

'Ah like you, Webster,' he said, putting his arm back round Mark's shoulders and steering him towards the entrance. 'You've got spunk!'

Mark made a face. That was exactly what had got him into all this trouble in the first place.

～

Sophie Jones sat on her stool and peered at the impressive selection of multicoloured bottles that filled the mirrored shelves behind the bar, trying to decide what cocktail to order next. Sophie was a huge fan of cocktails, despite the innuendos – she'd lost count of the times she'd been out and some slimy creep had materialised beside her, fixed a leering smile on his face, and asked her if she fancied a 'slow, comfortable screw against the wall', or a 'screaming orgasm'. And while she still hadn't lived down the time she'd been flirting with this guy on Tinder and she'd meant to type 'I love cocktails' in a message and her autocorrect had left off the 'tails' part (though Sophie hadn't noticed until much later, and only then realised why the conversation had taken such a sudden lowbrow turn), it hadn't put her off.

'What can I get you?' asked the elaborately tattooed barman, who was also sporting the most impressive beard Sophie had ever seen.

'What's good here?' she asked, fighting the temptation to reach across the bar and stroke it.

The barman shrugged. 'Everything?'

'What can you make?'

He shrugged again. 'Anything.'

'Well, what do you recommend?'

'What do you like?'

Sophie was about to reply 'everything', but she wasn't sure what that would say about her, so she decided against it. 'Something . . . sophisticated.'

'Wah are mah ears burnin'?'

Sophie turned round with a start. A breathless Tony A. Wood was climbing awkwardly up onto the adjacent stool as if attempting to summit Everest without oxygen, a somewhat bewildered-looking Mark Webster downing a drink as if he really needed one behind him.

'What's your poison?'

Sophie jabbed a thumb at the barman. 'He was just asking me the same question.'

'And what's your answer?'

Sophie thought quickly. Cocktails were classy, so this was her chance to impress Tony with her classiness (if that was even a word). And while she didn't know what they drank in San Francisco, she knew at least one with an American theme.

'Manhattan.'

Tony A. Wood raised both eyebrows. 'Good choice,' he said, then he turned to the barman and stuck two fingers up at him, which Sophie thought was a bit rude even if he *was* paying for the whole party, until she remembered that the American way of indicating 'two' was the other way round to the English one.

'Two Manhattans coming up,' said the barman. 'Bourbon in both?'

Sophie frowned – or at least, according to the mirror behind the bar, narrowed her eyes. Sticking a biscuit in a cocktail seemed a little strange, but then again, Americans did have some funny food combinations, like bacon and maple syrup, or peanut butter and jam, so she nodded. 'Why not?'

As the barman filled a cocktail shaker with something Sophie was a little embarrassed to note was actually called 'bourbon', and not the chocolate finger sandwich she'd been picturing, Tony A. Wood swivelled round to face her.

'This is a lovely party,' she said, relieved Mark Webster seemed to have disappeared – the last thing she wanted was for him to over-hear her flirting with their new owner. 'Though it must be costing you a fortune?'

'Depends on your definition of "fortune".'

'Well, *your* definition is surely a billion dollars?'

Tony A. Wood laughed. 'Whatever. It's just a number.'

'It's a *big* number.'

'Too big, perhaps. No one can possibly spend that amount of money.'

Sophie let out a short laugh. She'd be more than prepared to give it her best shot. 'You spent a fair bit of it on buying us, though.'

'True. Though there's still a bit left for what you could call a "rainy day". Which you have kind of a lot of this side of the Pond.'

Sophie smiled politely, though the British weather would be one thing she wouldn't miss when she was living in California.

The barman had placed two cocktail glasses on the bar in front of them, so she helped herself to the nearest one. It looked good, the liquid a deep red-brown colour, a frosting on the pre-chilled glass, and with what looked like a cherry on a cocktail stick balanced across the top. And though she wasn't particularly fond of cherries, she decided against asking Tony if he'd like hers, unsure whether the phrase meant the same in American as it did in English.

With a silent 'cheers', she chinked her glass against his, and took a sip. 'Wow. That's . . .'

Tony A. Wood grinned. 'A bit rich for you, eh?'

You? Or the drink? Thought Sophie, then she shook her head. 'Not at all,' she said.

'Well, there's more where that came from.'

'First the vodka, now this! Are you trying to get me drunk?'

'Yup.' Tony A. Wood grinned. 'But then again, ah'm tryin' to get *everyone* drunk,' he said, nodding towards the middle of the hall.

'So, are we all going to lose our jobs?'

'You sure are direct, aren't you?' Tony A. Wood paused, his drink halfway to his mouth. 'And why would you think that?'

'Because that's what you people do, isn't it?'

'*You people?*'

'Billionaires. You come in, take over the top floor of some posh hotel, drive around in your fancy sports cars while you buy companies, break them up, sell all the pieces for more than you paid for the whole thing, unless somebody can convince you that you can make something of one—'

'Hey, Purdy Woman.'

'Thank you. But don't try and change the subject—'

'No – that's the plot of *Purdy Woman*. What you just described. Life's not like the movies, Sophie. That's not what ah do.' Tony A. Wood took another sip of his Manhattan, then smiled. 'In case you hadn't heard, ah'm a billionaire. That means not having to worry about tryin' to save a few dollars here and there by firin' people. Ah bought Seek because what you do complements what ahFeel does – not overlaps. Everyone who wants to stay can keep their old jobs.' He waved the hand holding his glass around the room, stopping when he saw Mark Webster, who appeared to be frantically searching for someone. 'Some people maht even get new ones. Ah promise.'

'Pleased to hear it.' Sophie took another sip of her cocktail. 'So, what *are* your intentions?'

Tony A. Wood looked a little startled. 'Mah *intentions*?

'Towards us. Seek, I mean,' she said, quickly. 'Are you going to try and make another billion from this merger?'

'Ah am.' He cast a disparaging glance towards the dance floor, where the Seek and iFeel staff were dancing in two separate areas, as if someone had erected an invisible fence between the two groups. 'Assumin' you people actually start mergin' before ah'm as extinct as one of them dino-fellers y'all are dancin' round. Tell me somethin', Sophie. Are you a golfer?'

'Not really. I've been to the driving range once or twice. But I've never actually played a round.'

'That's a shame,' Tony said. 'Because ah'd love to play a round with you some time.'

Sophie blushed, unsure if Tony was being rude or not.

'Anyhow, mah point is this: some folks think business is a little like golf,' he continued.

'How so?'

'Well, since you ask, the objective with golf is to get better at golf in order to play less golf, if you think about it.'

Sophie thought about it. Then thought about it some more. 'You're better, so you don't have to take as many . . .' She hesitated. What was the technical term: hits? Goes?

'Strokes,' said Tony A. Wood, patting her lingeringly on the thigh. 'Precisely. And that's exactly how ah see business, except for one subtle difference: the better ah am at business, the more time ah'll have to do more of it.'

'And what exactly is the "it" you want to do more of?' said Sophie, though the way Tony A. Wood couldn't seem to resist staring at her chest every five seconds, she suspected a better question might have been 'Who?', and that she already knew the answer.

'Ah don't know yet. Ah've been too busy with ahFeel to come up with somethin'. But buying Seek should mean ah'm well placed for whatever di-rection the industry wants to go in.'

'So you're not planning to build a reusable space rocket, or make electric cars, or eradicate disease, or anything like that?'

Tony A. Wood laughed. 'Ah leave that "savin' the planet" bull to them other folks. Besides, ah've got one or two more important things to do first.'

'Such as?'

'Drink this, for example.' Tony A. Wood chinked his glass against hers, then peered closely at her face. 'You're one cool customer, you know? Hard to read.'

'That'll be the Botox,' blurted Sophie.

'What?'

'Nothing.' Sophie took another sip of her cocktail. It really was going down rather well, as were all her gambits so far this evening. For good measure, she picked up the cocktail stick and tried to eat her cherry as suggestively as she could, though given her face still felt a little numb, she was sure she was probably dribbling down her chin, but when Tony A. Wood's eyes widened as if she'd pressed a button, she began to giggle.

'What's funny?'

'You.' She looked aghast, realising she'd just called her new boss 'funny'. 'I mean, not actually you. It's just . . . I've never met a billionaire before.'

'Ah hope ah'm not a disappointment?'

'Oh no,' said Sophie, quickly. 'Though I don't know what I was expecting, really. The only billionaires I've ever seen have been on TV or in films, and they're either master criminals who want to take over the world only for James Bond to come and kill them in some ingenious way, or crime fighters who dress up at night in rubber costumes, or, you know, sexual perverts. Though those last two could be the same.' She stopped talking. Vinay had told her once she could take three hours to tell him about a two-hour film, and the last thing she wanted to do was to babble on.

'Ah'm glad you think ah'm neither.'

'Well, it's still early days . . .' Sophie slapped her hand over her mouth. 'I'm sorry. I didn't mean it like that at all.' She stared, embarrassed, into her glass, then realised it was already empty.

Tony A. Wood drained the rest of his Manhattan. 'Did you want another?'

'I'd better not.' Sophie put her glass down. 'Unless *you* did? You're the boss, after all.'

'Well . . .' He clambered off his stool. 'Do you know what ah *would* like?'

'What's that?'

'Another dance.'

Sophie obediently climbed down from her seat – a move that put her chest level with his face, something that he didn't seem too displeased about. 'Your wish is my command!'

And as Tony A. Wood took her by the hand, and led her onto the dance floor, Sophie congratulated herself. Surely it was only a matter of time before he was saying those exact same words to her.

᠀

Nathan Field was in that happy place between being slightly drunk, and knowing one more drink might well take him over the edge. This was a problem, not just because he already suspected he'd be popping ibuprofen like Tic Tacs tomorrow morning, but because so far Stacey had matched him glass for glass, and if he *was* going to miss out on the top job, there was no way he wanted to lose this particular contest.

Not that he worried it would actually have some bearing on who got the support director's job within the new organisation. Nathan had a suspicion that he wasn't even in the running. Stacey was more qualified than he was, more experienced – even if Tony A. Wood wasn't making the final decision (and given the way he'd been following Sophie around like a puppy dog all evening, Nathan already suspected the billionaire's judgement could be swayed by a pretty face, and the more time he spent with Stacey, the more he realised she had one of those), it was already clear to him that she deserved it. What was also clear to him was that working underneath her – if you excused the phrase – would be a position Nathan would happily settle for.

'Okay,' he said, as they sat at the bar, recovering from their last dancing session. 'Windows or Mac O/S?'

'Windows. I try to be as PC as possible.' She leant over and dug him in the ribs. 'You?'

'Same. Apple or Android?'

'Windows phone, actually. You?'

'In theory, Windows phone. In practice . . .'

'Fair enough.' Stacey smiled. 'I'm sensing a pattern here.'

'As am I.' He pointed at Stacey's empty glass, and when she nodded, signalled the barman for a refill. 'It's all about compatibility for me.'

Stacey raised one carefully plucked eyebrow. 'Really, Nathan?'

'Really. Try plugging a micro-USB into a firewire port . . . No – scratch that. Silly example, especially with USB-C on the way. But if your two systems can't talk to each other, can't connect . . .' The waiter had refilled his glass too, so he took another sip, the bubbles making his brain feel like he had too many tabs open, and Nathan wondered how many glasses – or was it bottles? – he'd had this evening. 'Then what's the point?'

'So, you don't believe in this "opposites attract" stuff, then?'

Nathan glanced over towards the dance floor, where Tony A. Wood was engaged in a vigorous bout of what could only be described as 'dad dancing' in front of a bemused-looking Sophie. 'I think the jury's still out on that one.'

A passing waiter was offering them a tray of snacks, and Stacey gladly helped herself to a mini hamburger. 'Thanks,' she said, stuffing the whole thing into her mouth and chewing it hungrily, followed by an indignant 'What?' when she noticed Nathan's expression.

'Sorry.' Nathan took one himself. 'It's just nice to meet a woman who actually *eats*.'

'As opposed to?'

Stacey was eyeing his burger, so he handed it over. 'Pushes a lettuce leaf around her plate all evening because she's scared of getting fat.'

'I don't really go in for all that "my body is a temple" stuff,' she said, her mouth full, and Nathan took the opportunity to cast his eyes slyly over her figure. From where he was sitting, it looked more like an amusement park.

'So,' she continued, washing it down with a mouthful of champagne. 'Shall we hit the dance floor again, or what?'

'What?' said Nathan, then he grinned. He was having a good time, he realised. He just hoped it wouldn't go wrong soon. 'Come on, then.'

They made their way onto the floor, to an enthusiastic 'thumbs up' from Tony (although Nathan suspected it could simply have been one of his 'moves'), but just as he was preparing himself for that always-awkward transition from walking onto the dance floor to actual dancing, the music changed.

'Ah,' said Nathan, turning to go, but Stacey grabbed his arm.

'What are you doing?'

'Well, unless you want to slow dance to "Lady in Red", I thought—'

'You're going nowhere, mister. I was promised a dance. And I'm wearing red. So suck it up,' She waggled a finger in his face. 'And no singing.'

Nathan reached for her awkwardly, not quite knowing how (or where) to hold her. He hadn't slow-danced with someone since Ellie, possibly a good five years ago, at a friend's wedding (and to the same song, he remembered with a shudder), and he was a bit rusty as to the mechanics, particularly with someone he hardly knew. But Stacey didn't give him a chance to be bashful, as she grabbed him by the wrists, placed his hands just above her hips, then rested her hands on his shoulders.

As they started to sway slowly to the music, Nathan careful to avoid any frontal contact, he told himself to relax. Stacey smelt, well, *good*. Issey Miyake, or one of those citrusy perfumes, with a sweet hint of alcohol on her breath. And she was certainly fit – he could feel the tight band of muscle at her waist as her hips moved from side to side. Then – and he didn't know if it was her pulling him closer, or just that the suddenly crowded dance floor was making them stand less further apart – their bodies were almost touching, and it was awkward to keep holding her hips because that made his elbows stick out, so he slid his hands round and linked his fingers behind the small of her back, careful not to touch anything that could technically count as 'bottom', and she looked up at him, so he bent his head down, and . . .

'Great to see you kids gettin' on.' A sweaty, panting Tony A. Wood had sidled up to them. 'Good for inter-company relations,' he said, leering down the top of Stacey's dress, before slinking off in pursuit of a hurriedly retreating Sophie.

'There's only one person on this dance floor who's getting on,' said Stacey, and Nathan laughed.

'Is he always like that?'

'Like what?'

'With women. He just tried to look down your top,' said Nathan, conscious he'd done the same countless times this evening.

'Sometimes he's worse. But he's harmless. Unlike you, Mister Field?'

Nathan felt himself blush. 'What are you talking about?'

'You were about to try and kiss me!'

'No I wasn't.'

'Yes you were.'

'No, I wasn't.'

'Well, what were you doing?'

'Er . . .' Nathan thought quickly. The truth was, he *had* been about to kiss her – although now he feared the moment had passed. 'I think I must have been about to drop off. The champagne, and Chris De Burgh . . .'

Stacey gave him a sceptical look.

'But say I had been?'

'Had been what? Trying to stick your tongue down my throat on the dance floor in front of everyone, after only knowing me for a couple of hours?'

But that was the thing, Nathan thought, as the music changed to something more up-tempo. *I feel I've known you all my life.* 'Well, yes.'

Stacey steered him over to the nearest table, picked up a Christmas hat that some bright spark had fixed a sprig of mistletoe to the front of, and slotted it onto her head. 'There's only one way to find out,' she said.

❦

Julie Marshall pulled the jacket tighter around her as she shivered on the bench. There was no sign of Mark, and she wasn't surprised. Her news had obviously thrown him, but by the looks of

Tony A. Wood, he'd had big things he wanted to discuss with Mark too, and – ever the corporate man – Julie suspected she knew where his priorities lay.

She wondered whether she should go back inside, but they needed to finish this conversation, and in front of everyone was the last place she wanted to do that – though surely even that was better than dying of hypothermia. Resolving to give him another five minutes, she stuck her hands into the jacket's pockets, desperate to find a bit more warmth. Though in the inside one, she *actually* found what felt like a jewellery box.

Julie fished it out and stared at it in the moonlight. Surely this wasn't what Mark was planning to 'discuss' with her? Or at least, *had* been planning, until her news had somewhat trumped his.

Her breathing quickening, she glanced back towards the museum's entrance, and told herself to relax. It couldn't be a ring. Well, it *could* be a ring – the box was certainly the right size and shape. But that didn't necessarily mean it was an *engagement* ring. In any case, she should just put it right back where she found it. It was up to Mark to decide when – sorry, if – she saw whatever it was, not her. Though she immediately knew she wouldn't be able to resist having a peek.

Nervously, she opened the box, gasping when she saw the diamond sitting on the band. Okay, the stone was perhaps a little smaller than she might have chosen for herself, especially given what Mark earned, and the ring itself looked a little big for her finger, but . . . She stopped herself. She and Mark hadn't even discussed this. They'd been dating for nine months. Nine months! And she'd only just got divorced. Today!

Perhaps he'd already found out about the baby. Maybe this was his way of convincing her to have it. That everything would be alright, and they'd bring it up together as husband and wife . . . But how on earth could he have? He couldn't have seen the testing kits, and unless he'd talked to Sophie . . . Julie doubted it. Sophie wouldn't have said anything, especially not after the mix-up she'd gotten herself into on Valentine's Day, and double-especially not about something so sensitive. In any case, she'd hardly been in the office all day, so when on earth she'd have had an opportunity, Julie couldn't think.

It occurred to her that Mark didn't do anything without thinking it through first, so maybe this was his casual way of proposing: Not in the traditional way, but to let her find it like this. No pressure; she'd make the discovery in her own time, on her own, and therefore be able to respond to it in a considered manner, rather than in a (down-on-one) knee-jerk reaction to the emotional impact a formal proposal might provoke. After all, he'd done the same thing on Valentine's Day. Not that *that* had quite gone as planned.

She quickly considered her options. Out here, in front of this beautiful building, with this wonderful snowy setting, and in the moonlight – you'd have to be stupid to not realise that this was the perfect opportunity for a proposal. But after only nine months, and with the two of them not even sure what they'd be doing any coming weekend, rather than for the rest of their lives . . . Besides, he didn't even know she was divorced now – another thing Julie felt ashamed of not telling him – and she knew Mark well enough to know he wouldn't even think about proposing until she was legally able to accept.

She could go back inside, of course. Pretend she'd never seen it, and head off any other attempts he might make this evening. Or she could take the ring now, and hide it in her handbag. After all, no ring would mean no proposal . . . But that would be mean. Not to mention stealing.

With a loud sigh, Julie decided it was cards-on-the-table time. She'd tell him about the divorce, explain that she'd found the ring, and then . . . Well, romantic it wouldn't be, but the two of them would just have to have a full and frank discussion until they'd made some decisions.

She gritted her teeth – as much to stop them from chattering as to confirm her resolve – picked up her still-full glass of champagne, and headed back inside.

♋

Calum Irwin led Mia-Rose to the far end of the great hall and up the right-hand part of the staircase, desperately trying to find a quiet spot. He'd given up on the idea of a public gesture, deciding instead that taking Mia somewhere completely private might be more appropriate, firstly to remove any chances of someone – or something – interrupting him, but particularly to spare his blushes if she (as he was now almost completely convinced she would) said 'no'.

Still sweaty from his dancing, he'd not dared to put his jacket back on yet in case the perspiration might ruin it, but – wanting to propose in it for maximum effect – he'd rescued it from the back of his chair. Now, he was carrying it carefully, making sure the ring wouldn't fall out of the pocket as he did so, reassured by the solid feel of the box in his grip.

'Look,' said Mia, pointing at a glass case at the end of the landing, and Calum suddenly felt he might be getting his first break of the evening. Mia's favourite animal was the gorilla, and although proposing to her next to the dead, stuffed version in front of them might not be the most tasteful thing to do, at least it made him look small in comparison. He could only hope he wouldn't be *feeling* small, once he'd done the deed.

As Mia gazed through the glass at the gorilla, which had a rather surprised expression on its face, as if being stuffed (though Calum assumed that had happened after it had died) had taken it completely unawares, he took a couple of breaths and did his best to slow his heart-rate down to something that wouldn't alarm them in an emergency room. He'd read somewhere that the average heart was the size of a fist, and he could well believe that, given how his was thumping against the inside of his chest. Checking Mia was still distracted, he surreptitiously reached into his pocket and removed the ring box, then quietly prised it open, wanting to check the ring was the right way round, its diamond pointing upwards to ensure the museum lights would produce the optimum amount of sparkle, and almost had a heart attack. Where his one-short-of-three-thou-sand-pound ring had been sitting was now what looked like a *Yale front door key.*

He stared into the box in disbelief, then took the key out and searched underneath it, removing the box's foam padding for good measure. How had this happened? Had it been stolen, and replaced by something of equal weight so he wouldn't notice, like when Harrison Ford replaces the statue with a bag of sand at the start of *Raiders of the Lost Ark* in an attempt to avoid being crushed? Except he'd certainly noticed. And now he was feeling crushed.

Desperately, he reached into his trouser pocket for his house keys, in case in some drunken moment he'd put the ring on his key ring and *his* key in the box, but to no avail. Besides, he already knew that the key wasn't one he recognised. And he'd never felt more sober.

His mind began to race. Had someone switched it for a 'laugh'? Why had he made that joke to Mia about the 'thing' pressing into her being his keys earlier? More importantly, why had he let the jacket out of his sight? But he hadn't, really. It had been on the back of his chair all this time, and he'd been dancing nearby, so unless someone had known it was there – and the only person who'd known was Nathan, though this was a practical joke too far even for him – something beyond his comprehension must have happened.

His legs started to wobble, and he looked around anxiously for somewhere to sit. How was it possible that this evening was going so wrong? If he was the kind of person who believed in signs, then so far this evening, he'd had a whole Highway Code's worth full of indications not to propose. What's more, the ring had been expensive. Two months' salary. There was no way he could afford to buy another one like this – not for ages, at least. And by then . . . Well, Mia was bound to have left him for someone less . . . stupid.

As he hurriedly slipped the box back where it had come from, Mia turned round and caught sight of his ashen expression.

'Are you okay?'

'Yes, I'm . . .' He quickly turned replacing the ring into making Mia think he was putting the jacket on, slipped one arm into a sleeve, then flailed around as he struggled to locate the other hole, though as Mia helped him into it, Calum was disappointed to find he couldn't get the jacket on properly. This was *all* he needed – either the sweaty atmosphere caused by all the dancing had made his brand new jacket shrink, or – even worse – he'd eaten so much of the (admittedly delicious) finger food and drunk so much champagne between arriving here and now that it didn't fit him any more.

As he struggled in vain to get the buttons anywhere near their respective holes, let alone do them up, Mia began to giggle.

'What's so funny?'

'I bet someone else is thinking they've shrunk.'

'Huh?'

'You must have picked up someone else's jacket by mistake.'

Calum stared at her as what she'd said began to sink in, then he frantically tore the jacket off as if it was on fire and hurriedly checked the label. *M&S Man!* It *was* someone else's, and being someone else's, then logically, what was in the pockets couldn't be his, which meant he hadn't lost the ring! Except, of course, he *had* lost the ring, because it was in the pocket of *his* jacket that this someone else was possibly putting on right now, and wondering how it had stretched so much.

'Mia, I could kiss you!'

'Well, go on then.'

Calum did as told, then with a 'Wait here!' he turned and quickly retraced his steps, intending to find his jacket, find the ring, and get back to propose almost before she knew he was gone. But when he reached the main hall and saw approximately a hundred people dancing, half of whom had left identical dinner jackets draped over the backs of their chairs, his heart sank. What to do now? He couldn't go around trying them all on, or even try to pat the pockets down in an attempt to find his ring.

In desperation, he ran back to his table, but the one jacket left there was Nathan's Hugo Boss, and of all the people here this evening, Nathan was the one most unlikely to have made the mistake of picking up someone else's. Then Calum spotted Julie Marshall striding in his direction, draped in a jacket several sizes too big for her, and for once, he was grateful for his girth. He hurried across to meet her, and pointed at the jacket.

'I think that's mine.'

Julie shrugged it off her shoulders, and looked at it quizzically. 'Whatever gives you that idea?'

'This,' said Calum, slipping on the jacket he was carrying as best he could.

Julie smirked at him, then her face seemed to go through a complex series of expressions. 'Oh, Calum!' she said, and then, to his astonishment, she enveloped him in a huge hug (which Calum would have returned, had it not been for the popping sounds he heard coming from the jacket he was wearing's seams when he tried to put his arms round her).

They exchanged jackets, Calum trying his on just to be sure, then he reached for the ring box in his pocket, inhaling loudly when his fingers located it, then exhaling in relief when he opened it up.

He took a moment to compose himself, nodded a 'Thank you' to Julie's 'Good luck!', then he sprinted back to where he'd left Mia, and looked around for his fiancée-to-be. But when he spied her in the corner, throwing her arms round the neck of an older black man, he thought his legs might just give way.

12.

Mark Webster's head was swimming from a combination of the evening's events and chugging back the drink Tony A. Wood had insisted on 'buying' him (though he needn't have bothered, since Tony had turned his attention back to Sophie Jones – or rather, Sophie Jones' chest – the moment the billionaire had spotted her at the bar). Still, his uncharacteristic feistiness had succeeded in buying him a week's reprieve – enough time to talk things over with Julie *and* properly consider moving to San Francisco, though Mark had worried even that might not be enough; it had taken him two months to ask her out, and the best part of a year to convince himself that moving one postcode further out of London was a good idea.

Realising he ought to action the first part of that plan as soon as possible, he rushed back outside, but Julie had gone – which probably made sense given the temperature. He considered waiting for her, just in case she'd gone for a walk, but that was unlikely; it *was* cold, especially if you were still in your shirtsleeves. Besides, her champagne glass was missing too, and given the look on her face when he'd left her, Mark hardly thought she'd be walking the streets, giving a celebratory 'cheers' to everyone she passed.

He walked back into the great hall, standing back as Calum Irwin came barrelling past him, then peered around the room.

Nathan Field was – to use one of his favourite phrases – 'playing tonsil tennis' on the dance floor with that girl Mark had seen on his laptop earlier, Sophie Jones was dancing with Tony A. Wood – again – but the one person he wanted to find was nowhere to be seen.

He spotted Mary at one of the tables, wolfing down what looked like a whole tray of mini hamburgers she'd evidently stolen from one of the waiters, and tapped her on the shoulder.

'Seen Julie?'

Mary peered up at him, her eyes seemingly unable to focus. 'Wo'yu'say?'

'Julie Marshall. Have you seen her?'

'Mine!' shouted Mary, forming a protective fort round the tray with her arms.

'No, I don't want a burger. I—'

'Mine!' shouted Mary, louder this time, causing a couple of people at a nearby table to glance in their direction.

'Never mind,' said Mark, making a mental note to change Mary's name on his 'fire' list from 'pencilled-in' to 'underlined', though as he looked up at the ceiling in dismay, he suddenly spotted Julie, sitting on one of the balconies overlooking the main hall.

He grabbed a drink from the bar, then hurried up the stairs, wondering how best to resume their earlier conversation. Maybe he should lead with Tony's offer – but then again, Julie might tell him to go because it was good for his career, or she might want to come, which could mean she definitely wouldn't want the baby . . . He almost laughed. This morning, his only concern was where they'd be spending Christmas, and who with. Now it was where they'd be spending the rest of their lives – and the 'who with' was a completely different ball game.

At least he hadn't given her the key yet, though it was still in his jacket pocket. The jacket he'd left her wearing when he'd gone off with Tony . . . For a moment, he panicked. What if she'd found it? Perhaps he should suggest she could move into his when he was in the US? Though maybe he could turn it around, make a joke of it being a 'Yale' key, tell her it was symbolic of her moving to San Francisco with him . . . Or was Yale in Boston?

He'd reached the top of the stairs now, and realised it was probably too late to check. Particularly when Julie's loud 'There you are!' meant she'd spotted him. Besides, making a joke of anything right now, given Julie's expression, would probably be a waste of time.

❦

Sophie Jones was beginning to have second thoughts. Close up, Tony A. Wood looked a *lot* older than his Wikipedia bio made out. Everything about him – particularly the slightly too regular and overly white teeth that she wouldn't be surprised spent their nights in a glass on his bedside table, what was quite possibly a fake tan, and his hair (both the colour and texture of it; Sophie wasn't sure if he was wearing a wig, but she'd heard that sometimes bald people had hair transplants by taking hair from other parts of their body, and if that was the case, Tony was possibly as naked down below as she was) – just didn't seem quite right. Plus, maybe it was just because he was drunk, but there was something funny about his eyes – and not only the fact that he couldn't seem to tear them away from her cleavage. From a distance, he looked the part. But for Sophie's plan to work, she'd need to spend more time than she might like at close range.

Eventually, and to her relief (she'd been concerned he was about to collapse), Tony A. Wood grabbed her by the arm – though she suspected it was for his benefit, not for hers – and led her off the dance floor.

'Phew-wee!' he said, removing his handkerchief from his pocket and mopping his forehead, and Sophie had to stop herself from shuddering when it came away brown. 'Ah'm not as young as ah used to be.'

Or as young as you say you are now, thought Sophie, pleased to be off the dance floor. Or rather, out of Tony A. Wood's slightly clammy grasp. 'None of us are.'

'True, true. Though when you hit sixty . . .' Tony held both hands up in a 'slow down' motion. 'Ah know, ah know, surely not, ah demand a recount!' He looked at her, expecting Sophie to nod in agreement, but when she didn't, he took the opportunity to leer at her chest again – something that had happened so many times this evening that Sophie was sure he'd be able to draw her breasts from memory if it was called for. He reached into his pocket, and withdrew a small tubular metal device. 'Tell me somethin', Sadie,' he said.

'*Sophie.*'

'Sophie. Do you vape?'

Sophie did a double take. Was this some *Fifty Shades*-type practice she hadn't spotted in the film? 'I'm not sure.'

'Ah mean, ah know ah shouldn't smoke. But little and often won' hurt us? Don' you agree?'

Sophie looked at him in horror. On her list of boyfriend no-no's, smoking was pretty near the top, alongside being shorter than her, and (and after this evening, she'd just promoted it to the number-one spot) being older than her, or at least, not having children who were. And while Christian Grey was none of these, *and* good-looking, which might have made some of those other, ahem, *practices* worth putting up with, could she really do this – do *Tony* – just for the money? She suspected she already knew the answer to that. And, she knew, she ought to bring this evening's events to a close. And fast.

'Actually,' she said, 'I think smoking's really dumb.'

'Somethin' else we have in common!' Tony A. Wood grinned, then took a massive hit on his e-cigarette, and a cloud of funny-smelling steam enveloped the two of them. 'Which is why ah only do these nowadays.' He grinned. 'And ah'm down to about twenty a day. Gotta have a few pleasures.'

'Yes. It must be a life of pure torture, being a billionaire.'

'It's not all it's cracked up to be, Sophie.'

Sophie made a face. 'Sure. I can see how it's really tough, being able to do exactly what you want. Buy what you want. Whenever you want. My heart bleeds for you.'

Immediately, Sophie regretted mentioning her heart, as Tony took a long, lingering look in its general direction.

'Mah ex-wives are all screwin' me—'

'You mean in the financial sense, right?'

'—mah kids don't speak to me any more. And mah friends – well, when you get to this level, it's hard to keep in touch, because the people you grew up with resent your success, and the ones you meet nowadays, they're really only interested in what they can get out of you. And as for women . . .' He sighed, then smiled. 'Ah'm sorry, Sophie. Ah don't mean to bring the evenin' down, but some-times . . .' He shook his head, and Sophie had to stop herself from looking to see if his hair moved separately. 'Ah must be drunk. And you seem incredibly easy.' He licked his lips, the way a lizard might on spotting its prey. 'To talk to, that is.'

'Is that a line?'

Tony A. Wood laughed. 'No. Although thinkin' about it, it sure sounds like one.' Tony A. Wood laughed, then he scanned the room and looked at his watch. 'Call me crazy, but do you wanna get outta here?'

Sophie realised that yes, she did. But not with him. 'Are you sure that's allowed? You've hardly spoken to anyone else all evening, and I'm sure they'd all appreciate—'

'It's mah party. And ah'll fly if ah wanna.' Tony A. Wood grinned. 'Hey, how about you come outside and ah'll show you my chopper?'

Sophie's jaw dropped. Tony A. Wood's ongoing charm offensive had suddenly become downright offensive, and before she knew what she was doing, she'd slapped him.

'What was that for?'

'How dare you!' The sudden movement had caused one of the straps on her dress to snap, and Sophie was desperately trying to protect her modesty, though gravity wasn't doing her any favours. 'Just because you're rich, you can't expect to get away with saying things like that!'

'Jeez. Can't a guy even offer a girl a ride in his helicopter?'

'Your . . .?' Sophie wanted to ground to swallow her up. 'Oh. Sorry. I thought you meant, well . . .'

'What?'

'Your penis.'

'*What?*'

'Chopper. It's slang for, well, I've just told you what for.'

'Given me what for, more like.' Tony touched his cheek gingerly, then eyed Sophie's slightly-more-on-display chest for what she resolved would be the last time. 'Though of course, if you wanted to see that too . . .' He reached into his pocket, and pulled out a small plastic packet of blue pills. 'Viagra!' he said, rhyming it with 'Niagara'. 'One of modern medicine's li'l miracles. Ah can go all night!'

Sophie stared at him in disbelief. There was only one place she wanted to go, and that was home. 'No,' she said, as evenly as she could. 'Thank you.'

'You're a feisty one, aren't you? What's your sign?'

Sophie rolled her eyes. Did people still ask that? People in their sixties, maybe. '"No Entry",' she said, sternly. Though she realised, to her surprise, that she should have said 'Not For Sale.'

'Another drink, then?' asked Tony, desperately. 'Ah might even tell you what the "A" stands for in Tony A. Wood.'

Sophie half-smiled. She could already guess, and it wasn't complimentary. 'I think I've had enough,' she said, in a tone designed to let Tony know she didn't just mean 'to drink'.

'Jeez! Don't make me 0 for 2 this evenin'!'

'Pardon?'

'First Webster turns mah offer down, then *you*—'

'Ewww!' said Sophie, loudly.

'That's what ah said,' said Tony, confusedly.

Then, with a last lingering look at her chest, he clicked his fingers, his entourage appeared at his side, and he turned and stalked out of the hall.

With her pride intact (though her dress *and* her dreams may not have been), Sophie watched him go. Then she collected her coat and bag from the cloakroom, held her head high, and strode confidently in the opposite direction.

❧

Julie Marshall reluctantly waved Mark Webster across to where she was sitting. Not because she wasn't glad to see him – more because she'd thought she'd managed to find a place where she could have a few minutes alone to think (though the bench she'd chosen, in front of a display of a nest full of fossilised eggs, perhaps had a little more symbolism than she'd have liked). But somehow Mark had tracked her down. He always seemed to be able to find her. Which was probably a good thing.

'I'd say "cheer up, it might never happen", but I'd be a little late, wouldn't I?' he said, smiling down at her.

'I'm sorry. I'm still trying to get my head around . . . everything.'

'Everything?'

'There's more.'

'*More?*'

'My divorce came through. This morning.'

Julie braced herself for what she was sure was going to be an angry outburst, but instead, Mark was beaming at her. 'Why didn't you tell me?'

'I was waiting for the right time.'

'And this is it?' He indicated the vacant spot on the bench next to her. 'May I?'

'Of course.' She edged over to make space for him, careful not to knock over the still-full glass of champagne by her feet. 'You must think I'm being very—'

'Silly?' Mark smiled as he sat down. 'A little.'

'I was going to say "matter-of-fact", but your description is better.'

'And are things becoming clearer?'

'I don't know. It's all just . . .' She took a deep breath. 'I've never been good with babies, Mark. Never seen myself as the motherly type. My career's always been the thing I've planned. Nurtured. The *only* thing . . .'

'Hey.' He looked around to check no one could see them, then took her hand. 'There's nothing to be ashamed of.'

'But it's not *normal*, is it? All of my friends, they've always been desperate to be mothers. And when they finally were . . . My God, they *loved* it. Even though it turned them into the most boring, baby-obsessed people you could imagine. Every time the child did so much as go to the toilet for a *number two*, they'd be bragging about it on Facebook.'

Mark grinned. 'At least there weren't photos.'

'But there *were*.' Julie made a horrified face. 'And these were intelligent women, Mark. With university degrees, and careers, and all of a sudden, they became . . .' She made a face, as if the memory was too horrible to comprehend. 'It was like some *disease.*'

'But it wasn't contagious?'

'God, no!'

'So what are you worried about? That that'll be you?'

'No – that it won't. I just don't *feel* it, Mark.'

'Well, it has come as a bit of a surprise, hasn't it? And like you said, everything else you've done in your life, you've planned. Thought about to the nth degree. Anticipated even the tiniest of details. Prepared yourself for.'

'Except for me and you.'

'And look how well that's turned out!'

Julie peered at him closely to see whether he was being sarcastic, then she remembered he didn't have it in him.

'I mean,' he continued. 'It's no wonder you're a little bit thrown by this new development. It's like . . . Say someone suddenly offered you a new job, somewhere you'd never even considered. It could be a fantastic opportunity, but it wasn't what you were expecting—'

'Less of the "expecting", please.'

'You're bound to be a bit thrown by it initially. Then, after you've had a little time to get used to the idea, you might start to think, well, San Francisco's not so bad . . .'

'San Francisco?'

'For example,' said Mark, hurriedly. 'Like I was saying, you might stop being shocked, and become a little intrigued. So you start doing a bit of research. Looking into it. Maybe you even speak to a few people who live in, you know . . .'

'San Francisco?'

' . . . for example,' said Mark, staring awkwardly at his shoes, 'just to get a feel for what it's actually like. And then, finally, you can make an informed decision as to whether you, you know . . .' He gave her hand a squeeze. 'Go for it. Or . . .'

'Or?'

'Other stuff might come up that's more important.'

'Mark, this is a *baby* we're talking about. Not some hypothetical move across the ocean that, quite frankly, if it doesn't work out, you can simply come back. What am I supposed to do if I don't like it?'

'Who doesn't like their baby?'

'*Motherhood*, I meant. But I suppose there's always that possibility too.' Julie sighed. 'The thing I didn't tell you, the one thing all my friends who were desperate to be mothers said, was how much hard work it was. How difficult. How their brains just got frazzled. And they *wanted* to do it. Imagine how it's going to be for *me*.'

Mark turned to face her. 'Do you want me to try and convince you to go through with it? Because that's not fair. On either of us.'

'No, I . . .' Julie stared up at the ceiling. 'I'm just worried that I don't care enough.'

'About us?'

'About the baby.' It was the first time she'd said the word out loud, and Julie was shocked at how unfamiliar it felt.

He nodded at her untouched champagne. 'And yet, you care enough to not even have a sip of that all evening?'

Julie stared at her glass. 'Well, yes. But that's just being . . . practical.'

Mark smiled. 'Practical's not a bad place to start. No one knows what it's going to be like for them. What you're going to feel the moment that bundle of joy comes barrelling into the world—'

'*Barrelling*?' Julie winced. 'Thanks for the imagery.'

'My point is, there are just some things you have to go with in order to find out what they're like. And while that might seem counter-intuitive to someone with your preference for . . .' he grinned. '. . . forward planning . . .'

'Shame it wasn't family planning.'

' . . . this might just be one of those things. And remember, these big, um, *moves*, are much easier if you've got someone else to make them with.'

'Mark, I . . .' Julie rested her head in her hands. 'Are you saying you want this baby?'

'That's hardly—'

'Hypothetically. Is it – you know, *fatherhood* – something you could see yourself doing?'

Mark shook his head. 'Julie, you don't get it, do you? This isn't something I see *me* "doing". Or you. It'd be something *we* did. As a family. The three of us. Assuming it's not twins . . .' Mark stopped talking as a look of terror flashed across Julie's face. 'Sorry, bad joke. But asking me if I want to be a dad isn't how it's done. Asking me if I'd like to be a parent, with you, bringing up our child . . . Well, that's something I'd leap at. With both hands. Or rather, legs.'

Julie exhaled loudly. 'But I'm worried what it'll do to us. To me. You won't fancy me when I'm fat, and haggard, and complaining about swollen ankles, or asking you to rub my feet—'

Mark made a face. 'On second thoughts . . .' he said, and Julie reached over and gave his leg a quick squeeze.

'Just when it was all going so well.'

'What do you mean?' Mark broke into a grin. 'It's still going well. This morning, your divorce comes through. And now . . . I'm going to be a dad!'

'Maybe. A lot can go wrong. And, you know, we might still decide, you know . . .' Julie cleared her throat awkwardly. 'Not to, you know, have it.'

'Oh. Right. Sure. Whatever you think, obviously.'

'Mark, for once, please try and come out with an original opinion, rather than always trying to say what won't offend people.'

Mark looked a little offended himself, and Julie immediately felt guilty, then he scratched his head. 'I'm sorry. You're right. I do that, don't I? But this? It's really not my decision, is it? I mean, you're the one that's going to get fat—'

'Thanks a lot!'

'—and have to carry it for nine months, whereas I? Well, I don't really know what I have to do, except support you in whatever you decide to do. And for me to say "Yes, I want to have a baby – this baby, our baby . . ."' – he reached a hand out and gingerly touched Julie's stomach – 'seems a little unfair, if you think about it. Do I want to have a family with you? Of course I do. And whether that family's just me and you, or we have a whole football team of kids—'

'No chance!'

'—then that's fine. But that's why it – *this* – has to be your decision. Because it's not right for me to ask you to go through with it just because it's something *I* might want.'

Julie folded her arms and mock-glared at him. 'Why do you always have to be so sensible?'

'I'm an accountant, remember?'

'So you'll be happy to put up with me getting – how did you put it – "fat"?'

'I refer you to my previous answer. Large figures don't worry me at all.'

'And the mood swings? And the grouchiness?'

'No change there, then.'

She dug him playfully in the ribs, then leaned across and held him close. 'Because this morning, when I first found out, I was sure I couldn't do it. And it's only now that you've reminded me how great you are that I realised it was something I could actually do. With you.'

'Well, don't feel you have to make a decision now.'

'I think I already have.' Julie held his gaze for a moment, then she picked up her champagne glass, clinked it against his, then emptied it into a nearby plant.

'Christ!'

'I'm not sure we'll be calling it *that*.'

Mark hugged her tightly, and Julie could feel his heart hammering under his shirt. Or maybe, it was hers.

'So, we're going to be parents?'

Julie shrugged as dismissively as she could. 'Looks that way.'

Mark beamed at her. 'Well, that definitely calls for champagne – for me, at least. Come on,' he said, downing half his glass, then leading her back down the stairs. 'The party isn't over quite yet.'

'Let's hope so.' Julie flashed him a look. 'Oh, what was it that Tony wanted to talk to you about?'

Mark thought for a moment. 'Just work stuff. Nothing important.'

'No moves I need to know about?'

'Not now. Well, except for . . .' He reached into his pocket, removed the ring box, and pressed it into her hand. 'Merry Christmas.'

'Mark, I . . . Wow. I don't know what to . . .'

'I hope you're not going to be choosing a name for this baby without knowing what sex it is?'

'Pardon?'

'That was a metaphor.' He nodded at the ring box. 'In other words, you might want to find out what's inside before you make any decisions.'

Julie smiled, then without opening it, she slipped the box back into his pocket. 'The answer's yes. Whatever it is.'

She took Mark by the hand, and – in full view of everyone – led him onto the centre of the dance floor. 'I do love you,' she whispered into his ear. 'You do know that, don't you?'

Mark blushed, then he leaned down and kissed her. 'I do *now*,' he said.

∾

Calum Irwin sat miserably at the bar, staring into a glass of what had earlier been the nicest champagne he'd ever had, although now he seemed to have lost the taste for it. He'd thought he'd be celebrating by now, cheers-ing countless times with various well-wishers, but instead, every bubble that rose excitedly up the glass, only to burst on the surface of the liquid, seemed to be representative of his dreams of married life.

The party was all but over now – just like his and Mia-Rose's relationship, he feared. Sophie had strode purposefully out through the door a few minutes ago without even saying goodbye to anyone, Nathan had just left with some gorgeous woman in a red dress. Mary from accounts was asleep, face-down in a plate of mince pies at the next-door table. And as for Benedict – Calum scented the air, like a dog might, but the lack of any unpleasantness meant he'd probably gone as well. In fact, Mark Webster and Julie Marshall were the only people left (and conscious) that he knew, the two of them slow-dancing in the middle of the dance floor, despite the fact that the DJ was playing 'Merry Xmas Everybody' at full volume. As for Mia? Well, M.I.A. just about summed her up.

How had it all gone so wrong? He'd planned this evening out from start to finish, rehearsed what he had to say, yet for some reason, not once had he had a proper opportunity to get down on one knee. So much for going for the close – the only thing that *had* closed was his window of opportunity. And now Mia was . . . Well, he wasn't sure where she was, to be honest, though he couldn't blame her for wanting to be off with someone else, rather than sitting around staring at his miserable face.

He'd have to leave his job, too, he knew. There was no way he could just come into work every morning and walk past Mia on reception as if nothing had happened. The shame, the hurt, would be too much for him, especially on a daily basis.

Plus, being with Mia had made him popular. The two of them had been like a great double-act, though in reality, she'd been the one with the talent, with the personality. Without her, he'd be the one they all felt sorry for, but nobody wanted to know, a bit like Ernie Wise when Eric Morecambe had died.

And women treated you differently when you were coupled-up. Being with someone gave you a sort of endorsement, as if you were a worthy member of the male species; one of their number found you attractive, so you were off the ignore (or at least, treat with disdain) list. Now, all he had to look forward to was a life where the only women who spoke to him with any kind of enthusiasm were his mother and the female shop assistants who welcomed him whenever he went into a Uniqlo.

A plate of crust-cut-off sandwiches, their edges curling up as if in an attempt to escape their unappealing grey filling, was sitting on the bar next to him, so Calum picked one up and sniffed it tentatively (mushroom, he'd guess, if he had to). Before he'd met Mia, his diet had been like that of an unsupervised child at a birthday party, though since they'd started going out he'd been watching what he ate, but right now, Calum was considering polishing the whole lot off.

As he picked the first one up and licked his lips, he heard someone clearing their throat behind him, and – assuming it was one of the bar staff wanting to collect the plate – he reluctantly put the sandwich back and turned round.

'Hi,' said Mia-Rose.

She was looking a little flushed, and Calum tried to banish his worst thoughts from his mind. And failed. 'Where have you been?'

'I'm sorry. But you'll never guess what happened.'

'No?' Calum didn't want to guess. He wasn't sure he even wanted to know.

'Well, as I was waiting for you, I saw someone I hadn't seen in a long time.'

'A man?'

'Yes, a man.'

'The one I saw you hugging?' Calum felt himself bristle. 'The one who was old enough to be your *father*?'

Mia-Rose let out a surprised laugh. 'He *was* my father,' she explained. 'Or, should I say, *is* my father.'

'*Wha . . .?*' Calum stared uncomprehendingly at her. He might have worked for a software company, but right now, he was sure that 'does not compute' was written all over his face.

'He works here. What are the chances?'

'I'd say they were pretty small,' said Calum, before realising that probably hadn't been a question. 'You're sure?'

Mia nodded enthusiastically. 'Well, I haven't asked him to take a paternity test, or anything. But I happened to see his name badge, and of course I've seen old photos, and . . . Well, you know your own father, don't you?'

Calum shrugged. He didn't.

'It's incredible! I knew he was a security guard somewhere, but my mum was always a bit—'

'Guarded?'

'Ha ha, very good. Yes. No, but seriously, she'd always left it up to me if I wanted to have anything to do with him. And I didn't, because I kind of thought it was being disloyal to her. Which was silly, really, because she was the one who kicked him out.' Mia was babbling, but Calum didn't care. He was simply glad that she was still talking to him, although 'at him' was probably a more accurate description. 'So I thought it was time to find out more about him. After all, everyone deserves a second chance. Don't you think?'

Calum smiled. He thought exactly that.

'Do you mind?'

'Of course not. He's your dad.'

'Great. Come on.'

'What do you mean, "come on"?'

'I've told him all about you. And he wants to meet you, silly.'

Before he could reply, she'd grabbed him by the arm, and led him excitedly towards the far corner of the hall, where the man he'd seen earlier was waiting nervously on the edge of a bench.

Calum cursed his luck. Having no dad had been something else they had in common, and while he knew it was extremely selfish of him, he'd loved the fact that he was the only man in Mia-Rose's life. But now that her dad was back on the scene . . . Well, he supposed he'd just have to deal with it, even though this probably meant that proposing might be a bit inappropriate at the moment – after all, how could he possibly compete with what had just happened?

'This is Calum,' said Mia-Rose.

The man looked him up and down warily. 'Don,' he said, after a pause, adding, 'Mia's father,' as if he was still getting used to the phrase.

'Calum. Mia's boyfriend,' replied Calum (even after nearly a year, he was still getting used to it). 'Nice to meet you, sir,' he added, and Mia's dad looked impressed.

'Good to meet a young man with some manners.'

Calum grinned. 'My mother's influence.'

Don shook him by the hand. 'Well, your mother should be very proud.'

'She is,' said Mia-Rose, who was still clasping Calum tightly by the arm. 'Imagine: bumping into your dad after twenty-five years! What a surprise. Don't you think?'

Calum nodded. 'Well, my dad's dead, so yes, for me, it would be.'

Mia was grinning from ear to ear, despite what Calum just realised was quite a downer of an observation. 'Sweetie, if you don't mind, we're spending the day together tomorrow.'

'Oh. Of course. I've got some stuff to do, so . . .' *Take the ring back to the jewellers, possibly*, he thought.

Mia was hopping from foot to foot with excitement. 'No, I meant *we're* spending the day together. The three of us. If that's okay with you?'

Calum grinned. It was more than okay.

'Well, listen,' said Don, nodding towards the exhibits. 'The building's about to close, so I'd better go and put these fellas to bed.'

'We'd better go too,' said Calum. 'Not to bed, I mean. Um—'

'There's loads more I want to ask you,' said Mia-Rose, sparing Calum at least one blush on what had been a very red-faced day. 'Tomorrow. *Dad*!'

'Tomorrow,' said Don.

He gave Mia a tentative hug, then shook Calum's hand again, and as they watched him go, Mia let out a small squeal. 'What an amazing evening!' she said. 'First of all, I get to spend it with you, my very own secret agent, and then I only go and see my dad.'

'No, that's . . . something.'

'I'm not sure tonight could get any better.'

'So, you had a good time?'

'Do you really need to ask?'

As he led her back into the centre of the hall, Mia stopped him. 'What's the matter?'

'Your shoelace is undone.'

'Oh. Thanks.' Calum knelt down to tie it, and as he did so, the ring box tumbled out of his pocket. He picked it up and popped it open, just to check the ring wasn't damaged, then looked up to find Mia staring, wide-eyed, at him.

And while Calum Irwin had never been certain about of anything in his life, the one thing he *was* sure of was that Mia's shriek of delight could probably be heard throughout the whole building.

❧

Nathan Field was more than a little drunk, but even so, he could tell he'd arrived at a crossroads. Still, it was probably the best place to find a taxi – though a taxi to *where* was what was troubling him the most.

He stared out into the traffic rumbling along Exhibition Road, hoping to spot a cab with its 'For Hire' light shining, while just in front of him, Stacey Garrity was doing the same on the Cromwell Road, though neither of them were having much luck. In the weeks before Christmas, everyone was having – and therefore looking for a cab home from – their office parties, and as for flagging down a taxi at midnight on one of the main routes in and out of London? Nathan suspected they'd have better luck thumbing a lift from the helicopter that had just taken off from the museum's roof, and right now was passing noisily over their heads. He waited until the din subsided, then walked over to join her on the street corner.

'Brr,' said Stacey, stamping her feet on the pavement.

'Where?' Nathan made a play of looking over his shoulder. 'Should we climb a tree?'

'No, not "bear". *Brr*. It's cold.'

'It's England, it's December,' said Nathan, resisting the temptation to make a 'duh' face. 'Here.' He took off his coat, and wrapped it around Stacey's shoulders, enjoying the excuse to get close to her again. She really had the most kissable neck. And, he suspected, the rest of her was quite appealing too.

'Always the gentleman, eh?'

Nathan almost laughed: if Stacey could read his mind, she might revise her opinion, though at the moment, in his mind was where it was going to stay. He didn't have a clue what his next move should be. A more confident man would look at all the signs – the fact that they'd spent most of the evening together, the couple of slow dances they'd had, the fact that he'd kissed her during the last one (and she'd kissed him back). And now they'd left at the same time – though most people had left at the same time, seeing as the party had kicked them out at twelve on the dot. If he believed in love at first sight – and Nathan had only felt that once before, when he'd received his first company iPhone – then he'd have said that today's experience with Stacey was pretty close. But surely he had too much hurt in his past to risk going for it after knowing her for less than a day?

A black cab flashed past, its light off, but Nathan waved at it anyway, and the driver waved back apologetically. 'There's always Uber?' he suggested.

Stacey shook her head. 'I've just checked. '"Unusually high demand, so fares have been quadrupled",' she said, showing him the message on her phone. 'And anyway, it won't even give me a projected arrival time for one.'

'Night bus?'

Stacey let out a short laugh. 'If I wanted to get vomited on by someone I'd never met before, I'd have gone to that bar some of your lot were suggesting moving on to.'

'Fair point.' Nathan thought for a moment. 'Where do you need to get back to?'

'Walthamstow.'

'Ouch.'

'It's not that bad.'

'I meant it's a long journey. Not . . . Actually, it *is* that bad.'

'Hey. We can't all live in . . . Where do you live, Mister Smarty Pants?'

Nathan hiked his trousers up. 'Thanks. And Bayswater. Just up the road, really.' He hesitated, then thought *what the hell*. 'It's actually walkable from here, so if you wanted, you could come back to mine . . . You know, just while we called you a cab. Much nicer place to wait than on a street corner. It's warm, and there's coffee. Or tea, if you—'

'I'd better not.'

When Nathan's face fell, Stacey rested a hand on his arm. 'I don't mean it like that,' she said. 'I just . . . have to get home.'

'Right.'

'Nathan . . . There's something I haven't told you.'

'You're married.'

Stacey let out a short laugh. 'God, no. Though sometimes it feels like that. But you're right, in that there's someone I need to get home for.'

'What's his name?'

'Carlos.'

'*Español*, huh?'

'My, you're perceptive!'

'Well, with a name like that . . .' said Nathan, glumly. He'd known tonight had been too good to be true.

'Did you want to see a photo?'

'Not particularly.'

'You not a fan?'

Of other people's boyfriends? 'Um, no?'

'Spaniels in particular?'

Nathan did a double take; he'd evidently had too much champagne, because this conversation wasn't making any sense to him. He replayed their last few exchanges in his head, but even after that, 'What?' was all he could come up with.

Stacey laughed as she pulled her phone back out of her bag. 'My dog?' she said, scrolling through to show him some photos. 'He's a spaniel. And if I don't get home and give him a walk . . . Well, I won't go into details, but I don't want to have to get my carpets steam-cleaned again. And no, that's not a euphemism.'

Before Nathan could reply, a Ford Mondeo that had seen better days pulled up by the kerb next to them. Nathan was about to berate the driver for what appeared to be some rather offensive hand movements, until he realised he'd simply been rolling the window down manually.

'Minicab?'

Stacey leant in through the window, offering Nathan a rather nice view of her pert backside. 'How much to Walthamstow?'

The driver thought for a moment. 'Fifty.'

'Forty.'

'Forty-five.'

'Forty,' insisted Stacey.

The driver thought for another moment. 'OK.'

As he wound the window back up, Nathan took Stacey by the arm, and led her a step away from the car. 'Are you sure? These guys are unlicensed. And you never know who you're getting in with.'

'Well, there is one way you can make sure I get home safely.'

'Which is?'

Stacey opened the car's back door, clambered inside, and turned to face him. 'Come with me?' she said, patting the vacant seat next to her.

As Nathan stood on the kerb, the driver wound the window down again. 'What are you waiting for, mate?' he said. 'Christmas?'

Nathan smiled, then he climbed in next to Stacey. As far as he was concerned, Christmas had come early this year.

❧

Sophie Jones sighed wistfully as she watched Tony A. Wood's helicopter disappear over the horizon, before resuming her search for a cab. Maybe she'd been stupid turning down his offer of a ride, or flight, or whatever it was you did in a helicopter, but Sophie had been too worried about what Tony might want *her* to do in his helicopter, and in the end, taking flight like she'd just done was probably the safest decision.

She stood beside the Cromwell Road and peered out into the slow-moving traffic, trying desperately to spot a cab, and noticed Nathan and that girl she'd introduced him to doing the same on the other corner. Even if one did miraculously appear, given the direction of the traffic, they'd get it first, a development which came as no surprise to her. Sophie knew she'd never be at the front of the queue where anything to do with Nathan was concerned.

As what looked like a minicab pulled up in front of them, Sophie almost laughed out loud. Trust Nathan to get lucky. And judging by the look on the girl's face as he climbed in after her, that was exactly what was going to happen whenever they got to wherever they were going.

It had begun snowing again, more heavily than before, and her feet were hurting, so Sophie made her way to the shelter of the nearby bus stop, and lowered herself onto the bench. She reached into her bag for her comfortable shoes, but as she fished the left one out, she frowned – on the inside, at least. *Where was her other shoe?*

She turned the bag upside down, shook it, and emptied out the contents, but there was no sign of the right one. Somewhere deep in Sophie's brain, a cog turned, and meshed with another; she'd had them when she'd rushed out of the salon, and was pretty sure she'd put them with the rest of her work gear, so . . . She suddenly sat bolt upright. *Tony.* She'd virtually chucked her bag in his face when she'd arrived at the party earlier: maybe he was a pervert after all, and his particular fetish was *shoes*. He must have gone through her bag and stolen it . . . No wonder he'd been chasing her all evening!

Sophie almost wanted to cry – not just because this was the end of her favourite, most comfortable pair of work shoes, but because she'd also blown the chance to go out with a billionaire with a shoe fetish! Imagine: Jimmy Choo, Manolo Blahnik, Louboutin – brands she'd lusted after whenever she'd taken a walk through Selfridges' shoe department, brands she hadn't even dared try on, given how expensive they were – she could probably have had as many pairs of each as she wanted! Maybe she'd only have worn them the once before Tony would take them away to . . . Well, whatever it was he did with them. She certainly wouldn't be wearing them *afterwards*.

As she stared miserably at her feet, picturing how they might look cocooned in something considerably more upmarket than the pair of Clarks that weren't a pair any more, a bicycle bell rang out from the road in front of her.

'Nice evening?'

For the second time that evening, Sophie tried not to smile at the leather-jacket-and-wings combination, and failed. 'It was . . . interesting.'

'Pleased to hear it, I think. At least you got there in time.'

'Thanks to the fact that you're Lance Armstrong.'

'The drugs cheat? Thanks very much!'

'Sorry. I don't know any other cyclists. Not that I know Lance Armstrong. Personally, that is.' She glanced back towards the museum's entrance, where a steady stream of well-dressed people were staggering, zombie-like, out through the door, like a combination of *Downton Abbey* and *The Walking Dead*, and spotted Mark Webster and Julie Marshall walking arm-in-arm along Exhibition Road, Mark's free hand resting protectively on Julie's belly. 'Are you stalking me?'

'You left this in the back.'

He was holding Sophie's missing shoe, and Sophie's jaw dropped open. 'How did you know it was mine?'

'I didn't. But I've been riding round, tracking down all tonight's customers, getting everyone to try it on, and you're the only one left.' He smiled as he handed it to her. 'So if it fits *you* . . .'

Sophie laughed. Today was turning into her very own Cinderella story – although the prince she'd been after hadn't turned out to be that charming. She quickly changed back into her comfortable shoes, then noticed the rickshaw driver was watching her intently.

'You're Rich, right?'

'I do okay. As long as I don't offer too many free rides.'

He flashed her a smile, and Sophie was reminded how good-looking he was. Perhaps not her type, but to tell the truth, in all her years of dating, having a 'type' hadn't really got Sophie very far. She shivered, then jammed her hands into her coat pockets. 'You haven't been waiting for me out in the cold all this time, I hope?'

'Nah. These things normally kick out around midnight. Thought I'd take a chance and come back just beforehand.'

'Right. Well, thank you.'

'No problem. My pleasure.'

'So . . .'

'What are you waiting for?'

Sophie stared at him indignantly. 'I'm sorry, but if you're expecting a kiss or something just for bringing my shoe back, then you'll—'

He glanced up at the digital screen on the bus stop. 'What *bus*.'

'Ah. Oh. Sorry.' Sophie fished her phone out of her pocket, and consulted her Citymapper app. 'The 70. Then the 52. Then the 18. Then, um, the H17 . . . Assuming they're running. Which is what I'll have to do if they aren't.'

'Sounds complicated.'

Sophie sighed. 'Isn't it always?'

Rich shrugged. 'Doesn't have to be. I could take you back to the centre of town. It'll be easier to get a cab from there.'

Sophie thought for a moment. While at least she had her comfortable shoes back, neither the prospect of four buses *or* a midnight jog appealed to her. 'Well . . .' She paused as a loud scream pierced the night sky – a scream with Caribbean undertones. *Good for you, Calum*, she thought.

Rich patted the rickshaw's handlebars affectionately. 'It's the only way to travel.'

Given the lack of cabs, and no sign of her bus, Sophie couldn't argue with that.

'Especially at night, in the snow.'

Sophie hesitated, then she spotted a single white feather lying on the back seat. And while she knew it had probably just fallen from the back of Rich's jacket, it was enough of a sign for her. It might not have been the same as seeing San Francisco from a yacht, but somehow she had a feeling it would be just as fun.

'You're sure you don't mind?'

'It's on my way. And I wouldn't, even if it wasn't.'

'Thanks,' she said, climbing in gratefully.

As they pulled out into the traffic, Sophie shook the light dusting of snow from the blanket on the seat next to her, and wrapped it tightly around her shoulders.

'You okay back there?' said Rich.

'Fine. Just a little chilly.'

'Well, we could call into Bar Italia for a coffee, if you like?'

Sophie smiled, and decided she'd like that very much.

ACKNOWLEDGEMENTS

Thanks to Emilie Marneur, Sana Chebaro, the Amazon Publishing team, and editor extraordinaire Jenny Parrott. Another book! My tenth! Who'd have thought?

To the usual suspects (Tony Heywood, Lawrence Davison, Tina Patel), for their ongoing support, and every one of the lovely people I'm extremely lucky to call my friends, and who (unknowingly, hopefully) continue to provide me with material. And, of course, the Board (shh!).

To everyone who made a donation to Streetwise Opera for the chance to have this book dedicated to you. You may not be the winning dedicatee (if that's even a word), but I was thinking of you while I was dedicating it to them, honest.

To Steve Garrity, whose generous bid won the Authors for Nepal auction (and who named the character he 'won' after his wife). I hope she's still speaking to you after reading this!

And lastly, as ever, to you, my fantastic readers, in particular everyone who read, reviewed and recommended *A Day at the Office*. If you hadn't, you wouldn't be reading this, mainly because I wouldn't have written it. I thank you all (yes, even you at the back) for allowing me to go on doing this *nods towards work-in-progress on laptop screen* for a living.

ABOUT THE AUTHOR

British writer Matt Dunn is the author of ten (and counting) romantic comedy novels, including *A Day at the Office* (a Kindle bestseller) and *The Ex-Boyfriend's Handbook* (shortlisted for both the Romantic Novel of the Year Award and the Melissa Nathan Award for Comedy Romance). He's also written about life, love and relationships for various publications including *The Times*, the *Guardian*, *Glamour*, *Cosmopolitan*, *Company*, *Elle* and the *Sun*. Before becoming a full-time writer, Matt worked as a lifeguard, a fitness-equipment salesman and an IT headhunter.